CW01560594

GEORGIA HARPER is a psychologist who has worked with both serious violent offenders and victim-survivors of crime. Her career spans correctional, forensic mental health, mental health and rural psychology roles. She advises on LGBTIQ+ workforce matters and, in keeping with her passion for animal welfare, was the Senior Inspector Prosecutions for RSPCA Queensland.

Born in Brisbane, Georgia currently lives and works on the beautiful Darling Downs, where she enjoys writing in her paddock under the supervision of her shire horse. *What I Would Do to You* is her first novel.

GEORGIA HARPER

WHAT I WOULD DO TO YOU

VINTAGE BOOKS

Australia

VINTAGE

UK | USA | Canada | Ireland | Australia
India | New Zealand | South Africa | China

Vintage is part of the Penguin Random House group of companies whose
addresses can be found at global.penguinrandomhouse.com

Penguin
Random House
Australia

First published by Vintage in 2024

Copyright © Georgia Harper 2024

The moral right of the author has been asserted.

All rights reserved. No part of this publication may be reproduced,
published, performed in public or communicated to the public in any
form or by any means without prior written permission from Penguin
Random House Australia Pty Ltd or its authorised licensees.

This is a work of fiction. Names, characters, places and incidents either are the
product of the author's imagination or are used fictitiously. Any resemblance
to actual persons, living or dead, events, or locales is entirely coincidental.

This work does not constitute health advice, and is in no way intended
to reflect the author's views on any health profession or health
service, nor that of any organisation she works for or with.

Cover design by Christa Moffitt, Christabella Designs © Penguin
Random House Australia Pty Ltd
Cover photography by Magdalena Wasiczek / Trevillion Images
Typeset in 11.5/17 pt Sabon LT Pro by Post Pre-Press Group, Australia

Printed and bound in Australia by Griffin Press, an accredited
ISO AS/NZS 14001 Environmental Management Systems printer

A catalogue record for this
book is available from the
National Library of Australia

ISBN 978 1 76134 212 7

penguin.com.au

MIX
Paper | Supporting
responsible forestry
FSC® C018684

We at Penguin Random House Australia and the author acknowledge that
Aboriginal and Torres Strait Islander peoples are the Traditional Custodians and
the first storytellers of the lands on which we live and work. We honour Aboriginal
and Torres Strait Islander peoples' continuous connection to Country, waters,
skies and communities. We celebrate Aboriginal and Torres Strait Islander stories,
traditions and living cultures; and we pay our respects to Elders past and present.

For Suzanne, my little sister.
This book has always been for you.

. . . little girls don't stay little forever.
They grow into strong women that
return to destroy your world.

Kyle Stephens, victim impact statement
at the sentencing of Larry Nassar, 2018

PROLOGUE

I'M EATING HER ASHES EVERY DAY NOW. IT'S USUALLY WHEN MUM IS asleep and Mattie's outside with the cows. I open her urn and unfold the thick plastic inside. Then I lick the tip of my index finger and dip it in so it gets coated with the grey powder. It's impossible to say which bits of what parts of her I've got in that dust, and I hope there is enough of her to keep me going for as long as I need. I dab her onto the front of my tongue and let her mix with my saliva. Then I move my tongue all around my mouth so she touches every part of it. She feels soft and chalky and gritty, but she doesn't taste like anything much. I don't have a drink after; I let her linger there while I go about my day.

1

OCTAVIA

SOMETIMES YOU FIND A PIECE OF YOURSELF YOU NEVER KNEW existed. Scary, isn't it, when that happens? Unsettling. Like the time that, on my fiftieth birthday, I felt a sharp prick deep under the skin of my heel. Turns out it was glass. I remembered instantly the broken wine bottle I stood on when I was a kid. I never knew a tiny, spiky green fragment had remained in my tissue all this time. It had been with me most of my life. A part of me. Yet I was shocked when I found it.

Is that how they'll each feel if they do this? As if they've discovered something jagged below their surface, something they didn't know belonged to them, something that could do damage?

These thoughts distract me while I sit sideways in my armchair, legs draped over the edge, the coffee table pulled in close as I prepare for tomorrow. The towering stacks of papers on the table are the sentencing transcripts. They tell of the whos, whats, wheres and hows, but so far they seem unable to account for the whys. There is something else always notably absent from these documents: a certain record of human experience. They describe the proceedings, sure. But they do not capture the visceral experiences of those listening to them unfold. They do not mention the haze of emotion which hangs unseen over the courtroom at the judge's weighing-up of the crime; an invisible, suffocating fog creeping above the gallery of bowed heads. An insidious fog which follows you home afterwards and hovers over you as you collapse, wrung out, into your bed. A fog which settles over your body as you fall into a twitchy slumber, drifting up your nostrils to create a disorienting murk-world of dreams.

I wonder what it will be like to meet the first two family members tomorrow. Will they even want to talk to me? I wonder if they'll be afraid that I'll share their secrets with the others. I can't, of course, not without their permission. Maybe they'll be fearful that I can stop them. I picture myself explaining it while they assess me watchfully: I can't prevent you from doing this. Only the judge can do that. I do need to advise him if I'm concerned you can't make an informed decision to participate, though; for example, if you have advanced Alzheimer's or are acutely psychotic. I imagine them nodding at this, dismissing what I say because they don't have dementia and they certainly aren't crazy. Then I would add that I must also tell Judge Gorski if they say that doing this might cause them to inflict harm upon themselves . . . or someone else. Again, I see them nod, saying they would never do that, exceptions being what they are.

Perhaps they will want my guidance about what they should do. I plan to explain up front that it's not my role to steer them, one way or the other, in making their decision; I'll tell them that I will merely hold a place open – like a bookmark keeping a journal page – for them to consider their course.

At a time when everyone's eyes are on them, perhaps they will find comfort in my neutrality, see me as their safe land. Their Switzerland, blanketed and nestled snug, separated from France by treacherous ranges, from Germany by an icy river. If I am not confident in the fortitude of my borders, I will not betray them by letting it show.

I gulp a mouthful of cab sav from the cheap tumbler I received in an office Secret Santa. The one that reads *Wine: Because punching people in the face is illegal.* I snooped around and uncovered the gift-giver. My receptionist. I still have mixed feelings about the glass. Was it intended to be generic and funny, or targeted, a passive-aggressive way of letting your boss know what you'd like to do to her? Anyway, it's bottom-heavy and I've only knocked it over twice since I've had it, which makes it my drinking mainstay.

As I turn page after page, living out this courtroom drama in excruciating detail, I wonder if it was a relief even for him when the legal proceedings finally exhausted themselves. Four years and six days from the day when everything was decided for her to the one after which little was possible for him. Is he the one having the terrible dreams now? Is he woken in the sharpest, deepest part of the night, torso sweaty-slick, heart thundering, mouth gaping, suffocating like a freshly caught fish? Does he picture the tacky silver tape that he kept, shaped like a hill and a valley?

When the reading gets too tough, I soothe myself by stroking Bob's wiry ear-and-a-half. The mats in his fur are just starting to re-knot after my last hack job. You'd never tell from how little I brush him how pathetically obsessed I am with this dog. My friend Susie helped me pick him out from the shelter four years ago. There he was: enormous and bear-like, sucking on a baby's pink dummy. Seriously. We figured that some unlucky toddler must have pushed it through the bars of his pen. He held that damn thing between his teeth the whole car ride home. Sitting on the back seat with drool thick as stalactites hanging from his cave of a mouth, his honey eyes met mine in the rear-view mirror, a slow-blinking mix of shame and defiance. His coat is so grizzly-thick that it wasn't until I sudsed him up for his first bath that I realised half his left ear was missing. Susie said I should have requested a partial refund, but I view imperfection – in the right context – as an upgrade.

He looks at my hand pleadingly as I return to flipping pages. The weight of the paper I turn over is nothing, almost a feather, but as the story unfolds each white slip becomes a fraction heavier than the last, until my hands feel as if they are lifting unhewn bricks from the bottom of the ocean. I glance at the clock: 11.47 pm.

As I snuff out the pooling candle and get up to toss the dregs of red from my tumbler into the sink, I think about the concept of neutrality; about how I need to avoid taking a position on the terrible thing on which they must decide. I must remain detached, avoid being drawn, monitor my words and expressions so they neither encourage nor deter. As I pad down the hallway to the bathroom, put a blob of toothpaste on my toothbrush and remember that I need to replace the shaggy-bristled thing, I wonder whether this unbiased state can extend to my own mind.

●

I awake with my brain and body feeling bright: no twinges to remind me of the heavy emotional weights I lifted last night. Bob snores on the rug, his vibrating black nostrils highlighted by the sun that peeps through my haphazardly drawn curtains. My neighbour – a lady with hair down past her bottom, called Shirley – once warned me, awkwardly, face slightly flushed, that she can see me getting undressed at night because my curtains don't always meet in the middle. I expect in making me aware of the situation, she intended that I would obscure future nakedness with correctly drawn drapes. I can empathise with how unsettling it might be to witness a nightly display of breasts that are now more like the dough than the cupcakes. But, to be honest, I can't be bothered to change the way I close the curtains. I hope she remembers to look away.

The muscles in my neck become taut when I think about the day ahead, and I tell myself to relax; I can handle this. I am driving two hours south-west of Brisbane, to a property near Warwick. There, I'll meet the mothers, Stella and Matisse. It is unusual for me to see clients outside of my consulting rooms, but this contract requires me to conduct appointments at a place of the client's choosing. This, for the mothers, is the family home on their cattle farm. The time spent out of the office – which will go on for at least a year – means reducing my overall client load, but the government remuneration for this job is generous.

Besides, I am doing this for me. As I plod down the stairs to make my first flat white of the day, I reflect on how much my career feels like the men's underpants I wear until they are faded and saggy. It's not a fetish or anything; it's just a habit that started decades ago after a chance discovery. I was in my second year of uni and, after two days of smoking weed and having mediocre sex in my boyfriend's musty man den, he suggested we attend a lecture to avoid being kicked out of our course. He offered me all he had in the way of clean clothes, which was a pair of faded black briefs with a small hole at the waistband. And what a discovery that was. Soft cotton. Giving elastic. So practical. So freeing. Such a departure from my assortment of nylon lace and dental-floss G-strings. I'd never realised men had it so good – at least not in this particular way. Since that revelation, I've been wearing men's undies until the colour is blanched and the elastic waistband is saggy. The pouch barely gets to me. I've contemplated swapping over to women's boylegs, but after all this time I'm too attached to the briefs. And so it is with my career: once an exciting discovery, it is now comfortable and familiar and hard to change. But in these past couple of years, I've realised I need to let go of convention again. Switch it up. Now I've come home with something new and wildly risqué to wear, something that makes me feel exposed, nervous and anticipatory as I slip into it.

•

I dress hurriedly and check that the doggy door is unlocked. Realistically, I may as well leave the house wide open, because Bob's entry is big enough for any small adult with a regular yoga practice to crawl through. After kissing Bob on his furry head and telling him not to miss me too much, I rush out to the car, managing to drop my satchel twice on the way. I open the door of my Mina Electrica and say a silent prayer that the battery will make it there and back without a recharge. Even though the range is much better than back when we all did the big swap, I tend to push things to their limits. I start the engine and see I have plenty of charge. I tap the address into the GPS and I am on my way.

About thirty minutes out of the city, I notice I am the only vehicle within eyeshot. This feels oddly freeing, as if I finally have space, as if when I inhale the air into my lungs nobody else is fighting me for it. I have my windows down. I cannot remember the last time I did that, and it is a double freedom because I recently cut my thick hair to a shoulder-length bob, and the cool air brushes against my scalp as the strands lift in the wind. I suck the air greedily, taking great breaths between choruses of 'Take Me Home, Country Roads'. It was the first song I learnt in primary school choir. On our initial attempt at a full rendition, Raelene – who was sitting next to me and who herself sang terribly through a long, ferrety nose – covered her ears and then relocated to sit next to Janice, leaving me in no doubt that my vocals were the cause. This was especially insulting because all the kids knew Janice smelt like a lunchbox-sweaty egg sandwich, poor girl, and thus we avoided her as much as possible. The memory doesn't stop me though: I crack out the song every time my sister and I take a day trip. In a predictable countermove designed to shut down my performance without saying it directly, Olive, who works in a nursing home, explains that she can't stand to hear John Denver because it's all they play on Seniors' Music Morning. Though I'm not fooled by her flimsy ruse, I usually take pity on her and turn on the radio instead.

Nobody's here to stop me now, and I let my mind drift to the task ahead as I belt out the lyrics. I wonder what Stella's daughter – Matisse's stepdaughter – is like. Just a touch younger than I was when I had my underwear revelation, she still lives at the family home. Hannah's chosen not to see me today, which is what provokes my curiosity. Unlike the other family members, she is not compelled to attend sessions, and I have been instructed that she will contact me if she wants to make use of my services. The son, Sebastian, is a veterinarian who lives in Brisbane. He is electing to visit my rooms on Monday evening for his first appointment. As well as being convenient for me, this choice makes sense for him. If I were a young man, I would not want an unvouched-for middle-aged woman poking around in my home as well as my head.

My attention is drawn back to the road when a wayward peewee swerves at the last second to avoid flying in the driver's-side window. I'd not previously considered the possibility of a collision with a bird in midair, and immediately re-engage the glass shield between me and the world. I notice a sign that reads *Welcome to the Township of Aratula* and realise I'm near the halfway point of the drive. I love the sound of the placenames on the signs that line this strip of highway: 'Ara-TULLE-a', 'Tanny-more-RELLE', 'Mudda-Pill-eee'.

As I come into town, I touch my foot on and off the accelerator, equivocating. Probably nobody would stop at Aratula if not for the bakery flanking the highway. My parent–angel and toddler–devil argue on my shoulders.

Should I stop?

NO, I told you last night. You're. Not. Going. To. Stop.

But I didn't have breakfast. I'm huuungry.

Well, whose fault is that? You're not stopping.

What about an apple turnover? They've got fruit. I could just eat half – throw the other half away.

No, that's wasteful. Distract yourself. Look: lovely old trees.

Ten minutes later, with the comforting tastes of cinnamon-y apple and sweet cream flashing across my tongue, I do look up at the century-old bunya pines towering over my picnic table. *Take me home, country roads . . .* I roll the lyrics across my mind to distract from my guilty mouth.

Standing up, I brush the dandruff-like pastry flakes off my pale pink shirt. I'm making an attempt at looking country. Nothing excessive: dressy jeans, long-sleeved shirt, belt and a pair of scuffed brown riding boots. I have these because Susie insists that our annual holiday together is always spent on the back of a horse. Luckily, she doesn't mind where we go so long as her hips are swaying to that clip-cloppedy rhythm, and I enjoy getting to choose the scenery even if I could take or leave the horses. This year, it was the Canadian Rockies on quarter horses. Next year, it will be the west coast of Scotland on Clydesdales. These boots are the only true farm item I own, and I hope they'll keep me from looking out of place.

I walk back to the car and turn on the radio. The ABC national news top stories draw me in as I rejoin the road. The reporter's polished voice tells of remote horrors we listeners – at least the fortunate majority of us – realistically cannot digest. A train crash in India kills one hundred and eleven people. An Adelaide man stabs his wife and three-year-old son before slicing his own throat. He survives, they do not. Then the usual autumn public-service announcement from a concerned fire chief, reminding us there is 'plenty of time over winter to prepare for what might be the worst summer bushfire season yet'. I picture myself standing in my suburban backyard, watching the tiny patch of crisp shrubbery go up in flames while I fumble with the mini fire extinguisher from the kitchen. Even as I make a mental note to refresh my knowledge of its use, I know I won't. Summer is a long way off.

The presenter wraps up the news and introduces *Environment Hour*. I'm usually at work when this program is on. I'm tempted to turn it off; what person experiencing the afterglow of a morning pastry wants to face the fact that their earthly home might expire? The presenter, a man with a phlegmy voice, tells me that today we will look back on the Australian legislative changes of the past fifteen years and ask ourselves the question, 'Was it enough?'

My hand hovers over the 'off' button as he lists the ways we've tried to save ourselves: shutting down coal mining, swapping to almost completely renewable energy sources, removing petrol vehicles from the roads. But then he mentions beef production, and I think instantly of where I'm going today – a cattle property – and let Mr Post-nasal-drip drone on in the background while I contemplate Stella and Matisse's farm. Well, I don't even know that it is their farm. Are they simply managers, or were they one of the tiny 15 per cent of beef farmers who won the government lottery and were granted a perpetual production licence? One of the small-timers who resisted selling out to the big corporations in exchange for the long-term gains of being part of a production chain that now sells a steak for the same price as a pair of R. M. Williams boots? Which is perhaps the somewhat frivolous exaggeration of a fillet mignon–deprived woman, but then I think about the seriousness of the protests, the chaos in the streets when the government announced it was spending billions upon billions of dollars to buy up farms and livestock-related businesses, and to compensate farmhands, transport drivers, saleyard and feedlot staff, and abattoir workers for lost income and retrain them to work in other industries. At the time, it seemed unfathomable that we could give up our Big Macs, our beef in black bean sauce, our $19 pub steaks and our Bunnings sausage sangas, in exchange for savouring a T-bone as an annual birthday treat. Still, those of us not directly affected by the industry changes adapted and moved on to the next thing within months.

If they're not licence holders, perhaps Stella and Matisse were raised on the land, and have the requisite skills to manage someone else's enterprise. Or maybe they'd proven their management skills in other industries, then chose a tree change so their family could live a freer, safer, more wholesome life. Given their current circumstances, I hope this wasn't their motivation. Being surrounded by the natural beauty of the land and the animals and the vast blue skies would be a daily reminder of that dream turning to a nightmare.

The country gets drier the further south-west I travel. Farmers have piled dead wood in pyres that dot the surrounding paddocks. Fields stand fallow. Crisp stalks of flaxen grass and moistureless tree branches cling to life and would carry a blaze through here faster than stampeding brumbies. My GPS is routing me around Warwick – known as the Rose City, although I'm sure it's closer to a large town, with a council that's highly unlikely to permit its finite water resources be used to cultivate roses.

I'm prompted to take a left turn and then a right. The roads narrow. I dip down over a creek choked with duckweed, then I follow the bitumen up, up, up the side of a mountain.

After a few minutes I am up high. The greenness here is in stark contrast to the dust bowl below. Thin veils of cloud, fine as spun sugar, blow over the car. Having calmed myself from the near-miss with the bird, I wind down my windows and the freshening air touches me, making little bumps on my forearms. The land on top of this mountain looks as if it's been tucked into bed with a green blanket, Mother Nature slipping her hands into the creases and folds, making sure no part of the earth is left exposed. The grass – almost vulgar in its shamrock glory – clearly has its own invisible watering can hovering above it, freely giving sips of water while half the country dies of thirst.

Around a bend, ten or fifteen red-and-white cattle appear, raising their heads at the sound of the car, little green moustaches of grass poking out the sides of their busy mouths.

The GPS tells me the next right is Sullivans Lane, which appears on cue. I turn onto the lightly corrugated dirt road and rumble along for a few hundred metres until I reach the dead end which Matisse, giving directions on the phone in a lightly accented – South American? – voice, had told me to expect.

I cross the cattle grid and see a sign to its right featuring the peaceful head of a Hereford, underneath which is written *Heathwood Farm Highest-Welfare Beef.* I wonder what makes it *highest*, but am distracted from this thought as I round a bend and see my path is blocked by a white pony. Though I know from Susie that most white horses are referred to as 'greys', as they are born a darker colour and lighten to white over time while their skin remains dark or pigmented underneath. This one has a dark mane and tail, and stands a few metres from my vehicle, right in my path, staring off into the distance and paying me no mind. I drive a bit closer, thinking it will move, but it doesn't seem to notice. I drive closer still, cautiously, my car almost touching its ample belly. The single acknowledgment of my presence the pony gives is a pinning back of its dainty ears. I wonder if it will kick the Mina if I beep. Just as I place my hand on the horn, the pony drags its feet a few steps forwards, sloth-slow, throwing me a backwards glare. It wants me to know it only moved because it was planning to anyway.

I duck around its hind end and continue for a couple of hundred metres, and there, set up on a hillock, nestled between two camphor laurels, is a white cottage. With its corrugated-iron roof, worn sandstone chimney and blooming garden, it is picture-book lovely. I rattle over crushed stone into the fenced yard. Weatherboards gleam with fresh paint. Two sizeable windows front the house, and I squint to see what I think is a stained-glass fairy-wren on each.

Between the windows there is a glossy vermillion front door. The raw wood planks of the wide verandah support a rocking chair, a pair of Adirondacks and a daybed. This place is old-school Australiana with a dash of modernity. It is a cosy hidey-hole where you could devour mystery novels while sipping endless cups of tea, made in a pot; a refuge where you could take satisfying naps under a crocheted blanket that smells comfortingly like your grandma's lavender drawer sachets. This is my fantasy retreat. I want to curl up inside this cottage's walls on a rainy day, snuggle in front of the fireplace and disappear. But, alas, I cannot continue this daydream because a woman with a huge mop of black hair emerges from the door, waving, a red dog at her heels.

Her hair moves as a separate animal. It bobs and billows as she approaches the Mina, smiling with warm brown lips. I take in the denim overalls, floral-print gumboots and giant earrings – blue and gold macaws. I grin inwardly. This woman looks fun.

As I get out of the car, she beams at me as though I'm a good friend, and her olive skin crinkles at the edges of her eyes. I feel warmth radiating from her, as if she has been basking in the sun and now exudes the solar energy she absorbed.

'Welcome,' she says in her soft lilt.

I extend my hand to shake hers, but she pulls me into a hug. I never usually have this type of physical contact with clients, but I'm caught off guard and I sense that bringing it up now could disrupt any tentative rapport we've established over the phone. She steps back without self-consciousness, as though embracing a stranger is the most natural thing in the world.

'I'm Matisse,' she says.

'Octavia Tate,' I say, smiling.

'I've been looking forward to meeting you, Dr Tate.'

'Octavia, please.' I wave my hand.

'Do you mind dogs?' she asks.

I notice that the dog, a shiny kelpie, is sitting a couple of metres behind her. It's wriggling on its haunches, shaking with the desire to get loose.

'I love dogs. I probably have dog hair on me right now,' I say, laughing and automatically wiping my jeans.

Matisse gives a hand signal, which frees the dog. It bursts from its spot and makes it to me in three big bounds. It leaps up, front paws on my chest.

'Down,' Matisse commands.

Immediately, the dog withdraws its paws and sits, but does not look chastened. Its tail wags so fast it becomes a blur.

'Sorry,' she says. 'He's only young. Still learning.'

'It's fine,' I say. 'He's gorgeous.'

'His name is Arnold,' she says.

Arnold the kelpie. I love pups with daggy human names – hence Bob. I reach down and pet his head. His ears are dusty and silky. His eyes, translucent green, stare into mine as if he knows my secrets.

'How was the trip from Brisbane?' Matisse asks.

'Good,' I say. 'But it's sad to see everything looking so dry. It's beautiful and green here.'

'Yes, we're lucky. The part of the farm that's on this side of the mountain gets higher than average rainfall, which is what sustains the national park. Did you see the entrance as you came up the mountain?'

'Yes, on the left,' I say.

'You can bushwalk in the park, but camping's prohibited. That's why Stella put the B & B here. People wanted a nice place to stay after hiking all day. It was popular when it was operating.'

'Ahh,' I say, nodding. I knew about the B & B from the court documents, but I didn't realise it had closed.

'If you kept going up the road past our place, you'd have come to a dead end. That's where the prettiest rainforest is. There's a locked gate that only the ranger's meant to enter, and there are no walking tracks, but one of our paddocks backs onto it.'

She pauses as though she's about to say something further, and then shakes her head.

'Most of our land is actually on the other side of the mountain, which is much drier,' she explains, gesturing to a ridge a few hundred metres past the house. 'It gets less rain and more sun, and it's heavily cleared. We're planting trees, though the kinds that can survive those conditions take forever to grow.' She shrugs. 'Mr Molly-Pants's place is at the bottom of that side of the mountain, and he says he's never seen the drought so bad.'

'Mr Molly-Pants?' I ask, intrigued by the name. She chuckles and shrugs again.

'Nobody knows why he's called that. He's lived there his entire life. I don't know how old he is, but he looks ancient. Hannah says he's a wrinkled avocado seed that's been left to dry out in the sun.'

I smile, hoping I'll have the opportunity to meet her step-daughter one day.

My view lingers on the front garden. Flowers ramble over each other. Lavender and roses and dahlias, and other pink and pastel beauties whose names I don't know. Bees buzz, and the air smells divine.

'It's beautiful,' I say, inclining my head in that direction.

'Thank you. I love being in the garden. The flowers won't last much longer, though, being May. We're not that far from Brisbane, but it's got as low as minus seven here in winter. But

I wait for spring, and they come again. And I enjoy having them inside the house, you know? Bringing in something wild. Will you come in?' She holds her hand out to the verandah steps.

As we walk towards the cottage, I wonder where Stella is, as she has the first appointment.

As if answering this thought, Matisse says, 'Stella's inside. I'll introduce you, and then go over to the cattle and come back for my appointment at eleven.'

'Maybe give it until eleven-fifteen. These first sessions sometimes run slightly over,' I say.

'Sure,' she says.

I told Matisse on the phone that it was important they each felt as though they had privacy for their sessions, even from each other. She said we wouldn't need to worry about Hannah, because she's usually at school in Warwick on weekdays. I said that I hoped Hannah would ask to see me if she wanted to. She explained that Hannah is reluctant to talk, that she is quite a self-contained young woman who doesn't tend to share her thoughts and feelings openly. She said she'd see what she could do. It didn't sound promising.

2

OCTAVIA

I FOLLOW MATISSE INTO A LIGHT-FILLED HALLWAY WITH SHINY timber flooring. Hats and jackets hang off horseshoe hooks nailed to the wall, the steel genuinely eroded from being worn by actual horses. I think of the mass-produced versions sold in country furnishing stores and decide I much prefer these. Pink and apricot roses give off a delicate fragrance from a vase on the hallstand.

'Come through,' Matisse says. 'Stella? Octavia's here.'

I follow Matisse into a lounge room to the left of the hall and see a thin woman sitting on a sofa in a baggy grey track-suit that pools around her waist and elbows. Her blonde hair is unbrushed and hangs limply around her face. Her grey eyes are flat. Her expression is tight, strained. Like lightning, the word *constipated* enters my head. She makes a slight effort to rise from her position and then sinks back down, as though getting to her feet takes too much energy.

'I'm Stella,' she says levelly.

'Hi, Stella. I'm Octavia,' I say with a smile.

She nods but does not return the smile. 'I'm not sure where you want to do this . . .?' she says.

'Just wherever you feel comfortable. All we need is two chairs.'

'Okay, let's do it here. Sit wherever you like.'

It is too familiar to plonk myself down on the couch next to her and, even if I wanted to, the cushions on either side of her are strewn with various items: a pilling blanket, a single sock, a crumpled tissue, a TV remote. The only other spot that faces her comfortably is the grey armchair across from where she is seated.

'I'll make coffees before I head over to the farm,' Matisse says. 'We have a machine: what would you like? Flat white, cappuccino . . .'

'Flat white would be great.'

'We only have oat milk.'

'Fine with me,' I say, although I hate that shit and wonder for the millionth time how I can make myself like it, so as to avoid the insane premium I pay to drink cow's milk. It's 2039: can't someone invent a milk alternative that doesn't involve any variety of nut, grain or bean? Also, I get that these people breed beef cows and that they're somehow different from dairy cows, but they must still lactate, right? Surely they could squeeze a bit of milk out of one of them for guests?

'Won't be long,' Matisse says, heading out of the room, Arnold close behind.

The contrast between the two women is striking, not just in their appearance but in demeanour. If I had to pick which one of the two was a distraught, grieving mother, it would easily be Stella. Matisse, on the other hand, looks as vigorous as her garden. But I remind myself to check my judgement. Some people are good at hiding their wounds.

I settle in my chair and face Stella. I smile at her again, and this time she responds with a weak upwards turn of her thin lips. I can hear Matisse clunking around loudly in the kitchen.

'Your house is beautiful,' I comment. 'Have you recently renovated?'

'Last year,' she says. 'Matisse's idea. Looking towards the future or something . . .'

'Well, you've done a gorgeous job. And that painting is stunning,' I say, pointing to an abstract work in purples and mauves hanging above the fireplace.

Stella does not follow my gaze, and that's when I notice the urn that sits on the mantelpiece. I unconsciously avert my eyes.

'Matisse did it,' Stella says. 'Her father is a devotee of Henri Matisse's cut-out doves. He loves art and he races pigeons. Quite an unconventional man. He insisted his daughter be named after the artist. Mattie says being raised with that history shaped her desire to create.'

'Well, I don't know much about art, but she's certainly able to produce things of beauty, like her namesake. There's something about such outlets that reinvigorate the spirit,' I say. 'What about you? What are your hobbies?'

Stella shrugs. 'Matisse says I don't have any interests now. I guess I'm pretty boring.'

She glances away from me then and starts blinking fast. Oh god, I've made her cry and we haven't even begun the session.

'I said I wouldn't do this,' she murmurs, hand touching her temple.

I lean forwards in my chair, but stop myself from reaching out to her.

'It's okay,' I say gently. 'I know this must be hard.'

She inhales deeply; gets control of her emotions. 'It's just . . . I don't *do* anything anymore. I don't even help around the farm. Mattie's always encouraging me to take an interest in something. It makes me feel useless—'

Matisse returns then, Arnold at her feet, a steaming mug of coffee in each hand.

She looks at Stella's pained expression and then at me. She gives me a nearly imperceptible nod that says, 'Don't be alarmed. This is how it is.'

She places a pottery mug on the table in front of me. It's a rotund owl, glazed emerald green. She hands Stella a matching owl in burnt orange. Gentle wafts of sandalwood drift from her skin as she leans over the table.

'I'm heading over to the farm, Stell,' she says, looking at her wife. 'I'll see you soon. I have my phone if you need me.'

Stella bobs her head weakly.

We watch Arnold play-biting at Matisse's ankles as they head towards the door.

I retrieve a notebook and pen from my satchel. The action of picking them up generally works as a sign that it's time to get down to business.

Stella reads the signal and subconsciously squares her body to mine.

I must have repeated my 'first session spiel' hundreds, maybe thousands, of times. This time, a few things are different.

'Thank you for letting me visit your home today, Stella,' I start. 'I know the court is mandating that you see me, but I still appreciate you trusting me to come here. Being required to talk to a stranger about such personal things must be confronting.'

'It is,' she says.

'Let me explain my job here. My role as the court-appointed psychologist is to support you and your family during your decision-making and preparation process. I'll also be here for as long as you need afterwards.'

I am skirting around saying it. The term that the court uses to refer to this thing.

'As I said to Matisse on the phone, I won't be sharing anything any of you say to me with the other family members, at least not without your permission. No matter how much we love someone or how close we are to them, sometimes it can help to talk about things privately with someone who is a step removed from the situation.'

'Okay.'

'However, there are rare instances when I may be required to disclose information to someone else. Like, if you're at imminent risk of harming yourself or another person.'

'Does that mean—' she begins.

'No,' I say, reading her mind and responding automatically, without intending to. 'That provision doesn't refer to you executing the sentence.'

There. I said it. She doesn't show any signs of discomfort at my use of the term. Maybe it's just me who feels awkward using the words.

As I will with each of the family members, I run Stella through a long list of information about my role and the legal, safety and ethical issues involved, and I clarify that while I'm not contracted to provide any mental health treatment for the family, I can help them find those services if needed.

'Any questions?' I ask at intervals, but she says no each time.

'Please let me know if any do come to mind,' I say. 'Now, if it's okay with you, I'd like to spend the rest of today getting to know you a little, so I can understand how best to support you through this process.' When Stella nods her agreement, I say, 'Let me start by asking whether you've ever seen a mental health professional before?'

'Yes. Two,' she answers. 'Never prior to Lucy – I was fine before then – but after.'

'Okay. Would you tell me about that?'

'Well, the first time was straight after Lucy. The police got a counsellor in. I couldn't concentrate on anything she said. She gave me her card so I could call her later, but I didn't.'

'How come?' I ask gently.

'I had nothing to say. To anyone. About anything. What was the point? They couldn't undo what had happened.'

I nod. 'And the second professional?'

'A psychologist in town – Geoff Hartman. Matisse arranged for me to see him because of my nightmares and stuff.'

'Ahh,' I murmur. 'What sort of "stuff"?'

She inhales deeply.

'Seeing images of . . . the scene when I was doing everyday tasks. Not sleeping. Being jumpy. Avoiding going into town, or to certain places on the farm.'

'Did Geoff diagnose you with anything?'

'Yes. PTSD.'

'I can't imagine how painful it would've been to experience that on top of your grief,' I say, feeling for her.

'He gave me some good strategies,' she says. 'But everything felt so overwhelming back then, and I . . . stopped seeing him.' She looks almost guilty.

'It sounds like it was an incredibly difficult time,' I say, 'and sometimes it takes a while to feel ready to receive help. You're certainly not alone in that.'

Relief crosses her face.

'What happened after you stopped seeing him?'

'Things got much worse. A few months later, Mattie and Sebastian dragged me back to his office. They couldn't live with me like I was, and that motivated me to stay in treatment.'

She leans forwards as though to tell me a secret. 'I went to a private psychiatric hospital in Brisbane for a couple of months. Geoff was very worried about me and he thought I'd benefit from the extra support. The therapists there were lovely, and I coped with the interventions much better than I'd anticipated. Then, after I came home, I kept working with Geoff for about eighteen months.'

'That takes a lot of commitment,' I say. 'Did it help with your symptoms?'

'Yes, actually. Quite a lot. I go most places on the farm now, which I couldn't before. But I won't go . . . down there.'

She gestures behind her head, in the direction of the place where the rainforest adjoins the farm. My brain had formed its own images of certain places while reading the court documents, and they return to me now in flashes.

'I go into town if Matisse makes me. Just last week, I said hi to Mr Taylor in the supermarket. He's known me since I was born, and yet he looked at me as if I was a stranger dressed in a clown suit. That's why I hate going there.'

'Yes. I've heard from people who've had family members killed how painful those awkward interactions are. It's as if the other person's discomfort gets in the way of them knowing how to respond to you.'

She nods.

'How's your sleep now?'

'I get three or four hours of unbroken sleep a night.'

This is such a meagre number that I struggle not to raise my eyebrows. It shouldn't come as a surprise, though – there are purple smears under Stella's eyes and, although the natural undertone of her skin is warm, her complexion looks chalky. Is she just tired, though, or weary? There's a difference, I think. Tiredness is because you are sleep-deprived. Weariness is

25

tiredness plus the exhaustion that comes with carrying a heavy burden for too long.

'What about your appetite?' I ask. She looks like a fragile bird. There are hollows under her cheeks, and her collarbones prick at her skin.

'I've always been slim,' she says, immediately sounding defensive. 'And I'm tall, which makes me look skinnier. Hannah's the same. But, yeah. Food tastes . . . yuck.' She screws up her nose like a toddler.

'Have you lost weight recently?' I ask, thinking of the looseness of her tracksuit on her body.

'I'm not sure. I haven't weighed myself,' she says, evasive.

'Have you bought new clothes? Smaller ones?' I gently persist, worried that a significant weight loss may be related to her mental state; that perhaps things have deteriorated since she stopped seeing Geoff.

'Um . . . I don't know,' she says, readjusting herself in the chair in a way that suggests that she does know. I want her to feel comfortable with me, and this line of questioning clearly isn't helping, so I decide to change direction for now.

'How did you come to live here?' I ask her.

'I grew up here. I lived in this house with my mother and father when I was a baby, but I don't remember it. Mum died of brain cancer when I was two. Dad moved us over to the cottage, which is where the main farm is.' She points towards the ridge.

'He couldn't keep up this place as well as doing his farm work, and the cottage was smaller. It was just me and him, and the day workers.

'When I was a toddler, a local lady would watch me while he was working. Once I turned six, she drove me to and from school, but I was on my own when I was at home. Even then, I couldn't wait to get out of here.'

She speaks fluidly now, without my having to probe. Maybe the distant past feels safer for her to discuss.

'My dad was a difficult man. Taciturn. Angry. A drinker. I only saw him in the evenings. Being so far away from everything, I couldn't go anywhere except school, and we rarely went into town. It was a lonely existence for a little kid, and no life for a teenage girl.

'I tried helping with farm jobs, but nothing I did was right. One time I was leading his horse through a gate, and it saw a plastic bag and bolted. The saddle caught on the gate and tore off.'

She uses her hands to make the action of the saddle ripping off the horse. I know from my riding holidays about horses' penchant for being spooked by plastic bags.

'Dad said I didn't open the gate wide enough. He wouldn't talk to me for days. I was – maybe ten? I don't think the saddle was even that badly damaged. But a mistake was a mistake, and he wouldn't forgive. There were scores of things like that over the years.'

'You were just a child, and he was so critical,' I observe. 'Was he ever physically abusive?'

'No, never. It was the unpredictability of his emotions that was frightening. You didn't know if he'd wake up hating you, liking you or being completely indifferent. It's like a dog that doesn't know if you're going to kick it, pet it or forget to feed it.

'But it wasn't even Dad, or the isolation, that really got to me. It was the cattle. I loved them. Even as a girl of three or four, I'd toddle into the middle of the paddock and plop on the grass, and they'd all come towards me, curious, and I'd sit there with a grin on my face while they worked up the courage to inch closer. I still remember them sniffing my hair; their slimy, rough tongues on my arms, licking me as if I was a newborn calf. I loved the sweet, dusty smell of them.'

She is smiling now, caught up in a good memory. Life in her eyes.

'It was my good place, you know? I felt safe with them. I know that seems strange. But I didn't feel love anywhere else. It sounds so stupid, but they became like my family. I knew every heifer, every cow, every steer in our herd. I knew when there was something wrong with them before Dad did. I'd tell him, "Whitey's getting lame again," or "I think Red Spot's getting the three-day sickness." I knew when a calf was on its way, or if a heifer was having trouble with her first pregnancy. It was the only time Dad valued my opinion. I know he was proud of me in those moments, even though he never said it.

'So, when it was market day, when the cattle truck turned up to take them, it—' Stella pauses, sucking her top lip under her teeth, biting it.

'I'd get sick the day before the truck came, knowing what was about to happen to my beloved friends. I wouldn't eat. My stomach churned. I'd vomit in the night. Just like I do sometimes now, about Lucy.'

She furrows her brows and glances away. I can see the shine of tears in her eyes.

'I'd toss and turn, trying to think of a way to stop that truck. And I never could.'

A tear comes down her face. She brushes it away with her hand.

'And then, one day when I was about twelve, Dad took me to the abattoir. I believe it was out of spite because I'd begun refusing to eat meat. He told me one of his mates managed it and wanted to "show us through". I didn't want to go, but he insisted.'

She stares down at her hands in her lap.

'It wasn't the same as dad shooting a steer at home. The cows were all queuing up, confused, overwhelmed. Some of them were terrified. There was a dairy calf, he was probably only a week old, and this worker was trying to get him to move, shoving him around and calling him a "little cunt". I know they're not meant to be treated like that, but this man was just doing what he wanted, and the poor thing was so . . .

'Anyway,' she says, flicking her hand in the air as if to swat away the memory, 'I left as soon as I finished school. Went to university in Sydney – to study psychology, actually.' She says this sheepishly, as though she thinks I might doubt her capability. I want to ask why she reacted this way, but I also want her to finish her story, so I simply smile encouragingly.

'It was excruciating to say goodbye to the cattle. There was an itty-bitty calf I named Maizie. Her mother died at birth and I hand-raised her. She was red with a white splotch, heart-shaped, on her forehead. She followed me everywhere. I asked Dad to make sure she didn't end up at the abattoir and he laughed. I told him I'd save the money – buy her off him – but he just laughed again.

'He could be cruel like that. When he was drunk and pensive, he occasionally told me stories about what a tyrant his father had been – always pointing out that I got a better deal with him. From what I could make out, Dad was punished heavily as a boy for showing any weakness. To survive, I think he became hyperalert to it in himself and others, and was driven to stamp it out. If I showed sadness, I was too sensitive. If I got upset, I was melodramatic. If I displayed compassion, I was a "big girl"; that was an insult to him. Daring to single out a piece of livestock to care about was a type of tenderness he could not tolerate. He always said life would eat me up. I guess he was right.'

Soft tears fall from her eyes now, but she seems angry too. She pulls a handful of scrunched-up tissues out of her pocket and dabs at her cheeks. Tears prickle behind my eyes, and I will them to retreat. Stella is sensitive to the pain and suffering of others. She thinks of it as a flaw; I hope one day she will see it as the superpower it is.

'I'm so sorry that happened,' I say. 'How hurtful that your father belittled your feelings and wishes that way. I'm curious: how did you end up back here?'

'Ha!' she exclaims, the loudness startling me. She stuffs the tissues up her sleeve. 'I never intended to. I thought Dad would lose this place when the cattle-licence lotto happened. Expected him to take the money and drink himself to death out of purposelessness. I couldn't believe it when he won the licence. He called me. It's the only time I can ever remember him sounding joyful. Of course, he was furious at the government for thinking they could tell him what to do, and I know he would have rebelled against the rules and regulations at every opportunity, but I think he was relieved he could stay. He had nothing else in his life, knew nothing else. I was certain he'd never sell the place, no matter what he was offered for it. So, I figured there were fifteen or twenty years left in him, factoring in the drink, and that he'd work until he dropped dead. But he had less time than I'd guessed. He was gone five years later. Rolled the tractor over on a steep part of the mountain. It crushed him, and I inherited this place.'

She shrugs unapologetically.

'By then, I had Sebastian and Hannah. They were eight and twenty months. I'd met a bartender – Cole – in my first year of uni. I was sitting in this grungy bar, waiting for a friend, and he served me a beer. He seemed so attentive and worldly. It was a slow night at the bar and my friend bailed, so we chatted for hours. Looking back now, I didn't have much in common with him, other than the physical connection you have with someone when you're nineteen, tipsy and in lust.'

I smile, thinking so many of us have been there.

'He asked me out and I jumped at it. He was my first, and after a few months of dating I accidentally fell pregnant. I couldn't face a termination, even though I wasn't financially or emotionally set up to have a baby. He pressured me to get rid of it, but I refused. Eventually he accepted his pending fatherhood, at least on the face of it.'

I nod to show I'm still listening.

'He wasn't ready to marry. I see that in retrospect. But I felt I needed the societal validation, and so nagged him to propose to me. I'm still surprised he went along with it. Commitment wasn't his strong suit. He turned out to be a tolerable father, mostly, and a shitty husband.

'At the start, he adopted the facade of a good man. He was kind and thoughtful and he did the little things, like cooking me scrambled eggs for breakfast and rubbing my feet. But it barely lasted. Within a few months of us getting married, he was going out drinking with his mates almost every night, sometimes not coming home. His clothes – which he'd chuck on the bathroom floor for me to pick up and wash – smelt like bourbon and this sickly sweet odour I couldn't identify, until one of my friends told me it was a gimmicky pheromone spray that strippers wore. I still remember how hard I blushed when she said that.

'As the pregnancy progressed, he became more and more critical of me. He started saying that I'd puffed up like the Michelin Man, and he began pointing out women in the street who he thought were overweight, commenting on how unattractive they were. He'd ask me whether I thought the stupidity gene was carried on the mother's side, and whether I reckoned eight months was too late for an abortion. Then, seemingly at random, he'd be nice for a day, or an hour. Bring me an almond croissant or some flowers.

'Strangely,' she says, 'I felt pretty comfortable with how he acted. He treated me in a way I was familiar with. I'd known that mix of unpredictability and contempt my whole life; it felt like home.'

She pauses, puffing up her cheeks with air and then exhaling through pursed lips. 'This is the first time I've ever made that connection.'

'It sounds like an important one,' I say. 'There was something in the way Cole treated you that echoed the only other close relationship you'd ever known. Sometimes our brains are drawn to things that are familiar, even when they're bad for us.'

'Hmm,' she says, contemplative. 'But then Seb was born, and Cole faded into the background. I was in love. A different kind of love. I couldn't remember my own mum, and I'd always wanted to be one. Do you have kids?' she asks.

Some therapists will answer this question, and some won't. I try to judge what feels right under the circumstances. Today, I simply shake my head and gesture for Stella to keep talking. Perhaps she wonders if I have lost a child, because a sad look briefly crosses her face before she continues.

'Well, I didn't want just one kid because I'd felt so alone as an only child. Even though Cole was an arse, he wasn't terrible with Sebastian, and I figured I could put up with the relationship to give my son a sibling. The problem was, I couldn't get pregnant again. We tried for years and it just didn't happen.

'Eventually we did IVF. I was shocked that Cole went along with it. I think the idea that he couldn't produce didn't sit right with his ego. Or maybe he just got sick of me going on about having another baby. He wasn't thrilled about the IVF and he certainly wasn't going to pay for it, but he was willing to ejaculate into a jar periodically, and that's all I needed. I'd dropped out of my degree when I had Sebastian, and I worked in an admin role that paid next to nothing. Cole dipped into my wages as though they were his personal drinking fund – his work was always sporadic – so after the decision had been made to do IVF, it took me almost three years to save up for one round of treatment. I couldn't believe it when it took on the first try, with a bunch of embryos left over. I still remember doing a happy dance around our apartment, swinging Sebastian in my arms, although he was far too big for that.'

Stella's face lights up as she relives the memory. Then it drops again.

'A couple of weeks before I was due, Cole left me for another woman. I hadn't even suspected he was seeing someone; I mean, someone in particular. I came home one day and his stuff was gone. When I tracked him down, he told me he wasn't coming back. He met Hannah once – when she was six weeks old – at my insistence. He "goo"-ed and "gaa"-ed and made all the right noises, and then he never asked about her again. He took Sebastian out to the footy a couple of times for the first year after he left, but as soon as I asked him to help with school costs, he was gone.

'So, there I was, alone with a baby and a seven-year-old, a poorly paid job and childcare fees, wondering what the future would hold. Even though Cole was unreliable, it genuinely hadn't entered my head that he'd completely abandon us. But then I got the phone call saying Dad had died.

'I was sad and relieved and – I'm not even sorry to say – delighted. What a windfall, to inherit the farm, which I could sell to give the kids a secure, comfortable life.

'One of the casual farm workers, John, was overseeing things until I could sell it. I hadn't been back once since I left, and I decided to come here to take stock. I drove up from

Sydney with the kids. We stayed in Warwick with an old friend of mine, Beth, and she watched them while I came out here.

'When I arrived, it looked like it always had, only a bit more tired. And it hit me that Dad was dead. I sat on the steps of the cottage for the longest time, looking out over everything. It dawned on me how beautiful it was. I'd honestly never realised that before.

'Just as I was relaxing into the silence, I noticed there were a few cows milling around one of the sheds, trying to reach the hay. I knew they weren't meant to be there. Someone had left a gate open, or a fence was down. I didn't want to deal with them, but I'd told John to have the day off and I knew they couldn't stay there. I felt unreasonably angry, and I strode towards them, waving my arms, yelling at them to get away from the hay. They all scattered except one mother cow with a calf at her foot. She just stood there staring at me with her liquid brown eyes, completely unfazed by my carry-on. I opened my mouth to yell again, and then I noticed the white heart on her forehead. It was Maizie, all grown up. With a baby. I couldn't believe she was still alive. I had grieved for her long ago, certain Dad would have sent her to the meatworks out of spite if nothing else. In that moment, I felt a surge of overwhelming love and gratitude towards him.

'I stood rooted to the spot, not sure what to do next. But Maizie walked right up to me. Her calf a solid red boy watched me without fear. Maizie stretched her head towards me and I held out my hand. She sniffed it so gently, then she licked it. I just started crying.

'I knew then, immediately, that I couldn't leave her. I couldn't leave them, the cattle, to whatever was going to happen next. The trucks, the meatworks – it all became real again. And there was a licence on this place that was never going to end.

'I'm not sure if you know about this, but there's a rule that the licensed cattle properties must produce a quota every year. If you're under quota for more than two years in any five-year period – unless there are exceptional circumstances – ownership of your licence and property is transferred to the government. They reimburse you at market value, less a penalty, and sell it to a new producer. I knew there were only two options: keep the property and continue to produce beef, or sell to someone else who would do the same thing.

'It sent me into a real spin. I grabbed a few biscuits of hay and lured Maizie and her calf and the others back into the paddock, through the gate that had been left open. My mind was racing with thoughts of what to do, but I couldn't find a solution.

'I didn't want to choose either of those options. I had no answer, and I felt pure panic. I paced around the property, up the hills, down the sides, everywhere, not really seeing anything, trying to figure it out. Eventually, after a couple of hours, my heart rate slowed a little, and I decided that eating might help me think. I took a peanut butter sandwich out of my esky and sat on the front steps of the cottage to eat it.

'While I was unwrapping the wax paper, I felt this intense sting on my calf. It was only a green ant bite, but it was like that split second of pain sent a fragment of memory slicing through my brain. This old fantasy from my childhood flashed into my mind. I'd come up with it when I was a girl, when the cattle truck was coming the next day. I'd be sitting up, sick, not being able to fix it, and I'd wonder, if people had to eat meat, why couldn't it be done differently? Done in a way where the animal didn't suffer needlessly? Dad had told me that when he was a kid, they only kept a few cows for meat, and they were all well-handled and not scared of humans. When the time came to slaughter one for the family to eat, his father would lead the chosen cow into the shed with a bucket of feed and shoot it while it contentedly munched on a mouthful of grain. The other cows might have been confused, maybe even sad, when it didn't return to the herd, but the animal didn't suffer. That seemed preferable to the stress and fear the same cow might experience being loaded onto a truck, when it's never been near one before, and being transported for hours with all the unfamiliar noises, sights and smells, only to arrive at the abattoir and be unloaded to go through the process of everything that happens there.

'In my childhood fantasy, we set up a beef farm where all the cows died like they did when Dad was young. And that's where my answer lay: I would set up my own abattoir on the property, slaughter the cattle at home, where they lived, where they were comfortable, and in a way where they wouldn't feel fear. I would produce the minimum amount required to meet the quota, and to keep the business afloat and pay our living expenses, and I'd market the beef to people who wanted to eat meat but who also cared about the animal's welfare. I knew there were people out there who wanted animals that are killed for meat to live a good life right until the end. Obviously I realised it would be a difficult business to set up – and painful for me, personally – but I was certain it was the way forwards. So, I did it.'

Stella looks reluctantly proud of her achievement.

'Wow,' I say. 'That's an amazing story.'

I am genuinely impressed. What a strong woman, to have done something so hard. I thought about how, since the beef restrictions, I'd marked every birthday with a big fat steak but had given no thought to where it had come from.

'I don't judge anyone, you know, for eating meat,' she says, as though she could hear my thoughts. Now I feel judged.

'To each their own?' I say, not disclosing whether I'm a meat-eater or not.

'Absolutely,' she says. 'I mean, I ran a diesel truck for years. I still put the toilet paper roll in the rubbish bin if the recycling is full. I use plastic. I used to buy fast fashion, back when I cared about clothes. We all do things that are bad for others and for the planet. I just chose to do this one thing that I think is right. Or right*er.*

'I'm also privileged to be able to choose this set-up, and I certainly don't think worse of people who do it the usual way: farmers, transporters, abattoir workers. They all play a role in feeding people, and it is a way of providing for their families. I have farmer friends who are fiercely proud of the efforts they make to care for the cattle they rear. I also know transporters and abattoir workers who do their best to provide the least stressful experience they can for the animals . . .'

She seems open to seeing all sides. I wonder how she's coped with the pain of killing the animals she loves to uphold this principle of lesser harm. I open my mouth to ask when I hear footsteps on the verandah. It must be Matisse. Our hour is up. I glance at my watch – more than up.

I see Stella look towards the verandah and then visibly pull back into herself, like a snail tucking its head back into its shell. A shutting down and turning off. The constipated expression returns. I regret allowing her to open up so much without leaving enough time to wind things down, to gently ground her back in the present day. Without being guided to do so, she's simply switched off.

We didn't even touch on much of the important background information I like to collect, or on Lucy's death, and the unthinkable dilemma Stella and her family face. That will have to wait. It's Matisse's turn now.

3

HANNAH

'I'D SAY, 'I'M HANNAH, AND I HAVE A SISTER-SHAPED HOLE IN MY heart. A dark, yawning crater, with edges too jagged for a surgeon to repair.'

It's a melodramatic way to introduce myself, but it's the only important thing I'd have to tell her. I might also say that I don't want to be a teacher like everyone thinks I do – but that would only be to lighten things up a bit. So, really, what's the point in us talking?

I mull it over as I twist my way up this tired old mountain. Right now it's the gloom-time, but this place feels just as shadowy at noon.

It's dark when I pull into the yard in front of the house. Mattie's got candles going in the lounge room, and I can see the outline of her body moving around, a shadow against the glow.

I close the car door softly, stealthily. Even Arnold doesn't hear it. As it clicks shut, I think about why Mum bought me this car. She said that she doesn't want me to be stuck here like

38

she was. And it's true that I would feel trapped without it. Still, I know it's only a token of freedom.

I thought Mum would harp on about me making it home before sundown, remind me that it's dangerous coming up the mountain in the black: all the edges, no streetlights. She hasn't said anything yet, and it's been weeks.

I think back to something a girl told me when I was in grade nine, a few months after Lucy died. She said: 'Your life as a teenager is over now. Your mum will never let you out of her sight. No sleepovers, no parties, definitely no boys.' I didn't care, when she said it. I couldn't picture a future where I'd want those things.

She was wrong. Some of the time, anyway. When Mum's in zombie mode, as she is now, she barely notices what I do. Zombie mode can last for weeks, or longer. After Lucy, it lasted for seventeen months straight. What happens eventually, though, is that she drives past a car crash or hears about someone who went splat after their parachute failed, and that switches her into You-Are-Going-to-Die mode. Then it's, careful in the bath, Hannah, you might fall and crack your head open. Chew that well – did you know a lady died from choking on her peanut butter toast? Keep the car charged, Hannah. If you broke down on the side of the road, well . . . She never finishes that one.

I know that she'd hate that I've been running in the national park. And sometimes it does feel scary out there, all alone. It's often silent, except for the birds and the sound of my feet crunching on the path. The canopy barely gets any sun by late afternoon, which makes the place feel ominous. Like there could be bad things lurking in the bottomless shadows between the ancient boulders and gargantuan trunks. But I have moved beyond avoiding things out of fear. So far beyond it that I am actively seeking out fear. I am learning, too, that the more you step into your terror, the less afraid you become.

The low light is also helpful because it creates a tougher running environment, where I can barely see the uneven gravel track.

When I first started – back when I could only run a few hundred metres, not endless kilometres like I can now – I'd trip in the dimness. Land on those sharp pebbles, and then have to cover up my skinned knees. Now, when my eyes don't make out a rock or a pothole and my foot hits it, I feel my ankle twist, flex to the side and then correct itself. I barely stumble.

I sneak across the yard, tiptoe up the steps. Nobody's heard me. I can't go inside to suffocate just yet, so I lower myself onto the wooden planks of the verandah and stare up at the blank sky. There's barely any stars to be seen.

There was nothing in the mailbox today. It's a sign of how reliant I am on it that every time I check it, I fear that snarky Mrs Porter will call out from behind the counter, tell me she made a mistake and has realised I was only seventeen when I applied for it. Australia Post rules say I should have been eighteen, blah blah blah. I'm catastrophising, I know, given that I am eighteen now and she can hardly cut me off because she was distracted when she processed my application.

I got lucky that day. It was the day the whole town found out Reverend Porter was having an affair with Mary from the gift shop. That took Mrs Porter down a peg or two, and she was preoccupied when I filled in the application form. I always smirk when I think about his mistress's name being Mary, of all things. Anyway, even though I didn't need to use my preparations, I don't regret all the books I read about bargaining and negotiation and winning people over, or the role-playing I did in front of the mirror, where I acted out both sides of the imaginary interaction I'd have with Mrs Porter. If she had argued I couldn't have the box because of A, I would have smiled and offered B; if she had objected with X, I would have complimented her and countered with Y. Would it have worked?

Maybe. But probably not because of my influence skills. It'd be the same old reason: I'm Lucy's sister, so you feel sorry for me and want to appease me. Placate me. Make me go away. Therefore, you do what I want.

I used to feel embarrassed when that happened. For you and for me. But you know what? Now I use it. I recognise your weakness and exploit it. Like when I'm buying treats for Arnold at the pet store and big-nosed Boris calls me to the front of the queue simply because I yawn or look somehow impatient. I step right up, even though old Mrs Morrie is squirming because she's about to wee herself if she doesn't get served soon and then make it to the bathrooms. Or when Samantha Sloan lets me buy a pair of jeans at sale price just because I ask, even though the sale ended the day before and she'll probably get into trouble for bending the rules.

I do it because it feels uncomfortable, and pushing through the discomfort makes me stronger. But that's not the only reason. Part of it is about taking something from you, too: something you're not quite sure that you should be offering; something you feel ambivalent about giving. I'm not sure why I want to do that. Taking advantage makes my soul feel dirty, to the point that sometimes I have to do something nice – like dropping tins of dog food in the rescue collection bin at the supermarket – for absolution. Then I feel weak, and the cycle starts again.

I killed a frog today. A green one, the colour of ferns. He was lying on the track. He tried to hop away from me but he couldn't. He felt squishy when I picked him up. Not frog-squishy – insides-squishy. He had tooth marks that went all the way through his body. I grabbed a cold, mossy rock from under a tree. I smashed it over his head until his brains came out, and then ran on.

4

OCTAVIA

I OPEN THE DOOR TO MY WAITING ROOM AND, *THUNK*, I'M HIT IN THE stomach. It's not painful, more like a rush of air. I look down to see a foam toy dragon at my feet.

A mother's voice, shrill: 'Logan, now you've hit that lady. *Sit. Down.*'

A red-faced youngster, wearing a T-shirt with a spiky yellow speech bubble that screams *POW!*, whines indignantly, 'It's not a *toy*, it's the Dragon Crusher. Ugh.' He runs back to the toy box that I provide for our child clients.

'Sorry,' the guilty-looking mother whispers to me.

'It's perfectly fine,' I say, smiling, I hope reassuringly. This lady reeks of the shame that often radiates from parents who find themselves here.

A different toy whizzes towards the receptionist's head. She ducks with practised skill and gives the child a steely look.

The waiting room is buzzing, as it often is on a Friday morning. Any morning, actually. Even on the increasingly frequent 'groundhog days' – the ones that blend into each other because they feel like the same scenarios playing on a loop – I experience a surge of pride when I look at the busy practice I've established. I love that clients can choose from a number of psychologists to find someone who meets their needs. And, most importantly, I'm confident our clients will be seen by someone who is warm and empathic. I look for these innate qualities just as much as qualifications and experience when I'm recruiting, because they can't be faked. I want a therapist who can genuinely connect, hear secrets, burdens, mistakes and confessions, and still help the person feel safe, and accepted, and hopeful about their future.

At this thought, he pops into my mind – as he frequently does of late – and I wonder if a therapist is doing that for him, right now, in prison. Helping him come to terms with what he's done, as well as what awaits him. Perhaps, although I can't imagine he'd be interested in that sort of assistance, at least not without some ulterior motive.

As I stride towards my therapy room – I'm cutting it fine for my first client, as usual – I think about the documentary I saw about him on Boxing Day. It included a jailhouse inter-view. It put me off my Christmas dinner leftovers, which I still hold against him. Along with the other stuff, obviously. He did not give the impression of being in need of help with his conscience.

I know there are prisoners who reach a point where they are filled with regret for their crimes, and put in tremendous work to make sure they do not repeat the past. The pain and suffering they have caused can never be undone, but through providing them with the treatment they need and giving them the right support along their reintegration journey, our communities are hopefully made safer. But he is an extreme case. One of the worst. Even if he actually wanted to change,

I don't know who could be convinced it would be worth trying. Not that there is any point now, anyway. No matter what happens, he will never again see outside those prison walls.

I banish thoughts of him as I sit at my desk, turn on my computer and open my calendar. My day is packed, and this job feels like hard work right now. It's not that I don't get satisfaction from helping clients improve. It's more that, although everyone's reason for coming to me is different, and despite the connection I make with them, they will eventually exit my life – hopefully on a better trajectory – to be replaced by someone else at their own low point. I'm on this journey of struggle with multiple people at once, and the dance is repeated over and over from year to year, starting at square one with each client in a never-ending queue of those needing – deserving – help.

I tell myself I will do things to protect my energy today: take breaks, eat the pasta I've packed for lunch, perhaps read a novel while I eat. Maybe I will even meditate for a few minutes, I think as I run my hand through my hair and remember with satisfaction that it's so much shorter now. And that I let it go grey, even though my friends warned me I'd look frumpy and prematurely aged. My version of self-care was saying 'fuck it' to caring about what others think, although it did help to discover that the type of grey I have is the steely, fashionable kind, and I can smile smugly at my friends every time it is complimented by a barista or a theatre usher or a sales atten-dant half our age.

I mentally review the histories of each of today's clients. A couple who lost their infant twins to a rare genetic disorder and can't decide whether to risk trying for another baby. A 73-year-old man with bladder cancer and a major depressive disorder, whose wife of four decades has just left him for his younger brother. A 17-year-old boy who is struggling to come out as gay because his evangelical Christian family will ostracise him. A 43-year-old woman with a cockroach phobia so severe that she duct-tapes the gaps around her bedroom door before going to sleep each night. And, finally, a thirteen-year-old girl with type one diabetes whose parents heard the term 'diabulimia' in the media and realised their daughter was restricting her insulin in an effort to reduce her tiny frame to a complete nothing.

On top of that, I have three letters to write to doctors and a phone call to return to a client who is attending her son's funeral today. He died by suicide.

If it were Monday, I would repeat this day again four more times – hopefully broken up with a few cancellations – before I rested properly. Thankfully, tomorrow is Saturday. I can sleep in, luxuriate with a breakfast of French toast with Nutella, and escort Bob on a proper walk, one that takes us further than to the end of the street and back.

Then I groan, remembering that I have clinical supervision with Henry tomorrow. We try to see each other during the week, so we can have a complete mental break from work on the weekend, but our calendars are both so full right now. Sometimes I feel as if this requirement of our profession is an imposition: spending your entire career – no matter how much experience you have – reviewing your practice with a supervisor. But, in reality, I get so much from these meetings, where I can discuss complex cases, brainstorm solutions to tricky presentations and ethical dilemmas, and, more recently, share strategies to counteract the professional malaise that has overcome me. No, nobody should be doing this work in a bubble: unseen, unaccountable. And besides, tomorrow won't be our typical supervision catch-up, because Henry's joining me on something of an outing afterwards.

•

I raise my voice to yell even louder, but Henry still can't hear me. I silently mouth, 'Talk later'. He simultaneously nods and ducks as the placard of the beetroot-faced man in front of us tips backwards. The man rights the lightweight sign with determined, hairy hands and continues to chant 'Execute justice, not people!' along with the crowd. I see a woman holding a placard with an image of Lucy's face on it, underneath the words, *Killing won't bring her back*. I feel ill.

A megaphone squeals, and Henry taps me on the shoulder and gestures for me to follow him. The chant has changed to 'Abolish the trial! Abolish the trial!' We squeeze our way to the back of the crowd, where there are more parents with children – I wonder at the wisdom of bringing them here – and less yelling. One woman has brought her white poodle and holds it in her arms, the dog intriguingly unperturbed by the chaos. It looks old, and I wonder if it might be deaf.

With perfect timing, a young couple vacates one of the handful of wooden benches positioned at the back of King George Square. Henry grabs my arm and pulls me towards it with such force that I almost lose my footing. I realise, as she stares me down with a face that says 'low move', that we've narrowly beaten a mother with a pram and toddler to the seat. I turn to Henry with my mouth ajar, and he shrugs, muttering, 'Kill or be killed.' I elbow him, and he mock-winces.

Someone is testing microphones as the speakers assemble behind them on the podium in front of the town hall. We both raise our voices to make affirmative noises when they

47

ask if people can hear. Incongruously, given the purpose of the protest, my mind fixes on an image of gallows and a robed executioner, surrounded by raucous mobs of peasants baying for blood to satisfy a primal need for release from the drudgery of their existence.

I notice a sheen of perspiration on Henry's forehead. It's a mild day, but I know he doesn't like crowds and is probably feeling anxious. However, when I mentioned the protest, he said he wanted to join me – something about it being important to 'understand both sides of this thing'. He'd never admit it, but I think he's simply intrigued by anything taboo.

I wouldn't have come to this event at all, except that Matisse was originally planning to attend. She wanted to hear what the speakers – particularly those who had also experienced the murder of a family member – had to say. She asked if I would join her for emotional support, which is one of the services I am contracted to provide if the family requests it for such outings. After further consideration, Matisse decided to skip the protest because of the risk of being recognised, but suggested I might still attend. In the end, and after checking to see that Stella and Sebastian had no objections, I decided to come as a private citizen – not in my contracted capacity – to understand more about the experiences of the victim-survivors who will be speaking.

Henry wipes sweat from his forehead with the back of his hand and grins at me. I take in his pleasing features – inherited from his Scottish mother and Japanese father – and have a flashback to my initial feelings for him six years ago, when he became my clinical supervisor. Something about his graceful assuredness and long fingers, combined with his cool logic and mercilessly dark humour, resulted in a mortifying schoolgirl crush. It was certainly not acted on in any way – and I'm confident remained undetectable to him – but was compelling enough that I briefly contemplated getting a different supervisor. Then he mentioned his partner, Tom, and all sorts of boring domestic routines they shared, and the fantasy shrivelled up like cellophane against a flame. Although we're friendly in a collegial sort of way, we are not friends, per se, and it hasn't been difficult to maintain professional boundaries. Mostly I think of him as my shrewd and thoughtful peer, and someone whose experience I greatly benefit from. Although, on the occasion I find myself physically close to him – such as now – his scent of the ocean and lime zest, perhaps aided by an undercurrent of pheromones, still causes a tiny flutter in my chest. It feels harmless and just a bit naughty.

Our supervision session started a couple of hours ago at my place with him asking, 'So, how did it go?' with no other context. By 'it' we both knew he meant my first my appointments with Stella and Matisse.

The government required the family to consent to me revealing their identities to Henry during supervision. I can't conceal who they are because, like everyone else in the country, he's aware of this high-profile case, and he needs to understand what I'm dealing with to provide proper clinical support.

'It went well,' I had said, smiling.

'And?' he'd said, leaning in.

'They're just normal people, Henry. I don't know what I expected.'

'You must have something more interesting to report than that.'

'Well, I saw Stella first. She's terribly affected, of course, she and Matisse losing their daughter that way. I don't think she's bounced back much in the past four years. Her mood seems quite low, and she's very shut down at times.'

I'd filled him in on the rest of Stella's story, including the origins of Heathwood's highest-welfare beef. I am reflecting on this conversation when my thoughts are interrupted by someone introducing the first speaker. Then we hear the soft yet strong voice of a middle-aged woman carried to us over the speakers. We can't see her actual face from our bench, but we can view it on the oversized LED screens that hang conspicuously from the sandstone walls of the city hall.

'The government says that executing people will give justice to the families of victims,' she starts. 'They claim the process will help families find peace. But as the mother of Milly Peterson, I can say from experience that the pain can never end for the families, no matter the outcome for the perpetrator. There will always be an empty bed, a vacant seat at the kitchen table, a missing voice when we sing "Happy Birthday" to our other children.

'Killing another person won't end that pain. It will simply cause more pain. There is no place for bloodlust in modern justice. Just look at the US. Look at the cases of Cameron Todd Willingham and Ruben Cantu: innocent men whose lives were brutally taken by the state, only for them to later be exonerated of their alleged crimes. Think of the suffering of the victims' families in those cases. The guilt they might experience on top of the pain of losing their loved ones. We are not immune to such travesties here. The courts make mistakes all the time. Connor Robinson was convicted of Milly's murder until DNA results later proved he didn't do it. Now her real killer is sitting in prison, where he should be. But what if my family had killed Connor? Murdered him, in fact. How would we feel now?'

Henry leans towards my ear and whispers, 'She makes a good point.'

I nod in agreement.

'Also,' he adds, 'even if the perpetrator is unequivocally guilty, like McDermott, do you think we are taking what should be a societal responsibility – making decisions about justice and punishment – and unfairly handing that burden to those most affected by the crime?'

'What do you mean?'

'A client told me something the other day,' he says quietly, so as not to disturb the people around us listening to the speech. 'Their son was badly bullied by another kid at his high school, and the school asked the son whether he wanted the bully to be stood down as captain of the football team as punishment. The bully is apparently an exceptional player who is being scouted by professional football clubs. But the school didn't say the bully would be stood down as punishment; they wanted the victim to decide if he should be. And everyone would know it was his decision. The son was *beside* himself with the responsibility of choosing his perpetrator's fate. His parents felt that the school only made things worse by putting all that on a bullied kid, instead of taking responsibility themselves. Isn't this like that, but on a larger scale?'

I sigh and shake my head as if it might help to sort out my thoughts. There is honestly so much to this situation – victims, justice, trauma, accountability – that it hurts my brain.

We return to listening to Milly's mother's compelling speech. By the end of it, I am almost entirely swayed to her way of thinking.

The crowd shuffles and murmurs while the next speaker is introduced. I smell beer and look around to see a man a couple of metres away casually holding a can. Under the circumstances, I understand his urge to numb himself.

I covertly point it out to Henry, who suggests we find a pub after this wraps up. I agree enthusiastically. After that, we sit and listen to two more speakers. They share their thoughts on the questionable morality of punishing the act of murder with sanctioned murder. They present the evidence from overseas jurisdictions about capital punishment having no greater deterrent effect than life sentences, and the potential for systemic biases against non-white peoples and those from lower socio-economic backgrounds.

As the final speaker takes the stage, a hush descends over the previously rowdy crowd. He is a young man whose partner and infant child were murdered by her ex-boyfriend. Before he even opens his mouth, I can feel the weight of his loss.

'I am a soldier,' he says, and for some reason I am surprised by this. Although he's a tall man, he appears compressed somehow – without the stereotypical military bearing – as though he has been squashed in on himself by grief.

'During certain army training scenarios,' he continues, 'you prepare for what you need to do if you're ever taken prisoner. Ever subjected to torture.'

I notice a tag sticking out of the blouse of a woman in front of me, and I find myself intently focused on the upside-down lettering of the discount chain store brand written across it. My eyes run over and over the bold black letters, my inner voice sounding out the word.

'There's a reason soldiers don't discuss the atrocities they are trained to face with members of the public,' he says. 'They are not for public consumption, because they are in-human acts.'

I see the woman with the exposed tag nodding, the small white rectangle bobbing slightly in time with her head.

'And now we are asking families – ordinary families, who are already suffering – to consider inflicting grossly violent punishment on another human being. No matter how detestable that human being may be, we are opening the door to these families not only taking a life, but potentially plotting, and then enacting, the torture of another person.

'What benefit can possibly come from that,' he asks, 'no matter the original crime?'

My internal state has shifted from sombre to something else. Something shadowy. Unclean. I need to leave.

I tap Henry on the shoulder. He looks at me, his expression morose, and I mouth, 'Let's go?'

He nods, and we stand and walk away from the crowd. He suggests a particular pub we both like and we walk purposefully and silently towards it, both caught up in our own thoughts.

After a couple of blocks, Henry says, 'I think I'm going to have a whisky *and* a beer when we get there,' and then promptly trips over nothing. We laugh and make predictable jokes about him not needing anything to drink. With this, the mood lightens, and he announces that he's going to treat me to a steak sandwich. This seems wildly frivolous – it's not my birthday and I haven't achieved anything vaguely important recently – and it also makes me think of the sweet cows dotting the Heathwood pastures.

When I don't answer immediately, he looks at me and says, 'I knew it! They've gotten to you.'

'What?'

'I could tell you were getting all mushy when you told me the story about the cows. They've guilted you into becoming a vego, haven't they?' He's grinning now.

'Shut up,' I say, stopping myself from giving in to the urge to whack him on the arm. 'I was actually trying to work out how you can afford to shout me a steak when you haven't put up your fees for five years.'

Henry and I share a list of topics that we have wordlessly negotiated to be fair game for teasing; his lack of business acumen being one. For all his talk of good boundaries and assertiveness, he's a softie when it comes to asking to be paid what he's worth, or even accounting for basic inflation.

'Three years,' he says. 'And I'm putting them up by four dollars a session from next month. Now, you haven't finished telling me about the family.'

'Four dollars?!' I say as we walk in the door of the pub.

'Octavia! The family.'

'*Okay*,' I say, knowing I will return to the ridiculously meagre fee increase later. 'But are we doing supervision, or enjoying a drink and a break from this whole topic?' I ask.

There is a long pause from him, because he knows we can't properly do both. He sighs heavily, then says, 'I guess we need to find a quiet table and swap our beers for Cokes.'

'Thank you,' I say. I think we both know I need to talk about this even more than I need a drink.

Once we've ordered our food and drinks, and settled ourselves at a table in a corner away from other patrons, I say, 'Where shall I start?'

'Start with the basics. Tell me about the other mother, the kids.'

'Well, Sebastian, the son, is twenty-five and a vet here in Brissy. Hannah's eighteen, living at home while she finishes her final year at school.

'And Lucy's other mum, Matisse . . .' I smile. 'She's a real woman, you know? Warm and fiery. In touch with her emotions. She seems more adjusted to the loss. She was born in Peru. She met an Aussie guy, a backpacker, there when she was nineteen. They moved to the Sunshine Coast together, got married and eventually divorced.

'Matisse was an ER nurse but had a passion for home renovations. After her marriage ended, she got a job renovating Stella's old farm cottage into a B & B. She said the connection between them was instant. She'd never felt "right" with anyone before.

'Stella's kids adored Matisse, and she them. Stella longed for another baby, and Matisse always wanted to be a mother. Stella had embryos left over from when she had Hannah, who was an IVF baby. Her ex, Cole, relinquished them. Apparently he didn't care what she did with them. And Matisse got to carry the baby.'

'Huh. A truly modern family,' Henry says. Then he asks, 'What's involved in executing the sentence?'

'Well,' I start, 'the sentence is due to be carried out on Saturday the fifth of November. That morning, the participating family members will go to the prison. There's a purpose-built unit that's been designed especially for this case and the ones that will follow. The offender will already be inside when we get there. The family will get a briefing from correctional staff before they enter. They are allowed to be in the room with the offender for up to twenty-four hours, and what they choose to do in there is completely up to them. There's no one else in the room, no one watching them on CCTV – but there will be panic buttons in case they need assistance. They're allowed to take in any implements they want – weapons, tools, whatever – so long as they are legal items in Queensland. So, a kitchen knife is fine, but mace isn't. And guns aren't allowed, even if you're licensed, because the risk to the family members is too high if there is a misfire or if shrapnel ricochets.'

'Geez.' Henry exhales. 'So, what happens if they change their mind halfway through the execution?'

'Well, if the family doesn't enter the unit – if they fail

to show, for example – then the sentence is automatically converted to life in prison. That's what he'll be hoping for. But as soon as one of them goes in, the sentence must be executed. So, if they maim him but don't kill him – freak out in the middle of it and leave, say – a doctor will enter with corrections officers to determine if the offender is still alive. If he is, a government-appointed executioner will administer a lethal injection to complete the sentence.'

Henry looks at me, upper lip curled in apparent disgust.

'Pretty intense, isn't it?' I say.

He nods. 'What about if the family can't agree on the method of killing him?'

'I honestly don't think the government's thought through those things. What if one wants to kill him immediately, and another wants to toy with him for the full twenty-four hours? Maybe they think that's something we can work out with a couple of family team-building exercises?'

Henry raises one side of his mouth in a wry smile.

'The family members sign a form indemnifying the government of responsibility for any trauma, or exacerbation of existing trauma, that is caused by participating. The underlying principle is that by letting the family administer the punishment directly, they will feel justice – whatever their personal concept of that is – has been served, and that in turn is supposed to help them cope with what they've done.'

'I can't see it working like that,' Henry says.

'Me neither,' I say. 'That's one of the reasons I wanted to be involved. I want to support them to decide what's right for them, not simply what the public'—I think of all the people at this morning's rally—'and the lobby groups want them to do.'

'Will Sebastian participate?' asks Henry.

'I don't know,' I say. 'I haven't met him yet. Hannah's out, though. She was a minor at the time of the offence, which means she's ineligible to participate. I count that as a good thing. She's only eighteen. Can you imagine being involved in something like this at that age?'

Henry sits back and shakes his head.

'She can still see me for support throughout the process if she wants to, but Matisse says she's noncommittal. They both describe her as a self-possessed, responsible young woman. She was the one the family didn't have to worry about after Lucy died. She just got on with it, they say. Held things together, helped look after the house, cooked meals and picked up extra chores around the farm when everything was chaotic.'

'Hmm,' says Henry, sounding unconvinced that a teenager could truly cope that well following the brutal murder of her sister.

'Matisse says Lucy was the polar opposite of her sister. She was a little firecracker, running all over the farm, climbing trees and riding horses. Always in trouble at school for being cheeky – one of those kids that teachers struggle to discipline because they are privately entertained by their antics. She was also sensitive, kind and great with animals . . . God, if I had a kid like that and someone murdered her, and I was given the legal option, my instinct would be to mush his features into a dog's dinner.'

I surprise myself with the vehemence of this statement, and how quickly I've swung away from Mrs Peterson's way of thinking.

'But you wouldn't actually do it, would you?' asks Henry.

'I don't know,' I say, shrugging. 'I might be tempted.'

'Yeah,' says Henry. 'I probably would be, too.'

'There is one other thing,' I say, glancing up as a waiter

walks towards us with two plates, 'but I'll tell you next time we meet, because I'd really like to block out all this misery while I enjoy my steak sandwich.'

'*Whaaat?*' Henry whines, drawing out the word like a five-year-old. 'Tell me now.'

I smile at the waiter as he puts our plates down, and wait for him to leave.

'Matisse has already killed someone,' I whisper.

5

HANNAH

IF I SPOKE TO THAT WOMAN, I'D TELL HER THIS: I'M ONLY A GIRL BUT my bones ache as if I've been on this planet for two hundred million years. And if I once walked with theropods, why do people treat me like a helpless pinkie plucked from the pouch of a road-killed kangaroo?

I'd tell her that I'm about to go for a run in the rain, partly to distract myself from the hunger pains that are prying my insides apart like the jaws of life. Biting my arm – where nobody can see, of course – also works, but reading doesn't help anymore; it's not intense enough.

I mark off day three on my calendar. My goal is to make it to day four this time.

I allow myself water, but only three glasses a day. Afterwards, I'll drink litres of Gatorade and stuff my face with bowls and bowls of pasta.

If I spoke to that woman, I'd tell her I heard Mum on the phone yesterday. She was talking to a man. I have no idea who he was. I came out of my room to get my first glass of water for the day. She was making porridge in the kitchen. It's all she likes to eat now. Mushy food. Because she's reverted to being a baby.

She had the phone on speaker. She probably thought I'd gone out. I stopped in the hallway when I heard his voice, a bellow, like the sound of our bull when he can't get to the cows in heat: 'I'll tell them what you did, Stella. Don't think I won't. You need to make this right.'

And Mum, like a mouse pleading with a cat not to eat it, was all, like, 'Okay, okay. Don't do it. I'll sort it out. I don't have it available just like that. Give me a couple of days. I'll call you. I promise.'

And him: 'You'd fucking better, Stella. You're a useless fucking bitch, and I'll make sure everyone knows it if you don't make it happen. Soon. *Slut*.'

He drew out every letter in the last word; the 't' crisp, like an ironed shirt. And then the phone went quiet. Mum started crying, making this heavy, heaving sound. I'd never heard anyone talk to her that way. I was only partially surprised that she let him.

I turned around and tiptoed back to my room, and silently closed the door. About ten minutes later, I noisily walked into the kitchen and Mum jumped because she hadn't realised there was anyone else in the house.

'Have you been reading, honey, with those headphones on?' she asked.

I shrugged. It felt good to withhold the comfort she was seeking – the certainty I hadn't overheard whatever was going on in that conversation.

6

OCTAVIA

I LIVEN UP THE DREARY COMMUTE BY PUTTING ON THE *WHO'S KILLING Who?* podcast. It's part three of an ABC series exploring the introduction of 'survivor-led capital punishment' in Queensland. A smooth-talking voiceover tells me that episode four will go into Lucy's case but, in this episode, Taylor Hayes will be interviewing a political scientist from the University of Canberra about the social and political climate that led to the legislation.

Hayes introduces Professor Adamik in her smooth, polished voice.

'Professor Adamik, can you explain how this came to pass? There are many Australians who say they thought capital punishment would never happen here.'

'Exactly,' responds Adamik. 'We were, most of us, shocked when this law passed. But if you look back at the political and social landscapes leading up to this time, it's actually not that surprising. Think back to how vulnerable we were as a nation twelve years ago. The climate falling apart. The federal government acknowledging – finally – that extreme action must be taken to save us from catastrophe. The huge unrest that followed as industries were shut down. The jobs lost, finances drained from the economy. We'd already lived through the decade of uncertainty that started with the pandemic in the early 2020s. Then the record-breaking floods, then droughts again. Year after year of catastrophic bushfires destroying houses and taking lives. The victims were angry, the farmers were angry, the *people* were angry. And we had unprecedented international unrest, the skyrocketing oil prices, the housing crash, the increased crime . . .

'Then there was the rise of the underground extreme-right terrorist groups. We know the consequences of that, and I won't delve into them today. Even though most Australians were, and still are, horrified by these ideologies, we experienced a general rise in conservative sentiment. People were feeling afraid and that things were out of control – you can see that in surveys conducted at the time. Altogether it created something of a boiling pot, a fault line of anger running through—'

'You think we as a people have a repressed rage?' Taylor asks.

'That sort of sentiment, yes. And I haven't yet touched on the huge frustration with the court systems, the criminal justice systems. For years, voters said we were going too lightly on serious offenders. The media has reported on a number of cases where repeat sexual and violent criminals with significant histories of offending, and compelling evidence to suggest they continue to present a threat, have been bailed or paroled, only to commit more horrific crimes.

'As a nation, we were clamouring for change for decades. Think back to Jill Meagher in 2012. The public's reaction epitomised their disgust in the system. Yet similar scenarios repeated themselves over and over. In the past ten years we've had Amira Ahmad, Sara Delaware, Timmy Chan, little Melanie Walsh-West. All killed by repeat serious violent or sexual offenders who were on bail or parole. Add in the statistics about family violence: women and children being subjected to the most brutal abuse, and murder, at the hands of their partners and fathers, despite multiple AVOs and DVOs being in place.

'People believed their voices were not being heard. The community, the families, the survivors, were crying out, "No longer." Calls for change via advocates' groups grew stronger. We had the fringe-dwellers – or so they seemed, initially – calling for victims' families to have a say in the punishment. A direct role in the punishment, even. The biblical "eye for an eye".

'Most of us dismissed these groups as a radical minority. But then – and this was the pivotal turning point – six-year-old Mikala Matthews was murdered by paroled offender Tyrone Newman. And who did Mikala happen to be the daughter of? Mega-tycoon and conservative political donor Brett Matthews.

'We were bombarded with media images of a distraught father: this once powerful, controlled man who led enormous companies – headed a multibillion-dollar empire – reduced to a puddle of despair. A man so devastated he stood down from his business roles, stepped out of the public eye. And then, three years later, we saw Matthews and his entire family regrouping and lobbying for the strongest possible changes to the justice system. Forcefully calling for states to move to the model being used in Texas, in Oklahoma. Giving victims' families, quite literally, the power to execute justice.'

'Matthews was the catalyst?' asks Hayes.

'Matthews had powerful relationships in the right places, as well as the support of far more Queenslanders than anyone predicted. And so, here we are, with this trial of survivor-led capital punishment. For the next three years, judges have the opportunity to consider this penalty at all relevant sentencings. The . . .'

I start tuning out. My mind turns to this evening and my first session with Sebastian. I strain to picture him: a 25-year-old man who lost his sister at the hands of another man in the most dreadful way. This man, who unleashed the most terrible power all men hold, but most never use, was rejected by his own father when he was a fledgling boy – just as Sebastian had been. I wonder, will this young veterinary doctor want to back up his mother inside that killing cell?

•

The man sitting in the waiting room is huge. Both tall and broad, but trim, fit. I take in his wavy, honey-coloured hair and warm brown eyes. His face is put together in the right way – a handsome guy, but not intimidatingly so. Open features, approachable. He is wearing aqua-coloured scrubs with a logo of a cartoon koala on the right breast, underneath which is written *Friends of Wildlife Hospital*.

He stands when I call out, 'Dr Heathwood?'

His smile is genuine, and he reaches out his hand to meet my offered one. 'Sebastian, please.'

'I'm Dr Octavia Tate,' I introduce myself.

'Good to meet you, Dr Tate,' he says.

'Please, call me Octavia,' I say.

We both laugh at the mildly nauseating banality of two doctors in a room saying, 'Please don't call me doctor.'

Ice broken, I lead him down the hallway to my consulting room. It is a good room. Glorious light, no matter the weather.

But it is particularly beautiful right now because it is lightly raining, which is a rare thing. Under the enormous picture window, an overstuffed leather tub chair and a double-seater couch huddle around the edges of a worn rug I picked up in a market in Turkey more than twenty years ago. The bookshelves are lined with reams of knowledge. The lamps glow golden, and coral-hued snapdragons brighten up the coffee table. I display colourful artworks from Sardinia, Istanbul, the Solomon Islands and Australia around the walls. And there is an electric fireplace, which you can enjoy with heat or just the flame effect as the weather dictates. Of course, there are boxes of tissues on every reachable surface.

Whenever I enter this room, I'm glad that I've designed a space with the comfort of my clients and myself in mind. Place is important: the feeling of warmth – the cocooning of souls – creates a sense of safety within this room. I think of it as being womb-like. Most clients comment on how they like being in here. Sebastian is no different.

'Nice room,' he says approvingly. 'Cosy.'

'It is, isn't it?'

He settles into the tub chair in front of the window, dwarfing it with his frame. A streetlight glows over his shoulder, making each tiny raindrop illuminate in the darkness like a Christmas bauble. '*Le ciel il pluet*,' my high-school French teacher would have said. The sky is crying.

I have a Japanese teapot between us. Cast iron. Two small ceramic cups. Steam rises in a twirl from the spout. 'Tea?' I ask.

When I happened to mention this touch during a supervision session, Henry teased me. He feels it's a bit over the top, this little tea ceremony. 'Wanky,' I believe he called it. But I like to drink tea throughout the day, and my clients often have some too if I offer. It's a tiny connection formed between us.

'Lovely, thank you. Perfect weather for it,' he comments as I pour the tea.

'Yes,' I agree as I hand him a cup. 'I adore the rain. But I must admit, it makes me daydream about skiving off work to drink hot chocolate and take naps.'

This back and forth about the weather might seem hackneyed, but it serves the purpose of building rapport before we get into the real stuff.

'I'm glad I'm not the only one,' he says. 'You should see my mums' place. It's the ultimate rain retreat. It's up in the hills and – oh, sorry, you've been there, haven't you?'

'Yes, I have,' I say. 'And I was charmed by the cottage. The perfect place to enjoy the rain. If Arnold's anything like my dog, though, they must spend the whole time mopping up muddy footprints.'

'Actually, Arnold's a giant baby when it comes to wet weather. He refuses to go out in it. Can't tell you how many pee puddles have soaked that carpet . . .'

Sebastian glances down then and, as though suddenly realising what he is wearing, he says, 'Apologies for turning up in scrubs, by the way. I hoped to get changed, but it was a hectic one.'

I am liking this man. He is affable, warm.

'You work in a wildlife hospital?' I ask, the scent of jasmine tea wafting up between us.

'Yup. Mum hoped I'd go into large-animal medicine. Wanted free call-outs for the cattle, probably – as if I don't provide them anyway.' He shrugs with his palms face up, grinning.

'But wildlife's always been my thing. It's usually our fault they need help. You know: car strikes, dog attacks, exposure to rat bait. I believe it's up to humans to set it right again, if we can. Often we can't, and that's the downside of the job.

66

Lots of euthanasia. But, when you bring a baby sugar glider back to health or fix a pelican's wing so it can fly free again, it's the best feeling.'

'A sense of justice for helpless animals. That's something you and your mum have in common,' I comment.

He nods. 'Yes.'

At this moment, my office phone rings. Damn. Reception knows I don't like calls coming through when I'm with a client. I apologise, striding across to my desk to answer it. It's a brief and unimportant query about tearoom supplies from Joseph, the new receptionist. I tell him I will discuss it with him later, but I say it kindly; it's hard to remember all the rules when you're learning a new job.

I sit back down, deciding it's time to crack on. I orientate Sebastian to the purpose of our sessions together and take him through all the same information I went over with his mother and Matisse. He has no questions. Then I ask him how he feels about seeing me.

'To tell you the truth,' he starts, 'it's come at a good time. It will be the fifth anniversary of Lucy's death in November and – except for the police, and at the trial – I've never spoken with anyone about what happened.'

'Nobody at all?' I clarify.

'Nobody. I mean, everyone who knew me knew what happened, and everyone I've met since then – well, either they realise who I am and are too polite to raise it, or I haven't felt the need to bring it up.'

'Why is that, do you think?'

He pauses briefly, then says, 'I guess it can be so over-whelming that it's easier to tuck it away, out of the light. Even now, it feels impossible that it happened. That day seems so distant. Not four and a bit years ago – more like ten, or twenty. I can remember everything clearly, though. It was such a normal day on the farm. I'd just finished the second year of my veterinary science degree. I was excited that I wasn't due back at uni until February, and had come home because Mum had a few cows who were due to calve. She had this one cow, Heidi, who she especially loved because she was a daughter of her favourite childhood cow, Maizie. Heidi was getting older and had given birth to twins the year before. Both died, and Mum was worried she was going to have twins again. Once they have one set, they tend to have them again, and twins have a higher mortality rate than singletons. There's also a higher risk of death for the cow. Mum hadn't actually meant to breed Heidi again – she was going to retire her, but there was some mix-up, and she was mated.

'So, anyway, she was huge. Her udder was seriously almost grazing the ground when she walked. And on that day, Mattie – Matisse – noticed that Heidi was looking uncomfortable, pacing, pawing, all signs of early labour. Then Mattie saw her lie down on the ground a couple of times and get back up, so she came to grab Mum and me.

'We weren't that surprised. We thought she'd deliver that day or the next. And Mum had said in the morning that it'd be today. She's got this weird connection with the cows; you know if she says something's about to happen with them, it probably will. In fact, I don't ever remember her making a wrong prediction.

'So, when Mattie arrived at the house, it was about four o'clock in the afternoon and we were in the kitchen, making coffee. Hannah was in her room, where she always is, reading her books, headphones on; she's a bibliophile. We asked her where Lucy was, because Lucy loved watching the calvings. We didn't try to protect her from the difficult ones, where we thought something might go wrong. She just dealt with them. She was a tough kid. Hannah, on the other hand . . . Anyway, Hannah said Lucy'd already gone to the treehouse. It wasn't a normal cubby house up in a tree – it's this place Lucy built, out of branches and stuff, in the national park at one end of our paddocks. She'd been going there most afternoons after school since she was seven or eight. We didn't know what she did down there, really. I mean, just kid stuff – make-believe and dress-ups, we figured. It was her special place, and she was private about it. None of us were allowed to go there.

'She'd ride her pony, Lil' Sis. She's this ancient grey Arabian that just hangs around the farm now, being stroppy.'

'Oh, yes. She and I have met,' I say, smiling.

'Mum and Mattie got her for Lucy's sixth birthday. Lucy'd been asking for a pony since she was in nappies. Mum used to say "gee-gee" to her – the old-fashioned nickname for a horse – whenever they saw our horses, and it was one of her first words. So, on her birthday, Mum and Mattie turned up with this thing they'd bought off some guy in Killarney. It was instant love between them, Lucy and that mare. The only thing Lucy wanted more than a pony was a little sister, so I think that's where the name came from. It's a terrible creature, though. Came barrelling out of the truck that first day as if a snake had bit it. I wondered what the hell Mum and Mattie were thinking. She should never have been a little girl's pony: she kicks, bites, pins her ears, looks pissy all the time. I thought she'd break Lucy's neck.

'Lucy was the only living thing that horse liked. And Lucy cared for Lil' Sis as if she was a Melbourne Cup winner. It was a weird love story. Lucy had no fear of her.

'We can't get near her, and none of us want to try. Farrier visits are a nightmare since Lucy's gone. Lil' Sis has to be sedated. I'm slightly ashamed to say that I tell Mum and Mattie I'm busy whenever she needs a vet. They've had every vet in a fifty-kilometre radius out to see her, because nobody ever wants to come a second time.' He chuckles. 'We can't even keep our other horses in the same paddock as her, because she'll take their faces off.

'We used to tease Lucy, calling the pony "Lil' Sass". Behind Lucy's back we called her "Little Bitch". Lucy once overheard Mum saying it, and there was screaming and tears as though Mum had said it about an actual grandchild. I don't know if they mentioned it, but she was an emotionally expressive kid.'

I nod, imagining this brave, slightly wild child.

'Anyway, that day when Heidi was calving, there was no time to get Lucy from the treehouse. We didn't bother asking Hannah to come, because she's so squeamish. So, I grabbed my vet bag and headed down to the paddock with Mattie and Mum.'

I am engrossed in Sebastian's words, and there is momentum to them, so I have simply allowed them to flow, but – perhaps because I am somewhat weary at the end of a long day – it only now dawns on me that he's launching into the story of the day Lucy died. This is not ideal for the first session. Aside from not getting the background information I need, I know nothing about his general state of mind or level of resilience. I worry that he could be adversely impacted by telling that story right now.

'Sebastian,' I say, holding my hand up in a gentle stop sign. 'I don't mean to interrupt, but I notice you're starting to talk about what happened on the day Lucy was killed. I don't want you to feel as though you need to tell me, especially right away. There's a lot of information we need to cover today, and it might also be helpful for us to make sure you're emotionally prepared before you recall the specifics of that day, particularly if you haven't discussed this with anyone before.'

'No,' he says, shaking his head. 'I'll be fine. I want to tell it, actually. Get it off my chest.'

I sense a resolve within him, as if he's been bottling up this memory for so long that there is pressure to expel it.

'It's just,' I go on, 'sometimes people aren't ready—'

'No,' he breaks in. 'Honestly, I can deal with it. I've thought about it that many times.'

He is clearly determined to tell me what happened when Lucy died, here, today. At least there's nobody left in the waiting room. People are understandably self-conscious about a bunch of strangers seeing them leaving a therapy room with the telltale puffy features and blotchy skin that come with vigorous crying. Also, if I have a new client in the waiting room, it doesn't do much for their confidence to see the previous one exiting my care looking like that, although I do my best to help the person recompose themselves before returning to the reception area.

'Okay,' I say, tentatively trusting this young man's judgement. 'If it gets too much, you can stop at any time.'

Sebastian nods, gazing into the near distance to find his train of thought.

'So, when we got to the paddock, I could see the cow was standing over something pale on the ground, which I knew would be a calf. As we got closer, I saw that Heidi was licking it. She wasn't bothered by us. She's tame, like a pet. All Mum's cattle are. She handles them from birth so that human contact – for routine care or slaughter – isn't stressful. It takes many hours every season to achieve. Mum still helps with it, even though she's let most things go.'

I smile, glad Stella still does something to connect with her beloved animals.

'The calf was a small fella, all white, which is unusual for the lot we breed. He was still. The amniotic sac had broken, but it was still wrapped around his middle. I touched his flank, and it was already cooling. I cleared his airways with my fingers. Mum passed me a towel and I rubbed him vigorously, but nothing. No respiration. I checked his heart and there wasn't a beat. Mattie ran up to the shed to grab a bucket of water while Mum did this thing where you tickle the calf's nose with a strand of grass to stimulate the sneeze response.

'It didn't work, so Mattie poured the bucket of water over his head to stimulate the gasp response. He still didn't move, so I went straight into mouth-to-nose resuscitation. Kind of gross, I know, but I had some PPE in my vet bag.' He crinkles his nose and looks at me with a bashful grin.

'You're committed to your craft,' I say.

He nods, and says, 'I noticed out of the corner of my eye that Heidi was getting restless. I looked up and saw two hooves poking out from under her tail. She was having twins again. I wasn't getting anywhere with the calf, so I called it and focused on the baby being born. The feet were a good ten centimetres out, so I knew the head had cleared the pelvis. Heidi started pushing again and the calf just slithered out, and Mattie and Mum caught it and lowered it to the ground. She was a little heifer, moving vigorously, her respiration strong. We were pretty buggered by then, so we all sat on the ground to watch Heidi sniffing and licking her until she fed.

'Mum told us she'd leave the dead calf's body in the paddock for a few hours so that Heidi realised he was gone. Mum reckons that's the worst part of slaughtering cattle on our farm: not the process, per se, because it's set up so it's totally unanticipated, instantaneous and out of sight of the rest of the herd, but the fact that the others don't know what's happened to one of their own. You can see how unsettled they are for a few days after one of them disappears. We've had mother cows break though fences and travel for kilometres in search of missing calves.'

I'd never thought of cattle as having feelings, like a domestic animal such as Bob does, for instance. I can sense the weight of an inconvenient truth descending on me, and I push the idea away.

'Anyway,' he continues, 'we headed back to the house for dinner. We were feeling jubilant because of the heifer. But as we turned the corner where the house comes into view, we saw it was in darkness except for Hannah's bedroom light. We all knew something wasn't right. The rule was that Lucy must be home before dark, and if she was home you knew about it, because she'd have every light on in the house to protect her from Cranky Cary, the Irish ghost she was convinced haunted the place.'

I smile.

'When we got inside, Mum called out to Lucy and there wasn't any answer. Mattie and I followed her through to Hannah's room. Hannah was lying on the bed, still reading, headphones on. Mum asked where Lucy was, and Hannah shrugged and mumbled that she didn't know.

'There wasn't much love lost between the girls at that time. Hannah being a young teenager – you know how that is – and Lucy being the pesky little sister. Hannah wasn't as obnoxious as some teens can be, but Lucy pushed her buttons. You know, going through her stuff, borrowing jewellery and trinkets without asking, hiding around corners and jumping out to scare Hannah. Just stupid stuff, but I recall Hannah was really touchy around that time – more easily frustrated and irritable than usual – and wasn't finding the humour in it. She tried to avoid Lucy if possible.

'Their relationship wasn't always like that. Hannah was so excited when Lucy was born. She was four then, but she wanted to be the third mother in the house. She'd mimic everything Mattie and Mum did to take care of Lucy. She learnt to help swaddle her, change her nappy, give her a bath. And as the two of them got older, Hannah would babysit her, get her dressed, make her sandwiches, read to her, take her out in the paddocks to feed the cows.

'But Lucy's independent streak showed up early, and Lucy insisted on doing her own thing while Hannah still wanted to mother her. Whatever it was – opening a farm gate, doing up her shoes – her favourite words were, "I can do it." I can still hear her little voice saying it.'

Sebastian smiles, but looks sad.

'I think Hannah felt rejected. Even more so when Lucy was on about wanting her own little sister to look after. Eventually she gave up trying to mother Lucy and went back to her books.

'It wasn't Lucy's fault, but she hogged the attention in our house, particularly drawing focus away from Hannah, who is so quiet. Lucy was a chatterbox and just commanded a room. Even when she was naughty, she was cute. I'm sure their relationship would've got back on track with time. Probably would've ended up best mates, as adults.

'That evening, Hannah would have assumed Lucy was occupying herself in her bedroom or somewhere else in the house. It was just a typical night. But we checked everywhere. Mum was opening the cupboards to make sure she wasn't curled up in there as a prank, but I knew she wouldn't go into a hidey-hole after dark because of Cranky Cary. Mattie was doing her usual thing, making excuses for Lucy. She was so soft on her – kinda like she is on Mum.

'I headed out to check the front paddock because, by this time of night, Lil' Sis was usually there eating the dinner Lucy had given her. But neither of them was there. I squinted down towards the national park to see if Lucy was riding towards the house, but it was so dark. There was no moon that night.

'I don't get uptight easily, but I had this knot in my stomach and an odd taste in my mouth, like . . . seaweed? Is that strange? I just knew something was wrong. I thought maybe she'd fallen off that stupid horse and was lying somewhere with a broken arm.

'I suggested to Mum and Mattie that we jump in the truck and see if we could find her as she was riding back. We grabbed some torches and I got behind the wheel, and Mum squished between Mattie and me.

'Mattie shone one torch out the passenger-side window, and I shone another out the driver's side. We were all calling her name. I beeped the horn a few times, but there was no response. By this point, the muscles in my scalp were tight. My palms were sweating. I remember nervously peeling bits of decal off the old steering wheel.

'Mattie kept muttering to herself, saying stuff like, "Thought she was getting more responsible . . . She's going to be in so much trouble . . ." You could tell she was worried because she's usually so chill.

'And Mum was just sitting there, kind of frozen. I heard her breathing heavily, like she usually did before one of the cows was going to be killed.

'As we got to the boundary fence, I made out Lil' Sis tethered to the high line. Lucy'd told me a few months earlier that she felt bad tethering the pony to a tree for hours while she was playing. So, I helped her set up a rope between two trees so the pony could move around and graze. Every time I was at the farm, Lucy wanted me to help move the line to an untouched area of pasture. The pony was standing exactly where we'd put the last high line.

'We parked near the line. Lil' Sis's head was up high, as if she was spooked, but she didn't look injured. Mattie ran for the boundary fence. I caught up with her and put a foot on the barbed wire so she could get through.

'It's weird how you remember all these details, isn't it?' he asks then.

I nod. 'Some people describe the feeling of everything being in slow motion.'

'Yes, it was exactly like that. And Mum was actually moving slowly at this stage, too. Dawdling. I yelled out to her to hurry up. Once we were through the fence, we didn't know which way to go. Lucy had shown us where she was building the treehouse a couple of years before, but after that none of us were allowed to visit. She'd even painted this sign on an old bit of fence paling saying *No Adults*. It was still hanging on the barbed wire. The writing looked so childish that night.'

He takes a deep breath before continuing.

'The way to the treehouse became obvious, because there was a well-worn path. Lucy had cleared vines and lantana. I remember feeling proud of her then, that she could fight back the bush like that, at age ten.'

Sebastian rubs his face. I can see his breath quickening. A vein on his neck stands out, pulse thrumming: *da-dum, da-dum*. Behind him, the rain has stopped.

'I was leading the way, Mattie was after me, then Mum. I saw the treehouse – which is really a section of forest where the branches of these giant old trees have tented together to create a canopy, with the trunks forming the corners of the house. I saw that Lucy had hauled in all these dead branches to almost completely close in the side and back walls. It's a pretty big area – probably the size of an average living room.

'Lucy always saved her pocket money to buy small pieces of used furniture for her house from the op shops in Warwick. She'd get me to drive them down to the boundary and lift them over the fence for her. We'd taken down a couple of stools, a pink side table, a dilapidated coat rack, a stepladder so she could hang things up, and this three-shelf bookcase. God knows how she hauled that through the forest; it would've been half her bodyweight, and she refused my help on account of her place being "top secret". I'd try to warn her that the furniture would warp in the rain but she wouldn't listen. We called her a bowerbird, because she was always getting trinkets and knick-knacks to decorate her treehouse: beads, ornaments, little mirrors. I pictured the national park ranger stumbling on this junk heap in the middle of the woods and thinking a crazy, homeless fairy had taken up residence.' He pauses for a second. 'Sorry, that's probably not appropriate.'

I wave away his comment. This is not the time to get bogged down in that discussion.

'Anyway, when I reached the front of the treehouse, I shone a torch in and was dazzled by a kaleidoscope of refracted light from all her objects. There were flashes of pink from beads she'd threaded through the branches, yellow glints from handheld mirrors she'd tied to thick twigs, blue tinsel from our Christmas tree. Mum had been so confused the previous Christmas when she went to put up the tree and couldn't find any. There was a rope strung above the entrance that had kitchen things hanging from it: tongs, wooden spoons, a purple whisk.

'Then I noticed the earth inside the treehouse was all scuffed up, and the pink table and one of the chairs were lying on their sides. There was a wooden rolling pin on the ground. We were still calling out for Lucy. I thought I might vomit. Something terrible had happened, I knew. I wanted to run back to the truck and sit with my hands over my ears and my legs up to my chest. So childish.

'Lucy wasn't in the treehouse – or so I thought, until I noticed what looked like a small alcove, an opening, at the back right corner. And I just had the strongest feeling that I didn't want to look in there. It was probably only for a split second, but it felt like ages that I stood still, stuck to the spot.

'I said to myself – and it's strange, because it's not how I was brought up – but I said, "You're the man here." It was my job to look in there.'

Sebastian is breathing rapidly now, and I feel queasy just listening to his description. It transports me to the scene in a way the court reports don't. He has that fixed stare. He is there, in that treehouse, right now. I don't want to be with him, but I am.

'My legs felt like weights as I walked towards that corner of the treehouse. I don't know what Mattie or Mum were doing then. I think they were watching me. The opening did enter into a little alcove of sorts . . .'

He leans forwards now, puts his hand over his mouth, thumb rubbing the side of his face.

'I shone the torch in. And she was there. Naked. Her body was hanging from a branch.'

He stops again, gathering himself. He inhales slowly.

'She was facing away from me, but I knew it was her, of course. I was frozen to the spot. Matisse was saying, "What, Seb? What?"

'"Stay back," I told her. I tried to use my body to block

the entrance to the alcove, but she must have looked over my shoulder or something. She started yelling, "Oh my god. Oh my god." Then she was crying out something in Spanish, as well as Lucy's name. And then she pushed me out of the way. Literally shoved me.

'She started grabbing at Lucy's legs, jumping, trying to reach up to the rope she hung from. "Quick," she was yelling. "Get a knife." I turned around to grab the old stepladder, which I'd seen leaning up against the back wall, and I saw Mum standing there with her hand pressed over her mouth. I think I told her not to come in. And then I put the ladder next to where Lucy's body was hanging and stepped up.

'I saw straightaway the rope tying her to the tree was this old red-webbing dog lead that had been kicking around the farm for years. It'd belonged to Bernie, the border collie Mum gave me when we moved to the farm.'

When I hear him say that, I recall this item being important during the sentencing. The prosecution argued that the fact that the perpetrator had stolen it from the farm and brought it back for the crime was evidence of premeditation. In fact, he made an admission about that.

'The lead was clipped to Bernie's rusty old choker chain, which was around Lucy's neck. It was pulled so tight. So tight.'

He shakes his head back and forth, looking down at the ground.

'I thought, *Oh my god, she's killed herself. Do kids this age kill themselves? Why did she take off her clothes?* I said to Matisse, "Hold her weight. Hold her up by the legs." I wanted to get the collar loose enough to pull it over her head. It was cold, and the rust flaked off as I tried to prise my fingers under it. I discovered later I'd torn a couple of nails down to the nail bed, but I hadn't felt any pain.

'Matisse was able to support Lucy enough for me to get the collar off, but neither of us had thought about the fact that once the collar was off, she would be propping up Lucy's full weight. So, unfortunately, when that happened Lucy's body fell backwards, going over Mattie's shoulder. I heard this thump as she hit the ground.

'She landed just inside the main area of the treehouse. That was when Mum first saw her. It was horrible. I'll never forget the sounds she made. She started screaming this shrill scream that echoed through the forest. It just went on and on, and the sound completely overwhelmed me. I was trying to concentrate, to think what to do next.

'I yelled at Mum to shut the fuck up. I'd never sworn at her before. I shouted at her, saying to call an ambulance. She did stop screaming then. She didn't move to find her phone, though. She just stood there, fixed to the spot, staring at Lucy. She didn't go to her or anything. I think she was so horrified she couldn't move. I'm certain she knew it was too late. I think we all knew that, but I just had to do something. Anything.

'I turned to Mattie and told her to ring the ambulance. I thought that by letting Lucy fall over Mattie's shoulder and hit the ground, I'd probably killed her. I mean, it was obvious to all the world that she was dead before that, but for some reason blaming myself felt better in that moment than the thought that she'd taken her own life.

'I'm not sure what I did then, but the next thing I remember is hearing Mattie some way away from the treehouse, talking on the phone to the ambulance people. I was relieved that she'd found mobile reception; it's incredible now that I think about it, given how patchy the service is all around the property. The lighting was dim inside the treehouse because she'd taken her torch with her. Mine was lying on the ground somewhere, and

Mum had dropped hers and the beam was facing out of the treehouse. I saw the outline of Lucy, but not the details. I went to her body and felt around for her shoulders. I started talking to her, saying her name softly, but there was no reaction. I can still feel how her shoulders felt. They were tiny, like a little bird. She was cool to the touch but not cold, which I told myself was promising given the chill of the night. She smelt sweet, like her strawberry bubble bath.

'I found her chest and put my hand on it. For a second, I thought I could feel a faint heartbeat, so I put my hand to her neck to take her pulse. Because of the way her neck was, from the chain and things'—he furrowed his brow—'I couldn't do that, so I tried to find a pulse in her wrist, but there was nothing. I found her mouth and nose, and put my ear over them, but I couldn't hear her breathing. So I did exactly what I'd done with the calf only an hour or so before. I cleared her airway and went to start CPR. I located her sternum and found the right place to start chest compressions. I did thirty pumps and then breathed my first breath. I immediately tasted blood.

'In between me doing all these things, Mattie was calling out to me, repeating the questions from the ambulance service: Is she breathing, can you feel a heartbeat, a pulse? Then the ambulance person must have told Mattie to come and help me, because at some point she was beside me, getting ready to take over chest compressions, the phone on speaker on the ground. It was unbelievably lucky that the phone continued to work inside the treehouse.

'Mattie used to be an ER nurse, but I wasn't thinking about that. I was just thinking, *God, I hope she's doing this right*. Every time Mattie would stop compressions so I could do breaths, she'd be puffing from exertion but would still be asking the ambulance lady questions. I recall her asking repeatedly if the ambulance had been dispatched, and from where. I was thinking there's no way they're going to find us here, in the middle of the bush, where there's no road. So, between breaths, I yelled at Mum to go to the farm entrance to meet them. I also remember telling her to call Mr Molly-Pants for help – Molly, I mean. He's an old dude who lives on the next property. But she just stood there. I yelled, "Fuck, Mum! Go! Go!" And I felt around for the rolling pin, which I'd accidentally knelt on when I crouched down next to Lucy. I threw it in Mum's direction. I didn't think about what I was doing, just that I needed to get her moving. I heard it connect with her body, her leg maybe, and she grunted. Then I fished around in my pocket for the truck keys and threw them at her. I think she picked up her torch and the keys and left.

'Mattie and I kept doing CPR; we swapped so I was doing chest compressions. I heard the noise of Mum driving off in the truck, and it suddenly occurred to me that we should have put Lucy in the truck, taken her to the hospital, or at least to meet the ambulance. I jumped up and started running out of the treehouse. Mattie yelled out to ask me what I was doing, and I told her we needed the truck. She said, "No, we can't move her. Her neck."

'It seemed as if we were doing CPR for hours. We'd swap positions so we could take breaks from the chest pumps. My hands were numb. I'm not sure if it was from shock or because the temperature had dropped so low by then. By the time the ambulance arrived, we were completely spent. People say they'd just keep going forever if it meant saving their loved one . . . Our endurance had been extended by adrenaline, but we were reaching our physical limits.

'I was so relieved to see the ambos coming through the bush with Mum. They brought this giant portable floodlight.

They faced it into the treehouse and turned it on. I was blinded for a second, blinking in the brightness. I turned back to Lucy and my eyes landed on her stomach. And that's when I saw it: the big, dirty boot print.'

7

HANNAH

IF I SPOKE TO THAT WOMAN, DR TATE, I'M NOT SURE IF I'D TELL HER this: that disgusting pig only knew where the treehouse was because I showed him. I revealed it because I was a spiteful bitch who wanted to hurt her own sister. I took him there because Lucy took my brooch, the one that Mattie's mum – Lucila – gave me when we visited Peru; the one in the shape of two doves kissing, tiny turquoise stones making up their feathers and the flowers of the branch they perch on. The one that Lucy liked better than the butterfly brooch she was given. The one she felt entitled to, because she believed she was Lucila's favourite, because she was her namesake and came from Lucila's daughter's womb.

I knew she would have taken it there, to the treehouse. I didn't bother going there to get back my skull bandana, or the pink kitty earrings I'd had since I was eight when Mum let me get my ears pierced. She could have those. But there was a line. She was not having the brooch.

I waited for Wednesday, when I had afternoon study period; the day Mattie dragged Mum to do the groceries before picking Lucy up from school. My heart was thumping as I headed through the paddock, because I didn't usually do stuff like this. I mean, I wasn't going to do anything bad – I was just going to take the brooch and hide it somewhere where she couldn't get it again. But I knew it was wrong, somehow, to enter her treehouse. It was her sacred space.

As I was opening the paddock gate, I heard him yell out to me. 'Hannah!' I looked up, and he was bent down in the shadows of a gum tree, doing up his shoelace. I hadn't even noticed him there. He smiled that big, friendly smile and his teeth were the whitest I'd ever seen. I felt my tummy flip-flop and I wasn't sure why. I'd spoken to him a few times, and he and his boyfriend – Christopher – had had morning tea on the verandah with Mum and Mattie and Lucy and me. He'd told us he was a mechanic and the two of them had met when he worked on Christopher's car. Christopher was much older than him, and very posh and obviously rich, but balding and flabby and quite boring. I wondered why he'd choose to be with a guy like that when he was so good-looking and funny, and could probably get whoever he wanted.

He knew how to tell a story in just the right way so that you'd want to listen to every sentence. I liked that he told adult jokes in front of me – clever ones, nothing too rude – as though I was mature enough to understand. And he had asked me about myself, and even though I was shy in answering he patiently paid attention, as if I wasn't just some stupid kid but was saying something interesting and worth listening to.

Even though he was so likeable, I felt uneasy around him. At first, I thought maybe I was getting sleazy vibes from him. But I reassured myself that he was very clearly gay, and that if he happened to possess any interest in females it would be directed towards worldly, glamorous, sexy women – who would probably flock to him – not skinny, pimply, dirty farm kids. Then I was stumped, because I didn't feel the same level of ill ease around Christopher. In the end, I put my unsettledness down to being intimidated by an adult who had such bold charm and charisma.

As he walked towards me across the paddock, the uneasy feeling swelled up to press on my sternum. When he reached me, though, he fixed me with such a warm smile that it bubbled back down again. He explained that Christopher was having a nap and he'd decided to go for a walk. He asked where I was off to and I said the national park, and he said he'd like to see that and asked if he could walk with me. I was thrown, because I knew I couldn't take him to Lucy's treehouse; that was her secret place. I figured I'd have to show him around a different area of the park and come back another day to search for the brooch.

I was uncomfortable about the idea of walking alone in the bush with a strange man. I wondered if I should let Mum or Mattie know where we were going, but it seemed rude to say that, and I also knew I was meant to be 'hospitable' with the guests and help them enjoy their stay so they would give us good reviews. I looked back over my shoulder towards the house, trying to decide what to do. He must have seen me equivocating, because he leant in, grinning, and whispered, 'I probably shouldn't be gone too long. Christopher has a sixth sense for when I wander off. He hates to be left out of any fun, and he always comes looking for me.'

This made me feel reassured, that someone would come looking for us if we were gone for too long, and so I started leading him towards the fence line that separates our paddocks from the national park, and we got talking. I was shy with most people outside of my family, but he started off asking me easy questions about myself, and he listened so closely and with so much interest that I noticed myself relaxing and opening up. Eventually, he asked about where my father was. When I told him my dad wasn't interested in me, in us, he acted horrified and said a father's number-one duty in life is to be there for his kids, and that I deserved so much better. He confided a bit about what his own dad was like and how abandoned he'd felt by him, and I felt so understood.

Then he asked me which of my mums gave birth to us, and I explained. He was surprised that Lucy wasn't related biologically to Mattie, because he said she looks so much like her, and nothing like me or Mum. I told him that even though Seb and I came out fair like Mum, my father has dark hair and olive skin and green eyes, just like Lucy. I said that Mum thought it was so nice that the baby Mattie gave birth to shares a physical resemblance to her, with the similar coloured skin and hair.

Then I said – and I'd never spoken this out loud before – that sometimes I looked at Lucy and momentarily thought of her as Mattie's daughter, and not related to Mum and Seb and me. I said I thought it was because of how different we looked, but he offered that it might also be because we were so different in temperament. He said that Lucy was outgoing and loud, whereas I was a deeper thinker, more sensitive and analytical, more self-controlled.

I looked at him then, and I saw something like sympathy in his eyes. He paused for a moment, as though summoning the courage to say something hard but true. Sounding almost reluctant, he said he'd noticed that Lucy seemed to get a lot of the attention from Mum and Mattie, and that maybe they overlooked my specialness and talents because I wasn't a show-off about them. I instantly wanted to defend Lucy, to say that she wasn't a show-off, but I knew it wasn't true, and it felt good to hear someone else say what I often thought. He added that it must be hard to go unnoticed when I had so much to offer, if only people – he meant Mum and Mattie – would take more time to see it and nurture it. Then he said – and I will never forget these words – 'Sometimes in life you have to take back what is rightfully yours.'

Was it the timing? The perfect timing? The way he delivered those words, with such conviction, right as we got to the fence line? Right at the point where I could lead us left, to Lucy's secret place, or right, into some other area of the park. Or was it that I really am a terrible sister? A traitor? In that moment, all I could think was that Lucy had what was rightfully mine, and that I was going to take it back. Right then. And why not take the one person who seemed to understand with me while I did it?

The words just tumbled out: I told him how Lucy stole my brooch – how she always stole my things – and how I was on my way to get it back from her secret treehouse, how she spent hours there every afternoon and how none of us were allowed to enter. He said that he had seen Lucy riding down this way the previous day and had wondered where she was going. He said that he wasn't sure if it was safe that a ten-year-old played so far away from supervision, or that they were allowed to have a secret place that their parents couldn't enter. He even suggested it was in Lucy's best interests that someone older at least see the place.

He asked then if I would have been allowed to have a secret place in the bush when I was Lucy's age. That's when it occurred to me that there's no way Mum would've let me disappear down here for hours every day, unsupervised. Why was Lucy allowed to get away with that? Was it because they thought she was more independent than I was at that age? More capable? More trustworthy? It didn't seem fair.

All I was feeling was indignation as I let him hold the barbed wire strands apart for me to get through the fence, and I did the same for him. I led him down the track to the treehouse, and I think we were both stunned when we saw what she'd done with it. It was actually beautiful, in a little-kid kind of way. It was like stepping into some chaotic, magical fairy world; like letting yourself slip through a door, unseen, into someone's wild mind, into their untamed imagination. Everything we had just discussed became irrelevant. This *was* a private place, in the most innocent and precious of ways. An intimate extension of my sister's body that deserved to be invite-only. I knew immediately that we shouldn't be there.

We had to leave. So, I pretended to look around for the brooch for a minute or two, and then said I couldn't find it, and that maybe it was somewhere in my bedroom after all. I took a few steps towards the path, but he just stood there, studying everything. At first he was motionless, touching Lucy's world only with his eyes. Then he moved into the space and started picking up her knick-knacks, turning them over slowly, with relish, in his big hands. He let his fingers glide across the surface of a dusty snow globe that I recognised as a gift from Sebastian to Lucy, leaving oily smudges on the glass. His expression had changed. His lids were half-lowered over his fish-coloured eyes, as though he were savouring a mouthful of the most delicious meal . . .

I experienced a whole-body sensation then that I still do not know how to describe. Premonition? Foreboding? My brain was whispering, '*Swim, swim, swim,*' like it had done before, but this time my body responded with action.

I was firm. My voice was steadier than I felt. I said I needed to get back to my homework and that we should go. I turned and walked back down the path. I heard him follow, and I told myself not to look over my shoulder or break into a run.

Once we were back out in the open paddock, the fullness of the afternoon sun on my skin, him chatting about all the trips he and Christopher planned to take, I realised I had overreacted. I had let myself get spooked by being alone with an unfamiliar man in the forest, and that, combined with the guilt of invading Lucy's treehouse, had caused me to panic. Nothing had happened. Everything was okay.

As we got close to home, he thanked me for taking him to the national park and told me he might have a word with Mum and Mattie about the dangers of letting Lucy spend so much time in the bush by herself. Please, please don't, I had said. I didn't want Lucy to be upset that we had gone there, that I had betrayed her, or to be the cause of her losing her treehouse. I hoped he would agree to remain silent, but he just shrugged, noncommittal.

I was feeling on edge right up until he checked out, scared that he would open his mouth, but he never did. He never intended to.

8

OCTAVIA

STELLA ISN'T CONSTIPATED ANYMORE. INSTEAD, I THINK SHE MIGHT have diarrhoea. She is sitting on the same couch where she sat for our first appointment, but she's squirming all around as if she's trying to hold something in. Legs up on the seat, legs down. Looks at me, looks past me, looks away. Bites her nails, stops. Gets up for some water, comes back. All this and she's barely said a word. I ask her if she's feeling okay and she says she's fine. I ask her various questions about her week, try to get her onto the topic of her cows, but she will not open up like she did previously. My frustration is rising the way it does when the supermarket queues are stupidly long and a pimply teenage boy stands stacking chocolates instead of opening another checkout.

I take a slow breath and remind myself that I'm here to help her, and she's obviously feeling uncomfortable for some reason. I focus on being curious about what might alleviate that. So, I ask if she'd mind if we walk and talk today. I say that perhaps she could show me the farm, seeing as Matisse has popped into town. I figure the movement of her legs might have an effect on the momentum of her mouth.

She takes me over to what they call the 'farm side', which is the working part of the farm, up over the knoll of a hill and not visible from the house. I ask her open-ended questions about the place as we walk, and she answers them in one or two words, or with the shortest sentence manageable.

'How'd it feel to grow up in a place surrounded by so much natural beauty?'

'Okay.'

'What sorts of things did you get up to on the weekends?'

'Patting the cows.'

'What else?'

'Not much.'

Once we get over the ridge it is much drier, as Matisse had said. The cattle are huddling around the few sparse trees, trying to get a fraction of shade. Even though it's winter, this side of the mountain is much warmer. Stella leads me through some old cattle pens and around some sheds. There is one shed that is much larger than the others, and it is so full of hay that the bales look as though they might be holding up the ancient corrugated-iron roof. One of the newer-looking sheds is adjoined by what looks like a commercial cold room. I speculate that these are the slaughter and butchering facilities, but I don't ask. Instead, I gulp in the sweet, musty scent of hay that is carried on the breeze.

A short distance from the sheds is a large patch of flattened red earth. I venture to inquire about it, and Stella says it was the B & B.

'The cottage where you grew up?' I ask. Stella nods.

I stare at the empty earth, and then out at the thousands of kilometres of fields and hills below this mountain. I imagine the breathtaking views she must have encountered every day from her bedroom or the lounge room.

'What happened to it?' I ask, perplexed, having assumed it still existed after reading about it in the court documents.

'I got it flattened after the police told us who Lucy's killer was. That he only knew about her because he stayed with us here.'

She scuffs her boot in the dirt, and for a second I think she is going to spit.

'Oh,' I say. It feels extreme, to flatten the whole building, your childhood home, but how can I possibly judge?

'Matisse is going to put a garden here once the drought is over,' she says, shrugging.

Perhaps it will be a sort of memorial garden to Lucy. I take the exchanged words as an opportunity to encourage Stella to speak about her emotions.

'How did it feel to see it gone? Your old home?' I ask.

Her expression is hard and hateful. 'I'm done talking for today,' she snaps. 'I want to go back to the house.'

With that, she turns on her heel and marches back towards the ridge. I'm mad at myself for deciding to ask that question. I don't call after her, as tempting as it is. This is akin to someone walking out on a session – which happens rarely – and I need to respect her space while simultaneously making sure she is safe. I follow her back to the house at a distance and am thankful to see Matisse's truck rumbling into the yard. Stella stomps towards the house, gravel crunching under her feet, then disappears inside.

Seeing this unfold, Matisse swiftly exits her vehicle. She looks towards the front door and then to me. She raises her hands palms-up in query.

'Hi, Matisse,' I say, walking towards her. I try to think of the minimum amount I can say without breaking any confidences. 'Would you mind checking on Stella before we start our appointment?'

'Ah,' says Matisse, understanding and looking concerned. 'I wondered what was going on.'

I wait for the accusing look, as though I've done something to upset her wife, but it doesn't come. Instead, she gestures to the white wooden chairs on the verandah, inviting me to sit.

'Hopefully I'll be back soon,' she says with a wry smile.

I try to relax the muscles of my neck and focus on the wind chimes being stroked by the light breeze.

Matisse reappears a couple of minutes later and reassures me that everything is fine. Says Stella gets like this sometimes; that she's perfectly okay, but just wants to be alone.

A second later, Stella stalks past Matisse and me, facing forwards, car keys and mobile phone in hand.

She mutters, 'I'm going for a drive.'

I look to Matisse, who whispers, 'It's all right. It's part of her process. She usually comes back in a better frame of mind.'

'If you think so,' I whisper back, conscious that Matisse knows Stella far better than I do.

Matisse nods and smiles reassuringly, gesturing for me to follow her into the house.

As we walk down the hallway, she says, 'You get used to it. She did this even before Lucy. It's as if driving soothes her.'

Matisse sits down on the two-seater couch, inviting me to sit opposite. She places her car keys on the coffee table, next to a pair of vivid-red reading glasses, and looks up at me. Something about the natural arrangement of her features cheers me. She pops on the glasses, red rectangles framing her brown eyes, which crinkle at the sides. She smells of sandalwood and straw.

'Octavia,' she says warmly, 'it's great to see you.'

She is obviously not thrown, like I am, by Stella's behaviour. It's nice to feel welcome.

'It's lovely to see you too, Matisse. Tell me, how's it been going?'

'O-*kay*,' she says, intonation dropping from high to low, head giving a nod in the direction that Stella just departed.

'Things are difficult right now?' I prompt.

'Just the usual, really. Stella's always in a mood these days. Or her mind's somewhere else. She's created this mental cocoon. She tucks herself up in it and will only emerge on her terms. It's when she feels forced to come out that she gets snappy.'

I comment that Mattie seems to deal with the pain differently. She sighs and pauses for a long moment.

'I once read,' she says, 'that you only ever have three options: You can change a situation, leave the situation or accept it. I can't change what happened to my darling Lucy, I can't escape it – and I've seen via Stella what happens when you try – so I only have one option left. To work towards acceptance, repeatedly. It's not minimising what happened, nor in any way lessening his culpability; it's merely acknowledging reality. Lucy was murdered, and I can't change it no matter how much I wish I could. It's a practice I started many years ago, in the aftermath of what I did. The thing I told you about last time.

'I hadn't intended to tell you that, by the way,' she adds. 'But I couldn't lie when you asked about past traumas. Taking someone's life is wretched. Thank you for not pushing me for too many details. You could tell that I wasn't ready to talk about it.'

I nod and give a small smile, but stay quiet. I get the sense there is more she wishes to say on the topic.

'The kids, Stella, they don't know about it.'

I'm not sure what I thought she was going to say, but it wasn't that. Matisse seems so open. I did not picture her to be a hider of things.

'Go on,' I say.

'It happened before I met Stell. I was still married to my ex-husband. I was working long shifts in the ER. Extremely long shifts. They were low on staff, and I was sometimes working for twenty hours straight. It never used to be like that – nurses weren't allowed to do that type of overtime because of the dangers of fatigue – but staffing shortages had become so severe by that time, the rules were changed to allow it.

'Between shifts, Dean and I were renovating our house at Peregian Beach. The pressure was on because I was flying my parents out from Peru for a visit, and we wanted to have the place finished before they arrived.

'I'd also had influenza a couple of weeks earlier. It wiped me out for a week. Afterwards, my body and mind felt unusually worn out, but I was guilty that I'd taken sick leave when work was already so short-staffed. And sick patients still needed the same amount of care. I was slammed with more double shifts as soon as I returned, and even though I didn't feel up to it, I didn't say anything.

'I'd had a restless night's sleep before my shift on the day it happened. I'd never felt so tired, and it was a huge mental effort to go in on that afternoon. I'd started at four pm and worked twenty straight hours. I was only meant to work a twelve-hour shift but when I was on the home stretch, in the early hours of Tuesday morning, one of the other nurses, Kylie, called in sick. When the nurse unit manager asked if I could please cover her shift until noon, I hesitated. I told her how wrung out I felt, but in response she pointed out that Kylie had covered three of my shifts when I was sick.

'I felt as if I was going to cry, but I was a people-pleaser back then and I gave in. I was meant to have a lunch break on the second shift, but we got hit with multiple emergencies. There was a girl who'd come off a four-wheeler and had massive abdominal trauma, and a six-week-old baby who had been thrown across the room by his mother's boyfriend. We lost the girl during resuscitation, and the baby was touch-and-go when I finished up.

'By the time I hopped in the truck to go home, I was incapable of mentally processing those events. All I could think about was drinking a cold glass of water – because I'd barely had time to drink anything during the shift – reheating the Chinese takeaway leftovers that were sitting in the fridge and falling into bed.

'I'd only been driving for about a minute when I hit her. A nineteen-year-old young woman. Claudia Schmidt. I'd seen a water bottle in the passenger footwell, and I was so thirsty that I quickly leant down to grab it. I vaguely noticed a couple of people on the footpath, but I remember checking the road was clear before I leant over.

'Apparently, Claudia's young brother had kicked a ball onto the road and she'd run out to grab it, probably thinking I'd slow down. All I remember seeing was a flash of pink as I sat up from the footwell – the colour of her shirt – then feeling a terrible impact as I slammed on my brakes.

'When I jumped out of the truck and saw her, I knew straightaway that she was gone. That type of injury to her head—' She waves her hand, brushing away the memory. 'I sank down on the road next to her. I could feel the bitumen biting into the backs of my legs. It must have been freshly laid, because all I could smell was tar. Everything after that is a haze.

'In court, the prosecution said I was this uncaring, irre-sponsible person, driving dangerously while fatigued, an ER nurse who didn't even try to save the girl she'd just mowed down. But I knew immediately that she couldn't be saved. The coroner confirmed her injuries were "incompatible with life". Basically, her skull was crushed.'

It's difficult for me to reconcile this wretched image with something Matisse could have caused, or to consider the possibility that anyone would find the woman in front of me uncaring.

'The judge said that if I wasn't speeding – they calculated I was doing eight kilometres over the speed limit – and if I wasn't fatigued and distracted, I would have had an extra two seconds' reaction time. Enough time to stop the vehicle or swerve to avoid her.

'He said there were mitigating factors: I had no criminal history; I was a nurse who helped save people every day; I'd been recently sick, was fatigued, and had worked an emotionally challenging and extremely long shift out of a sense of duty to my workplace and patients. He sentenced me to fifteen months in prison for manslaughter, plus a two-year probation period. I thought it was a light sentence, but my barrister said it was consistent with other convictions of a similar nature. It still seems like a minuscule punishment for taking another person's life.

'My nursing registration was suspended, but I didn't care about that. I didn't care about anything, honestly. My mind was hijacked by thoughts of Claudia and her family: her mother, her father. I thought day and night about the torturous grief that must plague them. And her little brother, seeing what had happened, growing up without his sister.'

Matisse's eyes are downcast and she is shaking her head back and forth, slowly, as though unbelieving even after all this time. I blink my own eyes a few times to hold back tears, both for her pain and for the terrible tragedy that befell Claudia and her family.

'Dean left me while I was in jail. Our relationship was already rocky before the accident. I wanted kids and he was having second thoughts. To tell you the truth, when he said he was divorcing me – and he was very kind about it, if that's possible – it didn't truly sink in. I was so caught up in the guilt of what I'd done that I couldn't process anything. It made sense that I shouldn't have someone who loved me by my side. I felt that I no longer deserved it.

'When I got out of jail, I didn't go back to nursing. But I had to get a job to support myself. I started working in a hardware shop, but I wasn't present in my mind. I was where Stella is now, which is probably why I understand it so well.

'It took a long time to come out of that fog. Eventually I wrote to the family through their lawyers, told them how sorry I was. They responded, saying that they held no ill will towards me, that they realised I wasn't a bad person and that a complex set of circumstances had led to what happened; that I'd been trying to save other people earlier that day, and that Claudia was a compassionate young woman who would not want me to spend my life tearing myself apart over what I'd done. They said they were a Christian family and believed Claudia was in heaven. They told me to thank god for my life, and to treasure it. They told me they forgave me.'

My chest feels lighter, as though I am personally experiencing the relief this must have brought Matisse.

'That letter set me free. Everything changed when I read it. My heart was – still is – enormously grateful to the family for the forgiveness they bestowed upon me. I was given permission to live again.

'And so, when Lucy was killed, I was wrecked again. The first year after her death was an inferno. But, after a while, I thought about Claudia and her family, and remembered their graciousness through their grief, their determination to embrace the life that god had given them, and their desire for me to do the same. I knew I couldn't throw away any more time.

'I also felt as if – and I know this sounds wrong – but I felt as if things had been evened out. I had taken someone who was loved so dearly, and now I was experiencing the same loss. Not that I was being punished by Lucy's death, nor that she died because of what I'd done to Claudia. More that everything was now balanced. I don't know, I can't explain . . .'

'Not quite karma, but a spiritual equilibrium?' I offer.

'Yeah, maybe,' she says. 'You might see me as a woman who is functioning, but that's because I make it so. I still wake up every morning with that cold fear gripping at my stomach – disoriented in that second between sleep and consciousness – as I realise again that she's gone. My brain tells me things like don't eat breakfast, you can't stomach it; don't close your eyes, even for a second, you won't be able to handle what you see; don't reach out and ask for help, you don't deserve it. But I fight those thoughts away. I strive to be present and appreciate each day. Nothing more. No real hopes for the future. No possibility of moving beyond. Just today: the breeze, the flowers, the colours I paint with. And I don't run from the pain. I let it wash over me. It comes when I'm at the sink brushing my teeth, when I'm walking in the paddocks or answering the phone. And I let it take me, even if it means falling to my knees. I give it a place to be, and it passes through me and then it is gone, until it comes again.

'But I have a wife who cannot allow herself to feel the pain, to be devastated by it in the moment and pick herself back up again. She shuts it out, squashes it down, pushes it away. It might help in that second, but it has a greater long-term cost, because it's shut down her whole being.'

I nod, noticing her keen level of insight.

'Even before Lucy, when Stella was killing the cattle – it's a sacrifice to snuff out the lives of your friends, day after day, even when you believe it's the moral thing to do – she was starting to fold up. She'll tell you she was the happiest she'd ever been before Lucy was taken from us. I believe she'd already begun closing the doors and windows to herself. Doors and windows that were only partially open to begin with, because of her childhood and her previous marriage.

'I can't get to her at all now. I still try to open those doors and windows, even just a crack, but how hard do you prise at them before you become an intruder?

'I wish I could talk to someone who's been through the same thing. The Homicide Support Group approached me, in the beginning, but I couldn't, could I? Because I've killed someone myself. Imagine them finding out what I've done. And so, I carry it alone. And I do okay, you know? I think of Claudia's family, and I manage.'

Looking at Matisse's pained face, I think, as I often do in these situations, that anything I might say will sound trite. I hope my facial muscles compose themselves in a way that adequately expresses my compassion.

'Matisse,' I start, 'that sounds so, so hard. Being so alone in your pain, feeling unable to share it. From a psychological perspective, what you're doing by letting yourself feel it – no matter how excruciating it is – and knowing you can tolerate it, and that it will pass, is likely helping you cope with all that has happened. Sometimes people need help to learn how to do that – how to be ready to do that – but it seems you have found your own way there.

'Despite your fortitude, it's clear that having this secret about Claudia weighs on you. Have you ever thought about telling Stella?'

Matisse presses her lips together for a moment, then speaks. 'I never intended to keep it from her. When we were first falling in love, I felt quite certain she would accept it as part of my history. But it was so painful to talk about that I put it off. Told myself I'd tell her tomorrow, and then tomorrow. Then the years flew past, and at some point it felt as if I'd been hiding this dark secret and it was too late to come clean. Tomorrow never came. Then Lucy was killed, and I lost the certainty I'd once had that she wouldn't judge me for what I'd done. I think there's a chance she might merge me and him as one in her mind. We're both killers.

'And exacting revenge from this guy is her entire focus. She wants to shred him into blood-soaked gristle.' She looks to her lap and then up at me. 'Sorry,' she says. 'It's awful to say, isn't it?'

'No need to apologise. You're simply stating the truth.'

'What I did to Claudia is the reason I'm certain I can't take another life. It also doesn't align with my spiritual beliefs. I feel this type of judgement is reserved for a higher power, not us.'

'But Stella hopes you might come around to the idea of taking part?' I ask.

'Yes. I've told her I can't. We talked about it even before Lucy's death, when the lobby groups were floating the concept. It was something people spoke about as a hypothetical. I told her I could never condone capital punishment. Even then, she said if anyone ever hurt the kids or me, she'd take them out. I remember the hardness in her face when she said it. I believed her.'

Matisse stops speaking when we hear a vehicle pull up in the yard and the engine cut out.

'So you think she can do that to Lucy's killer?' I ask quickly.

'I think she can,' Matisse lowers her voice, 'but I don't know what will be left of her if she does.'

9

HANNAH

I WOULD NOT TELL HER THIS: THAT I DREAM THE SAME DREAM, OVER and over. The dream where I am straddled across his lap as he lies on Mum's bed. He's wearing tight black jeans and his chest is bare. His wrists are tied to the bedposts – one with my skull bandana, the other with the old dog lead. I have my school sports-day skirt on: short and pleated. I don't know what I'm wearing on top. His lips are full and parted. I can feel the heat of him through my underwear, his hardness. I rub myself on him, grinding. A bloom of warmth spreads through my thighs and belly. I am open to him. He is looking at me with a yearning, a want. My eyes hold that intensity and I lean my face down to meet his.

He reads my expression, and his changes. To what? Is it fear? Swiftly, I draw my lips back beyond my red gums to expose a weaponry of pearls. I can see my own face as I cata-pult forwards. My mouth, forced to the limits of its openness, latches onto the hollow of his cheek. It sucks the flesh there from its holdings. He's frozen in place, cannot move. Then my teeth are ripping the sinew and muscle, tearing into that tender part of his face like a fox tearing at the hide of a lamb. I feel a yielding and a popping. Fluid – full-bodied, molten, ferrous – flows into my mouth, like the liquid centre of the chocolate balls we eat at Christmas. Then I release my grip and instead use my teeth to snap at his nose, twisting and jerking the bulbous cartilage. It comes away like a piece of gristle and I spit it back at him. Power flows through me. I rear back, a scarf of blood encircling my neck. I am flooded with a burning wetness between my legs as he pisses himself.

I return to his face with my hands now. Fingers prising apart a marsh of boggy wounds, nails bending back as I fight to claw deeper. He turns his face this way and that, trying to escape. His irises are encircled with white. His lips move, calling for his mummy. He shows himself to be prey, and it makes me wild with destruction. I sink my fingers into his terrified eyes, penetrating the sockets, pushing over the top and behind. I feel his eyeballs bulge in horror, and I take them from him and obliterate them in my palms. Then I wake.

Perhaps I would tell her there was a letter in my mailbox today.

10

OCTAVIA

a few minutes late. The waiting room is empty when he arrives. I arranged it so that he is the final appointment of the day again, to afford him privacy. He says people sometimes recognise him from the media coverage; I don't want him encountering any awkward approaches in the waiting room. Some people have an odd feeling of ownership over the stories of strangers who appear in the media, as though exposure to their intimate personal experiences creates a sense of familiarity. I can imagine that as the public's interest peaks the closer we move to the potential execution, so too will some peoples' inability to resist asking intrusive questions.

When he sees me, he smiles broadly and stands, unfolding to his full height. I notice a small smear the colour of Bordeaux on the front of his scrubs. He looks down in the direction of my gaze.

'Oh,' he says. 'Sorry about that. I didn't notice. It's not as bad as it looks.' He explains that an injured and bloody possum regained consciousness while he was examining her, and took off up the front of his chest. He grins and tells the story of how he and the nurses chased the possum around the room in order to capture and sedate her. After a successful surgery, he says, she is now resting comfortably.

'I'm glad to hear it,' I say, and then ask him how he has been.

'Good, actually. I felt a lot better after our first appointment. Getting what happened to Lucy off my chest.'

'That's great news. I was worried it might have been too overwhelming.'

'No, I needed it,' he says.

The phone on my desk rings. We've only just started. Joseph is on tonight. *Seriously, again?*

I give Sebastian an exasperated look and excuse myself.

'*Yes*, Joseph?'

I am surprised to hear the tinge of panic in Joseph's voice. My mind shifts from annoyance to concern.

'Dr Tate, I've got this lady on the phone. The one you drive out to see. Mat . . . Mattie something? It sounds urgent.'

'What's going on?' I ask. I wasn't expecting a call from Matisse.

'She's speaking fast, sounds kind of afraid. She's asking to talk to you, like, now.'

I ask Joseph to transfer the call to the empty consulting room across the hall and, with an apology, tell Sebastian I need to excuse myself for a minute.

I slip into the consulting room as the phone rings. I pick up the receiver and hear a familiar lilting voice.

'Octavia, it's Matisse. I didn't know who to call. Stella's hysterical. There's a man here. In our front yard. He's screaming at her. I don't know who he is. He just drove in—'

'Matisse,' I interrupt her firmly. 'Listen to me.'

'Okay.' She breathes heavily into the receiver.

'Is anyone hurt? Does he have a weapon?'

'No, but he's so angry and Stella's just—'

'Matisse, I want you to hang up and call the police, immediately. Call and tell them exactly what's happening. Can you do that?'

I don't know why she would call *me* in this situation, but now is not the time to ask.

'Okay,' she says.

'Hang up now. Text me to let me know when you've got through to them.'

'Okay, I will,' she squeaks, and the line goes dead.

I stand in silence for a moment, trying to consider what to do next. I suddenly wonder whether I should have kept her on the line and grabbed my mobile to call the police myself. It feels impossible to return to my room and pick up the session with Matisse's stepson without notifying him of what is occurring. In my head, I run through the rules for breaking confidentiality. Sebastian is an emergency contact for both Matisse and Stella. This is an emergency, albeit one of an unusual nature, and it feels as though it's in the best interests of all parties that he should know about it.

Making a rapid decision that I hope covers all the pertinent factors, I return to my room and tell Sebastian about the call from Matisse.

He is on his feet in a second.

'Oh, god,' he says, fear and confusion furrowing his brow. 'I'll go there now.'

He grabs at the baggy pockets of his scrubs, producing a phone and keys.

'Be careful,' I caution, thinking of him rushing the two-hour trip in the dark, speeding up that windy, unlit mountain road.

I want to tell him that perhaps it's not a good idea, but I realise that if I were in his shoes I would do the same. 'Maybe call them on the way to check she got through to the police.'

'I will,' he says, rushing out the door, looking over his shoulder with both concern and regret for the way he is ending our session.

'Good luck,' I say to his back as he disappears down the hall.

•

After receiving a text from Matisse to confirm the police were on their way, I get another from her at about 11 pm, which I read wearily:

> Sorry Octavia. I shouldn't
> have called you. I panicked
> and you were the first person
> I thought of, and your card
> was next to the phone. We're
> not hurt. The man left before
> the police got here.

A third text follows:

> Everything's gone to shit.
> Stella knows that man. Can
> we see you earlier please?

Given the time of night, and the fact that they seem safe for the moment, I send only a brief response thanking her for the update, saying I am glad they are unharmed, and letting her know I will be in touch tomorrow to discuss my next available appointments. I do not want to be directly embroiled in what-ever this drama is, although I am very concerned for their wellbeing, and curious about this man's identity. I also need to discuss with Matisse my decision to notify Sebastian of the emergency. I will inform her then that I cannot come out to the farm before Thursday, which is true, but will also establish a clear boundary around my availability and the fact that I cannot drop everything to travel to the farm on short notice. I want to support them, but it isn't the purpose of my role to be someone they look to for immediate bolstering when life emergencies arise. As a concession, I will offer them the open appointment I have tomorrow afternoon if they are willing to drive to Brisbane. For some reason, I hope the distance will make them wait until Thursday.

•

I enter the bustling waiting room to find Matisse and Stella squished into the corner like a pair of deer hiding from a hunter. Unlike Sebastian's late-evening appointment, there is no privacy: a terse woman is standing at the reception desk requesting the TV be turned down, two children squabble over something in their mother's handbag, a man booms sonorously to someone on his mobile and a teenager paces near the door, chewing her fingertips as an afternoon snack. Thankfully, nobody appears to be paying attention to the couple.

'Come on through,' I say, smiling. They follow me, silent and meek, into my room. Stella sits on the double-seater couch. Matisse chooses the single chair.

'I'm glad to see you're both okay,' I say.

They don't comment on my fireplace or bookshelves, so I know it's serious.

I look at their faces. I can see that Stella has been crying. Her lids are swollen; she looks as if she is peeking out from inside a pair of clam shells.

Matisse looks plain mad. Her arms are folded, her legs crossed and her body angled away from Stella.

'I'm sorry I called you.' Her words rush out before I can respond. 'As soon as I calmed down, I realised it was wrong to do that. Inappropriate.'

'Well,' I say, 'I'm glad you think of me as someone who can help. And you're right. In emergency situations, I'm not the best one to call. But it can be hard when you're afraid. Your mind tends to grab on to something it thinks can help. I was worried for you both. What's going on?'

Matisse turns to Stella with a glare. 'I think you should explain, don't you?' Her tone is steely.

Stella puts her fingers to her brow. 'I made a mistake,' she says softly.

'Okay.' I nod. 'Please, tell me about it, if you would like to.'

She looks to the side, rests her chin on her hand so her fingers are partially covering her mouth, then looks at me.

'Well, for Matisse to get pregnant with Lucy we used the embryos that were left over from me having Hannah . . .'

'Right,' I say, having been told this by Matisse in our initial session.

'And I told Matisse that the biological father, Cole, consented to Mattie and I using the embryos to have a child together.'

'Okay,' I say, wondering where this is going.

'Well, I lied,' she says. 'He didn't consent. I forged his signature on the forms. He didn't know we used the embryos. He thought they were still on ice.'

'Oh.' I am unable to keep the surprise out of my voice.

I didn't see this coming. Matisse's face is a concrete block. 'So, he didn't know, and then . . .?'

'Well, he was living in New Zealand, apparently – I didn't realise he'd left Australia, because we don't talk. He'd been there for five years, but a few weeks ago he moved to the Gold Coast. He was browsing an Australian news site and saw an article about Lucy. He saw her photo. He thought he was looking at himself when he was a boy, except with longer hair.'

Matisse looks at her wife in astonishment.

'It's true,' Stella says. 'His mum once showed me pictures from his childhood. Lucy looked a lot like him. A lot. Then he saw Lucy's last name was Heathwood-Chavez. He didn't recognise Chavez, of course, but he recognised Heathwood. So, he read up on the case and put two and two together.'

'He called the IVF place we'd used, pretending he couldn't remember if there were any remaining embryos in storage, and they told him no, they'd been used for the second baby. Meaning Lucy.'

'I see,' I say, trying to hide my shock at this turn of events.

'He knew how to contact me because I'd emailed him when I left Sydney with the kids, told him what had happened with Dad and how to reach us, on the off-chance he ever wanted to get in touch with his children.' She says this with a hint of bitterness.

'We never heard from him, of course. But then he rang me a couple of weeks ago, told me he'd figured it out. I was caught off guard. But I couldn't lie,' she says. 'I admitted it straightaway.'

Matisse is shaking her head, as though doubly frustrated with Stella because of her honesty laid over the top of such a huge lie.

'He went absolutely mental,' Stella continues, removing her hand from her chin and starting to pick the skin around the nails of the hand that is resting in her lap. 'He completely lost it. Screaming at me on the phone, calling me all these names he used to call me. It was like stepping back in time. I felt myself . . .'

She's tearing up now. 'Go on,' I encourage.

'I felt myself going to mush.'

Matisse opens her mouth.

'Then what happened?' I ask Stella, before Matisse can speak.

'He threatened to go to the police about what I'd done: impersonating him, fraud, stealing his baby. He said I'd deprived him of the chance to know his daughter. Which is ridiculous – he never gave a shit about the children he knew he had. He wouldn't have had one lick of interest in Lucy. Or, if he did, it would've only been narcissistic interest because she looked like him.

'He even said he'll tell the judge he wants to be there. At the execution. That he wants to be the one to kill the guy on the fifth of November.'

'Oh, wow,' I say.

I can feel the heat of Matisse's anger from my chair.

'So, I offered him money to leave us alone. Knowing him, I was sure this would be part of his plan. He immediately asked how much. I told him an amount, what I knew we have in the savings account, and he said it wasn't enough. He wanted more. A lot more. I didn't know what to do. I told him we didn't have anything like that in liquid assets. He was yelling, "I know you do, you fucking bitch. You inherited that property. You're a fucking millionaire."

'And, sure, the property licence might be worth a lot, but that doesn't mean we have money in our pockets. We only paid out the loan for the abattoir last year. So I tried to buy some time. Told him I'd talk to the bank, see what I could do. I was panicked. I was too scared to tell Matisse.'

Matisse gives her wide, sarcastic eyes and tips her head, as if to say, 'Yeah, you had good reason to be scared.' I guess even the most mature women have their limits.

Stella continues. 'What I did was horrible, and there's no way to fix it. So, I kept trying to buy time, hold him off. But last night he turned up on our doorstep, going mental. Threatening me. It was so scary.'

I nod to show that I empathise. It's a delicate balance, because I want to demonstrate I understand her emotions, but in doing so I risk losing Matisse.

I turn to her. 'And you obviously didn't know who this enraged man was?'

'No,' says Matisse, 'I didn't have a clue. I was scared out of my brain. I'd never seen photos of him. Stella said she threw out all photographs of him when he left them. We agreed that if Lucy ever wanted to see pictures, Stella would find a way to get some. But Lucy never asked.

'The other kids are so fair that I assumed he must be too. I always thought it was this magical thing, Lucy looking like me: olive skin, dark hair. I felt as if the universe made her look like *my* daughter, even though we weren't biologically related. Stella never told me she looked like Cole. And when he turned up, he was this frothy-mouthed, crazy man going off his brain. So, no, I didn't realise that he was Lucy's biological father.

'I did figure he must know Stella, though, from what he was saying and how much anger he directed at her. I thought he was going to kill us both. Find Hannah in her room, and kill her too.'

'That must have been terrifying,' I say.

'It was.' She exhales.

Stella looks at Matisse then. A broken look.

'Mattie,' she says gently, 'I'm so, so sorry. I never meant for this to happen.'

'I know you didn't,' snaps Matisse. 'You never meant for me to find out. You were going to let me go to my grave thinking Lucy's father knew about her being created and was fine with it. You didn't tell me I was pregnant with a *stolen baby*.'

Her voice is rising now. I paid to have the rooms professionally soundproofed but I've learnt – typically from doing couples therapy – that when it gets above a certain volume, anyone in the adjacent consulting room can hear.

'Matisse, I know this must be incredibly difficult,' I say, then attempt to redirect her by adding, 'Can you tell me about what happened after you called the police?'

'Not much.' She shrugs. 'Once he realised I was on the phone to them, he got back in his car pretty fast, yelling something about coming back, making us pay. The police said they were on their way, and I hung up.

'A second later, while I was catching my breath, Stella called the police back. She said everything was fine, it was just a misunderstanding and they didn't need to come.'

I look at Stella, thinking, *Really?*

'I don't want the police involved,' Stella says. 'If they get wind of it, this is only going to get worse. Can you imagine if this gets to the media? Or Judge Gorski? That Lucy wasn't meant to exist in the first place?'

'Oh, great,' Matisse mutters. 'My daughter wasn't meant to exist.'

Stella ignores this and says, 'What if I get in trouble for what I've done, and it affects whether or not I'm allowed to execute the sentence?'

'That's all you care about, isn't it?' Matisse's voice is getting louder again. 'Killing that guy. You literally don't give a shit about the fact that you fucking lied to me about our daughter's creation. And your other daughter – the one who's *alive*, Stella – is struggling. She's not eating. She's not acting right. I know you've seen it, but all you care about is taking him out. Tell Octavia what you want to do to him. Go on, tell her!' Matisse yells. 'You're fucked up.'

'I *do* care about what's happening with Hannah,' says Stella. 'I *am* worried about her.'

This is the first time I've heard this from Stella, and I want to ask her more, but Matisse makes a frustrated groan and returns to talking about the embryos. I can't help them when her emotions are so heightened. Things will explode. I ask her to take some deep breaths, which to her credit she attempts rather than telling me to go fuck myself.

I say to Stella, 'What do you think should be done about Cole's threat, if not going to the police?'

Stella shakes her head and says, 'I don't know. I mean, I know I can never make it right with Matisse'—she throws her wife a glance—'but there's got to be a way of stopping him from destroying everything.'

'What are your options?' I ask, trying to shift the focus to problem-solving.

'I think the only option is to give him money. But even if we could get what he's asking for quickly – which we can't – it's not going to stop him from coming back in a month and asking for more. The only thing I can think of is getting a contract drawn up by a lawyer, requiring Cole not to disclose the information to anyone if I give him the money. I don't even know if you can do that – if that's legal?'

'I'm afraid I have no idea,' I say, wondering if I need to get advice on whether I'm obliged to report this apparent crime of Stella's to the police. Then I realise that the potential victim appears well able to advocate for himself if he wishes to involve the law. If I did need to involve police, I would of course let Stella know in advance; we discussed at length my potential reporting obligations around crimes at our very first session, and she signed paperwork acknowledging her understanding of this, but I am sure she wasn't thinking about that when she just disclosed what she'd done. I feel slightly ill as I consider the complications reporting might create in my relationship with the family, as well as in their own lives.

'Have you got a lawyer you can talk to?' I ask.

'Yeah,' Stella says. 'Graham Kent, in town. He's been handling our family matters for years. He's good and he's level-headed. I think I could go to him.'

'When could you speak to him?' I ask.

'I could call today and ask for an urgent appointment,' she says. Almost as if it is an afterthought, she adds, 'I already transferred two thousand dollars into Cole's account to buy some time, and—'

'*What?*' Matisse hollers. 'What the *fuck*, Stella? You gave money to that disgusting man without even talking to me? This is . . .'

Her accent is strong. Her mouth is open and she's shaking her head back and forth like she's a sideshow-alley clown.

'I had to,' Stella says. 'Do you want him going to the police?'

'I don't know,' says Matisse. 'Maybe he should. I've got nothing to lose if he does.'

'Except your home, if he sues us,' says Stella. '*Hannah's* home. Our retirement plans.'

Matisse is silent, mulling this over. 'Could he do that?' she asks me.

'Honestly,' I say, 'I've got no idea. This isn't something I can advise on. A lawyer may be able to guide you—'

'I'll make an appointment this afternoon,' offers Stella.

'Fine,' says Matisse. 'But I'm coming.'

'I want you to come,' says Stella. Matisse stares at the bookcase.

'What about Sebastian and Hannah?' I ask. 'Do they know the details of all this?'

Thankfully, Matisse was fine with me notifying Sebastian of the emergency; however, I haven't spoken to Sebastian about what he was told when he arrived at the farm. I've never met Hannah, so I have no idea what she may know.

'Well, Hannah heard the whole exchange, given it was so loud,' says Matisse. 'We went to check on her after he left, and she was sitting on the end of her bed, wrapped in her doona, silent. Really still. She's just a kid, and she's already been through too much. And then that's how she hears her own father's voice for the first time . . .

'Sebastian called me when he was on his way last night and, after he arrived, Stella provided the backstory. Reluctantly,' she adds, acidly. She pauses for a second, considering, and then turns to Stella and says, 'You didn't even think of your other children when you did this, did you?'

'I did,' insists Stella plaintively. 'I thought they would want our baby to be their biological brother or sister. I thought that'd help them bond with—'

'Oh, so does that mean if it was my baby, my egg, you thought they wouldn't bond with it?'

'No, that's not how I meant it, Matisse. And I was also thinking of what would happen to those embryos – Hannah and Sebastian's potential brothers or sisters. I figured the kids would prefer us to bring one of them to life, rather than it eventually being thrown into some medical waste bin, headed for the incinerator. And I knew he'd never agree, so I just—'

'You just fucking let me go into that clinic and have them put a baby inside me that was never meant to be born. Without even telling me.'

I can see Matisse is getting tired now. The muscles in her face have sagged a little since she arrived; the corners of her mouth are turned downwards. The shock of Stella's betrayal, of Lucy's illicit existence, of all this emotional arousal, is fatiguing her. Even her skin, which is usually so luminescent, appears duller, sallow. I need to wrap this up – for my sanity as well. Even I need time to process what's occurred.

'Matisse, Stella,' I say. 'This situation's naturally bringing up a huge amount of emotion. I think our one-on-one sessions will be a good place to work through your individual feelings about how Lucy was conceived, and the current situation with Cole. Then, when you're both ready, maybe we can come back together for some joint sessions.

'It's to be expected that things will feel raw right now. And there's obviously the serious and pressing question of how to handle the threats from Cole. It sounds as if seeing the lawyer may be the first step in working that out.

'It might also be helpful to take some space for yourselves – to not be spending every moment in each other's pockets for the time being. Obviously you share the same house, but you're blessed to live somewhere with plenty of space.'

They both nod to acknowledge my advice.

'Of course, I cannot emphasise enough the need to ensure your personal safety, and that of your family. And it is *essential* that Hannah and Sebastian are informed of the potential threat to their safety, particularly given what we know of

Cole's history.' I shoot Stella a meaningful look and am glad she has been open with Matisse about her ex-husband's behaviour when they were married. 'Will you agree to have a frank and serious discussion with them about this, today?'

To my relief, they both promise to call Sebastian and Hannah to explain the situation as soon as they leave my office.

I hand them some printed resources about family violence, and encourage them to get advice about what safety options might be appropriate for themselves and Hannah, such as increased home security. 'And, please, as well as taking all available precautions, you might want to give serious contemplation to involving the police.'

Matisse and I both look directly at Stella. She looks away.

'Do you still want me to drive out for your individual sessions on Thursday, or is that too soon?'

'I think,' starts Matisse, 'that it's best if we see the lawyer first. Get some clarity on our options. Maybe our usual time the following Thursday?'

I look at Stella. 'Yeah, next Thursday,' she says.

'Okay,' I agree. 'I'll see you both then.'

I cringe at the thought of being either of them, trapped in a vehicle with the other for the two-hour journey home.

As I stand to signal the end of the session, Matisse says, 'Don't forget about the memorial day.'

In truth, the event had momentarily slipped my mind. I had agreed to attend when Matisse mentioned it at our previous session. She thought the family might benefit from me being there for emotional support, but she also said that attending the annual day their community holds to honour Lucy's memory might help me to fully appreciate the impact of her life and death on the broader group of people who knew and loved her. How could I say no to a mother asking that of me?

'I won't,' I reassure her, even though now it's the last place I want to be.

11

HANNAH

IF I SPOKE TO THAT PSYCHOLOGIST, I WOULD TELL HER I HATE MY mother for what she's done. I would also tell her I'm glad it can never be undone. Because a life where Lucy was never born is unimaginable. I would explain that I would willingly choose this defective, grieving, hollow heart – a heart that might fail at any point – over Lucy never having been born. I would say that those days – the blanket-fortress-making days, the snuggle-in-front-of-cartoons days, the bake-cupcakes-with-rainbow-icing days, the throw-shoes-at-each-other days, the sulking-silently-ignoring-each-other days – all those days were meant to exist.

I might tell her that when that seething, raging man was outside – the man who I didn't realise was my father – I thought we might all die. I thought he might fly into my room and rip the doona off my body, and put his hands around my neck until I stopped breathing. I didn't think about what he might do to Mum or Mattie before he got to me. Survival makes you selfish.

I would tell her that I am glad I heard my father's voice, contorted and poisonous. It means I can stamp out my childish delusions about what he was: a misguided, complex and tortured man who simply hadn't yet realised he needed his children in his life. Or a busy and distracted man who would track down his kids once he finally got through his hectic to-do list. Or a brilliant and studious man who had a more pressing obligation to save the world than to face the fact he'd contributed to its overpopulation. Mum never painted a picture of him at all, so I had to sketch out the possibilities myself.

Now I get to grab those tightly held pictures, tear them into disappointed shreds, set them alight and watch them curl as they burn in my mind.

12

OCTAVIA

HENRY AND I SIT IN MY GARDEN FOR CLINICAL SUPERVISION, HIS kitchen renovations apparently having turned into a full-scale home excavation. We eat camembert with apricot-fig crackers and drink mineral water with mint and lemon. I think about how delightful it would be to enjoy a glass of wine instead – something light and fruity to accompany the gloriously warm, clear-skied afternoon – but I know I mustn't offer. Instead, I chew on a lemon slice as we conclude the review of my treatment plan for a 67-year-old pensioner with obsessive-compulsive disorder who has an unusual presentation, including a compulsion to masturbate for up to three hours a day, doing herself some wince-worthy damage in the process. Then, just as our hour is almost up, I tell him how relieved I was to discover – after seeking professional and legal advice – that I am not obliged to report Stella's embryo theft to police.

Henry pauses, and then says, 'Tell me: what's *his* story?'

I sigh, because I know immediately that he is not talking about Cole. 'What are you doing now?' I ask.

'Avoiding going home to a bombshell.' Henry grins impishly.

I stand up, gesturing for him to follow me. 'It's probably easier for you to hear it from him,' I say.

Looking intrigued yet relatively confident I'm not harbouring a sexually violent killer inside, Henry follows me into the lounge room. I glance back over my shoulder to see Bob – who had been sitting on a third chair, staring at us – jump down to sniff the seats, searching for errant crumbs.

I direct Henry to take a seat on my soft-as-babies'-bottoms suede couch. As he settles down, I fumble with the remotes, mumbling to myself out loud, which is an involuntary by-product of living alone. Henry watches me in silence.

I select the show and start fast-forwarding to find the bit I'm looking for. 'I won't show you the whole thing, but this is the interview that *Deep Dive* did with him after he was convicted. You haven't seen it, have you? I know you don't watch—'

'Nope,' he responds. 'Current affairs still depress me.'

'I know. I wish I could stop watching. I don't know why I get sucked in to these investigations, murder mysteries, true crime. It's as if we're being entertained by others' suffering. I don't know why darkness fascinates good people.'

'We're just sickos,' Henry offers.

'Maybe,' I say. 'But I've noticed it's women who seem most interested. I actually heard someone theorise that it helps us feel safer to learn about the patterns men use to hurt us. If we study the warning signs, it makes us feel prepared to see the red flags and avoid harm.'

'Is there any research on it?' asks Henry, and I am quietly resentful that he chooses to focus on the science rather than empathise about what it must be like to inhabit such a world. I shrug and sit on the other end of the couch, and then hit play, quickly saying, 'This is where the interviewer asks him about his childhood.'

The screen fills with the face of a thirty-something man with a shaved head and a neck tattoo – prison-quality – seated at a desk in prison browns.

'*Wow*,' exhales Henry. 'I didn't realise he was hot!'

'I know, right?' I'm glad I'm not the only one to think it. 'It's so disconcerting.'

I study the handsome face of *him*, aka Lachlan McDermott. In another life he could have been a model. Although he is sitting down in the video, it is obvious he is tall and well-built. But it is his facial features that are the most striking. His golden skin is the perfect canvas for his symmetrical features, chiselled jaw and full, touchable lips. His eyes are particularly entrancing: pale, metallic grey – almost silver – with a dark limbal ring. They aren't steely in expression, but nor are they warm. They are 'come-hither' eyes. Seductive. Persuasive. The kind of eyes that should be staring out of the pages of a high fashion magazine.

The interviewer is midway through a question: '—anything in your childhood that would have contributed to what you did?' she asks.

I wonder, as I did the first time I watched this, how she's feeling to be in the same room as him.

'How I grew up probably didn't help,' McDermott replies, in a smooth voice. 'My earliest memory is of being in my cot as a toddler, because I still didn't have my own bed. It was dark and things were crawling over my skin and mouth and eyes. I guess they were cockroaches.' He shrugs.

'My stomach was always burning because my mum would forget to feed me. I remember once I was screaming because I was so hungry, and she gave me this sippy cup, but the milk wouldn't come out because it had curdled.

'I found out later that my speech was delayed, so I don't know if I had the words to tell her, but I remember crying and throwing the cup on the floor, and she just kept smoking her cigarette and staring out the window. She'd do that a lot: stare into space as if she wasn't even there.'

'Do you think she thought she was being an okay mum?' the interviewer asks.

'She'd claim she was doing the best she could. Which is a cop-out. I get that she was an eighteen-year-old junkie. I get that she left home because her dad was having sex with her. But she didn't try to make her life any better. If she wanted her life to improve after Paul – my biological father – went to prison, why did she let her old man start coming over to our place? Start having sex with her again?'

'Because she was probably groomed by her father her entire life,' Henry mutters.

'How do you know that happened, Lachlan?' asks the interviewer.

'I saw it,' he says, lip curled.

'It would happen in front of you?'

McDermott shrugs. 'They weren't particularly careful at hiding it.'

'And what happened after that?' The interviewer is leading him somewhere.

'He started babysitting me. Mum wanted to go out and make some cash, so she left me with him, knowing full well what he was like. He didn't discriminate between adults and children, males and females.'

'What do you mean by that?' the interviewer asks.

'I mean,' he answers, 'he started doing stuff to me. First it was touching, then it progressed.'

'How old were you then?'

'Three, maybe four? When it first started, I mean,' says Lachlan. 'Mum had to know what was going on. I had toilet problems – he injured me. He practically moved in, and he'd do things to me in my bedroom or the bathroom with the door open. And she did nothing.'

'And your father was in prison at the time this was happening?'

'Yeah. About a year after I was born, he did a break-and-enter and tipped an old man out of his wheelchair. Broke his hip. I was about six when Dad came home. I'd never gone to school – not even preschool – by then.

'When Dad found my grandfather there, he pushed him through a glass door. I remember seeing him hold a piece of glass to the old prick's throat. I never saw him again.

'I felt relieved, at the time, but that didn't last long. Dad had a bunch of guys coming and going from the flat, buying drugs, fucking – sorry, can I say that? – having sex with my mum for money. Half the time, Mum wasn't even with it.

'At first, Dad was kind to me. He brought me lollies and called me his "little man". He'd ruffle my hair. It was pretty amazing for a kid who'd never been touched by anyone in a good way before.

'But he got nasty really fast. Everything I did made him mad. He'd come at me for the smallest thing. Sometimes he'd say I wasn't his son. Call me an "inbred little c-u-n-t". I didn't understand what he meant then, but I know now – obviously – he was implying Mum got pregnant by her father. There's been DNA testing, though, which proves Paul is my biological father.'

The interviewer nods. 'You said your father would come at you?' she prompts.

'Yeah. Like, one time Mum hadn't come home for a couple of days and he hadn't fed me anything. He was pissed off about something and I knew I should avoid him, but I was so hungry I was dizzy and I asked for food. He grabbed me by the back of my hair and smashed my mouth into the kitchen counter. It injured my gums and I got this big lump on the inside of my mouth that wouldn't go away. It kept filling up with blood and pus. Then it would burst and come back even bigger. Mum must've known, because my face was swollen, and I couldn't eat and was crying all the time. I think it got infected, because I started getting fevers so bad that my bed would get soaking wet.

'Because I had no sheets – just the mattress – it started growing mould. Even now, the smell of mould makes me physically sick.'

'Did they take you to the doctor?' the interviewer asks.

'No.' McDermott shakes his head. 'My records were submitted as part of the trial. They showed I only ever got taken to the GP once, when I was three months old. It was some infant wellness check, and the doctor wrote that I was underweight. He wrote that the band was still on my wrist – you know, the one the hospital puts on the day you're born? Nobody'd taken it off, and it was cutting into my arm. There wasn't anything in the notes to say he followed up with anyone. Maybe if he had . . . who knows?'

'But child protection did become involved eventually?' the interviewer asks.

'Yeah.' McDermott nods. 'There was a drug bust at the house when I was six. They saw my living conditions and the state my body was in – I had a lot of bruises and old fractures and stuff – and they found out I'd never been to school. Mum and Dad both went to jail for drug offences, but also for child neglect and cruelty against me.'

'And what happened to you then?'

'I was put into foster care. My first foster family was

pretty good. I couldn't believe what normal life was like, you know? Having a clean bed and food and other kids around. Having a pet dog. Toys. But I didn't cope with school. I was doing some pretty extreme things: scratching myself, banging my head, breaking things.

'The family couldn't take it, so I got put in another home, which was more strict. They used a reward system to get us to do stuff, like only getting dessert if we kept our rooms tidy. The strictness worked better for me because I understood the rules. If I didn't want dessert, I didn't bother cleaning up my room. I could weigh up how important something was to me.'

'I guess you could interpret that as very self-interested,' Henry says. 'But don't most humans respond better to having some choice?'

I nod in agreement.

'In court,' says the interviewer, 'those foster parents stated that you started learning how to get what you wanted without following the rules.'

'Oh,' says Henry, looking dejected. 'So much for that. He just got smarter about how to manipulate his environment.'

'That's true,' McDermott said, not skipping a beat. 'I figured out how to scam the system. I could just swipe the dessert from the fridge after everyone'd gone to bed, and then I wouldn't need to clean my room. They couldn't prove it was me.' He grins.

'You started stealing things from your foster parents?'

'I mean, nothing of real value. I'd take coins out of their wallets here and there, maybe exchanged a few of their belongings with other kids at school for stuff I wanted. I'd never *had* anything before, you know?'

'Tell us about their daughter,' the interviewer says.

McDermott looks confused but, knowing what comes next, I can detect the subtle signs of disingenuity.

'Ah, which daughter?' he says, maintaining his bluff.

'Lisa. The youngest one,' clarifies the interviewer.

'Lisa? Oh, yeah, she was super cute and sweet. I taught her how to ride a bike and she caught on fast. She was so smart and—'

'And you molested her,' says the interviewer flatly.

I see a subtle shift in McDermott's face, but he hides it well. He doesn't like being accused.

'That's what she said in court,' he replies lightly, as though talking about ice cream and the beach. 'I'm not calling her untruthful, but . . .' He trails off.

'You didn't do it, then?' asks the interviewer.

'Well, I was ten years old, you know? I can't remember every moment of my life. But if anything happened, it would've been normal kid stuff. You know – you show me yours or whatever.'

'She said you straddled her neck and put your penis in her mouth and held her nose so she couldn't breathe. She said you could see that she was choking, and you laughed. She was four.'

McDermott gives a scoffing look. 'Well, that's a bit imaginative—'

'Let's move on to later,' interrupts the interviewer. 'The records show that you started getting caught for petty crimes and cannabis use when you were twelve. You were a frequent school truant, and a bully when you attended – dropping a boy who had his arm in a splint face-first into a wheelie bin and causing a concussion, for instance. Then, at fourteen, you were sent to juvenile detention following repeated car theft offences, and an assault occasioning bodily harm – that was against a shopkeeper who caught you stealing and tried to detain you until the police arrived. There were also several other charges against you – including some of a sexual nature – that were dropped for various reasons.'

'I don't think it's that surprising I went off the rails, with what I'd been through,' McDermott says.

Beside me, Henry shrugs, as if to say, 'fair call'. Before I can argue that not every kid with a horrible upbringing does the things that McDermott did, Henry adds, 'But a prejudicial childhood doesn't give someone a free pass to be a completely vile human, does it?'

'You went very much off the rails,' states the interviewer. 'The judge who put you in juvenile detention marked you as someone who could be a threat to society, noting his concern that you had the potential to commit serious adult crimes, didn't he?'

'He did,' McDermott says, nodding. 'And I thought he was right. I thought a criminal was all I could be.'

'But then you met someone in juvie who changed the course of things.'

'That's right. Freddie Montgomery. He was one of the detention officers, and a total car nut. He restored vintage luxury vehicles on the side. He got me interested in mechanics. Engines and stuff. He took me under his wing. He was the only person who ever took an interest in me. He talked the person in charge of the centre's fleet vehicles into teaching me how to do some basic servicing and repairs. It was the first thing I was ever good at,' he explains, genuine passion crossing his face. 'I felt as if I'd found – I dunno – my thing.'

'And so, when you were released at sixteen, you started a mechanic apprenticeship?'

'Yeah, Freddie helped me get one at this high-end car place. His mate was the owner. Sam. A really good bloke.'

'And what about Freddie?'

'Freddie kept tabs on me for a while, but I guess he got busy and—'

'The truth is that Freddie was arrested, wasn't he? Arrested for persistent sexual abuse of a thirteen-year-old boy in the detention centre? Would that have been why you lost contact?'

'Yeah, I'd almost forgotten about that,' says McDermott. Henry and I exchange sceptical glances at this.

'He never did any of that with me, though. I mean, it was all above board.'

'Did it feel as if another person in your life was letting you down?' asks the interviewer.

'Well, he didn't do it to me, so I wasn't that affected. Freddie helped me, set me on the right track. I have to give him credit for that.'

'Interesting that he didn't hold Freddie to the same standards as his grandfather, perhaps because Freddie's behaviour didn't harm him personally,' says Henry, 'and because Freddie was also kind to him in some ways, unlike his grandfather.'

'Or maybe Freddie was abusing him, but he chooses to deny it,' I add, thinking about how McDermott later had a sexual relationship with Christopher to get things he wanted, and wondering if he learnt to tolerate such trade-offs through an abusive dynamic with Freddie.

'And it seems that you stayed on the right track for a few years. Finished your apprenticeship, got employed full-time at the dealership.'

'Yeah, that's right.'

'But your life wasn't really on track, was it?'

Again, McDermott affects a look of mild confusion.

The interviewer continues. 'Isn't it true that you simply got sneakier? Found ways of taking advantage of people so you wouldn't be caught? You told the police about one man who owned a Jaguar . . .'

'Oh, yeah. That's true.' McDermott waves his hand as though having been reminded of something trivial. 'There was this client with a top-of-the-range Jag. He was an arsehole. Rude. Thought he was better than everyone else. Blamed me when his car wasn't ready on time, even though it wasn't my fault. He was ranting and raving, insulting me—'

'And he'd told you when he dropped the car off that he was flying out to New York in a few days with his family? For Christmas?'

'That's right,' answers McDermott.

'So, what did you do when this guy made you mad?'

'The only thing I'd ever learnt how to do. I took it into my own hands. Got his address off the system at work. Broke into his place when I knew they'd be away, chucked stuff around a bit.'

'It was more than "chucking stuff around a bit", wouldn't you say? You trashed the entire house. They found holes in the walls, food thrown over the kitchen, faeces on the bedsheets. You left the children's teddy bears in suggestive poses. You tipped their fish tank upside down, killing their pets. You turned the fridge and freezer off and left the doors open so the house smelt of rotting food . . .'

A cheeky smile flashes across McDermott's face, and he looks down briefly as if to say, 'You got me'.

'It was screwed up, I'll admit,' he says, shrugging.

'You were also committing other types of crimes, weren't you?' says the interviewer.

'I did tell the police I wrote down that other guy's credit card number and—'

'No, I mean you were committing a different class of offences, weren't you? Sexual offences.'

'I don't really want to go into that,' answers McDermott. He looks down, face still, as though he is perhaps about to cry. Was he ashamed? Feigning shame, more likely.

'You were jailed twice, weren't you? For indecent assault and rape?'

He shrugs, nods, rubs a finger over the steel prison table dividing him and the interviewer.

'And each time you did a stint in prison, you came back out and Sam – the "good bloke" – took you back at the dealership. He told the court that, despite everything, he liked you. He still felt he could get you on the straight and narrow. But in reality this resulted in a situation where you could go away for a number of years, then come out and return to your life as though nothing had happened. You'd report to your parole officer when required and had several other conditions to which you had to adhere, but other than those you were essentially a free man. Sam even helped arrange accommodation for you.'

'Yeah, that's true. Sam always supported me, even when—'

'And during a parole period – as you later admitted – you raped a nineteen-year-old university student in a park two hours from where you lived. She had found an injured duckling and was nestling it in her jacket pocket so she could take it to get help. You grabbed her and dragged her into some bushes, where you raped her. The duckling fell out of her pocket, and you stomped on it.

'She wasn't sure whether you planned to kill her too, but you were disrupted by a couple walking nearby and she was able to run away.

'Fortunately for you, through some unfathomable issue in the chain of evidence – which has been the subject of its own government investigation – no usable DNA was obtained. You obviously realised this was a lucky escape, though, because you modified your MO for a subsequent offence in an attempt to prevent DNA transfer. Which was unsuccessful, due to your lack of understanding of the science.

'Also unfortunate for you with regard to the rape of this nineteen-year-old were the impressive powers of observation she demonstrated. She was able to provide an excellent description of you to police, who in turn produced a photofit sketch and published it in the local newspaper, which you monitored.

'Even though you were calculated enough to commit the crime away from where you lived, you realised you might one day get caught via victim identification. That's why you decided never to let another victim live, isn't it? That was seven months before Lucy's death.'

McDermott opens his mouth to respond, but the interviewer fires another question. 'It was also around this time that you met Christopher, wasn't it? Christopher, who was a very successful but lonely gay man who brought in a vehicle to be repaired at the dealership.'

McDermott nods, his expression flat.

'A man much older than you, cultured, educated, extremely wealthy, but vulnerable because of his loneliness. You saw an opportunity, didn't you?' Again, she doesn't give him time to respond. 'Christopher was looking for love and he was interested in you. He describes finding you'—the interviewer looks down at her notes—'"insanely good-looking, witty and charming". He had no idea about your prison history. And you let him think you were interested in him, because you realised that if you returned his affections there would be a lot in it for you. Expensive gifts, clothing, cocaine, holidays . . .'

'He even bought me a vintage Mustang,' McDermott says with a grin, misjudging the moment.

'And you were with him that week, weren't you? The week

you first met Lucy. You took a holiday together, stayed in a charming little cottage on a working farm on the Darling Downs. A cottage owned by Lucy's mothers.'

I hit pause on the remote and turn to Henry. 'It doesn't go much deeper from here. McDermott says – and this is even though he's admitted his guilt and made an unashamed confession to police, and his appeals are completely exhausted – he says that his legal team have advised him not to talk about Lucy's case.'

'He's got the pay-off from the interview – cameras, attention and proximity to an attractive young journalist – and he doesn't want to deal with the stuff he knows will make him look bad,' Henry says.

'If that's true, it just shows how warped his definition of "bad" is, given everything that's been discussed. Get this, though: later in the doco they talk about police uncovering regular banking transactions from McDermott's accounts. For years, he's been donating to a charity that connects children from troubled homes with older buddies who offer mentoring and support. They take the kids out to do fun things they wouldn't normally get access to – you know, outings to the zoo, or ice skating, or whatever the kid's particular interest is. He never told anyone; he was doing it without praise or recognition.'

Henry looks surprised.

'But then, he says this one thing that really unnerves me. When he's refusing to talk about Lucy and the interviewer keeps pushing, she says something about him hurting innocent girls and it really riles him up. For a moment, he can't hide whatever seething venom is inside him. It seeps out. You know what he says? "Little girls aren't as innocent as you think."'

13

HANNAH

I WOULD TELL DR TATE HOW I PACED MY ROOM ON THE DAY LUCY died, before we realised she was missing. How I walked back and forth, sunlight streaming in my window, my lips moving like a hungry fish, mouthing the words I would say to Mum and Mattie later that evening after Seb headed back to Brisbane.

I would tell Dr Tate how I knew I needed to share what had happened to me because it was a slimy secret, a mossy, slick rock that was exposed at every tide, to be covered and uncovered again and again. I was sinking into the sand with the weight of that rock.

I planned my words. How to tell them about what happened on that night. It wouldn't be a difficult evening for them to recall: how many times had I ever asked them to take me to a party? They were so excited that I was going to socialise with other kids my age, because I so often preferred to do things on my own. I can't even remember what it was that made me want to go. Perhaps it was because it was the first proper 'teenager' party I'd been invited to; a rite of passage.

And Mum and Mattie weren't worried. They knew these kids. Had known them since we'd painted each other's faces with wonky butterflies in kindergarten. We were good kids from good families. Trusted kids. And, most importantly, still kids. I don't think they'd even noticed we were growing and changing.

But we were changing. Our bodies, our minds, the corners of our world all shifting. Part of the reason I hadn't told Mum and Mattie what happened straightaway was because I had lied. Lied by omission. I knew there would be other kids there. Kids we didn't know. Kids from out of town. Older kids. Maybe even ones who'd finished school – adult-kids, technically. I didn't tell them because I knew in an intuitive way that they probably wouldn't let me go. Perhaps I should have considered the reasons why it might have worried them, but I didn't. I don't know whether I would've even been able to conceive of the grounds for such worries. And no doubt I would've thought any reasons they gave me to be hysterical and baseless, because I was sensible and mature and knew how to follow the rules, and bad things didn't happen to kids like me.

So, Mum and Mattie didn't realise that they were leading their daughter to a familiar shore that was flanked by an unknown sea. They didn't realise that their daughter – the one who was never late, never lied, never broke the rules – would quickly find herself on uncertain footing, unsure of how to act in front of older, cooler, smarter, more worldly kids. That, in all her nerves and uncertainty, that girl would take the cheery yellow can of pineapple-flavoured premix she was offered. Then, liking the sweet taste and warm glow that followed, she would have another, and she would be calmer and prettier and chattier and more interesting than she had ever been.

That girl did not understand that she couldn't drink every drop in the sea and still dodge rudders, and rocks, and sharks. She didn't even suspect there were sharks to dodge. Had she known, she would have been on the lookout, certain that their murky energies would be palpable from a distance, and thus easily avoided. But the lookout would have been in aid of other girls, whom she could warn; girls who were silver and quick and shiny. She would have thought herself so ordinary as to make unappetising prey. She would have thought herself safe.

That girl had absolutely no idea that boys who reminded her of her grown-up brother – doling out cheeky smiles and teasing words and hair ruffles – could slip out of their golden human skins to reveal the rough grey coverings and sharp teeth of predators. She did not know that, before they showed themselves to be sharks, they could cut her from her familiar school of fish with mortifyingly blunt tools: fizzy drinks, yearned-for attention and artless ruse. She did not realise they could get her alone so easily. Without notice. Without alarm.

But alone she was. Alone as they revealed their real natures, as they pulled her down, down, down to the bottom of the ocean, controlling the movement of her limbs and neck and torso, hands like moist, dank tendrils of seaweed wrapping around her. Alone as the pressure of the ocean started crushing her, and she watched her mouth move while no sound came out, and she realised she could not breathe underwater. Alone while her brain whispered, '*Swim, swim, swim to the surface,*' but her body screamed for her to lie dead so the sharks would lose interest and leave her be.

Then, while she was that drowning, fightless thing – observer of her own pending consumption – something unexpected. Something from the shore. A hapless knock at the bedroom door, someone looking for them. Then, a low, guttural, '*Fuck*,' from one of their mouths, followed up by a loud and jolly, 'Out in a minute!' And – surprise! – those sharks slipped so quickly back into their human skins, slid their goldenness back over themselves like coats they had accidentally dropped on the floor. Rustle, rustle, they righted themselves and were off down the hallway, door closed behind them, the jingle-jangle of their blokey guffaws getting fainter – off to their next adventure. Finally, she was alone-alone. Abandoned prey, beached on a bed of salty, sodden sheets that smelt of bodies that were not her own.

Would I tell the story to Dr Tate like that? Tell her about that girl once removed, as if it wasn't me? Would she understand that choosing to think that girl wasn't me let me go on for days and weeks with my mind and soul somewhat intact? That it was easier to dust myself off, pull myself together and act the part? Because to admit straightaway she was me was too much. Too much reckoning: with my own stupidity, my naivety, my lack of understanding about bodies and boys and sex and right and wrong and silence and responsibility and where lines lay; with the fallibility of my innocent belief in a good world, a fair world, a world made up of trustworthy people who might occasionally be mean, but who rarely acted with intent to truly harm.

I let that girl be someone else for as long as I could, but reality finds its way through our nets. Would Dr Tate understand that, by the time the truth started seeping through my defences so cripplingly that I knew I needed to tell them, my story was overtaken by a faster-moving vessel? The Lucy Boat was caught on a larger swelling tide, in a more ferocious storm, on an ocean with waves so big that everyone was going under, and nobody had time for stories of little dinghies set adrift. I could barely process what had happened to my sister, let alone try to work out how to tell my mums what had happened to me and, anyway, how could I add to their pain? So, my story became the story of another girl again, and every time it threatened to engulf me, I reminded myself that dead girls trump wounded girls, and pushed it back down.

Would I tell Dr Tate that the only time I really let myself process what happened to me was in the context of my silly, hurt-little-girl-gets-rescued fantasy? The one where I lie in bed at night and think about tracking down my dad and telling him what those boys did. The one where I drop the bomb that activates his protective fatherly instincts, and then feel my worth and value grow in proportion to his outrage and defence of me? The one where he finds me and encircles me in his great bear-arms, then lets me go and looks into my eyes and says, 'I'm so sorry this happened to you, my darling,' before tucking me snug in bed and flying out the door to find those who hurt me, avenging me and restoring me to wholeness and goodness, and making my world safe.

If I told her that, then I'd have to tell her that three nights ago, when I figured out who that man was – the one screaming and threatening outside our house – I was forced to abandon the fantasy. My father will never protect me. He cannot make me whole. He is, in fact, only another species of predator.

It's time to face reality now. I *am* that girl. But I am not prey.

14

OCTAVIA

WHEN SEBASTIAN ARRIVES FOR HIS SESSION TODAY, HIS USUAL affable expression is gone. He looks pensive.

'What's going on?' I ask, already suspecting.

'Just the Mum thing,' he says. 'The Mum and *Dad* thing.'

'Tough, huh?' I say, guessing he knows I understand what he's referring to.

'Yep. I never considered that Mum would do something like that. Never even wondered, "Why would Dad agree to them using the embryos?"'

'Well,' I offer, 'you were only a teenager at the time. You were probably contemplating polocrosse, girls, getting into trouble with your mates. I'm guessing you weren't much focused on Mattie and your mum's fertility journey . . .'

'Yeah.' He sighs, a smile touching his lips. 'Probably not. I'm surprised Lucy didn't take more of an interest in who her father was, though. She was such a curious kid but, as far as I know, she never asked questions about him.'

'Maybe she would have given it more thought as she got older,' I say.

'I'm glad she didn't find out what her father was like. She would have only felt rejection,' he says.

'Is that how you felt? Feel?' I ask.

'From my dad? I guess. Although it doesn't sting now like it did when I was a kid.'

'How did it feel back then?'

'It hurt, a lot. Losing the father who I sometimes wanted to be like, who I thought loved me. And not because something terrible happened to him, but because we didn't mean enough for him to stay. I didn't mean enough.

'Part of me was relieved he left, though, because of how he treated Mum. Even the things he said to her were disgusting. I can remember knowing when he was going to say something vile, because his voice would go low and calm. He'd say things like her breath smelt so bad it made him gag, or her vagina was so mushed up from pushing me out that it felt like thrusting into a gutted pig.'

'They're extremely confronting things for a young boy to hear,' I say, trying to keep my repulsion towards this awful man out of my voice.

'It was also confusing because I'd see him do nice stuff, too. Like, once we were behind this old lady at the supermarket checkout – she was fumbling through her purse, struggling to find enough money for her order. He just pulled out his card and paid for her groceries.

'And I craved a father as I got older. A man I could look to for guidance, like, "How should I act here?" or "What do I do about this?" I tried to imagine what my dad would do in certain situations, but nothing my brain could conjure was reassuring. I knew the father I longed for was a different type of man to him. I wanted the kind of dad you see in family dramas: you know, amiable, principled, reassuringly lighting the path out of any problem, no matter how grave.'

I smile to show that I understand just the sort of fictional father he means.

'After losing Lucy, I wanted a man stronger than me to jump in and protect Mum. I was still just a kid myself, but I felt as if all eyes were on me to lead my family through everything that followed. Nobody said as much, but . . .'

'Is it possible that nobody expected that of you?' I ask. 'That perhaps it was your own expectation of yourself? Part of your internalised belief system about the role of men in society – that they should always be protectors, fixers, family figureheads?'

I see him consider this and then say, 'That has truly never occurred to me. I just assumed it was my role as a man, even one who grew up with two mums. That sounds pretty outmoded . . .'

I shrug as though to say, 'No judgement here', while silently wondering if I will ever in my career see a generation of men that has escaped the stranglehold of such weighty expectations.

'Then again,' says Sebastian, shifting course, 'I don't think it would matter what I gave, as a man or otherwise. Mum just takes and takes – sucks in your air until you're gasping – whether she means to or not. It's as if she's stuck in the hours and days after Lucy was murdered. She thinks nothing can be all right until she kills McDermott.'

'Can it be?' I ask.

'It won't change a thing about Lucy. The only thing it will make okay is that McDermott won't be here anymore. But that means his suffering ends. He doesn't have to spend the next forty years locked up inside a cold, grey box, thinking about what he did. He doesn't have to be deprived of, I don't know, a soft bed, the smell of the ocean, McDonald's.

'But perhaps Mum thinks the amount she can make him suffer while killing him outweighs the slow torture of life in prison? I find the idea hard to stomach, though. I don't believe my role is to mete out punishment, even to people I hate. It does make me wonder what Lucy'd want us to do, though.'

'What's your best guess?'

'I think she'd say'—he pauses—'"Take the motherfucker out."'

'Do you?' I reply, hiding my odd sense of pride in this brave girl I never met.

'I do,' he says. 'I can almost picture her face as she says it. Not that she swore when she was alive. And, you know . . . she was only ten.'

'And you wonder if imagining the wishes of a ten-year-old is the right way to make this very adult decision?' I ask.

He contemplates this and says, 'Yes. But, then again, when is it not right to listen to the victim? And when is it not right to support your mother? Mum wants me to be there.'

'She discusses the execution with you, then?' I ask.

'It's all she talks about.'

I picture Stella's tight-lipped visage and think about how the only time I've heard her speak at length was when she told me the story of how she came to own the farm. I wish she would talk to me more openly about the execution.

'She relishes describing what she's going to do to him.' He crinkles his nose.

'And that revolts you?' I ask.

'Yeah,' he says. 'I don't want to hear her describe the intricacies of torturing someone to death. It's as if I'm getting an insight into McDermott's mind when I hear her speak like that. There's a desire in her eyes that's almost . . . sexual, and it sickens me.'

'So, helping her do those things would be—'

'Disgusting,' he jumps in. 'I have nightmares about it. The guy tied up. Mum doing things to him, handing me things covered in red. The smell of blood in the air. Her yelling instructions at me: "Hold this. Stick him there." I can't imagine myself doing those things.

'Don't get me wrong: I am filled with a searing rage about what he did to my sister. And for others like him who still walk the streets. And towards all men, including myself, for standing idly by while this shit happens. It's a rage I don't know what to do with, but there's something about physical violence, even in this extreme context, that just doesn't sit right with me.'

'Do you know if your father was ever physically violent to your mother?' I ask, curious about how this may have had an impact on his views.

'Do you think that's why I can't stomach it?' Sebastian asks, then continues speaking before I can answer. 'Mum thinks she protected me from that, because it usually happened after I was in bed. But from my room, I could hear everything. There was a particular point in some of their arguments – usually on the nights Dad was drunk – where I could sense a shift in the dynamic. Mum's voice would turn from sounding loud and angry to soft and trembling. She would become conciliatory, placating. I learnt this was the moment before—'

He wrinkled his brow.

'Before what?'

'Before everything exploded. Before he grabbed her hair. Before he twisted her arm so far behind her back that I was sure it would snap. Before he put his hands around her throat and squeezed until her face was purple and her eyes bugged out of her head. Or, worse, before she would beg.'

'How do you know that's what happened?'

'Because sometimes I would sneak down the hallway and peek my head around the corner to watch them in the living room. Mum was always too caught up in the moment – terrified, I suppose – to notice me, but he saw me there twice. The first time, he was surprised. It caught him off kilter. He didn't acknowledge me, but he calmed things down, told her he needed to go for a walk to cool off.

'That gave me the idea that, if he knew I was there, he wouldn't hurt her. So, on the next occasion when they were getting into it, I poked my head around the corner again. But this time when he saw me he stared me right in the eye, then turned around and smacked her in the face. I took the message for what it was, and never got out of bed again when I heard them fighting.'

'Sebastian, that sounds like a terrifying and deeply disturbing experience.'

'It was,' he says, and I notice his bottom lip tremble slightly.

'And yet, you were a child, with no choice but to remain in that unsafe environment. Were there other instances of abuse you witnessed after that?'

'It did feel inescapable. Inevitable. And yes, it just kept happening. I did all sorts of things to try to get through. Covering my ears. Counting. Singing to myself. Pleading with some higher power that she'd be okay. But because she was always up and back to mum-stuff the next day – you know, cleaning the kitchen, getting me ready for school – my child's mind eventually concluded that she would always be okay. Which is stupid to think now, because she easily could have been killed.'

I nod, feeling sad for the little boy who witnessed all that. 'It's not surprising that you felt conflicted when your father left. And then you moved to the farm, and were completely without a male role model . . .'

'Yeah,' he says. 'From then on, I think I learnt about being a man from copying the boys at school. And those boys were different, somehow, from the boys I grew up with in the city. They were harder, tougher, more centred on traditionally masculine interests: rough sports, dirt biking and pigging.'

'Did you feel compelled to act a particular way around them?' I ask.

'Definitely. I distinctly recall becoming more focused on monitoring my emotional expression. I realised it was okay to show certain emotions, such as confidence, and determination, and anger, but never things such as sadness, or fear, or sentimentality.'

'Sounds bleak,' I say.

'I mean, there was good stuff: mateship, loyalty, adventure. But I constantly felt as if I was hiding parts of myself. I guess I've always been quite sensitive. Felt others' pain easily, seen beauty in things most people don't seem to notice, been moved by music and art. I found the coarseness of some of my peers . . . alienating. Still, I strove to fit in while I was there.'

'How so?'

'Sports. Endless sports. Playing pranks on your mates. Fisticuffs here and there. Alcohol. Like, really young: eleven or twelve. Cigarettes. Weed. Being passenger to your drunk-driving friends, urging them to go faster on back country roads. Parties. Bonfires. Sleeping with girls in the backs of utes, knowing you'd ignore them at school on Monday while giving lewd critiques about their bodies and their performance to your mates.

'I'm not proud of it, obviously,' he says. 'I mean, I lived in a house with four females. I knew when I disrespected the girls at school to fit in, I was disrespecting my mums and sisters. But sometimes – and I don't know if this sounds . . . sexist? – but I wanted to go home and not be surrounded only by women. I craved another male presence in the house. In retrospect, I can see it was because I was searching for a man who I could look towards to work out what I should be doing, how I should act. When I went to school on Mondays and the guys talked about what they did with their dads over the weekend, I was jealous. Not about the particular activities they did together, but about their connections to each other.'

'Did you have an image of the sort of father you wanted?' I ask.

'I had an English teacher for a few months when I was fifteen,' says Sebastian. 'He'd come from the city. In truth, he probably wasn't even old enough to be my father, but he was the sort of man I wanted to be: thoughtful, compassionate, principled. He had this way of getting us to think more deeply about things. Every Wednesday he'd set us a reflective writing assignment to hand in the following week. The assignment would always be built around a question, like "How will you know you've become the person you want to be?" and "What is the most valuable lesson you've learnt in life thus far, and how has it shaped you?"

'Some of the guys *hated* these assignments. Did everything they could to get out of them, or handed in the most haphazard, unconsidered responses. Their discomfort at having to think about or expose parts of themselves to someone else started coming through in their actions towards Mr Hussein; thinly veiled comments about his Middle Eastern heritage, mutterings of 'poofta' under their breath. But he seemed completely unruffled. In fact, the more their behaviour escalated, the calmer, the stiller, the more kind he seemed to become. That only made my respect for him grow, and I felt something like despair when he left the school after a semester. I believe the plan was always for him to stay only for a brief time, but I was resentful towards some of my mates for their behaviour and told myself they were responsible for him going.

'Still, even now, I notice myself critiquing my behaviour based on what I internalised from the guys I grew up with. Even to the point that I find myself asking what they would do to McDermott. What they would think *I* should do to him.'

'What would they say you should do to him?' I ask.

'They would say, without hesitation, that it's my job as a man to avenge my sister with every ounce of violence I can muster. And maybe they're right.

'I hate to admit it, but I'm scared to run into them when I visit home in case they ask about the execution. Thankfully, the rules are that nobody in the general public will be told which family members participate. But that won't stop them pressing for information. Fending them off will be hard enough. But can you picture how embarrassing it would be if I actually had to tell them I didn't do it? To say that I sat at home on the couch while the execution took place because I was prepared to let the man who raped and murdered my little sister live out his days in prison? To say, but, don't worry, my mum made sure he got what he deserved? Imagine being known as the big, strong man who sends his brittle, grief-stricken mummy into a prison cell alone to sort out his sister's killer, because he's too weak to do it himself. Because that's what they'd believe. I'm glad they'll never know, because I don't think I could bear the fucking shame of being that man . . .'

His voice wavers, and he grabs a tissue from the box on the coffee table. He squeezes it tight in his fist when no tears come.

•

It is one of those rare days when I arrive home to my cosy house – empty but for Bob – and wonder what it would be like not to be alone. What it would be like to have a partner or a child there with me. I remind myself that, most of the time, I enjoy my decision to be unattached. I like how much less complicated life feels; I find freedom in the space of only having to care for me, especially when I use so much energy caring for others every day. But there are days like this where I wish that I had someone to unburden myself to. Someone to whom I could say, 'This happened to me today,' and they would say, 'Ooh, tell me more,' or 'Geez, you poor thing.' Of course, I can do that in supervision with Henry. Or, if it's not work-related, I can choose someone from the group of dear, trusted friends I know I'm lucky to have. But it's not the same as having someone of my very own to unfold my heart to, someone who could maybe even tuck me up safe in bed on days like these.

15

OCTAVIA

AS MY CAR RATTLES ITS WAY UP THE LONG DIRT DRIVE TO THE heritage homestead that is Sullivan Downs, I see a green oasis peeking out from the centre of crisp, sullen fields. I park near a scattering of cars beside some dilapidated wooden yards where two alpacas stand under a parched willow. Their enormous, glassy eyes peer at me, evaluating, as I get out of the car. They blink their long lashes as if they have all day, and return to grazing.

I make my way past tin sheds, pulling my coat close to my body against the pinching fingers of winter in spite of the clear sunny day. I see a mammoth dam, half-full, to my left, and wonder if the edges freeze over at night. The homestead that appears to my right is a grander version of Stella and Matisse's cottage: quite similar in appearance but much larger, with sweeping verandahs and frothy wisteria vines draping the eaves.

The gardens are expansive, structured, traditional. Defined paths leading through rose beds, spiky bushes pruned obediently to shape. Huge trees – bunya pines and Moreton Bay figs – locate this place at a point in pastoralist history. The gardens are beautiful, but I wonder what the land looked like before the artificially neat lines and squares were imposed upon the place.

The green lawns roll on endlessly, the caretakers somehow defying the drought to maintain this emerald hideaway at the base of the Great Dividing Range. I wonder where the water is coming from.

Around fifty or sixty people move about like ants at an edge of the lawn that is flanked by a stand of the magnificent fig trees. They are busying themselves smoothing picnic rugs under graceful, weeping branches. Children dash around in clustered groups, squealing and playing. Some of them are around Lucy's age – her frozen age – and I let myself imagine her playing here among the other kids: shoes skidding on the grass as she runs, a small hand reaching out to grab the arm of a friend to steady herself, a high, sweet laugh piercing the air. Carefree, with the possibility of so many tomorrows ahead.

As I get nearer, I see Matisse. Or, more correctly, I see the huge topknot balanced atop her head, coiled tendrils fighting to spring loose. She is sprawled on a rug and saying her goodbyes to an elderly couple she had been chatting to: a man whose stoop is so bad his chin rests on his chest, and a robust, ruddy-skinned woman dressed in red, which gives her the look of a giant tomato.

Matisse notices me and calls a jubilant greeting. She is seated on a king-sized white bedspread. The lace fabric is weighed down with posh picnicware: porcelain plates, bone china tea cups, silver cutlery, floral linen napkins. She beckons for me to sit down and pulls camembert and strawberries out of an old-fashioned wicker basket. Giant pink-and-grey galahs swing from her earlobes. I had thought this would be a more sombre affair.

'How *are* you? Thank you for coming,' she says.

I fold myself into a cross-legged position, feeling my knees crack as they collapse into themselves.

When I am settled, Matisse produces a pale pink knitted blanket from a neatly folded pile and gestures for me to place it across my lap, as she has done with a similar one. I feel as though I am in a picnic scene from a film remake of *Emma*.

'It was minus one last night,' Matisse tells me, rubbing her arms. 'Our troughs froze.'

'Really?' I'm surprised: in Brisbane, only two hours away, it rarely drops below fourteen by the beginning of September.

'It's never usually this cold by now. But that'll be the last frost.' She gives a knowing nod. 'You watch, we'll be boiling our britches off before you know it.'

I laugh, feeling more and more as though I am on a Jane Austen film set.

'So many people,' I say, taking in the crowd.

'Yes,' she says. 'Beth – Stella's friend from primary school – organises this every year now in Lucy's memory. We choose the weekend closest to Lucy's birthday to hold the event. This year, her birthday falls on the weekend. It's tomorrow.'

She smiles sadly, and I can feel her pain and sorrow. She points towards the house, and I notice a large poster board with a photograph of Lucy, arm around her grey pony's neck, smile beaming. Lil' Sis leans in towards her, as though enjoying the attention.

'I feel touched that so many people turn out to remember Lucy. They all make donations to the Young Survivors' Fund, which helps kids who've experienced violence,' she explains.

'That's such a great way of honouring Lucy's memory.'

Matisse leans over and whispers conspiratorially, 'To be honest, Stella and I find it quite overwhelming. It's a lot of attention. Stella doesn't cope well in the lead-up.'

I nod. 'I can imagine.'

'And she's extra tense today, of course. So am I. We're worried Cole has got wind of the day and will show up.'

'Oh,' I say. I hadn't considered that possibility.

'That would be disastrous,' she says.

'Yes,' I agree.

'We were hoping that Sebastian might be here to take things in hand if Cole appears. But he was called into work on an emergency. Stella's talked to the lawyer; we're going to offer Cole a non-disclosure deal. It's far more money than we've got lying around, so we're trying to work out how to do it. We hope he'll accept. He seems so unpredictable, though. Who knows what he'll do?'

Matisse gazes into the distance towards the water.

'Hannah's taken Stella for a walk around the dam, as a distraction,' Matisse says. And then, after a moment, 'We're really quite worried about her.'

'About Stella?' I ask.

'No, I mean Stella and I are worried about Hannah.'

'Oh, right.' I am intrigued, but also not wanting to get into anything sensitive here, on a picnic blanket at her daughter's memorial day.

Matisse looks up, checking to see there's nobody in earshot, and presses on.

'John – I don't think you've met John? He's the butcher for Heathwood Farm. Since Lucy died, Stella hasn't been able to do the slaughtering, so we get him to do that as well. We trust him. He's kind with the cattle. Gentle and calming.'

'Right.' I nod, wondering where this is going and how to divert it.

'So, yesterday, John told Stella and me that Hannah approached him recently. She asked him to teach her how to slaughter and butcher a cow.'

'Really? I got the impression that Hannah was a bit . . . squeamish?'

'She is!' exclaims Matisse. 'That's what makes it so strange. That, and how many teenage girls – squeamish or not – want to kill animals and cut them up? She's always avoided anything on the farm that involves blood and guts. She won't even watch the birthings.'

'So, why the sudden interest then?' I ask, unable to help myself. It is odd behaviour.

'We don't know. John said she didn't give a reason. He said he was thrown, and he put her off so he could think about it. He asked us not to tell Hannah he'd talked to us. Said he doesn't mind teaching her if we're okay with it, but he's worried about how she'd handle it.'

I tell myself to try to change the topic, but instead I say, 'And is there anything going on with Hannah that would explain where this is coming from?'

'She's been distinctly different this past year or so. She's always liked her own company and kept to herself. Her safe place is her bedroom and her books. But recently she's become more . . . intense? She's started exercising and, trust me, she was never that girl. She's also been skipping meals. She thinks I don't notice, but I do, of course. And she seems – I don't know – secretive?'

'Has she had concerns with her body in the past? Body image issues?'

'Not that I know of.' Matisse shrugs. 'And she's a toothpick, skinny as anything. Always has been. I'm not sure that she's lost weight, but she looks more toned. Muscular, almost. She walked from the bathroom to her bedroom in a bra and underwear last night, and I swear she had a six pack.

'Speak of the devil,' Matisse says then, looking towards a pair of women walking across the lawn. As the two bodies come closer, I can make out Stella's features. She is accompanied by a tall young woman, gazelle-like, legs going on for miles in her jeans, and with red wavy hair – a stunning shade of copper – cascading down her back. This is not the image I'd conjured in my head of Hannah. Her family's description of her as retiring and bookish created in my imagination a squat, gawky adolescent with glasses, acne and mousy brown hair. How very judgemental of me, to both that girl and the one before me.

When they are a few metres away, Stella calls out a weak 'Hi'. I get to my feet and greet her, thinking she looks constipated again, but pretty, her features brightened by a touch of make-up. Then I turn to face Hannah. As my eyes meet hers I am taken aback once more, because I am faced with a wide, inquiring green eye, and one with the same expression in blue. Heterochromia.

'Hi, Dr Tate,' Hannah says, beating me to the introduction and self-assuredly reaching out a hand. 'I'm Hannah.'

I take her hand, which is soft, her fingertips cold, and say, 'Hi, Hannah. Call me Octavia. It's great to finally meet you.'

Matisse pats the blanket, indicating for us to sit, and Hannah gracefully slides into a cross-legged position on the ground. Stella and I join her.

'Aren't you freezing?' Matisse asks Hannah, and I take in the fact that the young woman is wearing only a fitted, long-sleeved olive-green top with her jeans. No jumper or coat, unlike the rest of us.

She shrugs in response to her stepmother's question and says, 'I'm fine.'

Matisse starts pouring glasses of champagne and orange juice as a group of ladies walks up to the picnic rug, all smiles and hellos. They are obviously old friends of Stella's, and they start catching her up on their families, jobs, the effects of the drought. They do most of the talking, while Stella answers questions as minimally as possible. She isn't rude, but she's clearly not engaged. Matisse intervenes in the conversation several times, saving Stella from social faux pas with warmth and diplomacy.

Hannah watches the interaction keenly. Subtly, I hope, I watch Hannah. Where is the shyness? The slumped shoulders from reading too many books? Hannah is no reticent mouse. She is a watchful fox, alert to her surrounds, blending in with them but aware of the slightest changes, body languid but poised, ready to respond in an instant. Her coat of glossy red waves makes her look as if she would be soft to the touch, but I get the impression that this is deceptive, and underneath she is weaponised with fox-sharp teeth that even she may not yet know she possesses.

Matisse passes me a mimosa, which I thank her for but do not drink. A minute later, Hannah sees a schoolfriend across the lawn and excuses herself. As she does so, her eyes meet mine again and I sense that she can peer into me and pluck out my thoughts, or look straight through me – whichever she chooses. Her presence brings up an unsettled feeling inside me. Not a bad feeling, exactly; more a sense of . . . disquiet.

The rest of the morning goes by in a blur. Person after person stops at the bedspread to converse with the women, who introduce me as a 'friend of the family'. Nobody questions this or engages me in conversation.

People are clearly curious about the upcoming execution date but are too polite to bring it up directly, and so talk around it. A beak-nosed woman in lavender goes so far as to mention she is going on a cruise in November and asks whether they have any plans for that month, to which Matisse replies that the woman has a green ant crawling on her skirt. This results in an unnecessary squealing and flapping of hands, and the moment is lost.

Matisse expertly dodges every attempt at extracting information: ducking, darting, redirecting. With the intensity of the media interest in the case over the years, she's clearly honed this skill. The mothers have told me they are grateful that the media is not allowed to approach them regarding the execution of the sentence; banned from doing so by the judge. It seems to me that there are pros and cons of this. If things go terribly wrong and they wish to speak publicly against the experience, the enforced silence could become a hand-icap. Then again, imagine family members turning on each other, publishing exposés about what happened in that room. Giving grotesque accounts of who did what and how. The prospect of this execution scenario seems more outlandish with each passing month, and yet the reality of it is getting closer by the day.

I wonder how Hannah feels about everything that is going on. She was at an impressionable age, thirteen, when Lucy was killed. The age of questioning who you are, of individuating yourself from your family, of opening up to the possibilities for your future, of meeting the friends and foes that are sex and love. And in the middle of this natural trajectory, a random man who visited the sanctuary of her home, the farm – a man she met and conversed with – destroys her baby sister. I wonder how she feels about the fact that she cannot participate in killing this man because of her age at the time of the murder. Does she find it unfair, or a relief? I'm glad she's not in the same terrible position as the rest of the family, but how would she handle it if she was? Would she weigh up the possibilities with a clear, still mind, then decide to tear him apart with her fox-sharp teeth and lick her coat clean afterwards?

A group of women leaves our blanket and a single woman approaches. Matisse beams at her and waves her over. She walks towards us, wearing a floral skirt with an elasticised waistband and a boa-constrictor-sized crocheted scarf. This is kind of how I expected Hannah to look, I think, except a couple of decades younger.

'Hello.' Matisse grins. 'I'm so glad you could come again.' Matisse turns to me and says, 'Octavia, meet Margie Moore, Lucy's fifth-grade teacher. Margie, Octavia is a family friend.'

Margie gives a serene smile and says, 'Lovely to meet you.'

'I hear Lucy was a gregarious little girl,' I say. 'You must have had your hands full with her in your class.' I give a teasing smile to let her know I'm being lighthearted.

'Oh, I had both hands full. She was a little monkey!' Turning to Stella and Matisse, she adds, 'I hope you don't mind me saying so.'

Stella gives a strained smile, but I doubt she's really listening.

'Of course not.' Matisse laughs. 'After all the parent–teacher conferences we had, it's hardly a surprise to us.'

The teacher giggles and says, 'You know, she was just so spirited. She kept me on my toes. I remember the time Tommy Kerr said something mean to one of the girls while he was taking his shoes off before gym, and Lucy got so mad with him she picked up his shoe and threw it on the roof of the change rooms. They had to get the maintenance assistant to get up on a ladder and retrieve it.'

'We got called to the school about that one,' Matisse tells me, sounding almost proud.

'You were at my office quite frequently,' says Margie.

'We were at her office *constantly*,' Matisse says, eyes wide in exaggeration. 'What about the time you had to send a letter home saying you thought she should get checked for a bladder infection?'

'Ha!' Margie laughs, and says to me, 'She was wanting to go to the bathroom four or five times in a day. I thought she needed to be seen by a doctor. But Stella asked if I could follow her one day, so I slipped out of the classroom – just for a minute – and saw her traipsing around the school grounds behind the toilet block, feeding magpies with crumbs from one skirt pocket and filling her other pocket with gumnuts and stones.'

'She told me later they were for her treehouse,' Matisse explains, and I see a flash of pain, unmistakable, cloud her face. But she immediately rallies and reminds Margie about how Lucy convinced another kid to sell his pet mouse, which he'd brought in for show-and-tell, to her for five dollars, some collectable cards and a packet of gum. Margie then recounts how she had to make Lucy give the mouse back when the boy's mother arrived, and how she overheard Lucy the next day demanding he return his spoils, plus extra collectable cards as interest for having kept them overnight.

I try to assess Stella's reaction, but she isn't with us. Her mind is far away, on other things.

16

OCTAVIA

I CAN BARELY BELIEVE IT'S BEEN ONLY FIVE DAYS SINCE LUCY'S memorial picnic, because it's now so hot that I am indeed sweating in my britches. I shift my position in my appointed armchair and regard Stella, who is in her spot on the lounge and wearing her usual tight expression. Her furrowed forehead is slick, but she has not deemed it warm enough to start the air conditioning or even open a window. I wonder if she's aware of the heat at all. Surely she can't have missed the candied smell of spring on the air.

She's giving me one-word answers again, or the most minimal responses possible. We have a pattern now: she will tolerate me for about twenty minutes, possibly twenty-five, before telling me she is 'happy to finish up here today'. We rarely cover anything of substance.

The first time this happened, I pointed out that sessions usually run for fifty minutes, and she countered that the court stipulated she see me, but didn't give requirements for the length of our sessions. The next time she saw me, she also mentioned that the court had not mandated the frequency of sessions, either; perhaps a not-so-subtle suggestion that my weekly visits were too . . . weekly.

Precisely eighteen minutes into the session, Stella pulls out the line. 'Thanks, Octavia. I'm happy to finish up here today.' It is delivered with a teensy, sweet smile and a dismissive tone.

The taut thing inside me – which has been fraying for weeks – finally snaps. I slap my notebook on the coffee table, more forcefully than I mean to. I lean forwards and gaze intently at Stella.

Her hand rises to her throat in surprise. I've startled her, which wasn't intended, and which I instantly regret. Although my brain is yelling at me to apologise immediately, my intuition says this isn't the time to do so.

'Tell me, Stella: what is it you want to *do* to Lachlan McDermott?'

Stella goes still and regards me for a long moment. Then she draws herself up, a 'now you're talking' expression on her face. Good.

'Come with me,' she summons, standing up and walking out of the room without turning to see if I follow.

I get to my feet and take a few quick strides to catch up to her, wondering what I've unleashed. I follow her down the hallway and she opens a door to the right.

She walks in and stands out of the way, making room for me to enter. Then she closes the door.

I know instantly that we are standing in Lucy's room. Unlike the rest of the house, which is freshly renovated in soft whites and greys, this room is a forest. The walls are covered with faded emerald-green wallpaper that is illustrated with fawns with spotted backs, masked owls, grey hares, red mushrooms, flowers and leaves. A dusky-pink canopy hangs over the bed. The bed itself is covered in a teal quilt, the dust-ruffle a pale blue. Above the pillow dangles a mobile of silver stars and white doves. There is a small wooden desk in the corner, over which hangs a whimsical painting of a red-headed girl hugging a fox. Blue-tacked onto the wallpaper to the right of the desk are photographs of Lil' Sis in various postures: head down eating, galloping, lying on her side taking a nap.

I look around, soaking in the magic of Lucy's presence. Then I notice Stella leaving the room. She closes the door behind her. *Okay* . . . I hear her feet stomp on floorboards, and then a drawer slides open somewhere, then thuds closed.

Footsteps retracing themselves, becoming louder, and here she is, back in the room, a large white envelope in hand.

'Sit,' she says, pointing to Lucy's wooden desk chair. I obey, sinking my bottom uncomfortably into the space meant for a child and hoping the legs don't give way.

'Read this,' she says, handing me the envelope before lowering herself onto Lucy's bed.

I open the envelope, which is not sealed, and pull out several sheets of A4 paper, stapled in the top left corner. The first few pages are already folded back, and I presume I'm meant to start at the text on the open page, which is highlighted in fluorescent orange.

12. To your credit, you pleaded guilty to those offences. This is evidence of cooperation with the administration of justice. Your cooperation, I accept, has been significant.

I know what this is. It's Lachlan McDermott's sentencing remarks. I've read these before, many months ago, prior to meeting the family. But I have not read them sitting in the bedroom of the little girl he murdered, with her mother watching me. I hold my breath and continue.

13. Your offending occurred several weeks after a holiday with your partner at a bed and breakfast at Heathwood Farm. A man, you subsequently admitted, in whom you feigned interest for the gifts and privileges he bestowed upon you. At Heathwood Farm, you met, talked to and even enjoyed morning tea with members of the Heathwood family.
14. During this visit, you were introduced to the youngest daughter of the family, ten-year-old Lucy, who by all accounts was an intelligent and spirited young girl, who was also naive, loving and very trusting.
15. You learnt through the family that Lucy played on most afternoons in what was referred to as a 'treehouse' – a makeshift play area located in a secluded and densely wooded area of national park adjacent to the farm, about thirty-five minutes' walk from the family home. Lucy would ride her beloved pony to the treehouse and tether it close by while she played.
16. This treehouse was an area of forest that Lucy had herself cleared and decorated over several years with carefully collected trinkets and bric-a-brac to create her own imaginary world. It was a sacred and private place for her; so much so that her family knew they were not to enter. She had even painted a sign and hung it on a nearby tree. The sign read 'No Adults'.
17. You, as a grown adult man, took no heed of this sign, or indeed of any other decently human convention. Instead, you entered the safety of this little girl's private playground and unleashed upon her the most despicable acts of evil.

18. *You told investigating police officers that you decided within minutes of meeting Lucy at her family home that you were going to return to rape her. You surreptitiously used the next few days on that farm to monitor her movements, and those of her family, so you could identify when and where to enact your plot. During this time, you learnt of the location of the treehouse and Lucy's schedule for attending it.*

19. *You returned home from your holiday and spent several weeks fantasising and planning your vile acts against Lucy. You applied in advance for several days' leave from work, with a plan to return to your apartment after the act and luxuriate in reliving your crime prior to resuming your workplace responsibilities.*

20. *Early on the afternoon in question, you drove past the Heathwood Farm to a dead-end road rarely used by anyone. Even so, you took the extra step of concealing your vehicle behind bushes. You brought with you a bag which contained items including latex gloves, rope, duct tape, cable ties, condoms, and a dog lead and choker-chain collar that you had stolen during your stay at the property and taken home to help build your fantasy of what you would do to Lucy. You had a hunting knife strapped to your belt.*

21. *You made your way through the forest, using a route you had practised during your stay, and located the treehouse. You concealed yourself behind nearby trees, indulging in thoughts of what you had in mind for that innocent ten-year-old girl.*

22. *About an hour later, you saw a slight figure dressed in a school uniform of white blouse, cardigan, knee-length plaid skirt, sandals and socks. You watched Lucy*

playing for a few minutes before you casually approached the treehouse and called out a greeting. You enjoyed the startled and confused look on Lucy's face as she recovered from the shock of someone being there, while trying to place your familiar face.

23. She said your name and asked what you were doing there. You did not answer but instead asked if you could come into the treehouse. She told you adults are not allowed in the treehouse. You ignored her and entered anyway.

24. She was immediately and rightly afraid, and attempted to run towards the path leading back to her pony. You grabbed her by her long hair and overpowered her with ease. She started to scream, so you covered her mouth with your hand. You produced the hunting knife from your belt and told her you would slit her throat if she kept screaming and would then kill her pony. This effectively silenced her for long enough for you to place duct tape over her mouth, before binding her wrists with cable ties and putting the choker-chain collar around her neck.

25. You used this choker chain and the attached lead to control Lucy's movements throughout the rest of her ordeal. You took your time stripping her clothes from her body, because, as you told police, you had set an alarm on your phone so you knew exactly how long you could spend with Lucy before her parents might notice she hadn't returned home. This demonstrates the particularly chilling level of planning that went into your crime.

26. You then proceeded to sexually assault ten-year-old Lucy in the vilest and most sadistic of ways; acts that were detailed extensively in your confession and require no further elaboration here. The nature of her injuries was explained in the expert testimony of gynaecologist Professor Paul Mason, and the knowledge of these has naturally caused enormous distress to her family.

27. You told police that Lucy was terrified during your assaults on her, as to be expected. You admitted enjoying her terror, being driven to continuously increase it by causing more and more pain and fear. You said Lucy never gave up fighting and struggling against you, and that at one point she managed to run free for a few steps before you tackled her and brought her down again.

28. When the alarm sounded on your phone, you knew you had fifteen minutes remaining before you should leave the crime scene. You used that fifteen minutes to put Lucy – who you said was still conscious but 'a bit floppy' – over your shoulder while you climbed a stepladder found within the treehouse clearing and tied the dog lead to a large, overhanging branch. You then let go of her naked body, climbed down the ladder and stood back to observe as she was strangled. You removed the cable ties from her wrists so you could watch her claw at the collar, trying to free herself. This desperate final attempt to save herself was, of course, completely futile. You told police she struggled for about one or two minutes before she stopped moving and presumably fell unconscious.

29. You then turned to checking the crime scene in an attempt to ensure you removed any trace of yourself from it. Of course, you could not undo the fact that a condom had broken during one of your vile rapes, leaving in Lucy's body the traces of seminal fluid which would later identify you. You were smug enough, however, to believe that because you did not ejaculate inside her after the condom broke, you did not leave DNA. Numerous additional forensic samples, such as touch DNA, trace fibres from your vehicle, and hair also linked you to the scene.

30. After satisfying yourself with the cleanliness of the crime scene, you checked Lucy's pulse. You told police you had to ensure she was dead because, if she lived, she may have identified you. Satisfied that you had indeed deprived this young girl of her life, you left the crime scene and returned to your vehicle.

31. You drove home undetected and spent the next several days viewing the almost three hundred photographs and videos you took during your assault on Lucy, and of her body in death. Even after returning to work, you continued to access these images multiple times a day.

32. You have described your crime as 'the most thrilling thing [you] have ever done', and said that, by the time police apprehended you, you had started contemplating how you might commit a similar murder. You had already brainstormed several 'improvements' designed to increase your satisfaction with your next kill.

I stop reading and, without looking up at Stella, slip the report back into the envelope. As I do so, I notice a small, stiff piece of paper inside. I pull it out. A photograph. At first, I have trouble deciphering the image. It looks like a contoured, silver papier-mâché art piece. I look at Stella. She stares at me with hard eyes. I look back at the photo and consider the context, and it dawns on me. This is an image of the silver duct tape the murderer placed over Lucy's mouth and nose; the very item he used to toy with her.

I become aware that I am shaking my head at the horror of what I am seeing. Not just the photo of the duct tape, but the mental image of Lucy, struggling and terrified. Her head shaking from side to side, *No no no no no*, blood in her mouth as she bites her tongue in a desperate bid to escape her binds.

In this stuffy room, with this mother, in this silence, it is too much. I feel as if I might be sick. I look at Stella and suddenly I too feel the tension always so evident in her. My neck and jaw feel so tight they might never relax again. As I place the photograph back in the envelope, she stands, turns on her heel and walks out of the room again.

Now, from some distant part of the house, I can hear clunking and thudding. Clanging. Stella reappears lugging a hefty oilskin sack, the sinews in her thin arms straining to hold it. She walks over to Lucy's little desk and dumps the sack on it. Metal clanks against metal again as the contents settle. What on earth?

I stare up at Stella as she stands in front of me. Her face is a challenge. She means for me to look in the bag.

I lean over and gingerly untie the knotted top. Then I pull the mouth of the sack wide to reveal the contents. I am perplexed to see what appears to be a variety of vintage metal tools: implements that might be scattered around any old farm. A brick hammer with its straight, sharp claw. A mallet. An old Phillips-head screwdriver with a wooden handle. Rusty secateurs. Some sort of nippers, like those a blacksmith would use on horse hooves. And is that a metal vice? And a . . . sickle?

My eyes search out Stella's, silently seeking clarification.

'This,' she says, in a voice as cold and steely as the bag's contents, 'is what I will do to him.'

17

HANNAH

I'M MEETING WITH OCTAVIA NEXT WEEK. SHE'S COMING TO THE cafe. We have to meet somewhere, and it seems right that it be a place where Lucy was happy. I won't tell Octavia about the last time we were here: Lucy's final birthday. Her little chipmunk cheeks flushed and chubby and full of triple-chocolate pancakes, a smear of ice cream on the side of her cheek, her squealing and shoving Sebastian's hand away every time he tried to steal a chocolate-dipped strawberry from her plate.

I've already booked the spot where we'll sit: the table in the garden that's behind the jasmine vine, so nobody can hear us or stare at me.

It was strange to see what Octavia looks like after all these weeks of imagining. How her face is kind but strong. Her skin is creased in places – the thing that happens to old people when they've made the same expressions too many times – but also glowy and bright, as though she is happy on the inside, and healthy enough to live for a long time if nothing bad happens to her. Her expression says there is nothing to hide. Not a thing. It's exactly the type of face someone should have when their job is to hear other people's secrets.

What am I going to tell her? Of all the things I've imagined confiding, which ones might I actually say? I think I'll tell her about my plan to spend twenty-four hours at the treehouse. I need to find a non-cheesy way to explain that I want to connect with Lucy's spirit.

I haven't been to the treehouse since that day. The day I took him there. The day when I saw the insides of Lucy's private hiding place; saw that it looked like a fairy cottage, so magical with its bits of tinsel and stolen baubles. The day I betrayed my sister by lighting a fuse to a bomb I didn't know existed.

What will it look like now? What did he do to it? I imagine her table and bookshelf upturned, her row of hanging kitchen-ware pulled to the ground, Lucila's brooch hiding somewhere, the little doves smashed into the earth. Did the forensic investigators leave anything behind from their work? Traces of white powder from fingerprinting? Sticky dots, like they use on crime documentaries to calculate blood spatter patterns? *Was* there blood spatter? I don't even know.

God, it's so hard to think about. Maybe I'll tell Octavia how much I've avoided it – ever truly imagining what my sister went through. Is it strange that I don't really know what happened to her? I know she was raped, and suffocated, and I know it was really, really bad, but I wasn't allowed to go to court and listen to the proceedings, or even sit in on the hearing when he appealled the sentence. Everyone said I was too young, that it would be too much.

Would they be glad to know how far I've come? That I'm ready for it now?

I've thought about going through Mum's stacks of court papers, but she keeps them locked up. Originally, she did it to protect me. She's such a mindless zombie now, though, that I reckon she'd hand me the key without a second thought if I asked. She's always rustling around in those papers, anyway.

That's what makes it feel gross to ask. It's as if I'm wanting to see something personal of hers. Something intimate. Like I'm asking to look at a stash of dirty pictures. I wonder if I can write to someone and request the court documents. My mailbox is working well now. I get letters at least once every two or three weeks.

I wonder how I'll escape to the treehouse for a full day and night without Mum and Mattie knowing. I've got to be careful, because Mattie had a little 'talk' with me the other day. Well, it was Mattie and Mum, although Mum just kind of nodded in the right places. The talk was about them being worried about me. Mattie spoke about my eating and exercise, and said I was 'acting out of character', whatever that means. I managed to fob them off, make a few excuses about stress and exams, but now I have to make sure I act 'normal'. I might tell them I'm staying at Jessica's. A sleepover so we can study for an exam together. I don't usually do sleepovers, but they'll be glad I'm spending time with a friend, even though I think they wish I would hang out with other kids in addition to Jessica.

To be honest – and this sounds mean to admit – Jessica wouldn't be my first choice as a friend. She's kind of . . . bland. The highlight of her week is netball practice, and her idea of conversation is showing me cutesy animal clips she's saved for me because she thinks I like them. The most terrible thing she's ever done is weeing in the school swimming pool when she was eight. I know, because I asked. She never asked me what the worst thing I've done is.

I can't remember exactly how we fell into this friendship,

but it seems to work for both of us in a transactional way. I need someone who can distract me with banality, normalcy. Jessica needs a person to agree with her that her mother is unfair and bossy, and to explain to her how to do her maths homework.

It's not as if I'm not friendly with other girls, it's just that I don't spend any time with them outside of class, so it's difficult to call them friends. I've never been particularly social, which seems to bother others more than it bothers me. I do sometimes crave a real friendship, though. One where we both understand each other on some deep, personal level. I've never believed I could find that, so I haven't put much effort into looking. And, since Lucy, I know I'm not an appealing prospect to get close to. Nobody wants a friend who might cling to them between classes like a stricken koala, dousing their uniform collar with the anguished tears of grief, while the threat of being invited to a sleepover – all morbidly silent family dinners and midnight dead-girl hauntings – looms in the air. Jessica doesn't seem to worry about any of those things.

I really have become so good at being alone that sometimes it scares me. My mind has become so cold I wonder if emotion will ever kick back in, or if I have lain on that part of me for so long that it's gone to sleep and lost circulation, and now cannot be revived. Then something will happen – a thought, a memory, an event – and I will be white hot, and I realise it is rage that is keeping me alive. Eventually, the caustic bubbles of anger that rise up burst and settle inside me once more, and I return to a state of perpetual numbness.

Perhaps the chill was creeping in even before Lucy died. Before the party. Because even then I couldn't sense a future. Sebastian always knew what he wanted to do. He was successful in every way a kid could be. And Lucy was full of passion for everything. I was just in the middle. Average. Boring. God, like Jessica.

I had no special skills or talents. I mean, I could tell you the plot of nearly every fiction book in the school library – primary and high school – but that's not a talent. That's just a sign of disconnection, or lostness, or boredom, or loneliness, maybe. Anyone desperate enough to escape can lose themselves in the delicious twists of novels, allow themselves to be transported into the bodies of wild women or small hungry boys, taken to strange cities or enchanted woods, dropped into wartime or the end of times.

Even though it's not a skill, some teacher once commented to me that because I read so much, I'd be good in an English classroom, and I took this and held on to it. I think that's when I started saying I wanted to be a teacher. Then, in tenth grade, I overheard Mum telling Mattie that teaching was one of the easier degrees to get into, so it would be a good choice for me after high school. To be fair, my grades were always pretty unremarkable, even before Lucy. I always gave the *impression* of trying, initially because I wanted to please my family and teachers, and after Lucy died because I didn't want to fail and give Mum anything else to worry about.

It was easy to say that I was studying in my bedroom; easier than admitting that I was crying, or panicking, or over-thinking, or escaping my life through yet another book. And when such purported effort produced only average results, it's not surprising that Mum and Mattie ascribed to me the qualities of persistence and dedication. They had to find something special about me. It's humiliating to be thought of as a studiously average non-quitter, especially because I know I'm capable of more. Only, I could never conjure a compelling vision of my future to strive towards.

But that's changed now. All the things I'm doing – the starving, the running, the letter-writing – it's all leading me forwards. I have vision. Purpose. Drive. I'm doing things I know for certain other kids my age can't. I'm doing things most adults can't. And it feels amazing.

Eventually I'll have to stop all these things, and real life will kick back in. I tell myself that I will go to university then, and that will be my unfreezing. People won't know me there. They won't know my story. I can start afresh and reinvent myself and be whoever I want to be. I can dream bigger now I know how much I'm capable of. Even though I'll start with the teaching degree, something will come to me, some inspiration for my future, and I'll shift over to studying my true calling. I'll make friends – real ones – and perhaps I'll meet a guy who's kind and sensitive – a good guy, like my brother – and we'll fall in love. Maybe I'll even have kids of my own one day, although I'm not sure I want them.

When all that starts to sound too scary, I just focus on my very next step. Right now, that's the treehouse. I've already decided I'm going to park my car where he parked his, where police found his tyre tracks. Off to the side of the road, behind the lilly pillies. Then I'm going to try to figure out what track he would have used, and follow his footsteps to the treehouse. It seems important to stay for the full twenty-four hours, to see her place in all its lights and shadows. I don't know whether I'll try to sleep. Even if I want to, my body might not let me. I'll take Seb's old polocrosse sleeping bag, although it's so warm now that I'll probably just lie on top of it. I'm going to take books, too. Lucy used to get so mad when I'd read instead of spending time with her, but I think she'd understand I need something to distract me if it gets too hard. I've downloaded some of Lucy's favourite bands and musicals so I can listen to them if I get too scared after dark. I remind myself I've come a long way since that night more than a year ago when Lucy should have turned fourteen, and when I decided everything. The very first thing I did then was to stop pushing my desk up against the door of my bedroom to sleep, and I haven't gone back – not even when I wanted to after the visit from my dickhead father.

18

OCTAVIA

THE WIND BUFFETS THE CAR AS I DRIVE. IT'S 12.42 PM, AND I HAVE A one o'clock appointment with Matisse. I hope I make it on time. It is so hot that a transparent haze hangs over the road. I observe the sky made smoky from distant bushfires while simultaneously listening to the news on the radio about how firefighters are struggling to contain blazes near Stanthorpe, with new spot fires starting all over the place.

I whizz towards the bald, nose-shaped hillock where, like clockwork, crackling static eats my radio signal. I sigh and glance across at the controls to select a local station. As I look back to the road, I catch a blur to my left before – *THUD*. My hands vibrate on the steering wheel as a massive force hits the front of the car. Heart bursting with adrenaline, I slam my foot on the brakes while trying to keep the wheel straight.

Everything goes dark as a blackness spills over the bonnet. I raise my arm to my forehead involuntarily while I wait for whatever it is to smash through the windscreen and kill me. But the light reappears as I hear a bang on the car roof. I briefly lose sight through the rear window as something slides off the back of the car. Then everything is still.

I am dazed. For a split second I don't know where I am or what has happened. As I come back to reality, a picture forms. The car is stopped nose-in to the verge, rear end still on the road. My hands shake wildly on the wheel. I realise I'm holding my breath.

I inhale deeply and look around. I check my rear-vision mirror. No vehicles coming up behind. I instinctively look to my right, beyond the road, for any clue as to what I might have hit. Nothing but paddocks, dead grass, dirt. The same to my left. I drive the car forwards a few metres and park parallel to the road. I take in the fact that I've hit something. I concentrate on slowing my breathing. In and out. In and out. Then I gingerly open my door and exit the car. A wall of hot air hits me.

I walk to the back of the car and see it. A wallaby, lying on the roadside. Grey-brown fur, light yellow chest, about the size of a medium breed of dog. I see its leg move and I freeze. It's still alive. I want to go closer, want to help, but I don't want to see the damage. I force myself to inch nearer to it. Its leg flicks again. I can't see any obvious injuries, but clearly it cannot get up. I try to think what to do. A towel – I remember something about putting a towel over the head to reduce stress. I go to my car boot and start rummaging. I can't find a towel, but my beige wool coat is there, intended to be dropped off to be dry-cleaned at some point. I worry momentarily about getting blood on it, then dismiss the thought. Helping this animal is more important than my coat.

I approach the wallaby slowly, coat under my arm, trying not to startle it, but it doesn't move. I watch for respiration and see its chest moving up and down. The rise and fall is achingly slow. I lean across and gently place the coat over its head. The hot wind plays with the edges of the coat, but the wallaby doesn't react.

I straighten up and take a deep breath. Try to think what to do. I wonder whether there is someone I can call. I'm still watching the wallaby's chest. The rise and fall is becoming more irregular. The movement becomes almost imperceptible, then I can't see any movement at all. I stare at the soft, fuzzy ribcage for what feels like minutes. Nothing moves. I hover my hand over the animal's chest, before placing my palm flat on the fur. It is warm and still. Holding my breath again, I slowly lift my jacket. I look at the eyes. Fixed. Dull. Covered with a translucent veil. The wallaby is dead.

A surge of guilt sweeps through me. What have I done? Is it too late to get help? Probably. I realise I'm going to have to leave the wallaby here, by the side of the road, to bloat in the hot sun and be filled with maggots and devoured by carrion. I whisper an apology to the animal.

As I reluctantly walk away, wondering how late I'm going to be for Matisse's appointment, I recall something I saw on the Wildlife Channel. I am meant to check if the wallaby is female. See if there's anything in the pouch. I wish I hadn't remembered this, but now I feel too guilty not to look. It is spring, I remind myself. If it's a female, there's a good chance she has a baby.

Having never checked the sex of a wallaby before, I look under its tail and can't see anything resembling testicles. I observe that there is sparser, darker furring on the abdomen and a slit in the skin. A pouch. Damn.

I'm not sure how I'm meant to do this. I touch my fingers to the opening and pull them away. I look around stupidly, as though someone will see me molesting this dead animal and yell out, 'What the hell do you think you're doing?'

I reprimand myself for being so squeamish and try again. I have to force my fingers into the surprisingly tight opening. I touch something nodular, rubbery. My face crinkles in slight disgust. As I feel around, I hear a car engine approaching from behind. I pull my hand out of the pouch quickly, furtively, and stand up.

A white ute appears around the bend. I hope the driver will stop to help, but then I realise they could just as easily rape and murder me. I tell myself I'm stupid for thinking someone would want to do that to a middle-aged woman in badly approximated country attire, but before I can finish the thought I remind myself that such things apparently do not deter. I suddenly hope they drive on by.

They don't. The ute slows, puts on its indicator and pulls up on the gravelly verge behind the wallaby, creating a low cloud of grey dust. I squint to evaluate the driver as they open the door and get out of the vehicle. It's a man, but he's not close enough for me to make out his features.

'Octavia,' a familiar voice greets me. I squint harder.

'Sebastian?' I inquire, just making out the blond waves.

'Are you okay?' he asks as he walks towards me.

'Oh, I'm glad you're here,' I say. 'I'm fine, but I hit this poor wallaby. I think she's dead, but her pouch . . . there's something in there.'

'Are you sure you're okay?'

'Yes, positive,' I say. 'I don't know about my car, though. Can you check the wallaby? I'm so glad it's you . . .'

Sebastian leans over the wallaby and looks at her face. Then he places his hand on her chest for a moment before giving a single shake of the head. He straightens up and, without saying anything, walks to his ute, pulls a black leather bag from the passenger seat, walks back and puts it next to the wallaby. He removes a stethoscope from the bag and places the ear-tips in his ears, then holds the bell to the chest of the animal.

'Definitely dead,' he says after a few seconds. 'I mean, it's pretty obvious just by looking, but alive people have ended up in the morgue, so I always check.'

His back is to me, so I can't tell if he's making a joke.

He pulls out a pair of blue nitrile gloves, snaps them on and deftly inserts his fingers into the pouch, feeling around.

'I thought you only had to be on the lookout for roos at dusk and dawn,' I say.

'Usually,' he says, palpating his fingers. 'They're more likely to cross the road in the daytime if something is chasing them. And they come closer to the road during the drought, trying to find every last blade of grass.'

'Oh.' I nod.

He pulls his hand from the pouch and looks up at me.

'There's a pinkie,' he says as he reaches back into his bag. 'Very small.' This time, he pulls out a small pair of scissors, like nail scissors.

'What are you doing?' I ask, panicked. Is he going to cut up the joey?

'It's okay,' he reassures me. 'It's best if you leave the mother's teat in its mouth when you remove the joey. You can do damage to the mouth if you pull it straight out. I'm just cutting off the teat while it's in situ.'

I feel slightly ill.

'If you have one, you can put a safety pin through the teat before you cut it off; makes it less likely that the joey will swallow it,' he explains. 'This one's tiny, though, I don't know why I'm . . .'

He pulls a delicate little creature out into the light, all pink and rubbery. He holds it out in his hand for me to look at. It squirms on his palm, and I wonder whether the sunlight is a shock to its system. I come closer and study its delicate paws, its hind feet with tiny claws, its front feet without any nails yet. Its blushing skin is wrinkled over its chest and abdomen, and I can see the fine veins carrying blood across its body. Its eyes are closed, the lids a bluish-purple, and its ears are turned inside out, their tips meeting together at the back of its scalp. There are tiny lumps underneath the tail. I wonder if this means it's a boy.

'Too small,' Sebastian says, shaking his head.

'What?' I ask, worried about what it is too small for. For surgery?

'Too small to save, probably,' he says.

'Oh.' My heart sinks. 'Are you sure?'

'Well, it's very unlikely . . .'

'But there's a chance it could be saved?'

'We'd put him to sleep at the wildlife hospital. You know, not enough resources or carers to gamble on such a young one.'

'But there's a chance?' I ask again, insistent.

'I suppose, but the reality is I'm not going to have the time to—'

'What would it involve? Maybe I could do it?' I say impulsively.

'Well – he's got no fur, so he needs a source of heat to replace his mother's warmth, and he needs frequent feeds. It would be a large time commitment for a very small chance of success. Even when they're with their mother, many joeys don't survive, especially in drought conditions.'

'Where would I get the stuff?' I ask, my mind turning to

practicalities. 'I mean, I've got appointments with your mum and Matisse . . .'

'I've got some gear in the back of the truck,' he says, 'and some at Mum's. But, Octavia, don't feel you have to do this because you hit the wallaby. It's not your fault.'

I look at the squirming little pinkie and then at his mother on the side of the road.

'I'll do it,' I say.

'Okay,' says Sebastian, in a tone that implies I don't know what I'm in for. 'You'll need to start by keeping him warm.'

'How do I do that?' I ask.

'Well, most women just put them down their, um, top,' he says. 'You know, sort of nestle the tail end in their bra, making sure not to squash them.'

I don't know if he means the breasts or the joey. I decide he must mean the joey. He can't be concerned about me squashing my breasts. Even so, he looks slightly embarrassed and stares hard at the joey.

'Okay,' I say, and carefully take the pinkie blob from his hand. It feels so delicate, I'm worried I will crush it. I turn my back on Sebastian and place the pinkie's tail and hind legs into my bra, his upper body gently nestled on my chest. He feels like part of my skin. I hold him in place with my hand over my shirt.

Sebastian walks to the front of the car, then, surveying the damage. I follow him and see that the bumper and bonnet are crumpled at the point of impact.

He lowers himself to the ground, rolls onto his side and peers up under the car.

'Looks okay to drive,' he says after a minute, getting up from the bitumen, brushing dust and grit off his tan moleskins. I always marvel at how clean farming folk seem to stay, for all the dirty work they do.

'I'll follow you up the mountain,' he says. 'It's only another fifteen minutes or so. Just drive slowly and I'll have a proper look when we get there.'

'All right. Thank you, Sebastian,' I say, genuinely grateful. Then, 'What are you doing here, anyway? Don't you usually work today?'

'Yeah,' he says. 'But I have a few days of overtime up my sleeve, and Mum has things she needs done with the cattle. I'm going to stay for a long weekend, help her out.'

As I lower myself into the driver's seat, holding my left hand protectively over Pinkie so he doesn't jostle out of my bra, I notice I'm still shaking. I start the car, and my fingers are red-and-white worms as I clutch the wheel.

About halfway up the mountain, I see clouds rolling across the sky – thin, grey and fast moving – flanked in the distance by darker, plumper, more sinister-looking clouds. I say a little prayer to Mother Nature that it will rain, for the sake of every plant and animal around here. I open the car windows so I can be soothed by the clear song of the bellbirds, but the air rushes in to assault me, hot, dry and blustery, and I hurriedly hit the button to close them again. It's always been cooler up here than down below, but not today.

My mind wanders to the conversations Hannah and I have had at our appointments – there is always so much to digest after these that I often find myself reflecting on them outside of session, looking at things from fresh angles – but then I am distracted by the tickling movement inside my bra. I instinctively move my hand to my breast to cradle Pinkie. Without any warning, I burst into a fit of giggles. I have a kangaroo – no, a wallaby – on my boob. Moments like this remind me how unpredictable life can be. When I woke up this morning there was no way to know my day was going to take such an improbable turn, was there? That, before the sun went down, I would become a surrogate mother to a baby creature of the wild.

Suddenly I feel more serious. How on earth am I going to care for this little thing? I've barely got time to care for me; and Bob; and my business, my employees and my clients; and my relationships with everyone else who is important to me. And this case. My sleep is already interrupted by thoughts of murder and retribution. Now it will be further consumed by the needs of this hairless imp. I can't let him die, I think – I killed his mother and I owe it to him to save him. I will find a way.

I check my rear-view mirror as I leave the road to drive into the farm. I can see Sebastian's face in the ute behind, but can't make out his expression. He follows me into the yard in front of the house, where I see Matisse standing on the verandah, her hair moving around in the wind like a swarm of restless bees. Her expression is one of mild concern. I remember that the wallaby debacle has made me late. There would have been little point in us trying to call each other, though, the mobile reception being what it is up here.

After we park, Sebastian comes to my door and offers to take care of Pinkie while I complete the appointments, saying he will show me later how to feed him. I delicately retrieve him from inside my top while Sebastian discreetly occupies himself by scanning the paddocks.

As I relinquish the blob, I whisper to him, 'You be good.'

•

Our session finished, Matisse has headed over to the farm side, as they call it. I sit in the lounge room waiting for Stella to arrive, reflecting on the past fifty minutes spent with her wife furiously processing her anger about the embryo betrayal and the Cole situation.

Matisse talked almost nonstop for the entire session, her hands gesticulating wildly and toucan earrings fluttering as if they were going to fly away with her ears. She told me that Cole had called Stella around sunrise, threatening that he was going to come up here if they didn't transfer the money into his account by ten o'clock this morning. He didn't say where he was, or what he would do if he did come to the farm. Stella told him they were trying to get the cash but didn't have it yet. Matisse is scared, worried he is going to show up on their doorstep. She wants to call the police, but she says Stella won't allow her to. I hadn't thought she would take orders from anyone – especially not someone with whom she's currently so furious. But, despite Matisse's generally well-adjusted approach to life, she seems to struggle to put boundaries in place when it comes to Stella. Babies her, almost. I know it's felt scary for Matisse when Stella's been at her lowest; perhaps she's got into the habit of doing whatever is needed to keep her wife away from that dark precipice. Those strategies might've made sense in the short term, but now they seem to be backfiring. I flag this topic in my mind as a potential talking point for a future session with Matisse. At the very least, she was left in no doubt that I am concerned by the decision not to involve law enforcement.

I hope Cole doesn't turn up while I'm here; partly because I'd like to give him a piece of my mind, but more realistically because I think he could be dangerous.

Pushing that thought to the side, I realise I'm alone in the lounge room of this house for the first time. I take a moment to enjoy the cool, crisp sensation of the air conditioner blowing in my face. The light outside is low now as the dark clouds move closer to the farm, and through the window I catch a zigzag of lightning in the distance. I look around the room, examining the vase of slightly wilted snapdragons, Matisse's vivid purple artwork and the fireplace, which is awaiting a clean after being used through the winter.

I notice there are no photos of any kind here. I thought perhaps there would be some pictures of the family together – a holiday snap from some faraway place, taken during happier times. Maybe a photo of Lucy, such as the one displayed at her memorial picnic. My eyes linger on her urn on the mantel: a smooth redwood box with a gold plaque on the front. Out of politeness, I have not previously studied that box for more than a millisecond.

I stand and meander over to the mantelpiece. I listen for Stella's footsteps at the front of the house, but all is quiet except the wind – which has grown quite vicious now – tearing through the trees, creaking the rocking chair on the verandah, making things whistle and clunk. I wonder whether rain – or even a storm – will actually hit, and whether I'll have a chance to outrun it on my way back to Brisbane.

I hope Stella comes soon, but I also want to spend more time alone in this room. I tentatively touch my hand to the top of the urn, feel the warm silkiness of the natural wood. *Lucy, our brave, wild heart. With us always.* Simple words gently curving across the shiny plaque.

Matisse told me they were able to have an open casket, that the morgue did wonderful things in covering up her injuries with make-up and strategic drapery, that she looked like a sleeping angel. I picture her face as she lay in the coffin, motionless, serene, the original death mask of terror moulded into one of peacefulness and rest. Not for the first time, I am overcome by a surge of hatred for the man who did this to her, who made such a precious, innocent child – so full of joy and appreciation for every living moment – into something forever cold and still. A man responsible for a family twisted in grief, with burdens too heavy to carry, on top of the ups and downs of life we all must negotiate.

What sort of human being is capable of this? What does he deserve? Everything that is coming to him, I think. What do *they* deserve? They deserve peace, but here they are, faced with another hell: the hell of deciding on the right justice for Lucy.

While I am considering this, Sebastian enters the house, calling out that he's back from the sheds, hot air following him down the hallway like a disgruntled ghost. I snatch my fingers away from the urn and return to my place in the armchair, making it just before he sticks his head into the lounge room, face red and sweaty, and tells me Stella will be over soon.

He lifts up his shirt to show me the baby harness he's created for Pinkie: a tie-dyed scarf draped diagonally across his chest, running under one arm and knotted behind his neck. I want to avert my eyes from his toned body, golden skin slicked with sweat.

'He's pretty comfy,' he says, smiling, pulling down his shirt.

'So, he's okay, then?' I ask.

'For now. But it's best we don't get our hopes up,' he says, clearly more for my benefit than his. 'Why don't you come through to the kitchen and I'll show you how to feed and care for him. You can look after him under my supervision for now, but I'll have to arrange for you to get your carer permit through a wildlife group pretty quickly so the legal requirements are met. They'll also give you plenty of guidance.'

I glance out the window, wondering when Stella will be here, but get out of my chair and follow Sebastian into the kitchen.

The kitchen's just how I imagined it would be: white, airy, honey-wood benchtops, a bowl of lemons from the garden, a gingham tea towel hanging on the oven door, a separate eating area with a scrubbed wooden table topped with a vase of roses, a few petals scattered on the wood. It feels good to be in here.

Sebastian explains how to care for the joey, showing me how to disinfect baby bottles, mix up feeds, make sure the liquid is the right temperature. I type his instructions into my phone as we go. I don't want Pinkie to die because I forgot some important detail.

When we're finished, we put Pinkie in a pillowcase with a heat pad, which delivers gentle, constant heat. Sebastian pins the case to the back of the armchair in the lounge room. He apologises that his mother still hasn't arrived and politely excuses himself, saying he's got to drive down to examine the bull, who has a skin condition on his hind legs.

I say that examining a bull sounds like a treacherous prospect and, with a smile, he assures me it is.

Alone again, I slip back into thoughts about Cole and the threat he might present if he showed up. I recall what Sebastian told me about his memories of his father. Stella had not shared many specifics with me, but she mentioned that Cole had put his hands around her throat when she was pregnant with Sebastian. She added that she had later seen a documentary that mentioned the correlation between intimate-partner strangulation and homicide risk. I asked her how it felt to learn that information, given what she had experienced. I could see the light dim in her eyes as soon as I said it – the shutting down I was now familiar with – and her response was that he only had his hands there for a moment, and he didn't really squeeze that hard. Then she changed the subject. She had taken initial steps towards speaking about the memory, but an in-depth discussion of the topic was too much for her. It later occurred to me that the memory might also trigger recollections of what subsequently happened to Lucy.

I am brought back to the present by the sound of footsteps on the verandah. Boots being removed, plonked onto the floor in the hallway. Stella appears in the door to the lounge room, looking hot and bothered, frowning, muscles tense.

'I don't want to do this today,' she says. No smile, no greeting. No 'Hi Octavia, how are you?'

'Why is that?' I ask, not bothering to greet her either. I try to keep the irritation from my voice.

'I don't feel like it,' she says, sounding like a child.

Well, I don't feel like it either, I want to say, yet here I am. 'I get that, Stella, but you know the deal . . .'

'There's a storm coming in,' she says, 'and you were late. I don't have time for this.'

'Yes, I'm very sorry about that,' I say. 'It was unexpected. I hit a wallaby on the way here. And Matisse and I finished our session early so yours could start on time.'

She says nothing. I'm tempted to add, 'Don't worry, I wasn't hurt in the accident,' but I tamp down on the urge.

'What's going on that you don't want to talk today?' I ask, making my voice warmer, more encouraging. 'Did something happen?'

She's not falling for it.

'No. I just don't want to.'

Petulant, surly, like a two-year-old. Her forehead a strained frown. I almost expect her to stomp her foot. Heat surges in my chest, like it does whenever I'm at risk of saying something I might regret. In my own moment of childishness, I want to yell at her to go take a laxative. Instead, I pace my breathing. No matter how I feel, I will not let my emotions betray me.

'How about we just do a shorter session?' I propose.

'Maybe you should go,' she says flatly. A challenge.

I didn't see this coming. Her asking me to leave. My indignant inner voice rises up. How *dare she*? I've driven all this way, I'm doing my utmost to support her – to give her help she desperately needs. Who is she to reject me?

I rein myself in, remind myself to consider the underlying reasons she might be behaving this way. I think the reality of this situation is getting too close for her now, and – combined with the stress about Cole – it's too much for her to tolerate, let alone contemplate discussing with someone else.

'Of course I will leave if you want me to, Stella. This is your home, and you have every right to ask me to go. But it's a requirement of my role that if you decline to participate in the sessions, I must advise Judge Gorski.'

I can see her brain spinning. It hadn't occurred to her that refusing to talk to me might truly jeopardise her chances with McDermott. Knowing I've got her, I offer a way for her to save face.

'You look as if you're hot and tired. What about if you get a drink, make yourself some lunch – it's probably been ages since you've eaten – and then we can catch up. I've got some work I can do out on the verandah.'

She is silent for a second, and then says, 'All right.'

'Why don't you come get me in, say, twenty minutes? We can do a quick session, and then you can get back to whatever needs doing on the farm.'

'Okay,' she says, sighing heavily.

Under normal circumstances, I wouldn't enter into these negotiations. If someone wanted to leave a session, it would be their prerogative to do so. Stella is a person who would never have walked through my door in the first place. Yet here

I am, cajoling and placating, dragging her through session by session. I'm starting to understand how Matisse has come to act the way she does towards Stella. And I wonder if all this is worth it: if this is the career reinvigoration I was really seeking. Right now, I want to ditch this new, risqué underwear and go back to my saggy-waisted, faded men's briefs.

The air outside the house is still unpleasantly warm, and the wind carries a faint tinge of smoke from the distant fires. I lower myself into a white Adirondack chair. A few kilometres away, lightning flashes across the heavens. Dark clouds gather conspiratorially overhead. Then their meeting is blown apart as new gusts of wind send them flying. Angry thunder grumbles in the distance, and my vision becomes completely white for a millisecond as a sheet of lightning brightens the yard. I wonder if I should go back inside.

Will I need to wait out this weather before I return to Brisbane? I hope Stella will be reasonable if I need to stay a little longer than anticipated. I normally love a good storm, but I am sticky in my clothes, and irritable, and uncomfortable about needing to loiter in a place where I know I am not wanted.

I'm not even going to attempt to use a notebook in this wind; I have work I can do offline on my laptop, so I retrieve that from my bag. As I open the first client file, I focus on mentally reframing this situation as a good opportunity to chip away at the many letters I need to write to general practitioners about their patients' progress.

I'm partway through my introductory sentence to a GP when I notice Matisse walking at a brisk clip from the direction of the farm. As she gets closer to the house, she starts to jog a little. I haven't seen her moving at this speed before. I can't make out her face. Has there been some sign of Cole?

I save my document, close my laptop and make my way down the verandah steps and across the front yard to meet her.

'You okay?' I call out.

She doesn't answer but waves in acknowledgement, then jogs towards me. She stops a couple of metres from me and puts her hands to her thighs. Her breathing sounds wheezy; I recall from my intake assessment that she has asthma. She straightens up and I notice beads of sweat on her brow. She is taking short breaths.

'You need your puffer?' I ask.

'Yes,' she huffs. 'I'll grab it in a sec. A fire's started down the bottom of the mountain. Looks as if it's near Molly's boundary line. It's small and a long way from his house, but he doesn't have a phone . . . Well, he does, but he refuses to pay the bill now the service fee has gone up. We'll need to call the Rural Fire Service, maybe drive down there, make sure he knows about the fire,' she puffs.

'Okay,' I say, concerned for the man the family refers to as Mr Molly-Pants, but more concerned about Matisse's breathing. 'We'll do that, but let's get your puffer first.'

She nods in agreement, and we make our way into the house.

'Stella's in the kitchen,' I say.

I follow Matisse down the hall and into the kitchen. Without saying anything to Stella, she walks to a cupboard above the bench, grabs a puffer and puts it to her mouth. Stella looks at her questioningly, but Matisse shakes her head, holding her breath while the Ventolin absorbs.

I repeat to Stella what Matisse told me about the fire.

'We need to call the RFS,' Matisse says to Stella, exhaling slowly. 'Can you get the number?'

Stella picks up her mobile, dials and hands it to Matisse, who says, 'Oh, hello, Gunter. It's Matisse from Heathwood

Farm.' She explains the situation and then I hear her say, 'What? All the way over there? . . . No one at all? So, what should we do? . . . Okay, okay . . . I'll call you back. Bye.'

She hangs up and says, 'Gunter says there are three other spot fires within twenty kilometres of here. Got started by the lightning strikes from the storm. They're out dealing with them. There are no volunteers left. He wants us to get a better look at the fire – see if it's moving – then call him back.'

'Come on,' she says to us, walking towards the kitchen door while taking another puff on her Ventolin.

'Where's Sebastian?' asks Stella, following.

'He's down with the bull,' I say.

'I'll try him,' says Matisse, pulling her mobile out of the pocket of her overalls. I cross my fingers that she'll be able to reach him despite the patchy reception.

Figuring I'm along for the ride at this point, I follow the women out of the house. The hot air hits my face like the blast of a hair dryer turned to high. I notice that the darkest storm clouds have moved past us and are now being herded across the valley by the brisk, dry wind. Any hope of rain is being ushered into the distance with them.

Stella starts striding up the road towards the ridge. I push my shorter legs to keep up with her longer ones. Matisse follows a few metres behind, holding the phone to her ear. I can hear her wheezing softly.

'Has this happened before?' I ask Stella. 'A fire near here?'

'Not for a long time,' she says. 'There's never been one on the house side, but Dad talked about a bad one on the farm side about five years before I was born. It's one of the reasons they cut back the trees so much.'

As we get close to the sheds, Sebastian's ute roars up behind us. We reach him as he's getting out of the driver's door. He looks worried but doesn't say anything. Matisse takes another dose from her puffer and strides towards the top paddock, the highest area of the mountain before it slopes down to the lower paddocks and finally joins Mr Molly-Pants's property.

The three of us follow her in silence, the only sound the wind whipping through the trees. It changes direction frequently, seemingly on a whim. When we get closer to the paddock gate, I see a group of six or seven red cattle nibbling on a round hay bale, seemingly oblivious to the small drama unfolding.

'Down there,' Matisse says, pointing off to the right. I can see an area of smoke at the foot of the mountain but no flames. She opens the paddock gate then closes it behind us, and we all traipse down the slope, my feet crunching on grass so dry it sounds like someone's biting into a piece of Kentucky Fried Chicken.

We walk for a few more metres before I see it. A distant glow running along the roadside at the foot of the mountain. A house – which I assume belongs to Mr Molly-Pants – sits about a kilometre back from the road. The driveway running between it and the road is bisected by fire.

At first the blaze looks to be about the length of a football field, but as we walk further down the slope my heart leaps as I see it is much more extensive than that, weaving around the side of the mountain like an orange snake, disappearing out of view. We all stand quiet, shocked and mesmerised by the extent of the fire.

After staring at it for a minute, squinting, I realise that the snake is wriggling to the left, growing fatter as it devours dead grass and shrubs. The flames are a very long way off, but the distant, reptilian part of my brain nudges me, letting me know that if this thing were to get close it would present a real threat. My heart beats a smidge faster. I remind myself about my tendency to catastrophise. In reality, I can easily walk to my car, get in it and drive away. Perhaps that's what I should do.

Then something else dawns on me. I turn to Stella.

'Where's Hannah?'

'She's staying over at her friend Jessica's place tonight. Studying for an exam,' she replies, distantly.

Fuck. The treehouse. Her plan. Maybe she really has gone to a friend's house? It seems unlikely, given what she has told me, and I know in my heart that she's chosen today to camp out. Would she be at risk if the fire got worse, or if another one started near where she is? Do I need to say something to her parents? My mind starts running faster, calculating. Stella said there's never been a fire over on the house side. I don't know exactly where the treehouse is, but I know from what I've read that it's in damp rainforest. It's hard to imagine it would be affected by fire like these dry paddocks. And this fire is still many kilometres away.

'Maybe we should try calling her, Mum?' Sebastian says to Stella, a touch of concern discernible in his voice. 'Just let her know, in case she decides to come home tonight or something.'

Stella nods vaguely, then mumbles something about needing to move the cattle up from the bottom paddock.

Sebastian bobs his head in agreement, then says, 'I'm really bloody annoyed about Mr Molly-Pants and his phone. I told him *I'd* pay the service fee, even though I know he could afford it if he stopped drinking so much whisky.'

It's the first time I've heard Sebastian sound irritated.

'The fire's still ages away from his place,' he continues, 'and surely he'd smell the smoke. He's usually out on the ute feeding up around now, and the ute's still parked by the house.'

'He's probably passed out,' says Matisse. 'Do you think if we all called out – really yelled – that he'd hear?'

'There's no way he'd hear us from here. He's half deaf as it is,' Sebastian replies. He pauses for a moment, then adds, 'But in my room there's that old megaphone we used for polocrosse musters. We could try calling with that. It travels pretty far.'

'Yeah, I think we should try,' says Matisse. 'Let's go get it, and I can call Gunter and update him.'

We look at each other in agreement, and then at Stella when her phone begins to ring in her jeans pocket. She takes it out, looks at the screen and presses a button to end the call.

'Let's go,' she says.

•

We move quickly but quietly back to the house, each of us lost in our own thoughts. None of us, I think, wants to cause alarm by expressing aloud what is going through our mind. Matisse's breathing reminds me of the way Hugo, the bulldog from the dog park, sounds after walking the hundred metres from his owner's car to the park. She takes another dose of her puffer.

As we reach the yard in front of the house, Sebastian turns to me and says, 'You should probably hit the road, Octavia. The fire's wrapping around towards the road side of the mountain, and there's no sense in you staying and risking getting cut off.'

We all stop walking. Something about the set of Sebastian's mouth tells me I should consider what he is saying.

'What will you all do?' I ask. 'Are you going to go too?'

'No,' he says firmly. 'We've got a stay-and-act plan in place. We'll need to think about putting it into operation if things get much worse.'

He looks at Stella, who remains expressionless. In the

commotion, I had completely forgotten about our earlier encounter, and I suspect she has too.

Matisse turns to me and says, 'Yes, Octavia, I really think you should go. We'll be fine. We've prepared for this. But you shouldn't put yourself in danger by staying.'

I nod. 'If you're sure there's nothing I could do to help?' I say, knowing the most self-preserving act would be to leave, but surprising myself that I am genuinely willing to remain if it means helping keep them safe.

'No, you should go,' Matisse says. 'But perhaps you could stop at the national park car park on the way down, call out to anyone you can see and let them know to leave, and count how many cars are there and call me. I'll let Gunter know. The ranger's in Borneo with his wife.'

Borneo seems very distant.

'Yes, I'll do that,' I say. 'But, please, all of you, promise me you won't take any unnecessary risks. You need to be safe. I'll call you tomorrow to see how you got on.'

I feel an overwhelming urge to hug them before I leave, but I don't. Instead, I get my belongings from the verandah while Sebastian fetches Pinkie and his supplies, and brings them to the car, confirming his earlier instructions.

I am hurtling down the driveway when the Hannah situation pops back into my mind. I'm shocked that it had fallen off my mental agenda in the unfolding drama. Thank god I've remembered now – but what am I going to do? Do I do anything? What would Hannah want me to do? I imagine our newly established trust being obliterated by my violating her confidence, telling her family where she is, them not understanding, the fallout it would create, and then the likelihood that Hannah would refuse to share with me again, right at the point when she needs a confidante the most.

I think of my legal and ethical obligations. Just how risky is this fire situation? There's a possible risk to her safety, sure, but is it an imminent risk? It's possible the fire could reach the treehouse, but it's still so far away that it doesn't seem likely. Then again, would Hannah want to know about the situation her family is facing? Damn. I wish I knew where the treehouse was.

I decide to drive down to the national park car park and buy myself some time to think. As I get to the cattle grid at the entrance to the property, I see Lil' Sis off to the side of the driveway, head up, ears pricked, looking around. In that moment I feel sorry for her, being so alone. I wonder what makes her behave so viciously that she can't have any of her own kind nearby. I wonder if she gets lonely, or scared. I wonder if she misses Lucy.

As I turn onto the road that leads down the mountain, I notice the wind has changed course again, the trees bending in the opposite direction than they were when I was coming up the mountain. Knowing the bends and curves of the road better now, I drive a few kilometres over the speed limit, feeling a sense of urgency to get to the car park and make sure people are safe.

I feel and hear my engine give a funny little skip, and I remember that Sebastian was going to check it. The wallaby incident seems eons ago now. I glance at Pinkie's pillowcase pinned to my passenger seat, and I realise how helplessly dependent he is on me. The car seems to be running as usual; I glance at the battery and reassure myself that it is half charged.

As I turn into the final long bend near the foot of the mountain, before the entrance to the national park, I hear a thunderous crack and jump in my seat. I look up at the bleak sky for the source of the sound, but there are no signs of the fast-moving storm clouds from earlier. Then the road straightens out and I am met with a wall of smoke.

My visibility is limited to about five hundred metres in front of me. I rapidly decelerate, then come to a halt. Staring directly ahead, through the smoke, I can see that both sides of the road are engulfed in flames. Angry yellow fingers reach metres high, licking the limbs of the hundred-year-old eucalyptus, the oils in the leaves and branches causing them to light up like candles. Even though all my windows are closed, the smell of smoke enters my nostrils. I check that my air conditioner is set to recirculated air. I jolt in my seat again as another enormous crack echoes through the dense forest on either side of the car. At the limits of my vision, I see an enormous tree fall as though in slow motion, a trail of flames following it like the tail of a comet as it crashes onto the road. Across the road. All the way across the road.

I become aware of a cacophony of sound around me. Everything is alive with it. A dull distant roar – churning and low – overlaid with a rapid, sharp crackling, and the high-pitched whistling of the wind fanning the flames. My heart thrums in my chest now, but I notice my thoughts slowing, becoming singular. My brain tells me to go. *Go. Go. Get away.*

I can see the tree has completely obstructed the road in front of me. The dense forest grows so close to the bitumen that there is no way to drive around it. Even if there was, there is a menacing glow behind the wall of smoke, suggesting the fire is worse on the other side of the fallen tree. The only way to flee is back up the mountain. Then I remember the car park. I am torn between a desire to escape and a moral certainty that I must find out how many people are there, warn anyone I can.

Quickly. Go to the car park. Count the cars. Drive up the mountain. Tell Matisse. Find Hannah. Go. Go. Go.

As my foot presses down on the accelerator pedal, I notice that my right knee is shaking, weak. Against everything my body is saying, I force myself to drive ahead another thirty or so metres and turn right into the national park. I follow a short road down into the car park. The roaring noise is now on my left. I pull into the car park and am momentarily confused. *You need to count the cars,* my mind tells me. It takes me a few seconds to realise I cannot count the cars because obviously nobody is visiting the park. The car park is empty.

Cognitively, I feel a rush of relief; however, my body is saying something else. *Run, run, go.* I urge my jelly-knee to press my foot onto the accelerator, and the Mina's tyres squeal as I make a tight, fast turn.

When I get back to the main road, I look to my right. I can't tell if the fire is worse than it was a minute ago. Everything is hazy. I feel heat on my right arm and leg, and I realise it is penetrating the car from outside. Despite the air conditioner being set to recirculate, all I can smell is smoke. I turn left and drive back up the mountain faster than I have ever driven before.

19

HANNAH

THE TREEHOUSE IS DIFFERENT FROM HOW I IMAGINED IT WOULD BE. It looks like someone's cleaned it up; there are still rake marks in the ground where the earth's been smoothed over. I wonder who did it. Maybe someone from the forensics team felt bad about the destruction of a little girl's hideaway and wanted to put it back to rights. Or maybe it was Mum. I'd like to think it was her. That would mean she did something to show her feelings, on the outside, in the real world.

My butt's going numb from sitting on the dirt floor, so I spread out Sebastian's sleeping bag and sit on that. The wind was up early this morning, but it's dropped a bit now. I stare up into the leaves of the trees, watching them flutter, and I wonder if Lucy did this too. Did she sit in this exact place, in her little chair, and watch the leaves? What was she thinking? Was she wondering about how the world works, about her future, about her friends, school, Lil' Sis? Did she worry, or just ponder? Did she feel happy in this world? I think she did. Every day, she would find things to laugh at. It didn't matter if it was a funny cartoon, or the pony doing something silly, or one of us getting a fright when she jumped out from around a corner. I feel bad now about being envious that she was always finding things to enjoy and be happy about. If something bothered her, she'd get mad and yell as loud as she could, or get sad and cry until snot ran down her face, and then let it go as though it had never happened and move on to the next thing. I can see now that was an art.

I decide to put my headphones in and listen to *Cats*, the musical. It was Mum's favourite when she was a kid and she introduced Lucy to it. They used to play the songs as loud as they could and dance around the kitchen while Mum was getting dinner ready. Mattie and I would just watch and smile at each other. We weren't included in this ritual, but we enjoyed watching them be happy.

I lie back on the sleeping bag, which smells like musty horses, slip in my earbuds and hit play on my phone. I put my backpack, which contains water, a bag of cashews, and a jumper – in case it gets cold tonight – under my head as a pillow. I notice that I don't have reception where I'm lying, but that doesn't matter. I'll walk out into the paddock later and send a text to Matisse to let her know that everything's going well at Jessica's. Mum won't try to contact me.

As I squirm around, trying to get comfortable on the sleeping bag, I am glad for the relative coolness of the forest, because this day is hotter and drier than any I can remember from springs past.

I let my eyes wander around the treehouse to the jolly tempo of Mr Mistoffelees's tale. I'm surprised that I'm not scared to be here. The arsehole's presence doesn't hang as heavily over the place as I had expected, and it doesn't seem as if anything bad happened here. Tonight I might feel differently.

The wind is getting back up now, and I picture it whistling through the branches in the dark like a howling ghost. Through the foliage above me, the sky looks bruised, and I wonder whether it will rain. I haven't prepared for that. It would be good to get cold and wet and shivery. If I do, I will set my mind to sitting through it. I won't squirm or try to escape the discomfort.

As I listen to the song of the original conjuring cat, my mind drifts to the brooch. I couldn't find it anywhere in the treehouse. A zap of electric panic flashes from my stomach to my fingertips as I realise I might have come here, brought him here, on a false assumption – that Lucy had stolen my brooch when in fact she'd never had it at all. Maybe I'd lost it myself. I will think about that later, I tell myself, blocking those thoughts for now.

I wrestle my mind over to a Lucy love memory. The little lamb cake. I think about how, for her fifth birthday, I gave her a book called *Little Lamb Bakes a Cake*. She loved reading it to me while we sat curled up on her bed: the story of the little lamb putting butter and flour into a bowl, having to visit a friendly neighbour to borrow some sugar. I recall how that book inspired her to make a cake for us one night after dinner. She copied what Lamb did in the book, following a list of ingredients with no quantities and no egg. In a bowl, she mixed up lumps of sugar, a mound of flour, a few globs of margarine, all stirred together with fat drops of food colouring: 'Pink for hearts, green for slime and blue for Lil' Sis's favourite colour.'

I picture her standing on tiptoe, pulling this multicoloured monstrosity from the microwave, all steamy in its silicone mould, smiling at her success. I can still taste her creation in my mouth, hot and rubbery, like chewing on an eraser that had been left out in the sun. I remember us praising her, telling her how artistic she was, her face bright with pride, and how this spurred her to cook the cake over and over, making us eat it maybe twenty times in the space of a year. I recall the day when we could no longer take it, and Mum had the idea to save us by writing quantities next to the recipe in the Little Lamb book. I can see Mum leaning over the book on the kitchen bench, blonde hair hanging around her face, blue biro in her hand, moving back and forth between her own recipe book and *Little Lamb*, transferring the formula. I remember how, after months and months of cooking it for us, Lucy only baked the cake once more after the addition of the quantities.

Why was that? Why had she delighted in making us that cake so many times, and then just stopped? I decide, today, lying here under her trees, that she wasn't prepared to fit her spirit into tablespoons and measuring cups.

•

I startle and open my eyes. There is a moving green canopy above me, and it takes me a moment to realise where I am. I must have fallen asleep. The light is lower in the treehouse and the music has stopped playing in my ears, but I can hear something: a voice. I pull out my headphones and listen. Silence, and then a faraway voice. A man's voice, muffled by strong winds whipping through the branches around me. A few words, then silence, then the voice again. It sounds like when you hear the events being announced at the Warwick Show: *Make your way . . . Angus heifers . . . starting at twenty-past . . .* You know they are announcing something, but you can't make out all of the words. Except now I can't make out any of the words. Just a distant sort of yell. I feel my jaw tense up. I've never heard anything like this on the farm before.

I sit up, and my body is clammy from the heat and stiff and numb from lying on the ground. As I breathe in the dusty, warm air, I detect a faint scent. Smoke? I search my mind for the reason. The Stanthorpe fires are too far away for the smoke to drift to the mountain. There's no way we'd be burning off on a day like today – it's too dry and windy – and anyway, there's been a total fire ban for weeks.

I stand up and walk out of the treehouse, towards the path Lucy made through to the paddock, sniffing the air. The track is overgrown, and I snap a branch of lantana with my shoe, its soapy scent spilling into the air. I take another step and a vine catches my sneaker. I snatch my foot upwards, twice, but it is still trapped. I lean down to unwrap the vine from my shoe and then, right in front of the toe of my shoe, I spy a glint of silver.

20

OCTAVIA

I DASH FROM THE CAR TO THE FARMHOUSE, HOLDING PINKIE against my chest in his pillowcase. The front door is open, so I enter, concurrently yelling for Matisse, Sebastian and Stella. Nobody answers. I run down the hallway, yell again – no answer. I realise they're probably on the farm side, so I quickly pin the pillowcase to the back of the armchair and sprint back to my car, jump in, reverse and head up the road to the ridge. I park between the sheds, where Arnold is sniffing around, and see the family walking up the top paddock, towards me. A red megaphone dangles from Sebastian's arm. When they see my car, their pace quickens. I jump out and run to them, my hand at my chest, hot wind whipping at my cheeks. The scent of smoke is strong here now, as though I'm visiting a bonfire, and the sky behind them has taken on a hazy hue.

'The bottom's on fire!' I yell. 'You can't get through!' I'm panting from exertion.

We quickly close the gap between us, and I see the worried

209

expressions on Matisse's and Sebastian's faces. Stella looks vacant.

'Where?' Sebastian asks.

'The national park,' I say. 'Just after the entrance. It's massive. It's like a wall of fire. It's so high . . . all the trees . . .'

I'm talking fast, and I hear my voice shaking.

'Could you see if there was anyone—' Matisse starts.

'I drove in there,' I say. 'There were no cars at all, thank god. It was so hot, driving out. The side of my car—'

'It's growing down there, too – moving closer to Mr Molly-Pants's,' Matisse interrupts, gesturing back over her shoulder. 'Seb tried calling out but he's not responding.' She still sounds wheezy.

'The RFS can't come,' says Sebastian. 'They're tied up with other fires, ones closer to more properties, more homes. Higher priority.'

'What? Is there anyone else you can call?' I ask, shocked.

'No,' says Sebastian. 'Other fires have started all around Queensland today, and over the border. Every single plane is already in use. Local crews everywhere are tied up. Gunter said they'll come later, if they can.'

I am not reassured by this, and I can tell they aren't either. I had expected resources to be readily available when it came to fighting bushfires. Yes, there were problems in the past, but with so many royal commissions and recommendations – and with the increasing impact of climate change – I thought surely these things had been fixed.

'It's unimaginable,' I say, still trying to appreciate the unreal situation I find myself in, having planned on doing nothing more today than some driving and talking, albeit probably tense talking.

'I have to get to Mr Molly-Pants,' Sebastian says. 'I can't leave him there.'

'No!' Stella turns to him, her face looking alive for the first time today. 'No,' she commands again.

'Mum, I have to,' says Sebastian. 'I can't let him die in a fire – for sure he's got on the grog and passed out. He won't stand a chance.'

Stella reaches out her hand, puts it on Sebastian's bicep, gripping it. 'No, you can't.'

Fear makes her pupils huge. Sebastian places his hand gently over hers.

'Mum,' he says, his voice steady, 'it's fine. I'm going to saddle up Mindy and Dylan. I'll be down there in ten minutes, put him on Dylan, and we'll be back up here in no time. Everything's going to be all right.'

I picture him riding down the steep mountain – a reluctant Man from Snowy River. He tenderly removes Stella's hand from his arm.

'I've gotta go now, though,' he says firmly. Stella still looks worried but seems to accept there's no point in further protest.

'You need to sort out the stock,' Sebastian instructs her. 'Move them over the front. I'll leave the gates open on my way back through so Molly's sheep can come up.'

I look at him and wonder if this self-assuredness is false bravado. How scared is he underneath? I admire him for his loyalty to his elderly neighbour. His courage. I am also scared for him. I don't know if I'd be able to do the same in his situation.

He leans in and gives Stella a quick peck on the cheek, then turns and does the same to Matisse. He briefly squeezes my shoulder and nods. Then he turns his back on us, and is running towards the sheds.

I look at Stella and then Matisse, wondering what we do now.

Matisse is looking around at the sheds, then over at the road leading to the house, and then back to the sheds, as though looking for the answer.

'We should, ahh – well, let's go back to the house and figure out what to do,' she says, her accent strong. Perhaps people feel the urge to revert to their mother tongue during periods of high stress.

Matisse's uncertainty about our next step is unnerving. I look to Stella, who has adopted her thousand-yard stare. Like a child gazing on the faces of two parents who don't know what to do in an emergency, I feel my fear rising.

'We can take the car,' I say, pointing to the Mina.

'Okay,' says Matisse, and as we stride towards it I wonder whether we should be running. We open the doors and Arnold, who has been sniffing around nearby, flies into the back seat.

'Sorry,' Matisse apologises.

'It's fine,' I say, not caring in the slightest about a dog being in my car, and feeling the urgent need to get moving.

I start the car and, as we rumble up and over the ridge towards the cottage, I realise that Hannah has slipped from my mind again. How can this keep happening? I know the time has passed for ethical dillydallying, and I must say something. I consider my words as I use my left elbow to steady Arnold – who has his front feet balanced on the centre console – and try to ignore the pleading alarm of the Mina, alerting us to the fact we don't have our seatbelts on.

As we approach the house, I see – with relief and glee – Hannah standing in the centre of the yard in shorts and a singlet.

'What's Hannah doing here?' says Matisse, turning to face Stella in the rear.

'Not sure,' says Stella, shrugging, as though she has little to no interest in the fact that her daughter has appeared out of nowhere in the middle of a bushfire.

I am not saying a word now that I know Hannah is safe. We pull up in the yard and exit the car.

'Hannah! What are you doing here?' asks Matisse. 'How did you get through?'

Hannah shrugs, as if she is also indifferent as to how she got here.

'And why are you wearing Granny's brooch?' Matisse asks.

I see that pinned to Hannah's pale blue singlet – partially covered by her long, red, wavy hair – is a silver brooch with turquoise stones. She puts her hand to it, self-consciously, as though she didn't realise it was there.

'Don't worry about that now,' she says. 'I'll explain later. How bad's the fire?'

'It's blocked off the road out,' I say.

Hannah opens her mouth, shocked.

'It's down in Mr Molly-Pants's paddocks too,' adds Matisse. 'We think he's in the house, but he's not coming out. Sebastian tried calling him on the old megaphone but it didn't work. He's taken the horses down.'

Hannah growls. 'Bloody idiot.' I'm not sure whether she's referring to Sebastian or Mr Molly-Pants. 'Anyway,' she continues, 'what are you all doing?'

Stella remains silent. She described to me during a session how she started to dissociate as a child – a turning off and numbing of her mind that allowed her to mentally escape her father's abusive rants, which could last for hours. I suspect she is dissociating now, seeing how blank her face is, how detached her responses are to the extreme events unfolding.

'Ah, we were just coming back to the house to figure out—' starts Matisse.

'Right,' interrupts Hannah, drawing herself up. 'Mattie, start hosing down the house, put the sprinklers on in the garden and then start wetting down the hay in the sheds. Make sure you really soak it.'

'The water pump to the house is broken,' responds Matisse, then turns to Stella. 'Stella, you were meant to fix it last—'

'I forgot,' says Stella weakly.

'Oh, for fuck's sake,' Matisse snaps.

'Stop it,' commands Hannah. 'You're going to need to fix the pump. You can usually get it going by jiggling the electrical cord around where it connects to the pump, but turn off the power first. And close up the windows in the house, and fill the bath and sinks with water.'

Hannah turns to Stella. 'Mum, we need to get the cattle from the farm paddocks and move them over here.'

Stella nods vaguely.

'Which horses has Sebastian taken?'

'Dylan and Mindy,' answers Stella.

'*Argh.* Okay, go and saddle up Goblin. I'll have to get Lil' Sis.'

Stella just stands there.

'What should I do?' I ask, realising Hannah is directing the show. Thank god someone has a plan.

'Go with her,' answers Hannah. 'Keep her focused.'

'Okay,' I say, and turn to Stella, suggesting we go.

She looks at me, not moving.

'Mum!' yells Hannah. 'Do what she says! Go! You need to saddle up Goblin. I'll meet you at the sheds.'

This seems to startle Stella into action, and she strides off towards the road that leads to the farm. I follow her, looking back over my shoulder to see Matisse rushing towards the house water tank, Arnold in tow. Hannah's gone in the opposite direction, towards the paddock in front of the house.

As I march along beside Stella, both of us silent, I wonder how Hannah's feeling right now about having to catch and ride Lil' Sis. I think about how afraid the whole family is of that pony, how Sebastian refuses to do her vet care and how they have to put sedatives in her food just for the farrier to trim her feet. I have no idea how Hannah thinks she'll be able to saddle her up and ride her. And who knows how much help Stella will be.

I turn to look at her. If she sees me doing so, she doesn't show it. Her face is impassive, her slow eyes squinting into the approaching smoke.

21

HANNAH

MY HANDS ARE SHAKING AS I ENTER THE SHED TO GRAB LIL' SIS'S gear. The leather of her bridle is stiff, and her saddle is covered in a thick layer of dust, which feels gritty as I brush it away with my hand. I quickly shake out the faded pink saddle cloth – white horse hairs come off it like a cloud – and then turn over the saddle and check underneath it, and between the flaps, for spiders. I can't see any, but I know from experience that doesn't mean they won't come crawling out later.

I go to the plastic bucket in the corner, bend over, pull out bits of bailing twine, old gloves, a hoof pick, a screwdriver, and there, right at the bottom, are the rusted old wire cutters I am searching for. I stand up and pause for a second while my vision swims, then put them into my shallow shorts pocket. I snatch up the bridle and throw it over my shoulder. The cheek piece catches on the brooch, reminding me it's pinned to my singlet: a little piece of Lucy with me.

I grab a bucket of feed and head into the paddock. Time is ticking as if I'm going to run out of it, and part of me wants

216

to dash towards Lil' Sis, but I know I can't do that if I want a chance of catching her. I approach quietly as she stands with her head in the air. She looks straight at me. I wonder if she's noticed the smell of smoke and is on higher alert than usual. My heart pounds in my chest and my legs feel weak as I near her, but I try to look calm and confident. *Please don't run, please don't run.*

The pony stands her ground and lifts her nose to sniff the bucket I hold out to her. She puts her muzzle in it, sniffs again, snorts loudly and takes a mouthful of pellets. Then she pulls her head out of the bucket and chews. I put the bucket on the ground and, as she lowers her head to take another mouthful, I slip the reins over her ears.

Please don't bite me, please don't bite me.

I move the reins further down her neck as she raises her head again to chew, and then quickly join them together under her neck with my right hand, making a firm loop so she can't run. She immediately pins her ears, her eyes narrowing to angry slits, the usual precursor to her biting someone.

'*Oi!*' I growl at her in a deep voice.

I surprise myself with how stern I sound. I hope she has heeded my warning, but I still expect her to spin around and take my arm in her teeth, like she did to the vet when she came out to vaccinate her. Dr Sue cried out so loud I heard it from inside the house with my headphones on. Her forearm was this purple, swollen sausage, with teeth marks denting it like when you bite into a piece of cheesecake. I have my left elbow ready to crack Lil' Sis in the head if she turns to bite, but I must have sounded scary enough, because she unpins her ears, pricks them forwards, and puts her head down to eat more pellets.

I wait patiently while she puts her head up again, chews

and finishes the mouthful. She goes to put her head back down to eat but I firmly tell her, 'No.' I hold the bit in my hand and guide it to her rubbery lips. She opens her mouth, accepts the bit, and I put the crown of the bridle over her ears. I do up the nose band and throat latch, fumbling with the little buckles, take the reins off her neck, and lead her up to the shed, where the saddle cloth and saddle are lying on the ground. I bring the bucket of pellets with me as a lure.

When I go to put the saddle cloth on her back, she pins her ears again, turns as if she's going to nip me, and I yell at her, '*NO!*'

I whack her neck so sharply with my open hand that it stings. She turns her head to the front as though nothing happened and lets me place the saddle on her back.

'You need to do this for Lucy,' I whisper to her, my voice shaking. 'Be good for me, please . . . Lucy would want you to. You need to help us save the farm. You need to live here too.'

Her expression is soft now, and I'm not sure if it's my words, my tone or the fact that I just slapped her. She allows me to tighten the girth. I unbuckle the stirrup leathers, which are short because they are still adjusted to Lucy's ten-year-old-leg-length. This hits me hard, but I have no time to stop. I run the buckles down the leathers until I reach a hole I think will be long enough for my legs. I'm not even sure I've made the leathers the same length on both sides, but there's no time to check.

I tentatively put my shoe into the left one, wishing I'd chosen jeans and boots this morning instead of shorts and sneakers. Then I remember the fire safety booklets the RFS sent us, which said you should never wear synthetic materials near bushfires. I picture my feet dissolving into pink puddles inside melted white plastic.

As I bounce on one foot, preparing to spring into the saddle, I realise it's been a lot of years since I've ridden a horse. I picture myself at eleven, bobbing around on Goblin's trusty back at pony club musters, sneaking glimpses at my watch while Mum wasn't looking, counting down the minutes until I could tie Goblin to the horse float and go get lemonade and lamingtons from the CWA stall, and eat them under a tree while reading my book.

And Lil' Sis hasn't been ridden – has barely been touched by anyone – in four years. She always threw in a few bucks, even with Lucy. If she tries to throw me, I'll be on the ground in a second. But I won't give her the chance, because this little bitch is going to do what I say, and I'm not going to take shit from her.

With that attitude, I spring from the ground into the saddle, swinging my right leg over the horse's haunches and slipping my right foot into the stirrup. I immediately pull the left rein until Lil' Sis's nose is at my left knee, making it hard for her to get her head under her so she can buck. She doesn't fight me and only takes a few seconds to relax into the contact before I release it. She turns her head to the front and just stands there. I pat her neck in appreciation.

'We need to get this show on the road, Lil' Sis,' I say out loud, and gently touch my legs behind her girth.

She moves off at a brisk walk. Thinking of the fire currently approaching the cows, I ask her to trot. Immediately she pig-roots, lifting her rear end into the air.

'No,' I growl at her, and apply my legs again, harder. She trots forwards again, in small, choppy strides, and we cover the ground to the gate without further argument. She manoeuvres herself expertly as I open the gate with sweaty hands. I leave it open so we can bring the cattle through when we move them over here. I aim Lil' Sis towards the ridge and ask her to canter. She launches forwards, then snatches the reins from my hands by thrusting her head down and arches her back in a giant buck.

22

OCTAVIA

I FOLLOW STELLA INTO A SMALL SHED, WHICH IS HOT AND CONFINED, and see a row of several Australian stock saddles, each with a saddle pad laid over the top, lined up along a railing that runs the length of the wall. A bridle hangs neatly above each saddle. There are two spaces where bridles and saddles are missing; I assume the ones Sebastian is using. I hope he's safe.

Stella pauses in front of the saddles and seems to deliberate, perhaps uncertain about which gear we need.

'Do you know which stuff we should use on Goblin?' I ask, hurrying her along.

'I used to,' she says, her brow furrowed. 'The kids got so much gear over the years, for pony club and polocrosse and mustering.'

Her hands are held out in front of her, at waist height, as though she's in a dress shop deliberating on whether to pick up a brown skirt or a black one. I notice her hands are trembling. I see the beads of sweat on her forehead, and realise I am sweating too.

'He's the Appaloosa, right?' I say, remembering she pointed him out to me the day we took a walk during our session; the pretty brown horse with the white hindquarters decorated in black spots.

She nods.

'So he's smaller than Dylan and Mindy?'

'Um . . .' She pauses as though I've put to her a challenging mathematical equation. 'Yes.'

I step forwards. 'This one, maybe?' I say, picking up a smaller bridle.

'Yeah, that might be it,' she says.

I take it off its hook and hand it to her. She stares at it blankly before taking it from my hand and slipping it on her shoulder. I remove the corresponding saddle and pad from the wall and hand them to her as well.

If we were in a session, I might use some sort of grounding technique to help her engage with the present moment, but there's no time.

'Where would Goblin be?' I prompt.

'Over in the side paddock, maybe?'

I have no idea where the side paddock is. I am impatient to get moving, and also to get out of this oven-like shed. 'Can you take me there?' I ask, making it sound more like an order.

Without answering, she walks out of the shed, then stands in the dirt yard that all the sheds face onto.

'Stella,' I say loudly, with more authority – and irritation – in my voice. 'The *side paddock*.'

'Yes,' she says.

Her eyes suddenly meet mine and focus, as though my tone has snapped her out of a reverie. She puts the saddle and pad on the ground and the bridle over her shoulder, then leads me out behind the sheds. We traipse through the red dirt where the cottage was razed, and I see Goblin standing in a paddock beyond, his head in the air, which now smells like a summer Saturday afternoon in the city, everyone with their barbecues fired up, ready to cook chargrilled creations for family and friends. But there is no amicable chatter here, no festive music, no clinking of glasses; only the sound of the wind thrashing the tree branches and using its invisible fingers to pry the corners of corrugated-iron sheets from the shed walls.

Stella approaches Goblin with the bridle. He appears happy to be caught, even takes a few steps forwards, letting out a soft nicker despite the fact she has no food. She slips his bridle on easily and leads him towards me.

When we get back to the tack shed, Stella hands me his reins without saying anything, and goes back into the shed. Goblin stands quietly next to me, and I give his silky neck a pat, breathing in his sweet, horsey scent. I'm not sure what Stella's doing in there. I wait for her to return, but a minute goes by and she doesn't come back out. I squint through the door into the dark of the shed and make out her shape, paused in front of the row of saddles.

'The saddle's on the ground out here, Stella,' I say.

I look up at the sky and see that darker clouds are blowing closer to us again. I wonder if another storm is coming, perhaps more lightning, which will create new fires. Or perhaps rain. My mind flashes to the menacing orange monster at the entrance to the national park, the smouldering snake wrapping around the foot of the mountain. We would need a lot of rain to put that out.

Stella appears from the shed empty-handed. She leans over the saddle, pulls the pad off the top of it and puts it over Goblin's back. She then grabs the saddle and places it on top of the pad. The girth hangs down the right side of the horse, and Stella reaches under his belly and grabs it, pulls it over to her side of the horse and tries to do it up to secure the saddle. Her hands are shaking badly, and she fumbles with the buckles and then drops the girth. It falls back into its hanging position on Goblin's side.

As she leans down and puts her arm under Goblin's belly to grab it again, I feel the ground start to shake rhythmically underneath my feet. We both look up to see Hannah riding Lil' Sis at a canter towards the sheds, her long, pale legs hanging down the pony's sides. She's far too big for her, but somehow still manages to appear graceful. This isn't hindered by the fact they are moving towards us sideways – almost diagonally – rather than in a straight line, as though they're performing a dressage manoeuvre for judges in a competition ring. I realise this isn't intentional on Hannah's part, though; Lil' Sis is being a shit.

The pony stops abruptly mid-stride, catapulting Hannah's body forwards onto her neck. As Hannah straightens in the saddle, Lil' Sis plunges her head down to buck. Hannah yanks the pony's mouth with the reins, rips Lil' Sis's head around to her left knee, then releases it and gives her a sharp kick in the ribs, followed by a whack to the side with a sapling branch – leaves still attached.

'Get up!' she rumbles, her voice deep and commanding.

The pony obediently closes the distance between us at a trot. Hannah tells her to halt, then slides off her back. Lil' Sis makes a face as if she's sucking on a sour Warhead.

'Mum!' Hannah yells. 'Why haven't you got Goblin saddled? Argh.'

She thrusts Lil' Sis's reins into my free hand, so now I am holding two horses. She shoulders Stella out of the way – not particularly gently – and secures Goblin's girth. She lets down the stirrup, walks around the horse's hindquarters and does the same on the other side, then grabs the reins out of my hands and throws them over Goblin's neck.

'Mum, hurry up and get on! We need to move the cattle or they'll die. Mum, I'm serious!'

Stella, looking like a lost child in a shopping mall, gathers up Goblin's reins in her left hand, her tremoring fingers wrapping themselves through a chunk of black mane. She lifts her jean-clad leg and places her boot in the stirrup iron. Her toe slips out. She lifts it and puts it in again. I can see now that her legs are also shaking. It looks as if she's standing on one of those circulation-boosting machines.

She puts her toe in the stirrup again; it slips again. She stands still then, defeated.

Hannah startles me when she leans forwards, grabs her mother by both shoulders and starts shaking her.

'*MUM!* Get on this horse or the cattle are going to die! I *need* your help!'

Stella's head bobs backwards and forwards loosely with the shaking, and suddenly tears sprout from her eyes. Hannah stops.

'I . . . I . . .' Stella stammers.

'For fuck's sake!' Hannah yells in exasperation. 'You're the one who won't use bloody bikes and quads like normal farmers. You're the one who wants horses to muster—'

I surprise myself then. 'Stella, move out of the way,' I instruct.

She takes a few steps back. I thrust Lil' Sis's reins towards Hannah. She takes them, unsure what is going on.

My heart starts pounding as if I'm going to have a heart attack. There is a faint whirring in my ears, and a distant voice questions me from the depths of my mind: *What are you doing, Octavia?*

I grab Goblin's reins, gather them up over his wither, thrust my boot – thankful I'm still dressing 'country' for my visits – into the stirrup and hoist myself up into the saddle.

Surprised at the ease with which I manage this, I turn to look at Hannah. She has the wonderstruck expression someone might wear when watching their partner strike up a conversation in fluent French, having had no idea they were bilingual.

'I have this friend, Susie—' I start, but there's no time. 'I can ride a bit. I'm not great. Hopefully I'll stay on.'

'Awesome,' Hannah says, smiling. She does not waste another second in mounting Lil' Sis. 'Goblin's a good horse. I learnt to ride on him. You'll be right. Let's go!' She turns Lil' Sis and takes off at a trot.

I swiftly reach down to double-check Goblin's girth is tight, remembering the time I came off in the Rockies because I didn't do this. Then my head was protected by a helmet, which I do not have today.

With trepidation, I touch my legs to Goblin's side to request a trot, and he responds instantly. He follows Lil' Sis without me needing to guide him. I look over my shoulder and see Stella staring after us. I realise we didn't say goodbye. She puts her hands up to her face to wipe away her tears. She looks like she must have done all those years ago, a chastised little girl, scared and alone on this farm.

23

HANNAH

I CAN NO LONGER SEE MOLLY'S HOUSE. I COULD STILL MAKE IT OUT when I was in the middle paddock, but in the minutes it's taken us to ride to the bottom paddock, the fire's eaten up the ground. I bring Lil' Sis to a halt at the boundary line, mesmerised by the sea of fluorescent orange only a hundred or so metres from the fence, flames wrapping around the few trees Molly has, their crowns lit up like the Olympic torch. The heat is enormous. The smoke is in my nose and throat, making me cough with each breath.

Things are moving so fast, changing so quickly, that my brain doesn't have time to analyse what's happening. The light is low now, almost like twilight, and the sky above us is black. The book cover of *The Hobbit* flashes into my mind: a pissed-off Smaug sitting on his mountain, inky sky lit up by the searing red flames roaring from his nostrils and mouth.

This is a different terror from the one I felt when Lucy was murdered. Not cold and clammy and useless. It's hotter, closer; tells me to act. This time, the raging, evil beast is after me personally, cornering me, taking my space, herding me as I herd the cattle. My skin feels as if I'm sitting too close to a heater, and I remember learning in school that you usually get killed by a fire's radiant heat before the flames even get to you.

I want to cry out for Sebastian, but there's no point. And no time. I say a prayer under my breath, even though god deserted us years ago: *Please, god, let him be okay. Please god. Please.*

There's forty, maybe fifty of Molly's dorper sheep banked up on the steep ground against our boundary line, bleating, coughing, desperate to get away from the heat and flames. Our cattle are circling, scared, snorting the ashy smoke out of their nostrils. I lift the neck of my singlet up to cover my nose and mouth, but it springs back down. My hair's come free from its knot and the gusts of hot wind blow it around my neck, where it sticks to the sweat, a light strangulation.

I reassure myself we're halfway to getting the job done – the cattle from the middle paddock are already herded up to join the group in the top paddock. Now we just need to bring up this final lot before we open the top paddock gate and flush them all over to the house side. I think about the fire Octavia told us is burning near the national park, and I hope I am right in assuming they'll be safer on the house side. Where else can we put them?

I picture the images of bushfire aftermath they love to show on TV: cows' bodies bloated and charred, lying on their backs, limbs in the air like the legs of a table. They never show the human bodies – if there's ever anything left of them – and I push the thought of our singed corpses out of my mind. There's work to be done.

Octavia's just catching up to me. Her smaller body suits Goblin's short, wide frame. She can ride. Like, properly ride. I knew from the moment I saw her that she's a woman who can do things. I just didn't realise she could do this thing. I silently thank god for that.

As she gets closer, I put my forearm up to my brow to wipe the sweat away before more of it trickles into my already stinging eyes.

'I don't know why these cattle aren't moving themselves up higher, like the others did,' I yell over the popping and crackling, the bleating, the low distant rumble.

'What?' she yells back.

I ride closer to her.

'You go round the back of them to the right. I'll go this way.' I gather my reins in my left hand, using my right hand to mime what I'm trying to convey.

It seems to work because she nods, gives a thumbs up and canters down towards the boundary line, behind the cattle, with Goblin ready to scoop them up.

I ride around to the left. Lil' Sis is thankfully doing what I say now – either subdued by our predicament, or realising her determination is no match for mine. It doesn't take much pressure for the cattle to start milling towards the open gate. Within a few seconds, they're at a run: big pregnant cows, red-and-white steers and heifers, freshly born calves following their terrified mothers. Their eyes bulge and some of them look at me wildly, as if I'm the threat. They're leaving a trail of dust for us to breathe in as they funnel through the gate into the middle paddock, the leaders already heading up to join the mob in the top paddock. Octavia follows them up at a controlled gallop.

Mum said last week that we have one hundred and twenty-three head, plus thirty-seven babies, but there's no time for counting now. I want to ride after Octavia, but I know I can't leave Molly's sheep to be devoured by the fire, so I turn back to the boundary fence. Lil' Sis doesn't want to go back. She's not just being a pain in the arse now; she senses danger. I feel guilty as I kick my heels into her sides, whack her on the rump with my stick, growl at her to 'Get up.'

She shifts her weight back to her hind end and lifts her front legs off the ground in a low rear. I lean forwards, so as not to pull her over backwards. When we come back down, I yell at her, 'Get up, you bitch!' I boot her again and give her three stinging whacks to her flank. She stands still.

Now my whole body is shaking. We're going to die if we stay here much longer. I plead with her, 'Lil' Sis, come on, do this for Lucy.' Finally, she moves forwards, and we cover the ground to the boundary fence with me kicking her in the ribs every couple of strides.

I refuse to look at the flames. Instead, I focus on the dirty, creamy mounds of sheep with bobbing black heads as I jump off. I grasp Lil' Sis's reins in one hand, feel behind me with the other for the handles of the cutters and retrieve them from my shorts.

I freeze as a brown snake streaks under the fence, hurtling straight at me. I hold my breath as it races between my feet, its side touching my left sneaker, then turn my head to watch it as it veers off to the right and is gone. I exhale. The sheep are pressing themselves against the hinged-joint wire fence, newborn lambs mixed in with terrified ewes, probably not even sure who their own mothers are right now. The sheep are taking short gasps of air, making little 'kah-kah' sounds, trying to clear the smoke from their airways. I'm coughing too, the smoke burning my nose and eyes and throat. As I cut through the bottom few strands of the wire, sheep start ducking down on their knees, pushing through the gap I've created. I cut more strands as quickly as I can, and a torrent of them fly under the remaining wires of the fence. Lil' Sis yanks backwards on her reins in fright as the panicked balls of fluff duck around and under her. Going against my old pony-club safety teaching, I wrap the reins around and around my arm so she doesn't run off. I yell, 'Stand up!' as I lean forwards to snip all but the top two wires, creating a gaping hole in the fence. The remaining sheep press together to funnel through it.

Then I notice a tiny lamb squashed at the bottom of the pile of sheep; they are using it as a stepping-stone as they push through the fence. I wait for the remaining sheep to clear it. It is only seconds until they are all running up the steep ground towards the middle paddock. I pull Lil' Sis over to the small, cotton-ball mound.

The lamb is lying on his side, panting. His visible eye stares up at me like that of a fish pulled from the ocean – wide and fixed, with a crescent of white showing below the bottom of his iris. I see that his leg is caught up in the fence wire and I quickly untangle it.

The lamb tries to rise, manages to wobble up on his front legs but has trouble lifting his back end off the ground. I slip my hand under his belly, guiding him to his feet, and see that his bottom hind leg is at a strange angle, hanging loosely, probably broken by the force of the sheep springing off his body in a panic to save themselves.

The lamb won't be able to walk on his own. I gently lower him back to the ground. I look up now, straight at the fire. It has moved closer, even in the few minutes I've been down here. The intensity of the orange hurts my eyes – which are already stinging as if I've got chilli in them – but it's the only colour I can see in front of me that isn't black. The sound is like standing at the railway tracks as a freight train passes.

Please, Seb, please be okay.

231

I need to get out of here. I'm not going to die this way. I look down at the lamb, trying to think what to do with him – there's no way Lil' Sis will have him on her back – when I hear a muffled call.

I turn around and see Octavia cantering down the steep ground towards me, Goblin balancing himself with the ease of a horse that grew up on this land. I can't see the sheep anymore; they must already be in the top paddock with the cattle. We've got to get back up there, move them all to the house side.

'You okay?' Octavia yells, coming to a halt a couple of metres from us. 'Oh, no. What's wrong with the lamb?'

I glance up at her bright red face, her neck wet, the baby-pink collar of her shirt turned magenta with sweat. Her gaze moves from me to the lamb to the fire, and back. She looks afraid, which scares me.

'I think he's got a broken leg,' I say.

'Quick,' she says. 'Hand him up here.'

'Are you sure?' I ask. 'Can you ride while you're holding him?'

'Goblin's a good boy. We can do it.'

Not able to see another solution except to leave the lamb here to perish in the fire, I scoop him up, his delicate body not weighing much more than a couple of bottles of milk. I hand him across to Octavia, and she loops the reins over her arms and reaches out to take him. She drapes him over her lap at the front of the saddle, pressing against him firmly with her left hand to hold him in position, and gathers up Goblin's reins in her right. Goblin turns his head to see what's going on and, unbothered, faces front again.

'Okay,' she says, looking up at the fire again. 'Let's get out of here.'

24

OCTAVIA

EVEN WITH THE DRAMA UNFOLDING ALL AROUND, I FEEL RUDE traipsing into the house in dirty boots. But I can't take them off; I've got a lamb in my arms. I use my booted foot to push the front door closed behind me to keep out the smoke. My throat feels raw. The coolness of the air conditioning hits me in the face, and I pause for a second to savour it.

'Hello?' I call into the hallway, but nobody answers.

I'm worried about Matisse, who I last saw at the sheds, hosing down the hay bales through wheezes and coughs. I don't know where Stella is and, although I vaguely hoped I'd see Sebastian and the infamous Mr Molly-Pants relaxing in the lounge room with beers in hand, the room is empty. Except, that is, for Pinkie, who is in the pillowcase pinned to the armchair. Damn, he probably needs a feed.

I stand holding the lamb, unsure what to do. I'm worried about putting him on the pristine lounge suite, soiling the smooth grey velour, so I lay him on the soft rug – which, I reason, can be dry-cleaned if needed. I put him down injured-leg up.

His mouth is open, revealing toothless gums. He's breathing in short, raspy gasps. Despite the heat outside, his body is cool to the touch, and I think he is in shock. It's so cool in here and I realise I need a blanket to cover him. I look around the room but can't see anything suitable, so I move quietly down the hallway like a thief, in search of a linen cupboard.

As I open and close cupboard doors in the hallway, I think about how surreal this situation is. In the beginning, I didn't even like coming to my clients' home to conduct our sessions, fearful it might blur the therapeutic boundaries; now I am rifling through their personal belongings like a burglar looting a house while the owners are out.

I jump involuntarily when I hear a cough. Then another cough. I freeze. I'm certain the sound came from Lucy's room. Someone is in there. My mind flashes to Cole. What if he managed to make his way through the fires?

I listen closely, then I hear the murmur of a female voice. 'Please let him be . . . I beg of you, Lord . . .'

It's Stella. She's praying for Sebastian.

I remember the lamb then and spring back into action. I figure Stella is best left alone for now. It's simply a relief to know she is safely inside the house. I locate the most ancient-looking blanket I can find – an ugly, brown, pilled thing with ribboned edges – and tiptoe back down the hallway.

I place my hand on the lamb's soft, springy coat. He still feels cool. I spread the blanket out on top of him. I'm not sure what else to do. I remember from a pet first-aid course I took when I first got Bob that you're meant to check the animal's mucous membranes, so I open his mouth and see that his gums are pink. I press on them, and they turn white for a second before the colour flushes back. I think this is a good sign. I'm pretty sure I shouldn't feed him, at least until Sebastian has looked him over.

Where is Sebastian? I wonder for the fiftieth time today. It's the same feeling as when I've lost something important and can't settle until I've found it. My brain kindly offers me an image of him and Mr Molly-Pants and the horses being swallowed by flames. Thank you, brain.

I walk over to Pinkie then, open the lip of the pillowcase and peer inside. He's curled up on the heat pad, and very still. For a minute I worry he might be dead, but then I see his translucent abdomen moving in and out.

I look at the clock on the mantelpiece to calculate how many hours it's been since the joey's last feed. Even though the outside world has been dark for what feels like days, I'm still surprised to see that it's only five past five. The past few hours feel suspended in time. Undersea hours, deep down in the depths.

My head feels fuzzy. I haven't eaten or drunk anything since leaving home this morning. I suddenly feel like sinking into the deep, softly cushioned lounge and taking a long nap.

I rouse myself back into action, heading to the kitchen to make the joey's feed. I sterilise the baby bottle and the teat, mix the correct amount of Wombaroo formula with warm water and test the temperature on my wrist. Then I drink a big glass of water – swigging it down and enjoying it as if I've been stuck in the desert for a week. I return to the lounge room with the bottle of feed and carefully remove Pinkie from his pouch.

I still feel nervous handling him, worried that I'll break something. He squirms and I wrap him in a corner of Sebastian's swaddle-scarf. Settling into the chair, I cradle him in my hand like he's a premmie human baby and offer him the teat of the bottle. He moves his muzzle away from it, but I persist, softly stroking the rubber on his lips, and soon he opens his mouth, takes the teat and starts sucking hungrily. The lamb lies like a stone on the rug, but I can see the rise and fall of the blanket in time with his breath.

My mind slips into a sea of numb nothingness, and so I startle when I hear the front door open.

'Octavia?'

Hannah's voice. She must have finished untacking the horses, counting the cattle.

'In here,' I call out.

She walks into the room, tall, taut, lean like a racehorse. Her face, usually a delicate ivory, is red from heat and exertion, and a smear of dirt or ash highlights her left cheekbone.

'Sebastian's not here?' she asks, looking around the room as though he might be hiding behind a chair or a pot plant.

I shake my head and say, 'Not yet,' trying to sound optimistic.

Her forehead crinkles. 'You okay?' she asks.

'Pinkie and I are fine. I'm not so sure about him, though,' I say, pointing to the lamb.

She bends down next to the lamb, peels the blanket off him and places a corner of it over his eyes. I mentally kick myself for not thinking to do this to reduce his stress. She puts her hand on his body for a second, and then runs it down his length. She feels his ribs, his abdomen, his spine. She gently touches his twisted leg and the lamb whines faintly. She withdraws her hand and uses it to prise open his lips and press on his gums. Then she stands up, walks out of the room and comes back with a tea towel. She places the blanket back over his body, and puts the tea towel over his head, leaving his muzzle clear.

'Nothing we can do till Sebastian gets back,' she says. 'Have you seen Mum?'

'Ah, I think she might be in Lucy's room.'

'Right,' says Hannah. 'Yeah. Probably the best place for her right now.'

We both look up then as we hear footsteps on the verandah.

Hannah trots to the door, calling, 'Seb?'

Matisse answers from the other side. I hear the door open and close, boots being removed, coughing.

'What can I do?' I hear Hannah say. No response.

They appear in the doorway. Matisse looks different; smaller, somehow. I realise that she has her hair tied back. She looks less . . . invincible without it. She is wheezing and has her hands laced behind her head, as though trying to open up her lungs to air. Her whimsical toucan earrings give the whole scene a surreal feeling.

'Do you have any other medications you can take?' I ask. She shakes her head.

'Sit down,' Hannah tells her. 'You'll start feeling better now you're away from the smoke.'

I'm not sure if this is false bravado, but Hannah makes her statement sound like fact, and that is somehow reassuring.

Matisse sits on the lounge, leaning over with her hands resting on her legs.

The joey's finished feeding and I explain that I need to take him into the laundry to toilet him. They nod, and I go down the hallway and hover him over the laundry sink, rubbing his genital area with a wet piece of cotton wool like Sebastian showed me. Then I bring him back to the lounge room, while he wriggles in my hand, and tuck him into bed inside the pillowcase.

Hannah announces that she will make us tea and sandwiches. Her words conjure up a high tea, with cups of Earl Grey and crustless white bread crowned with cucumber rounds and snow pea shoots. Instead, ten minutes later, she brings in a wooden tray with plates, paper napkins and a big stack of sourdough sandwiches filled, she explains to me, with a mixture of mashed chickpeas, avocado and garlic, chilli flakes, mint, parsley, toasted sunflower seeds, lemon juice and olive oil. I have no idea how she's had the time or energy to whip this up, but I'm salivating.

Hannah pops out of the room again and comes back with another wooden tray, this time carrying a steaming teapot covered in hand-painted pink peonies, a milk jug and three teacups.

We each take a sandwich and some tea, and sit in silence, chewing, sipping, processing. Matisse, breathing more comfortably now, puts the sandwich down every few bites to cough into her arm, and then returns to eating.

None of us speaks for the longest time, each lost in our own thoughts. I wonder how I got here. The day didn't begin with some sort of omen, did it? No, it started so normally: coffee made, breakfast eaten, dog fed and guiltily shoved into the backyard, before jumping in the car to make a drive that's become so familiar I can predict every turn and landmark before it comes into view. But now it's almost six o'clock and I've dinged up my car, killed a wallaby, rescued, fed and toileted its baby, almost driven into a tidal wave of fire, mustered cattle on horseback through smoke and ash, helped rescue a lamb and rifled through my clients' belongings uninvited. And now, here I am taking tea with them in their lounge room as if I'm an old friend, while they no doubt silently weigh the odds of losing another loved one – and only weeks before they are scheduled to execute the murderer of the other. I guess this must also be how the day Lucy died began; normally, blandly.

Having thought of Bob, I realise that he will probably be

hungry and howling because he's been left alone for so long, making me not only a neglectful dog mother, but at risk of being labelled a bad neighbour. I'm so thankful to have the lovely Cassie living only a few doors down. I make a mental note to contact her, because I know she won't mind taking Bob for the night, and he will behave himself because he'll be hiding in a corner, terrified of her Persian cat.

I wonder how Stella is, and whether we should check on her. But right now, I can't move. My body and mind are so heavy. Outside the house, the wind howls through cracks and crevices. Something falls on the roof – a small branch, perhaps. None of us reacts. We have finished eating but we don't shift in our chairs. Matisse's breathing is much slower now, an even in-and-out, in-and-out.

Hannah picks up her mobile phone and, a few minutes later, still seems transfixed by the screen.

'There's so many of them,' she says, breaking our silence.

My expression tells her I don't understand.

'I'm checking the RFS app,' she says. 'There are so many fires. Stanthorpe, Woodenbong, Millmerran, Yangan, here. I checked them earlier and ours wasn't on there, but it is now. It's bigger than most of them. But Seb said the firies were going to some of the others first, because they were closer to more houses. Maybe we should call them again?'

I look at Matisse.

'I'll ring Gunter in a minute,' she says, but doesn't move. 'How far does the fire stretch?'

'I'm not really sure,' says Hannah. 'It just shows a red blob over the general area. It's not clear where it starts and stops, or how close it is to Molly's place or ours.'

Matisse nods.

'I might go and check on Mum,' says Hannah.

25

HANNAH

I OPEN THE DOOR TO LUCY'S ROOM. IT'S DARK BUT NOT EMPTY. I TURN on the light. There's Mum, lying on Lucy's bed, curled on her side like a baby in the womb. Her hands are over her face. I sit down next to her on the bed.

I wonder if she's annoyed that I'm in here. She doesn't like us coming into Lucy's room. It irritates me that she thinks this room is only for her. It doesn't belong to Mum; it belongs to Lucy. And I love Lucy's room. I don't know if it's something to do with the way it's decorated – sort of like a forest – but I feel cosy and safe. It's almost like being in her treehouse.

'You okay?' I say softly, touching Mum's arm. She nods but doesn't uncover her face.

'We're still waiting to hear from Seb,' I say. She doesn't respond. 'Mum – look at me.'

She obediently moves her hands away from her face and I see that it's covered in tears. Somehow, the fact that she's showing her emotion – wearing the evidence of it – is a relief. It means something has reached her.

'He'll come back, Mum. He'll be fine. I know he will.'

I say this not only to reassure her, but because I can't stand to imagine any alternative.

'How do you know?' she says, fresh tears dripping down her face and onto Lucy's pillow. 'You don't know. Lucy didn't come back.'

'I know,' I say. 'But this is different. Seb's a smart guy – he won't have ridden into danger. He'll find a way to get around the fire and back.'

'What if he doesn't? What if he . . . All for that stupid old drunk. I can't go on if anything happens to him. I can't. I can't do this again.'

She's sitting up now, propping herself against the white enamelled bedhead that always reminds me of the ones you see in hospital scenes in old movies.

'Mum, he will come back. I know you're scared for him and I am too. But you'll see, he's going to walk through the door any minute.'

'You don't know that!' She sobs. 'I can't do this. I can't lose him. I can't lose him . . .'

I have a vague urge to physically comfort her, but I don't know how. She's really crying now. Big, heaving, gulping crying. I look around for something to give her to wipe her eyes and nose, but there's no tissues. Snot and tears run down her face and dribble onto her shirt, making a wet patch on her chest.

She mumbles something.

'What, Mum?'

'I . . . I . . . don't want to do it. I can't do it. I can't.'

'You won't have to, Mum. He'll be back.'

'No, I don't mean Seb. I mean *him*. I can't kill him.'

I pause. Breathe in.

'I know,' I say.

'But I can't *not* do it, either. I can't let him live. He doesn't deserve to live after what he did. I cannot fail Lucy. She deserves justice. But I think if I do it, it might . . .'

'It might what?' I prompt after a moment.

She looks at me, finally. Her skin is pink and splotchy from crying. 'I think it might break me.'

26

OCTAVIA

IT STARTS AS A *PIT* ON THE CORRUGATED-IRON ROOF. THEN A *PIT* ... *pit, pit* . . . *pit, pit, pit.* Matisse and I look up at the lounge room ceiling, as though we'll be able to see through it. Then a band of percussionists launches into concert on the tin above us. *PIT, PAT, PAT, PAT, PAT.*

Rain? Rain! It's raining! Matisse and I look at each other and simultaneously break into huge smiles.

'Thank god!' she exclaims, leaping out of her chair, toucans fluttering.

She dashes for the door, and I know she's heading outside to check that the sound is not deceiving us. I follow. She pauses in the hall to slip her feet into thongs before flinging the door open. Damp, fresh air hits us in the face. Matisse sprints down the verandah stairs and out into the garden. Heavy droplets of water – silvery from the house lights – fall onto her shoulders, her arms. I run down after her, the rain hitting my skin like a sweet, wet gift.

We both look up at the sky, letting the blessing fall onto

our dusty faces. We laugh with joy, and then Matisse throws her arms around me in a bear hug. I don't resist but instead hug her back, feeling the warmth of her body against mine like the comfort of a mother's. In this second, my mind is exhausted far past being able to consider my ethical boundaries. I am filled with relief, and hope.

We pull apart and look around us. We need to check that this rain is actually doing something to douse the fire. Because the flames weren't visible from the house, I consider suggesting we run up to the farm side to look. Then I remember Matisse shouldn't run at all and I stare into the darkness, considering what to do.

Then I blink. I blink again, harder. My heart, which I thought was so worn out it could not quicken another single time today, flutters and skips a beat. Keeping my line of sight perfectly still, as though not to break the apparition, I reach out to where I think Matisse's shoulder must be, and tap her. 'Matisse! Matisse! Look!' I point into the shadows.

'What?' she says, staring in the direction of my lifted arm. 'Is it . . .? Oh my god.' She starts bouncing up and down on the spot like a joyful child. 'Oh my god. Oh my god. Thank you, god. Thank you!'

And then she's off, running into the watery blackness.

I run after her, out of the front yard and into the paddock, as she calls out, 'Sebastian! Sebastian! Oh, thank god.'

I hear Sebastian's voice. 'Mattie! It's okay. We're okay.' Two shapes come into view. Centaurs in the night.

'What's all the fuss for, woman?' Another man's voice, cracked, slurring. I can't tell whether he's cross or making a joke.

We're close enough now that I can smell the horses, can distinguish their heavy shapes from their human riders.

The larger man dismounts, and I hear a thud, his weight causing the ground to vibrate as he lands on his feet.

'Mattie,' says Sebastian. His features are grey in the darkness. He throws his arms around his stepmother and they hold each other.

She reaches up and pats his hair, strokes it, kissing his face and murmuring over and over, 'Thank god, thank god.'

Finally, they separate.

'Octavia,' Sebastian says and turns to me. Suddenly, his arms are around me, and he says, 'I'm so glad to see you. Thank you so much for helping us.'

I hug him back and then we pull apart. 'Of course,' I say.

The other voice gruffly interjects with, 'C'mon, let's get this show on the road.'

'Molly, you just bloody behave yourself,' Sebastian chides. 'You're lucky to be alive.'

'Well, if it's bloody thanks you want, you won't be getting any. Don't need the likes of you riding in on your horse to save an old man. Would've been fine on me own . . .'

With that, he dismounts tentatively, knees creaking as he slowly lowers himself to the ground. Watching his feebleness, I know immediately he could not have saved himself.

The men lead the horses towards the house. I walk alongside Sebastian. Matisse breaks into a run again, this time towards the light – the house – calling out over her shoulder, 'I have to let them know you're both okay.'

The rain continues to fall, but less heavily, and I wipe it from my face. My clothes are wet through.

'Do you think this will be enough?' I ask Sebastian.

'Enough?' he says.

'Enough to put out the fires.'

He is silent for a moment, and then says, 'No, I don't think so. I think it'll slow them, at best. The bottom of the mountain's an inferno.'

'It's taken me bloody house,' says Mr Molly-Pants.

'I'm sorry,' I say.

'Me too,' he says. 'My father built that thing.'

We walk into the front yard of the house in silence, the rain and horses' hooves on the stones the only sounds in the night. Then the front door springs open, and Stella and Hannah rush through it, followed by Matisse.

'Sebastian!' The sound of a mother's gleeful voice rises into the evening air and bounces off the old fig trees. She races up to us, and the horses startle.

'Easy, easy,' Sebastian soothes them. 'Mum,' he says, his voice low, vibrating with emotion.

Without words, he hands me his horse's reins and throws his arms around Stella. They hold each other in silence. Hannah stands to the side, looking on, a smile I haven't seen before warming her face.

As Sebastian and Stella release their embrace, I can see tears streaming down Stella's face. Emotion, finally. She turns to Mr Molly-Pants.

'I told you to lay off the drink, you bloody old fool. He could've been killed saving your sorry rear end.'

The light of the verandah illuminates the old man's face and I see his features for the first time. Huge, wiry brows spread like eagle's wings above dishwater-coloured eyes, which are red-rimmed but alert. A beard – which would have been white if it wasn't so tobacco-stained – further elongates a long, craggy face. Deep valleys run down his leathery cheeks. His chequered shirt, stained with yesterday's dinner, hangs from his thin body like a crumpled tea towel, and his legs are bowed as though he just hobbled out of a Western movie.

He shrugs at Stella's comment, then says, 'You got a drop of Scotch, Stell?'

She sighs, and the sound betrays a bemused tolerance for the old man's behaviour. I guess they have known each other a long time.

'Come inside,' she says, 'but take off your boots at the door.'

'What do you think I am, woman? A bloody animal?' he grumbles as his shaky legs carry him up the verandah steps.

'I'll sort the horses out,' says Sebastian. 'You lot go inside.'

As I follow the family into the house, Hannah walks past Sebastian, rubbing his arm and whispering, 'I knew you'd be fine.'

As we all squeeze into the hallway, manoeuvring around each other to remove our footwear, Matisse says she'll be back with towels. She reappears with an impractically white, fluffy towel for each of us, and we set about dabbing our sodden, dirty clothes until the towels are muddy and limp.

I hear the rain start up again and think of Sebastian, wet, exhausted and alone outside.

'I'll be back,' I say wearily, squashing my feet into my boots once more and slipping out the front door. As I walk onto the verandah, I hear lively chatter – Mr Molly-Pants hurrying Stella along for a drink, Hannah and Matisse talking about making us all some dinner – and I'm not sure they even noticed that I left.

Back outside, I see Sebastian has closed the yard gate and the horses are tethered to bale twine tied in loops around the top rail of the wooden fence. Above the rain, I hear running water and the low, mechanical hum of a pump. Following the sounds, I walk around the side of the house, where I find Sebastian in the half-darkness filling a plastic tub under the tap of the water tank. He must be getting water for the horses.

'Hey,' I say. He glances up, and then looks straight down into the tub.

'Oh, hey,' he says. He continues to stare into the tub as water sloshes into it.

'You okay?' I ask, sensing there's been a shift in his elated mood of a few minutes earlier.

The rain dies down again, allowing me to better hear him. 'Yeah,' he says in a half-whisper, half-squeak, his voice cracking.

'Sebastian?' I prompt, wondering if he's suffering from a bit of shock in the aftermath of his rescue of Mr Molly-Pants.

'I'm okay,' he says, still staring into the tub.

'Look at me,' I say.

He lifts his face and there is enough light for me to see that his tanned and sooty skin is wet, although I'm unsure if it's from the rain or tears. His curly golden-retriever mop is soaked and flattened to his scalp.

'Are you crying?'

He puts his big hand over his eyes and nods.

'Sebastian, what's wrong?'

I hear his breath catch in his throat before a rattle emerges from his mouth. He tries to stifle a sob. 'Sorry.'

'It's okay,' I say softly, reassuringly.

'It's not,' he says, and leans forwards, turns off the tap, then abruptly swivels on his heel and walks back in the direction of the horses, leaving the tub behind.

I follow. The horses are tied a couple of metres apart, and he is standing between them, loosening the chestnut's girth. I walk up to him, into the dark alcove between the two horses, careful to let them know I am there.

'Sebastian,' I say.

He drops the girth and puts both hands on the railing of

the fence, facing out into the darkness. His shoulders heave as he is racked with sobs.

I squeeze up next to Sebastian so that I am also standing along the fence, his shoulder to the left of me, the chestnut's head to the right, its soft, warm breath tickling my arm. Up this close, I appreciate what a large man he is – or how small I am, my head only coming up to his shoulder.

'Sebastian,' I say. 'You're okay. Molly's okay. The stock are safe. We're going to get through this bushfire. The firefighters will turn up eventually. It's going to be all right.'

He looks down at me and brushes away his tears with the back of his hand.

'What's worrying you?' I ask.

'I dunno. I think I'm just overwhelmed. By today. But also by Mum, and the embryo situation, my father turning up, the execution. I want to have a family of my own one day, you know?'

I nod, confused. He has told me about his desire for a partner and children, about his struggle to find space for romantic relationships when he was a young adult, trying to cope with completing university and establishing himself as a vet against the background of Lucy's death, the stress of enduring the criminal justice system, and his worries for his mother's mental health – but I'm not sure why he's raising it now.

'I'm really, really lonely,' he says.

Oh.

'I just want to find a woman to love, someone I can share my life with. But how will she see me when she discovers I sent my mother in, alone, to kill my sister's murderer; when she finds out my mum desperately wanted me there? How could any woman ever be interested in me when I tell her I didn't stand by the one who raised me on one of the hardest days of her life? How—'

'Hey, hey, hey,' I say, holding out my right hand in a stop gesture. 'Sebastian, listen to me. You've had an incredibly stressful day that's not yet over. You haven't eaten for hours and you're almost certainly dehydrated. Your brain is exhausted, yet hyper-focused on danger. There's no danger directly in front of you, so perhaps it's throwing up these distant fears. But what I'm going to say to you is this: you *are* supporting your mother, while also remaining true to your own values. I'm not qualified to say what being a man is, but can I give you my best guess?'

His face is earnest and he nods.

'My guess is that being a man is caring enough to ask yourself these hard questions. That it's reaching conclusions about your values through deep self-reflection, and then standing by them. It's being strong enough to say, "No, I will not engage in terrible physical violence that is abhorrent to my soul." It's caring enough to want to support your family while staying true to your morals.'

I can tell he is listening intently, so I continue.

'A fine example of a good man, I think, is one who – when his conscience tells him to – puts his life in danger to ride through a raging fire to save another human being, even if that human being is also one he refers to as "a cantankerous old drunkard".'

He smiles a little at this.

'And the woman who is the right one for you, when you find her, will *value* you for your ethics, your compassion and your integrity. And, you know what?'

'What?' he says.

'I think many women would sleep better at night next to a

man who hasn't tortured someone to death with a bag full of steel implements.'

I see him open his mouth to say something, pause, and then let out an entirely unexpected chuckle. I pause for a second too, taken aback. What I said wasn't intended as a joke, but now, under these extreme circumstances, I can see a dark humour in it. Feeling exhausted and slightly hysterical, I find a laugh escapes my mouth. Sebastian's chuckle turns into a deep belly laugh, and I feel my chest starting to shake with irrational hilarity. Soon, Sebastian is cackling unreservedly, wiping the tears from his face, and I find myself doing the same. Then, without warning, he throws his arms around me in a strong embrace. Our laughter stops.

Releasing me, he steps back to properly take in my face. His is serious. 'Thank you, Octavia,' he says. 'Thank you for everything you've done for me, and my family.' His voice rings with sincere gratitude.

'It has been my absolute honour,' I say. Then I find myself brushing a tear from my own cheek while breaking into a smile again. 'But it hasn't been easy, you know, experiencing this country life: braving kangaroo collisions and riding through life-threatening fires on the back of wild broncos . . .'

'And Mum,' Sebastian says, laughing. 'Don't forget about braving Mum. I mean, I love her more than anything, but she can be kind of scary sometimes . . .'

As I picture Stella's constipated face, I know I'm not allowed to laugh, but I'm sure he sees the sly smile form involuntarily on my lips before I quickly banish it.

Taking advantage of this lightness in the air, I say, 'I'm going to go help with dinner.'

'Great. Thank you,' he says, smiling.

As I walk towards the house, I turn and say over my

shoulder, 'Don't get too relaxed yet, though. We've got a new patient for you in the lounge room.'

He chuckles, one hand massaging his forehead. 'Of course you do.'

•

Back inside the house, I see that Mr Molly-Pants has folded his thin, wasted body comfortably into the double lounge chair. A whisky glass is clutched in one cragged, dirty hand, and he is leisurely flicking through the local newspaper with the other. Seeing him in the light, I observe the grey pallor of his wrinkled skin: the complexion of someone who has had too many drinks, and probably not enough nutrition, for a long time.

He looks completely uninterested in the lamb – his lamb – which is still lying on the floor covered in a blanket. Someone, Hannah I presume, has propped towel-wrapped hot water bottles against the tiny creature's body.

The old farmer peers at me over the top of the newspaper pages with watery eyes and grumbles, 'The women are in the kitchen.'

I resist the urge to follow up with '. . . where they ought to be,' and walk through to find the three women working in amicable silence. Hannah is stirring a pot, Stella slicing sourdough, and Matisse sprinkling something onto a salad.

'Smells good,' I say, as they notice me enter.

'Just pasta.' Hannah shrugs. 'You don't have any allergies, do you? I didn't even check when I gave you the sandwiches.'

'Nope,' I reassure her. 'Allergy-free and stomach like a cast-iron pot. I survived a year in India and two in Uganda, so I can handle whatever you throw at me.'

'India and Uganda? Really?' says Hannah. 'I'd love to travel.'

'What?' says Stella, surprisingly alert, looking up from the breadboard. 'Since when? You'd hate to travel.'

'Mum,' says Hannah, pouring pasta into a large serving bowl and rolling her eyes in a time-honoured adolescent gesture, 'there's so much you don't know about me.'

I smile inwardly. How true. 'I'll set the table,' I offer.

Matisse points out the cutlery draw. As I am counting out knives and forks for the six of us, Stella says, 'Don't set a place for Molly. He says he'll have his in there, on a tray.' She gestures to the lounge room with her head.

'God,' says Hannah, 'he thinks we're his women-slaves.'

'He's always been that way,' says Stella. 'You won't change him.'

'It doesn't mean we need to encourage him.' Hannah shakes her head.

'Sometimes,' says Matisse, regarding her stepdaughter with clear affection, 'it is easier to keep the peace than to start a war.'

'Who's starting a war?' asks Sebastian, appearing in the doorway. 'We already have a war going on outside; we don't need another one, do we?'

'Sebastian,' Hannah says. 'There's a lamb in the—'

'I know. I've already looked at him,' Sebastian interrupts. 'Broken leg. Maybe internal injuries, probably just the leg. I'm going to get my euthanasia gear now.'

'What?' says Hannah in a high-pitched squeak. 'You can't do that!'

'Molly doesn't want the hassle, or the cost, Hannah. It's not a viable proposition.'

'So, that's all this is about?' she demands, hands finding her hips. 'Money?'

'He's a farmer, Hannah. I know this farm is . . . different, but that's how most farmers operate. He has to make a living.'

Hannah walks towards the door.

'Move,' she commands, and squeezes past Sebastian into the hallway. We are all silent, listening for what is going to happen next.

Then we hear Hannah's voice from the lounge room, her tone firm – demanding, even.

'How much for the lamb?'

The old man's voice answers. 'What're you talking about, woman?'

Hannah says, 'How much is that lamb worth?'

'That broken thing? It's worth bloody nothing.'

'It's worth *less* than nothing,' replies Hannah, 'because you're going to have a euthanasia bill to pay after tonight.'

'What? What bill?'

'The bill for Sebastian putting it to sleep.'

'He won't charge me for that,' scoffs the old man.

Then, 'Sebastian, come here.'

Sebastian winces jovially, then turns and thumps down the hall.

'Tell Mr Molly-Pants how much it's going to cost him to put the lamb to sleep.'

A long pause. A sigh. Then, tentatively, 'Well, at his weight . . . eighty bucks, I'd say.'

Now, a movement, the rustling of paper, a clunking of glass onto wood. Sebastian says wearily, 'Stay where you are, Molly.'

'You've got a nerve, son, after all I've done for you, charging me those ludicrous city prices for something I can do with a bullet.'

'You don't have a bullet here,' says Sebastian.

'Well, I'll get a bloody rock.'

'Whoa, whoa, nobody's getting a rock.'

Hannah interjects. 'What if I save you the money, Mr Molly-Pants?'

'What? How?'

'I'll take the lamb off your hands.'

'What the hell for?' says the old man.

'Well,' answers Hannah, 'I've got some money saved, so I'll pay for his leg to get fixed.'

'And what the bloody hell would you want to do that for?' Exasperation – and perhaps suspicion – rings in Mr Molly-Pants's voice.

'Lucy always wanted a pet lamb, Mr Molly-Pants, and I'd like to make that dream come true. It would help me to . . . feel better.'

There is silence now. Then the old man mumbles, 'Well, I don't want it, so do what you like with it. You've got more emotions than sense, woman.'

'Sebastian,' Hannah says, 'I'm guessing there's nothing we can do for the lamb's leg tonight. Can you please give him enough sedation and pain relief to last him until we can get an X-ray tomorrow, and put it on my bill?'

With that, Hannah practically skips back through the kitchen doorway, face aglow.

'Got myself a lamb,' she announces.

'We know.' Matisse smiles, raising an eyebrow. 'Did Lucy want a pet lamb?'

'Maybe,' Hannah says and shrugs. 'She probably just forgot to mention it.'

27

HANNAH

I WATCH MUM DURING DINNER. SHE LOOKS LIGHTER, SOMEHOW. HER face brighter. I wonder if it's because she told me her secret: she doesn't want to kill him. Or at least part of her doesn't. Maybe it's because Sebastian didn't die. Or because we've got the animals somewhere safer. Or because the rain might help stop the fire.

I look at Octavia, too. She's looked so put-together when I've seen her previously. So fresh, so . . . showered. Now her usually stylish hair is a cap on her head from sweat, her neck is creased with soot and her fingernails are black underneath. She still looks strong, though. I have to be careful when I watch her, because her eyes are all-seeing. You can tell her brain's working, summarising things, making judgements. Not bad judgements – judgements that let her help us. Hypotheses, she calls them when we talk. Hypotheses she will put to you for your thoughts.

'I wonder, Hannah, if your mother's regression to this child-role – your growing up and her growing down, as you've described – is what's causing your drive to protect her?'

I don't always know the answers to her hypotheses. She says I'm not meant to. She doesn't either. They're something to spark reflection, consideration, new ways of looking at things. Like sifting through dirt until you find something valuable.

Sometimes I know her theories are plain wrong. Such as when she suggested that maybe I don't eat because it makes me feel more in control. I mean, it does, and that's part of the reason I do it, but the underlying motivation isn't what she proposed. I told her it's not because I want to get thinner. It's got nothing to do with my appearance. And that's the good thing about Octavia: she listens and uses what you're saying to help you make new hypotheses; helps you turn them over until one feels right.

I told Octavia about what happened, at the party. She was perfect. It was as if I couldn't break her with my confession about that night, and yet she still experienced every tiny particle of fear and pain that I did. And, despite that, she could stand strong for me in that story, even when I lost my words and cried. I haven't cried for so long. She made me feel as if I told her the biggest thing in the world, but she also made that thing so light that we could throw it backwards and forwards between us like a ball, watching its colours, feeling its size.

I could tell she wanted to touch me, hold me, make it all go away, even though she did nothing to suggest those things. People say that when someone gets paid to hear your problems they don't really care, as though the exchange of money somehow negates human compassion. But I can see that some people, people such as Octavia, do this because they do care; they just can't care for free all week long, because they have bills to pay and stuff.

I asked Octavia what she thought about me telling Mum and Mattie what happened. Or maybe even Seb. She wasn't perfect there. She was frustrating. She wouldn't tell me. She kept putting it back on me, asking what I thought would happen if I told them, when I might tell them, where, how and, most importantly, why.

Why would I tell them? Honestly, I struggled to answer that, but I told Octavia it just felt sneaky keeping something like this back, as though I'd skipped over showing them a part of myself. I also gave her lots of reasons for not wanting to tell them yet.

The main reason for not telling them now surprised me: it is Sebastian. He doesn't want to help Mum with the execution, I know. And I reckon he should stand strong on that, because that kind of retribution is not him. But if I tell him, it'll make him waver even more than he is now. It will give him another reason to doubt himself, to think he *should* do it, that it's his job to do it, because the women in this family have been hurt by men and he needs to defend us. Because he's a man. How dumb is that? That we all somehow implicitly know that's the default role. To defend his woman-clan with his hands. Well, it's not, and I told Octavia I will not give him another reason to think it is.

In the end, the conclusion I came to is this: after this whole thing is over, after we can finally say our proper goodbyes to Lucy, when Mum can – and I really hope she can – be present again, then I will tell them. But not because I need them to know in order to survive it. God knows all of us in this family are capable of surviving things on our own. But survival is different to living freely, to being open to the world again. To do that, I need the people who love me to know all the parts of me.

Sitting here, seeing my family together, that feels like the right decision. My hands still feel a teensy bit trembly with everything that's happened today. I still can't believe I rode that crazy horse. Controlling something as wild as Lil' Sis, to face something even wilder – the fire – and surviving it, has created a new feeling inside me. Not power, but close to it. Certainty, maybe? Certainty that I can face the most difficult things that will come my way in life. Certainty that during those times, I will either perish or not perish, and if I don't perish, I will survive. If I perish . . . well, that's coming to all of us eventually, isn't it?

Despite Lucy being in the air around us, despite being able to feel her, I don't believe in god or heaven, or even an afterlife. So, I can't comfort myself by thinking I will be with her again, that I will get to say I'm sorry, that I will get to say, 'I love you, sis.' And I understand now: the things we believe to comfort ourselves about the fact that we're dying are just a band-aid for fear. I know we need to live *in* the fear to be at peace with it.

Matisse is speaking. Saying she has something she needs to tell us. She sounds serious. I try to pull myself into the present moment to hear what she has to say, but my brain feels like cotton wool. It's telling me there's no more space for anything else today. There's already been too much. My mind wants to nestle itself in a comfy pillow and switch itself off, surrender itself to the inky dreams that will wash over it and somehow refresh it for another day. I take a deep breath and tell it to focus. We have more work to do tonight.

28

OCTAVIA

MATISSE MEETS MY EYES ACROSS THE TABLE AS SHE SOLEMNLY announces she has something to tell the family. I know in an instant what she is going to say. *Now, Matisse? Really? After today? While the fire's still burning?*

Distressing events, I think, affect people in different ways. I know Matisse has been contemplating sharing her secret with her family, and perhaps it doesn't seem like such a leap to disclose something that intense after all the overwhelming emotions they've already shared today. Possibly she's decided it's time to put down this heavy burden to create some space for everything else she's carrying – to relieve herself of it before the execution. Maybe it feels safer to do it while there's someone else in the room who already knows and has still accepted her. I can't help but think that Stella's betrayal recently having come to light is also on Matisse's side, because Stella's not exactly in a position to be criticising anyone else about past wrongdoings. However, I think she's making a bold, and perhaps foolhardy, choice by raising it now. Part of me wants to ask to speak with her alone, to caution her, tell her to stop. But I'm just so tired that I can't think what I should do, so I don't do anything.

Everyone is looking at Matisse. I think they are surprised by her serious tone. Stella stops chewing, puts her fork down mid-mouthful. Matisse clears her throat and looks directly at her wife.

'I killed a girl,' she says.

Wow. She's not pulling any punches.

'What?' says Stella, with a look that says she thinks the smoke has gone to Matisse's brain.

'I am sorry,' Matisse says and reaches across to put her hand over Stella's, which rests on the table beside her plate. 'I know this is perhaps the wrong time, but I can't keep it from my family any longer.'

Stella stares hard into Matisse's eyes. Matisse meets her gaze. Sebastian and Hannah stare at Matisse.

'Years ago,' she says, taking a deep breath, 'when I lived on the coast, when I was a nurse, I worked a very long shift. A lot of very long shifts. After one of those shifts, when I was tired – too tired – I drove home. Chose to drive home. And on the way home, I got distracted and I hit a young woman with my car. She was nineteen. She ran out into the road to grab something, and I hit her. She died instantly. I killed her. It was an accident, but it was my fault. I should have told you – all of you – a long time ago. I always meant to. But I just . . . couldn't.'

Tears are running down Matisse's dirty face. I look down at the table, struggling to handle the intensity of the emotion, the weighted silence hanging in the room. I hear a chair shift and Stella stands up. Oh, god.

She spits her mouthful of food into a paper napkin, which she places on her plate. Her face is flushed red. She turns, looks at the door and then at Matisse. Then she stoops and puts her arms around her wife. Squeezes her. Rubs her back. Kisses her head.

'I'm so sorry,' she whispers. 'I'm sorry you've had to carry that alone. And then Lucy, on top of that pain. I know you would never deliberately hurt anyone. I love you.'

Stella lets go of Matisse. Matisse gets to her feet and they embrace again. Then wooden chairs scuff at the floor as Sebastian gets to his feet, then Hannah. They walk around to their mother and stepmother, and throw their arms around both of them. They hug in silence for a few seconds.

Then Sebastian says, 'Matisse, we are so lucky to have you, and we would never judge you for such awful circumstances. You must forgive yourself for this.'

I hear Matisse sob. Then Hannah says, 'Mattie, thank you for having the courage to tell us. We love you, and nothing could ever change that.'

Matisse murmurs, 'Thank you.'

With her family's arms wrapped around her, she says, 'Stella. I'm not mad about the embryo anymore. I realised that if you'd told me beforehand, I wouldn't have agreed to it, and that means we'd never have had our Lucy.'

At this, Stella squeezes her wife tighter, and says, 'I'm sorry. I know it wasn't right.'

I feel as though I'm watching something very special. Somehow, things in this family have just righted themselves. Perhaps Matisse did choose her moment well.

'What the bloody hell is going on in here? I called out for a drink, and nobody came.'

I look up to see Mr Molly-Pants standing in the doorframe, rheumy eyes ogling the scene, empty glass in a hand dangling by his side, a strand of pasta hanging off his beard.

Everyone separates as though they've been caught in a sordid act. Hannah turns, levelling her chin at the man, and says, 'Molly, you've had enough to drink. Go get your plate and put it on the sink.'

The old man takes a second to register this command, then obediently turns on his heel to collect his dinnerware. The family looks at Hannah. Sebastian raises his brows.

'Woman,' he says to his sister, 'you impress me more with every sentence you speak.'

After the tension of the past few moments, of the day, we burst into peals of laughter which are perhaps disproportionate to the humour contained in the comment. Hannah makes a mock scowl before joining in.

In the background, I see Mr Molly-Pants tiptoe around us and gingerly place his plate on the sink, and this makes me laugh even more.

After we recover ourselves, Hannah says, 'I think we should go check on the fires.'

I realise then how – over the past couple of hours, since the rain began – my brain has detached from the reality of the fire. The truth is that the rain will be thoroughly insufficient to stop the raging beast in its tracks, but it's as if my mind took that event, plus Sebastian's safe return, as a reason to scale down the threat – an opportunity to shut down and switch off. The most logical explanation is that my brain simply needed time to rest before it could continue. Strangely, I do feel somewhat refreshed after food and rest and laughter.

We each plonk our plates on the benchtop and traipse down the hall towards the strewn pile of boots.

'You just stay on the lounge, nice and comfortable, Molly,' says Sebastian. I can't tell whether he is being sarcastic or if he simply wants the old man to stay out of trouble. Molly grunts.

Then we are out under the night sky, which, behind the layers of grey smoke, emits an eerie red glow. I'm not sure if it's because we've been inside, in the comparatively clean air, but the smoke feels thicker, smells stronger, than it did earlier. Also, there's no longer any rain to dampen it down. The temperature does not seem to have cooled, although the winds are milder.

As we walk out of the yard in front of the house, Sebastian flicks on his torch and the beam of light exposes the level of air pollution. The air is dense with particles.

'Mattie,' Hannah says, 'I think you should go back inside the house. We're not going to be able to get help if your asthma flares up again.'

'I didn't even think of that,' says Stella. 'You should definitely go back, Mattie.'

I notice just how much Matisse's cough and wheezy breathing has settled.

Matisse pauses for a moment and then, sensibly, concedes.

'I'll go call Gunter. See if he can give us an update,' she says.

The four of us walk on in silence, the distant hum and crack of the fire filling the air. None of us says a word as we take in the fact that flames are now clearly visible from the road side of the property, where the cattle and sheep restlessly mill in their new surroundings. I remember Sebastian saying we could move them into the paddock near the treehouse if needed. I consider the prospect of getting back on the horses tonight and feel a new surge of exhaustion run through my muscles.

We slog our way up the ridge towards the farm side, and I jump as a *pop* sound ricochets through the air from the direction of the sheds. Sebastian starts to jog up the hill, and we follow suit. It is almost as light as day as we reach the peak, our faces and arms bathed in apricot light. We come to a halt on top of the ridge and each of us is silent as we survey the farm, which is alight, flames dancing along the post-and-rail fencing and lighting up the insides of various farm buildings. There is a sinister glow radiating from the tack shed where Stella and I stood only hours before. I can feel the heat of the fire on my face. Only the hay shed – stacked high with the scores of round bales that are needed for the cattle to survive this drought – is not burning.

I look over at Stella, whose face is as bright as if she were staring into the sun, and I am unnerved to see tears silently flowing down her sooty cheeks.

We continue to stand, mesmerised by the scene. Just as I wonder how long it will be before the hay shed catches alight, I see an orange ball of flame leap from the adjacent shed onto a round bale.

'We need to go,' says Sebastian in an urgent tone.

'No,' says Stella. 'We need to get the hoses, start wetting it down again.'

'Mum,' says Sebastian, 'we need to leave. That hay shed is going to go up.'

'Mum,' Hannah says, 'let's run back to the house, chuck some of the hoses in the ute . . .'

I realise this makes no sense, because there isn't any water over here to use for firefighting. The tanks are engulfed in the inferno before us, their plastic sides melting like marshmallows that have fallen off their sticks into a campfire. Water or no water, there's no hope of us fighting this fire, and it's obvious it's not safe to stay, even though it seems that Stella might insist on it.

'Okay,' murmurs Stella, and I realise Hannah is attempting to lure her mother back to safety, probably counting on the fact that Stella is sufficiently detached from reality to not realise the irrationality of what Hannah is proposing.

She puts her hand on her mother's arm and gently ushers her in a half circle so she's facing the road back to the house. 'Let's hurry, Mum.'

We take quick steps down the hill, the heat at our backs. Just as the road starts to level onto the flat, a deafening noise cracks through the night: a roaring, thunderous explosion from behind us. My heart jumps until it bumps into the roof of my mouth, and my hand flies to my chest as though to tell my heart where to return to.

We turn around in unison to see flames as high as an inner-city office tower licking the night sky.

'Oh my god,' says Stella.

'It's the hay shed,' says Sebastian, as another explosive crack sends us all jumping. 'It's not going to take long to reach the house side. We need to get on the horses, move the cattle again.'

'One of us needs to start wetting down the house again, the yard,' says Hannah. 'Mum?' she prompts.

Stella nods vaguely.

'Octavia,' Hannah says, and I turn to face her, 'do you think you can help on the horses again?'

My body and my mind are saying *No, no, I can't. I don't want to.*

I jump again at another thunderous crack. Then, the awful scraping sound of steel on steel. Metal buckling, bouncing off metal.

'The roof's coming off!' yells Sebastian.

'I'll catch Goblin,' I say immediately, wondering how Hannah's going to manage to recapture Lil' Sis, and wishing we'd had the foresight to have kept them tethered for this very scenario. I realise then, with relief, that at least there are still two horses in the house yard. Horses that are, presumably, better behaved than Lil' Sis.

With the light of the inferno behind us, we hurry along the road, and I force back tears of exhaustion and thoughts of lying down right here, curling up into a tiny ball on the crunchy, dead grass and sleeping forever. I force my feet onwards.

Through my mashed-potato thoughts, I vaguely notice that the low hum of the bushfire is getting louder, even though we're moving away from it. My feet continue to step in unison with the rest of the troops. The hum grows and, as though it is tapping me on the shoulder, my brain now properly pays attention to it.

Hannah, whose pale legs I am following, stops. She turns around, back towards the sheds. The rest of us mimic her action. The sky is like one of those drawings you do in school where you scribble all over a piece of paper with a waxy orange crayon, then go over the top of it with black, and then use your fingernail to scratch the black layer away to reveal the orange that still lurks beneath.

The noise continues to increase. It no longer sounds like the fire, but something distinct from the fire, something droning. I feel confused. I look to the others, trying to figure out from their expressions what's going on. The noise intensifies. It is definitely not the fire.

'They're here,' Hannah murmurs.

Who's here? I wonder. It's not until a helicopter appears like a bat against a sunset that I realise help has arrived.

We all watch silently as the noise of the chopper blades swells, the shape getting larger.

'Are they here to collect us or to fight the fires?' I ask, perhaps stupidly. 'I didn't think they could fight fires at night.'

'They can.' Sebastian nods reassuringly. 'I think they first started doing it during those big fires in California a while back.'

'Maybe they're just scoping things out,' says Hannah, as we watch the white helicopter hover directly above the sheds for a second, and then tilt on its side and swivel as though to leave.

This time my heart plummets down to my belly.

'Maybe they'll have to wait till morning to do anything.' Hannah sighs. 'By then, the cattle will be . . .'

I bite the inside of my cheek between my molars as the helicopter straightens itself again and a frothy fountain of purple-white liquid gushes from its centre. The liquid is tinged with the golden hue of the fire as it falls down, down, down, disappearing from view. Then I hear the sizzling sound of cold water turning to steam when it hits a hot frying pan.

Hannah squeaks with delight and, without warning, throws her arms around me. 'We're going to be okay!' she squeals.

I hug her back heartily. I feel the air leave my lungs in a long, slow exhale.

We're safe.

•

Matisse and Mr Molly-Pants already know about the heli-copter, they tell us when we arrive back to find them sitting in silence in the lounge room. Gunter's been in touch. Matisse says a second helicopter is leaving Mr Molly-Pants's house, which is beyond salvage, and heading towards the sheds. They are planning to work through the night. They will try to hold back the fire from the Heathwood home and front paddocks until the full firefighting team can be deployed on the moun-tain at first light.

'It may be a day or two until the way out can be cleared,' Matisse says, looking at me. I'm glad I got onto my neighbour, who is happily Bob-sitting.

Oddly, Mr Molly-Pants does not appear at all downtrodden about the news that his house – the home he has lived in all his life – could not be saved. Folded into the comfort of the lounge chair, he announces that he will be borrowing a caravan from Mac, who apparently has the cheek to own one but never use it. I feel quite confident he has not yet asked whomever this Mac is if he can borrow the caravan. I feel equally confident that Mac will, if only for the sake of a peaceful life, allow him to borrow the caravan for long enough that Molly will claim squatter's rights.

'Right,' says Hannah. 'We should get to bed. It's going to be another big day tomorrow.'

I watch her taking control again, posture poised and face brave, and I picture her as a leader one day: the manager of a team, or director of a company, perhaps. Whatever she wants to be. I don't see her as a teacher – she wouldn't have the patience.

Although she is undoubtedly squirming on the inside, to Hannah's credit she does not show it as she offers her bed to Mr Molly-Pants for the night, saying she will sleep on the couch. The old man grunts ungraciously to indicate acceptance of this offer. I wonder if she'll ever get the smell of whisky and old man out of her room.

'Octavia, you can sleep in Lucy's room,' Hannah says. 'I'll just change the sheets.'

'No!' erupts Stella.

We all turn to see her horrified expression. The thought of someone sullying Lucy's shrine with their presence, their body, their aliveness is an affront.

'It's okay.' I raise my hand. Then, aching body cursing me, I say, 'I'm absolutely fine with sleeping in the reclining chair.'

Matisse shushes me with a movement of her own hand. She gets out of her chair, toucans flapping, and walks over to where Stella stands.

She places her hand firmly on her wife's shoulder, and says simply, 'Stell.'

Taking a deep breath, and as though coming back to herself, Stella turns to me and says, 'Sorry, Octavia. Of course, you must sleep there. You've done so much for us. Lucy would want you to have a comfortable bed.'

Realising the momentous nature of her concession, and wanting to reinforce this newfound courage, I thank her as graciously as I can.

•

Everything seems to happen fast then – even feeding and toileting Pinkie doesn't seem to take long – and within minutes we are all tucked up in bed. After a day filled with chaos, the only discernible noises are the old man's arrhythmic snore – which comes within seconds of the lights being turned out – the air conditioner humming, and the distant, comforting whirr of helicopter blades. By the time I close my eyes, snuggled under Lucy's canopy, I am almost too exhausted to give thought to the fact that I am sleeping in a murdered girl's bed.

29

HANNAH

I WASN'T EVEN SURPRISED WHEN I SAW THE POLICE THROUGH THE lounge room window walking up our front path. There'd been so many different SES and RFS personnel at our door that one human in a uniform blurred into another. I was sitting on the floor at the boundary of the lounge room and hallway, holding a bottle as Lamby sucked greedily. I watched from the ground as Mum answered the front door. There were two male police officers: one was about Mum's age and looked almost as wide as he was tall. He seemed puffed from walking up our three verandah stairs. I sincerely hoped his job never requires him to chase anyone. The other cop was young and scrawny, and a carrot top – I'm allowed to call him that because I'm a ginger myself – with pink skin like a piglet.

The older one explained to Mum that they'd found a burnt-out car near the bottom of the range, and asked her if she knew anyone called Cole Haynes. That's when I knew they weren't part of the SES scene. Mum was quiet for a second, and then told them who he was. They asked if he had been planning to visit us on the morning of the fire. Mum paused for a long moment and then said, quickly, that he had mentioned something to her about a visit, but that it seemed more like a casual idea than a serious plan.

Then the older officer asked if the visit was about anything important enough for him to risk trying to drive through a fire.

'Not that I know of,' said Mum, shrugging. 'He's been out of our lives for a very long time until recently, when he just seemed to get a hankering out of nowhere to see his kids. But he's completely unreliable, so I wasn't really expecting him to turn up. Why do you ask?'

I noticed her wringing her hands as she spoke.

In a high, uncertain voice, the younger cop told her that they believed the burnt-out vehicle belonged to Cole and that a body had been found inside. But, he added, it would be days, or even weeks, before they could make a formal identification. He said they'd already been in touch with Cole's mother, who was his listed next-of-kin, and she said she hadn't spoken to her son in years, that he kept to himself unless he wanted money.

The doughy older cop added that there weren't any personal effects in the car, or, if there were, they all got burnt up, except for one thing: a large hunting knife under the driver's seat. I pictured a blade glowing red hot in the flames.

The younger officer showed Mum his phone then, asked her if she recognised the knife in the picture as belonging to Cole. No, she said, she didn't: she didn't know he carried a knife. I could see her get shaky at that point, even from behind, and it sounded as if she was starting to cry.

'I'm sorry,' he said, mistaking her reaction for grief. He gave Mum a pat on the arm, and added, 'You've been through so much these past few days . . . and years.'

Even though I know this cop isn't a local, it seems as if everyone who deals with us is forewarned of our history.

'I wish I could say that it's not going to turn out to be the kids' father,' he went on. 'It's the last thing they need. But my guess is, well . . .'

Mum told them she thought she needed to sit down, and the redhead asked her if she needed a cup of tea or something. Mum told them she'd be fine, that she was probably better off being on her own to process everything. The older cop said they'd be in touch if they needed anything further, and to confirm that it was him when the forensics results came through.

•

I lie on my bed with my legs curled around Lamby, who is snoring softly in his sleep. I snuck in here just before the cops left so I didn't have to talk to Mum. I'm not even sure how I feel about my father being dead. I have no memories of him, except of the night when he turned up here in a rage, screaming and threatening our lives. It seems, from the knife – and his determination to drive through a bushfire to get here – that he might have had the intention of carrying out his threat. I feel sick to think that Mum or Mattie or I – or even Sebastian or Octavia – could have ended up the same way as Lucy. Was the bushfire actually a blessing in some way?

I count on my fingers the things I know about him. One, he was horrible to my mum when they were together. Two, he deserted his wife and kids, including me, a helpless baby. Three, he never showed any interest in meeting his daughter or getting to know her. Four, he got to know his son, let his son know him, love him, rely on him and then, without a word,

273

left him minus a father – left him feeling like he wasn't worth hanging around for, not even worth sending a birthday card to. I mean, I'm guessing that's how Sebastian felt. Worthless. Abandoned. He's never said anything, but he's got to have felt that way. And he's a boy. He needed a role model, and all he got was that despicable piece of shit.

Yes, that's what he was. Suddenly I'm sure of it. I don't need to use my fingers to count any further. I know exactly how I feel: as if a despicable piece of shit is now gone from this earth. A despicable piece of shit who was nothing to me and never will be anything to me. He was the real worthless one. The only thing I can be grateful about is that he donated his sperm to create me and Sebastian and Lucy.

I think about how being sisterless and being fatherless are the most different feelings in the world. I think about how Sebastian might be the only man I will ever know, for a fact, isn't a danger to us, isn't out to hurt us, take what he wants from us and then discard us like a crumpled-up beer can. As soon as I think this, Lamby wakes with a start and looks up at me reproachfully. I pat his lanolin-soft head, and reassure him that he too will be a good man.

30

OCTAVIA

I'M ALREADY AWAKE WHEN MY 2 AM ALARM GOES OFF. I PAD DOWN the stairs, Bob at my ankles, and take the lid off the tin of Wombaroo. Pinkie's only been in my life for a week and a half, but it feels as if I've birthed a baby and then got up to feed it during the night for five months straight. It's becoming automatic: the feeding, the toileting, the pouch changes.

Sebastian connected me with a wildlife organisation so I could get my permit, and a tiny lady enveloped in a pink shirt covered in black bats – driving a pink car splashed with hundreds of bat decals – came to the house and ran through the rehabilitation training. Tina – 'Tina Batina', in my mind – has become like an AA sponsor: I call her whenever I'm worried or feel off track. Contrary to Sebastian's belief that Pinkie wasn't going to do well, his tiny body is growing and filling out, and Tina says he's thriving.

•

It's noisy when I arrive at the cafe in West End. Bottoms – petite, large, tight, flabby – fill every seat and stool. I weave my way through the tables, catching an animated but banal conversation between a group of businessmen about whether a dirty chai is better than a regular chai. Turns out yes, but only if you need caffeine more than you need flavour. As I make my way into the noisy rear courtyard, I see Henry neatly tucked into a shady corner under a Japanese maple tree. He greets me with a broad smile. We've already debriefed by phone, several times, about the bushfire experience, but he quips that he's glad to see me still alive. As I settle into my chair, he gets straight down to business. We only have an hour.

'So, tell me about these phone calls you've been getting from Stella.'

I sigh, picking up a delicate leaf that has fallen onto the tabletop and rubbing it between my fingers.

'She's distressed,' I say. 'She's saying she can't take it anymore. Not that she's suicidal. She's strongly denying that. It's more that she feels incapable of executing the sentence, but also incapable of not following through.'

'What's brought this on?' asks Henry, his brows furrowing. 'She's always said she's certain she wants to do it, hasn't she?'

'Yeah,' I say. 'She has, but she also has a huge amount of internal conflict about that intention. And now, with the bushfire, and Cole . . .'

'What does she say about Cole?' Henry asks.

'She says she feels guilty. She feels terrified – horrified – to think of what he might have done to her family, feels as if she would have been responsible for bringing that on them. She also feels as though her actions ultimately caused him to die.'

'As if she's responsible for killing him?' Henry asks.

'Yep,' I say. 'Even though she has all these feelings about

the man – anger, contempt, hatred, really – she reasons that if she'd never done the embryo thing, he would still be alive, and so his death is on her.'

'And then she's got another killing lined up in . . . how many weeks?'

'Three,' I say.

He purses his lips, and a whistling noise escapes. 'Pretty heavy stuff.'

'Yeah,' I say, feeling my forehead crinkle in a frown.

'Does her family know how she's feeling?'

'They do,' I say. 'All three of them have called me, worried about her.'

'And she's definitely not suicidal?' he asks.

'Well, I've been doing risk assessments throughout the time I've been working with them, of course. She's adamant she'd never consider it, would never want to leave her family. Her GP and I have encouraged her to get treatment for her mental health symptoms, but she won't. And she's not so unwell that she doesn't understand what's what, you know? So long as she sufficiently holds herself together until the execution, there's no grounds for me to contact the judge and say she's too impaired to proceed.'

'And if the judge thought she didn't have the legal capacity to make her own decisions, he could stop her participating in the execution?' Henry says.

'Yes,' I say. 'Even on the day, if she becomes so profoundly distressed that she can't think straight, I can call the judge. But unless that happens, she has the right to do this.'

'So, what do you think? Do you believe she's fit to kill that man?'

'Geez.' I exhale, rubbing my eyes with my hands until I remember I'm wearing mascara and am probably making myself look like a panda. 'It depends on what you mean by fitness. Do I think it would be good for her? Absolutely not. Do I think it might do her more psychological harm, and take her to a worse place than she is now? Definitely. Do I think that, by the relevant legal standards, she is capable of making that decision? As it stands today, yes, I do. She clearly understands and can articulate the nature of the choice she is making. She can reason through all the options, she has insight into the potential consequences for her and the family if she executes the sentence, and she ticks all the other relevant boxes.'

'And that's what it comes down to?'

'Yeah,' I say. 'Judge Gorski stipulated that I am to advise the court if it is my professional opinion that any party eligible to execute the sentence becomes impaired in their capacity to make the decision to do so, at or near the time of the execution date. If I advised that this were the case, he would likely remove their eligibility to execute the sentence, or at the very least arrange for a second opinion on the matter, which is what I would be asking for.'

'I wonder if you should write to the judge anyway,' Henry ponders. 'Let him know what she's going through, what you think it'd do to her mentally if she went ahead.'

'It would be a breach of confidentiality though, wouldn't it?' I say. 'Not to mention the ethics of betraying Stella like that, when I have no grounds to do so.'

'What about the ethics of letting this woman destroy herself?' Henry counters, playing devil's advocate.

I think for a moment. 'But people do that every day, don't they? Drugs and alcohol to excess, other risky choices, ruining relationships, affairs that break families apart. Except under rare circumstances, we don't dob clients in to the authorities when they tell us all the damaging things they do. And the reason we don't is that they are adults who have the agency to make those choices. Whether they are good choices is irrelevant to their ability to choose them.'

'Yeah,' Henry says, massaging the bridge of his nose. 'You're right.'

He suddenly looks small inside his crisp white shirt, as though he's shrunk with the weight of contemplating the situation. Seeing him like that makes me reflect on what I've been carrying around for months, day and night.

Perhaps he reads my thoughts, because he says, 'How are you doing, anyway?'

How *am* I doing? I've barely stopped to check in with myself for weeks. Feeling oddly put on the spot, I go to answer with the stock-standard response, which is to say I'm doing okay. I open my mouth to say the words, but it involuntarily closes without anything coming out. I open and close it again. And again. Like a gormless guppy. Then, to my dismay, tears prick my eyes. I grab a napkin.

'Sorry,' I say, blinking fast.

But it's not enough to hold back the tears, and they spill down my cheeks. I madly dab them away but they are instantly replaced by fresh ones. I realise I've never cried during clinical supervision before, and certainly never cried in front of Henry. In public, no less. I feel exposed.

Henry reaches across the table and puts a comforting hand on my forearm. 'It must be extremely difficult,' he says.

'Don't,' I say, shaking my head. 'Don't do that psychologist crap on me – you know it'll make me cry more.'

We both half-smile at this unavoidable fact. Showing empathy to a vulnerable person is a guaranteed recipe for tears.

'Seriously, Vee,' he says, using the nickname he pulls out when we're getting into something difficult. He used it when my father's death led me to struggle to work with grieving clients, when I lost a client to suicide, when my husband and I were divorcing and I didn't want to take on a client who was leaving his wife. Is this situation *that* hard?

Nope. Harder.

'I guess it is pretty challenging,' I say. 'I never thought it would get under my skin this much. The family, I mean. Getting to know them, learning what they've been through, and knowing what they're yet to face. Being there for the bushfire, helping them defend the farm, sharing meals with them, sleeping in Lucy's bed – it brought us closer. Probably too close. It's becoming more difficult to maintain professional boundaries, if only inside my own mind. I'm struggling to separate myself. I think about them when I wake up in the morning, when I'm having trouble sleeping at night. They're *real* to me, you know?

'I've seen them living their lives. Doing normal person things. Doing mundane things, hard things, scary things. They're more three-dimensional than the clients we see in our rooms for an hour every week or two. I know we think we get to know our clients pretty well, but this is . . . more.'

'Too much more?' he asks.

'Feels like it,' I say, concentrating on the salt shaker in the middle of the table and willing myself not to cry again.

'What about when this is over and done with? Once the sentence is executed?'

'My contract is to provide services to them for as long as is needed after the execution. The wording is very broad.'

'And they're going to require it for a long time, aren't they,' Henry observes.

I rub my lips over each other, tasting both strawberry lip balm and sunscreen.

'It feels as if this could go on forever. How do I extricate myself down the track? I know Stella's going to fall apart after the sentence is carried out, be a complete mess. And I have no idea how the rest of the family will cope with what does or doesn't happen on the day, or afterwards. I'm not sure how to make it okay for them.'

I notice the prickle of panic spreading across my chest as I speak.

'It sounds as if you're feeling personally responsible for their outcomes.'

I sit back for a minute, knowing I need to calm myself so I can gain perspective.

'Yeah,' I reflect. 'I guess I am.'

'You know it's not your job to make it okay, right?'

I have an urge to argue that he's wrong, but I say, 'It's just that they've been through so much pain already. I don't think Seb and Hannah have even processed what it means to lose a father. Then, after the execution date, there's the anniversary of Lucy's death, then they have to go through Christmas again. And then—'

'Octavia, stop.' Henry interrupts my spiralling thoughts, his tone and the stop sign he forms with his hand reminding me of my recent interaction with Sebastian at the water tank. 'You are responsible for providing the services you are contracted to provide, to the best of your ability, and I have personally observed the thought and care you've put into this case. However, you cannot be responsible for the terrible position this family's been put in to make this decision, or the choice Stella's making – to go through with the execution despite knowing full well it may negatively impact her and her already-suffering family. Likewise, you're not responsible for any fallout from the decision. Beyond providing the services you do, you have no control over this situation. You cannot determine how other people choose to think or behave, or what they do to make things better or worse.'

His words make me realise something I had completely forgotten: it isn't my job to fix everything for this family. 'I'm not responsible, am I?' I exhale. 'I'm not responsible.'

All the tight muscles in my body start to relax, and I suddenly feel overwhelmed with a great tiredness.

'I had a dream last night,' I say.

'What was it?' asks Henry.

'I dreamt I was in a slaughterhouse, operating the captive bolt gun to stun the animals. The cattle were queuing before me, restless and afraid, big liquid eyes pleading, and then the gate opened to let the next one into my killing pen. But when I looked towards it, it was McDermott. He was naked. Pale. Slicked in sweat. He met my eyes, and his face morphed into how it would have looked when he was a baby. Pink, downy cheeks. Rosebud lips. And he had the most peaceful expression: innocent, cherubic, resigned. My hand was shaking, and I put my finger on the trigger. Then I woke up.'

31

HANNAH

IT'S BEEN SIX DAYS NOW AND ALL THAT'S PASSED MY LIPS IS WATER, electrolytes, coffee, Lucy's ashes and my toothbrush. I told Octavia that even though I started fasting for one reason, I keep going for another: the numbness. I can't think about much else when I can feel my stomach eating itself up. The horrible, panicky sense of dread that was with me every minute is gone. It's replaced by a comforting light-headedness.

At first, all I could think about was resisting food; it took up all my energy. The first week I fasted, Jessica asked me to drive her through Western Wings. It smelt so good that, after I dropped her home, I went back through and bought six buffalo wings. I'd never eaten meat in my life. After I shoved the chicken in my mouth, I cried until snot ran down my face. Then I learnt how to use my will to control myself – I do it by picturing him. Now, it feels as if I could go on like this forever. But I won't. Tomorrow, I must eat.

Focusing on my weekly to-do list makes it easy to avoid food. I only wish I could avoid the stupid school formal as easily. But

I promised Jessica I'd be her 'friend-date' – because neither of us has a real one – and Mattie's so excited to take before photos. Even Mum's saying she wants to see me in my dress.

Exams finished a week ago, so studying – even the obligatory minimal amount – no longer takes up time. I need to review my list to make sure there's still enough on it to keep me constantly busy:

Task:	When/How long:
Run in national park; free weights	1.5 hours daily
Feed Lamby	4 x day; 2 x night
Help with fire clean-up	2 hours daily, forever
Check postbox	Tues, Fri
Pick up formal dress	Thurs
Watch inspiring movie (e.g. Hunger Games)	30 mins daily, before bed
Career planning	???
Tell Molly to 'fuck off'	Next time he calls me 'girlie'
Sit-ups, balance board, stretch	30 mins daily (during movie)
Chores (laundry, vacuum)	20 mins daily
Meditate in treehouse	When Mum and Mattie go into town
Ride Lil' Sis	30 mins daily (feel the fear)

I want to add 'Avoid Mum, daily', but it doesn't seem fair. All these words clutter into my mouth every time I see her. Words such as selfish, dramatic, infantile, sook, big fucking baby. They want to run out of my mouth and slap her in the face. I've almost slipped a couple of times, such as when she asked me to go to my dad's funeral and put flowers on his coffin for her. What the fuck, Mum?

I've been researching Matisse online. Reading about the girl she killed. It took me a while to find the articles, because I wasn't searching for her married name from her previous relationship. I can't remember if I even knew she was married before Mum. Maybe someone mentioned it when I was younger? In my head, I had this story going that we were her whole life; that she came over the seas to Australia and just landed here, on the farm. It feels weird to think she had a proper life before us, a husband and a different career. And secrets. Secrets she's kept even longer than Mum's one about Lucy and the embryos.

The girl's name was Claudia Lucy Schmidt. I thought Mattie wanted to call Lucy that because her mum is Lucila, but maybe that's only partly true. Maybe Lucy was named after the dead girl. And then became a dead girl. Did the name jinx her?

Mattie must've been so scared when she killed that girl. The arrest, the sentencing, her husband leaving her, losing her career, going to prison. I wonder if bad things happened to her in there. Did the other women hurt her? Did she make friends? Did she stay in her cell every day, or work in the laundry, or the kitchen? The only thing I know about prison life is what I've seen on TV. I hope it wasn't like that for Mattie, but I hope it's exactly like that for him. I think he's in solitary, though. So maybe he gets to escape the tall white guys with the shaved heads and swastika tattoos who want to kick him in the head and pin him to the bed and force things into his body. Maybe the guards do it instead. I picture him squirming on the floor, writhing and struggling to breathe with someone's big, sweaty hand over his mouth, and a warm flush prickles my toes and my private parts.

I'm loving my hair right now. It's really silky, and the red has got deeper somehow. I practise straightening it and tying it in a high ponytail. I don't usually wear it this way, but I want a look that makes me feel confident and powerful.

I stand in front of a mirror and pretend to stride around, and watch it swish back and forth, tickling my shoulder bones. I wrap it around my neck to make a sort of noose and pull it tight for a few seconds. Then I let it go and it smoothly uncoils like a snake. A memory comes to me so strongly that I have to sit down on the bed. It's of Lucy and me swimming in the creek, play-wrestling, her dark hair and my copper intertwining underwater, becoming a red-bellied black snake. I wonder if, wherever she is, Lucy is glad that monster will be dead soon. I also wonder if Lucy's not anywhere but in an urn on our mantelpiece; if her spirit simply does not exist any more. That's part of the reason I eat her ashes. I figure if my body manages to digest them, then she's in my blood and my organs and my cells. She's alive in me, at least.

32

OCTAVIA

I STARE INTO MY COFFEE MUG, BOB AT MY FEET. I DECIDED NOT TO GO to work today. There are three days until the execution date, and it's the first time I've chucked a sickie since owning my own business. Well, not exactly a sickie. A mental health day. Mine is the type of work where people count on you – sometimes life-and-death count on you – so I always prioritise that. But, this morning, I just couldn't. I'm exhausted. Sick of all this responsibility. So, when I reviewed my list of appointments and saw it – quite remarkably – consisted entirely of clients who have been doing well and are close to discharge, I called it. The receptionist will ring them to check they don't have anything urgent they need to talk to me about and rebook their appointments.

Still, even though I badly need downtime, I can't avoid thinking about Saturday. Stella needs to be at the prison gates by 7.30 am. Matisse and I are allowed to go with her for support, but only up to the point where the guards let her through the doors of the specially prepared unit where the killing will happen. I'm using these words more and more with myself now – execution, killing – perhaps as a way of desensitising myself to the reality of what will occur. I rehearse in my head, over and over, walking in to that cold, hard, concrete prison. It's a place I've only ever pictured entering in my 'life gone wrong' ruminations, with a sense of unreality. Like if I punched the guy at the airline counter when he told me my flight was delayed for the third time, or if I scammed pensioners out of their life savings, or if I had sex with an underaged client. Stories that are so improbable to me that I have no fear they will eventuate.

Truth be told, I have also fantasised about being in prison. It's been during times when my life was extremely challenging. When the decisions and responsibilities I faced were so heavy that I just wanted to escape to somewhere else. Somewhere where I had no decisions to make, and there would be someone who called all the shots for me. Someone who would tell me when to sleep, eat and work, someone who would pay my bills. In my imagination, I share a cell with a life-weary old-timer, her sharp tongue belying a soft and sentimental interior. I spend my days reading books off the library trolley, practising yoga in my cell and working in the garden. I don't have visits from anyone, but that's the point. Okay, maybe I'm confusing prison with a health retreat.

Anyway, I suspect that visiting a real prison will be a departure from my fantasy. We've received a long list of dos and don'ts from the facility: do wear clothing that covers the breasts, upper arms and knees – nothing tight or clingy; do wear closed shoes with heels less than three centimetres high; do not wear any jewellery other than stud earrings or a wedding band; do put any essential belongings in a transparent bag; do not bring anything to drink but water – in an unopened bottle less than 750 millilitres in volume; do have a letter from your doctor if you must bring medication, and bring only the dose you will need for the day; do leave any electronic devices in the lockers outside; do bring two forms of photo identification; do not bring Vegemite. *Vegemite?* I chuckled when I saw this. I said to Henry, 'What, do they think we're going to be having tea and toast while waiting for him to die?' But Henry explained that Vegemite can be used to make home brew, due to its high yeast content. My prison-innocent mind cannot imagine where an inmate might set up a distillery in a high security fortress where every move is supposedly monitored.

I mentally take stock of how each family member might cope with what's ahead. In my more optimistic moments, Hannah concerns me only mildly. She has shown a deep under-standing of herself and how the execution might affect her; an understanding beyond her years. Watching how she handled the bushfire – her leadership abilities, her problem-solving skills and her bravery – confirmed that she is a young woman of formidable stuff. Sebastian, I suspect, will continue to doubt himself about his choice, but I hope in time he'll be able to more comfortably separate the messages he has internalised about what a man is expected to do from his own deeply held personal convictions. Matisse worries me, but mostly because of the carer-style role she has adopted towards her wife. She's faced past adversities and carried the heavy burden of guilt, but she's forgiven herself, at least on the good days. She understands and accepts herself. What concerns me is how she will cope with the farm if Stella falls into an even bigger hole after this event. Is this the life she imagined – essentially alone, running a demanding, complex business single-handedly, on top of a solitary mountain? Sebastian's life is so busy that it's unlikely he'll be of regular assistance, and Hannah certainly can't be expected to give up her future to become a farmer, a life she's very unlikely to want, by my understanding.

And Stella? All this hinges on Stella. If what's left of this family is to stand a chance, she needs to be diverted from killing that man. But I know she will not abort this bloody mission, and so I must prepare for round two with this family. Which, I now see, could be harder than round one. I don't know if I can do it. I want my old life back.

•

I toss and turn all night on Friday. Pinkie is sleeping through without a bottle now, so even when I'm awake I have nothing to occupy myself with. Bob, lying on a soft mat next to my bed, sighs with my sighs, rolls over when I do. The call from Stella last night – in floods of tears – left me shaken. 'I don't want to do this,' she cried, 'but I can't not.' The usual refrain. I'd felt – I *feel* – so angry that the family's been put in this position. I wish they didn't have to make this choice.

I talked to her for over an hour. Matisse was in the background, cooing and soothing Stella when her sobs got so big I could hear the phone rattling against her cheekbone. By the end of our call, we were exactly where we started. Stella is going to kill McDermott: she must do justice for Lucy; there's no other way. At least by the time we hung up, she had cried herself out. Matisse said she'd stay at her side, make sure she was okay. Stella said she was going to take a sleeping tablet and go to bed. I'd wished I had a sleeping tablet.

As I drag myself out of bed at first light and stare at my apparition in the bathroom mirror – purple half-moons under my eyes, a pimple on my chin when I haven't had acne for thirty years – I wonder if Stella will look more haggard than I do. I dress slowly. I chose my outfit carefully for the occasion: long black business trousers with a sharp pleat up the middle of each leg, a white button-up blouse tucked into a slim patent-leather belt, and sensible black slingbacks with a pointy toe and low heel. A slight smile comes to my lips when I think of the jewellery requirements – I wonder whether Matisse will feel naked without her owls or parrots or finches today. Or perhaps she will attempt to flaunt the rules and wear them, little friends coming on the journey, protecting their nest in stormy weather. I had intended to leave my face bare, but I end up applying dabs of concealer, a touch of blush, a swipe of mascara and tinted lip balm so I don't appear too much like a corpse.

Stella is going to see a corpse soon, I think. An image flashes into my mind of McDermott's face, after. Not the cherubic baby face I dreamt of, but a handsome man's face. Stony. Still. Frozen in time. A garish thought occurs to me: will his face be his face when Stella has finished with him? Pale with the hue of death, but otherwise untouched? Or will she mash his features into themselves, so his face becomes the pulp of a blood orange? Will she pluck out his eyes so that dark, cavernous holes stare out? This is too much.

I reassure myself that I will never have to see McDermott's face after his death. I will never know what happens to his features. Or will I? Will Stella choose to relive her actions with me – detail the role of every object in that oilskin bag? Will she relive the thrusts, and thuds, and thumps until I want to cover my ears and ask her to stop? I can't tell her to stop – won't be able to – because my job is to help her process the event if she wants to. And she will. I know she will.

Be honest, I say to myself. When you felt the need for a

career reinvigoration, a new direction, something interesting, when you applied for this role, you didn't think of this day, did you? You thought this would provide revealing insights into the human mind, an opportunity nobody else in your field has experienced. You didn't think about walking a fragile woman into a concrete cave so she could kill a man and break herself in the process.

No, no, I didn't.

•

I meet Stella and Matisse at the back of the police station as arranged. If the media knows we are coming here first, there is no sign of it. No vans, no cameras, no journalists shoving microphones in the family's face. Gorski was clear: no direct contact is to be made by the media with the family on this matter, now or in the future.

But I still thought this would be too tantalising an opportunity for them to resist – that there would be at least one network who would walk the tightrope between court orders and the 'public interest'. Get some juicy quotes from the family now, say sorry later and hope to avoid a massive fine – or maybe even jail time – by arguing for the public's right to know.

Stella and Matisse are already standing next to a uniformed officer, all three of them uncomfortably silent, when I arrive. As I park my car and walk towards them, I can see that it would take more than a touch of make-up to fix Stella's face. Glazed blue-grey eyes peek out from between puffy, swollen lids, in a face the colour of – and as immobile as – concrete. I want to wrap my arms around her and gently lead her back to her car, pop her in the back seat and cover her with a warm blanket, all the while cooing to her like a mother soothing a small child with a fever. 'There, there, sweetheart. You don't have to go to school today. Let's get you home and tucked up in bed.'

Matisse acknowledges me with a silent, fearful nod.

A stone-faced officer hurriedly ushers us into the back of an unmarked police car and turns on the motor. The day is already heating up, and I can hear the incessant drone of crickets above the car's engine.

Squished between Matisse and the door, I wonder why the police officer didn't offer for one of us to sit in the front. Some sort of protocol, perhaps. Or maybe he feels the heavy energy we emit and wants to keep his distance. Maybe it is a skill he has learnt to survive his line of work. He mumbles something into a radio and, after a brief wait, two more officers appear in the carpark and get into a white four-wheel drive, also unmarked.

They follow us out of the carpark and tail us on our fifteen-minute drive to the prison. We are all silent during the trip. As we approach the prison driveway, I see a caravan of media vehicles parked alongside the road: ABC, Channel 9, Network 10, Channel 7. A well-known journalist – a tiny, pink-suited silhouette in front of the prison gates – is delivering a piece to camera. Jostling on one side of the journalists are Lucy supporters – or death-penalty supporters? – wearing T-shirts emblazoned with her image and holding placards with the same. On the other side of the journalists are the anti-death-penalty protestors with their own placards. One is dressed as a grim reaper. They are chanting something I can't make out. A blonde girl of about ten is holding a sign that says *Execution is Legal Murder.* Yes, I think, it is. I wonder if her parents – at whose behest she is no doubt here – have thought that she, too, could one day be a Lucy.

As we near the crowds, Stella and Matisse instinctively duck down and stay this way until we come to a halt at the side of the prison. Feeling self-conscious and unsure what to do, I simply shield my face with my hands.

The general manager of the facility opens the rear door of the police car with an odd flourish, as though we are arriving at a five-star hotel. He seems a jolly chap, with ludicrously plump red cheeks, a sharp nose and a defined widow's peak: Count Dracula hoarding acorns for the winter. He introduces himself as Marvin, which makes me want to burst into giggles for some reason. I think I'm becoming hysterical.

Marvin is proud of his facility, he explains, launching straight into what sounds like the pitch he'd give to any visiting dignitary. He uses expansive gestures to capture the various grey buildings huddled behind lashings of razor wire. He shares facts and figures about the prison. He seems oblivious to the purpose of our visit and to the growing beads of sweat on Matisse's lip, and Stella's ten-yard stare. He keeps us standing on the sweltering bitumen as he outlines his numerous improvements to inmate rehabilitation programs. The police officers sit listlessly inside their air-conditioned vehicles, waiting for us to go inside.

It isn't until Stella starts to sway slightly that Marvin seems to remember why we are here. I expect him to direct us through the side entrance into the prison, but he explains that we must enter through the 'gatehouse', which is the front door of the prison. I worry that the media will have their cameras pointed directly at us, but as we round the corner to the entrance, I see that we are too far away for them to get a good shot even if they decided to flout the court rule to do so. Then I think of the long-range cameras that have captured various celebrities in their most private moments – adultering, picking noses, pulling out wedgies – and wonder if they could use those on us. Perhaps they would blur out our faces, or at least Stella's and Matisse's.

Marvin opens the glass front door with a merry flourish and, as neither Matisse nor Stella steps forwards, I stride in, full of faux confidence. Entering the brightly lit foyer, which smells like a hospital, I see a hulking, moustached man at his post. Has someone pulled him off the front door of a night-club, squashed him into a neatly pressed uniform and told him to behave? His biceps look as if they're about to split the pale blue fabric that stretches over his arms, and he is wearing more Lynx body spray than a teenage boy. He nods at me but doesn't smile.

I see him look over my shoulder for a few long seconds, so I turn my head to follow his gaze. Stella is frozen at the door, with Marvin patiently holding it open. Matisse is in front of her and has her by the forearm, whispering gently to her, but she is stuck in place, trapped in her own mind.

As I deliberate about what to do, a shrill metallic screech cuts the air. Stella's face instantly comes alive. She snaps back into this world and toddles through the door. I seek out the source of the offensive noise and observe the correctional officer put his hand to his side, deftly silencing something hanging from his hip.

'False alarm,' he mumbles.

I instinctively look to Marvin, seeking confirmation that nothing is wrong. He is holding his mobile phone to one ear, murmuring something quietly, and gives a reassuring nod and uses his hand to indicate that we should keep walking. I'd thought mobile phones weren't allowed in prisons. Perhaps they make an exception for the top guy.

Whether the officer set off his duress alarm deliberately or by accident, it has done the trick, because Stella looks alert and aware. The officer guides us to a waist-height conveyor belt and gruffly explains, using as few words as possible, that we need to put anything that contains metal – such as keys, watches or steel-capped shoes – into the wooden boxes that sit at our end of the belt. We each set about pulling off our bits and bobs and placing them in the box. I ask the officer if we should also place our ID and water bottles in the box. He shrugs noncommittally, so I just do it, and Matisse and Stella mimic me. He then directs me to enter a person-sized Perspex bubble – a beam-me-up-Scotty-looking thing – and to stand still in there until it lets me out the other side. He doesn't explain what this is for, but there appears to be no other way through to the next section.

After I walk through the opening in the bubble, it closes behind me. I feel like a goldfish in a too-small bowl. The enclosed space is filled with the tang of stale sweat. A second later, the opposite side of the bubble slides open and I walk into an area with a reception counter, enclosed at the far end by another bubble machine. I turn back to see Stella in the bubble I've just passed through. Her gaze is impassive, unreadable.

The officer pulls my wooden box off the conveyor belt and clunks it onto the counter. As I fish out my belongings, he wordlessly slides a large, open book and a pen towards me. The book, I see, contains a row of perforated yellow slips with the words *Visitor's Pass* on top of each. I fill out my details and rip my pass out of the book, hoping I'm doing it right. A carbon copy sits underneath. The officer passes me a clear pocket attached to a chain necklace of tiny metal baubles: easily snappable, I think, if someone was to pull it taut. I deduce that I am to put my pass in the pocket and place it around my neck. I do so, and he says nothing, so I assume I guessed correctly.

I turn around and Stella is behind me, silent, staring at nothing. It occurs to me that she might have taken something this morning. A Valium, perhaps? Surely not – there are strict rules that the families cannot be under the influence of any mind-altering substances while carrying out the sentence. Still, if I were Stella, I could imagine being tempted to use a benzo-induced haze to survive this nightmare.

As I look back at the bubble, Matisse pops out. She tips her head sideways, to Stella. She's signalling to me that her wife's not right, in case I hadn't noticed. I stand back from the counter as Matisse and Stella retrieve their items from the boxes. Only Stella had to take off her shoes. She is wearing steel-capped workboots; they are not part of her usual wardrobe.

Marvin emerges from the bubble and sidles up next to me. 'She okay?' he whispers.

'Not sure,' I answer truthfully.

He shakes his head and looks almost sad as he says, 'The bag is waiting over at the unit.'

'Bag?' I ask.

Marvin shifts uncomfortably and says, 'With her tools in it.'

'Oh.' I hadn't even wondered how that awful oilcloth bag – full of sharp and clunky steel – would arrive. 'Right.' I nod, strangely ashamed, struggling to meet his gaze.

With our visitor passes hanging around our necks, Marvin leads us deep into the bowels of the prison, which is lit up like a hospital ward. Every few hundred metres there is a steel door, which he leans into heavily with his shoulder. The doors don't open automatically. Marvin explains that officers watch us by camera from a central control room, and when it's safe for us to go through, they remotely unlatch the door. The first door took five seconds to open, the second forty-seven, and the third twenty-two. I'm counting to calm my mind.

The third door leads us outside, into natural light and fresh air. We enter a long concrete breezeway, fenced on both sides with wire mesh. Through the mesh, I see verdant expanses of suburban-esque lawn. But rather than the lawns flanking bungalows and two-storey brick homes, they stop at the feet of cold, grey concrete rectangles, which are dotted with scores of barred windows, so I feel like I'm being monitored by the many facets of an insect eye.

As we follow Marvin's fast clip down the corridor, I can't see a single soul in any direction, but I know we are being watched.

'They'll be interested in you,' Marvin says, reading my thoughts. 'They see everything,' he goes on. 'Being observant helps you survive. A lot of the guys grew up in abusive, violent households, so they learnt young to be on the lookout.'

I nod, looking around, wondering what type of men are taking me in, what they've experienced and what they've done. Matisse and Stella stare straight ahead, as though wearing blinkers.

'We do our best to keep them busy,' Marvin continues as he walks. 'Industries running morning and afternoon, seven days a week. If they want money for buy-up – chips, chocolate, that sort of thing – they have to earn it. They do a four-hour work day. That's the rag block over there,' he says, pointing to a concrete box on the right. 'They rip up donated clothes and make rags for the hardware stores to sell for painting and things. There's a few other jobs to choose from. Cook and gardener are the most sought-after, and librarian, but there's a metal shop and a wood shop, too. Some of the lower-security places have farming jobs. Livestock, dairy cows. I wouldn't want some of these guys near my animals, though,' he reflects.

'There are some cruel bastards in here. Not a bit of good in them – skin you alive if there was something in it for them. But some fellas are hard done by, you know, never had a chance. Drug-dependent mums, dads who beat the shit out of them, or no dads, or seven different dads; grew up in poverty, dropped out of school young, can't read or write, became homeless, never got taught about making an honest living, got addicted to substances too young when their parents introduced them, or the people their parents brought into their homes. A lot have mental health problems, PTSD, you know. Some aren't that bright. We've got a guy over in Block Seven'—he points into the distance—'that they reckon has the intellect of a child. In here for manslaughter. Killed his carer during a meltdown. We can't leave him alone with the others. Gets taken advantage of, you know? He can't even understand why he's here. Cries himself to sleep like a baby.'

A cold ball is knotting in my stomach. What a sad, cruel, hopeless place. I want to turn around and leave, but I force myself to move forwards, do what I came to do. It's not about me. I am here to help Stella and Matisse. My distress is surely nothing compared to theirs.

After a few minutes of twisting and turning down various breezeways, waiting for doors to be opened by unseen people, we enter the solid confines of another concrete building. The floors are a shiny vinyl; so clean that my shoes squeak as I walk.

I notice a man ahead of us wearing a prison-issue brown tracksuit. It's an unflattering tone, and I wonder whether dressing people in the shade of excrement helps with their rehabilitation. This guy's brandishing an old-fashioned string mop and peering into a bucket.

He looks up and says, 'Morning, sir; ladies.' He smiles as we approach.

I glance furtively at his face and notice something smudged

across his forehead. As we get closer, I see that it's writing. What on earth? Closer still, and I can make out six cramped capital letters in faded green tattoo ink. They're fuzzy round the edges and clearly etched by a novice hand. They read 'DIGGER'.

'G'day, Chris,' says Marvin, and continues to walk directly past the man. 'Good job on the floors. Could eat off 'em.'

Marvin changed the way he spoke when addressing the prisoner; made his vowels more ocker-Aussie. I expect it was intended to make Chris feel more comfortable, but it sounds condescending.

'That's the idea, sir,' Chris returns. 'The rest a' the floors should be dry – no need for the ladies to worry 'bout slippin'.'

He draws out the syllables of the word 'ladies', but we've already walked past him, so I can't gauge his intent by reading his expression.

Once we are out of his earshot, I lean towards Marvin and whisper, 'Why did he have "digger" written on his forehead? He's too young to be a veteran of World W—'

Marvin gives his head a short, sharp shake, silencing me. 'You don't want to know,' he says simply.

I immediately believe him. His comment, and the tone of Chris's last sentence, reminds me of the reason we are here.

We walk in silence for about a minute, two-abreast, twisting and turning along miles of colourless corridors, not seeing anyone else. Matisse and Stella are behind Marvin and me, and I can hear rapid, nasal breathing. I know it's Stella. I want to remind her to practise the deep-breathing exercises I taught her, but I don't want to embarrass her in front of Marvin.

We pass through another airlock door, and then into a breezeway, a short one, maybe a hundred metres long, with a squat, single story Besser-block building waiting at the other end. There is unsettled red dirt around the edges of the building instead of the grass that flanks the other prison structures. The bright iron frames of the small, high windows glint in the sun, not yet dulled by the elements. This building is new. It is the only low-set building I have seen – an afterthought in a two-storey facility. They've built it for this. We're here.

Instead of Marvin leaning on the entrance door, waiting for the airlock to be popped, he thrusts his hand into his pocket and retrieves a single key, which, I notice, is attached to a strong chain secured to his belt. It's an old-fashioned skeleton-style key, like you might see in movies about Alcatraz or in horror films. My sense of unreality deepens; I am apart from my body, my limbs heavy, moving through molasses. I take in my surrounds, but they have a dreamlike quality, hazy around the edges. My own breathing becomes more rapid, and I work to lengthen my inhales and exhales. I tell myself I'm in control, although the environment begs to differ.

Marvin inserts his key into the lock of the solid metal door, but before he can turn it in the barrel, the door opens inwards with a heavy dragging noise. A man in uniform stands on the other side.

'Warren,' Marvin says, nodding. Warren is the opposite of Marvin: towering, solid, arms so big the veins are like tree roots. Unlike the bouncer at the gatehouse, this guy looks like a professional defender: ex-SAS or something like that. I'm sure he could pick one of us up and toss us across the room with one hand, but his strong jaw has a trustworthy set to it. I sense a protective aura, as if he's one of those American TV-show fathers who greets his daughter's first boyfriend with a shotgun and a warning to have her home by ten. Ordinarily, I would find this patriarchal approach – the sense of possession – off-putting, but right now, at my most vulnerable, it is disconcertingly comforting.

Warren, I say to myself. Warren and Marvin. Warren and Marvin. Warren and Marvin. The words play over in my head like a mantra, and I hypnotise myself with the names as we follow the men down yet another long, squeaky corridor. My mind has gone all slow and sticky, like it was in the bushfire.

Warren and Marvin say nothing to each other, but appear to share the familiarity of two men who have known each other a long while, been under fire together, covered each other's backs.

We reach an alcove decorated only with a stainless-steel water fountain, a steel coffee-sized table bolted to the ground, and several beige chairs of heavy plastic. A waiting area, perhaps?

Indeed, Marvin gestures for us to be seated. Stella almost melts into the chair nearest to her, as though she has been waiting for someone to slip it underneath her all morning. Matisse sits to one side of her, I to the other. I feel the hard plastic under my seat-bones. Have they forgotten we could be here for up to twenty-four hours, if Stella chooses to utilise the full time available for the execution? Even as my body protests, I hope the three of us spend a very long time in these chairs and that, during that very long time, there is some sort of magical intervention that diverts the course of things.

Marvin and Warren assemble themselves in front of us, the three seated women.

Their postures are erect, stern, militaristic. Marvin has gained a couple of centimetres in height, and looks less like a Dracula-squirrel and more like an army man.

'The prisoner is in there,' Marvin points to a door no more than five metres across from us. So close. I thought I would have known when I was in his presence, that my body would have alerted me, given some sign – my heart stopping for a moment, perhaps.

'The walls are thick,' says Marvin. 'He cannot hear us, and we will be unable to hear . . . whatever occurs within that room. That means,' he says, facing Stella directly, 'that we will be unable to hear if you call out for help.'

Stella stares at Marvin without giving any indication that she has heard what he said.

'That's why we're giving you one of these,' he says, as Warren unclips from his belt a black rectangular plastic box about the size of a deck of cards.

'A duress button,' says Marvin. 'To call for emergency assistance if you need it. In a moment, Warren will demonstrate how to use it. There are also multiple buttons mounted around the room. They look like this,' he instructs, pointing to a palm-sized red button on the wall in the alcove.

'Press it once and the officers will enter immediately. Warren will be stationed next to the door at all times. He's a man of great experience and someone you want on your side in the unlikely event of trouble. There are also two other officers who will remain within ten metres of this room. They are stationed just down the hall.' He points to his right.

'You will hear an alarm go off when you activate any of the duress buttons. If you do not hear an alarm, you have not activated the button correctly. Press again. We have tested the alarms today, and they are in working order.'

He takes a breath, as though thinking about what to tell us next.

'There are cameras here in the hall,' he continues, pointing to CCTV units installed in the roof, 'but there are no cameras in the room. Personally, it would make us feel much better if there were, so we could help you in an emergency, but the judge has ordered that you should have privacy at all times when with the prisoner.'

I remember Judge Gorski being explicit that whatever the family did in this room, did to the perpetrator, was their private business and not for public titillation. Surely if guards did monitor cameras in that room they would have a hard time keeping what they saw to themselves. Word would get around.

'So,' says Marvin, 'we will not see if you are in trouble. Do you understand?'

He looks squarely at Stella. I can tell he is worried by her presentation. Matisse elbows her gently, prompting her to respond to Marvin's question, but it still takes her a couple of seconds to nod.

'Good,' says Marvin, as though she has given a full and lusty 'yes'.

He fishes in his pocket and pulls out a folded piece of A4 paper. Unfolding it, he passes it to Stella. She takes it.

'This is the layout of the room,' he says. 'The diagram shows a computer-generated bird's-eye view of the area. This is the door where you will enter,' he says, pointing on the diagram to the door separating us from McDermott. 'The bag you provided us is directly on the inside of the door, to your left.'

My heart rate increases at the mention of the bag.

'In the centre of the room is the gurney,' he says, pointing to a shape on the paper.

It looks like a horizontal crucifix, but with a couple of extra bars for the legs to rest on, spread-eagled.

'The prisoner is strapped onto the gurney, facing upwards to the ceiling,' Marvin explains. 'His arms are strapped out to the sides, here and here. And his legs are attached to these two bars, here and here.'

He doesn't mention the ominous hole cut out of the steel at the point where the person's buttocks would lay. Blood rushes to my cheeks. My god, what are we doing?

'Each part of the gurney can move independently of the others, swivel in various directions, and the entire gurney can be turned upside down so that the prisoner faces the floor.'

I look to Stella and see that she is studying the picture intently. Acid burns my gut.

Without looking away from the diagram, she whispers, 'And there's a sink?'

Marvin nods and points. 'Yes, running hot and cold water.'

'And electricity?' she probes.

'Yes, power points here and here, and an extension cord here.' As though to make it more benign, he adds, 'There's also a bar fridge here that contains drinks and snacks. And noise-cancelling headphones, a chair, soap, towels, a first-aid kit, and a toilet for your use behind a privacy curtain.'

Noise-cancelling headphones – to block out the screams? Snacks? Wow, they've thought of everything. I try to picture Stella a few hours into the proceedings, getting tired, deciding to take a tea break. I see her soaping up her sullied hands and arms – suds streaked pink – before drying them off and throwing a stained towel to the ground. I see her sinking into the chair to unwrap a plate of plastic-wrapped salad sand-wiches, popping open the tab of a Diet Coke and looking for somewhere to put her feet up.

This is wrong. Surely this is wrong? My role, my job at its essence, is to keep this woman safe. Mentally safe. This is not mentally safe for her. This seems trauma-inducing in the extreme. I want to tell Stella it's time to leave. I want to drag her back down all of those grey corridors, plop her in an Uber and whisk her away to some generic, franchised coffee shop in a bland suburban shopping centre so we can defuse this psychological near-miss with a flat white on bloody oat milk and a slice of vegan carrot cake. We can laugh big belly laughs and she can say, 'Ha, isn't it funny to think I actually considered doing that? Anyway, what are you up to on the weekend?'

I sit in silence as Marvin finishes his instructions and starts talking about the arrangements for me and Matisse as we are waiting outside the room.

His words drone on almost outside my sphere of consciousness, but I pick up snippets: ' . . . toilets . . . meals served . . . emergency escape . . . two single cots down the hall . . .'

I tune back in to the instructions as I sense Marvin is preparing to leave. He points at the clock on the wall. He notes that it's ten-thirty, says we have half an hour before Stella can enter, that we should wait quietly here, that Warren will unlock the door when it's time, that Warren can call him in an instant if he's needed.

Having exhausted all of the information he has to impart, Marvin nods formally, even giving us a little bow. He turns to depart and walks a few steps down the corridor, then turns back to face us. He gravely regards Lucy's mothers, huddled together in this waiting room of death.

'Stella,' he says. 'We are all with you in there. Give that motherfucker hell.'

33

OCTAVIA

THE SECOND HAND OF THE IKEA CLOCK TICKS AS IT MAKES ITS TINY grasshopper jumps forwards on the clock face. I am connected to these jumps, each one bringing us closer to eleven o'clock. The only other sound is the low murmur of conversation from the officers stationed somewhere down the hall. Stella and Matisse sit completely still, like me, staring into nothingness. I feel an electric zapping up my arms and down my legs, as though my nerve connections are standing to attention. Ten forty-two.

Stella's right leg starts up. *Jiggle jiggle jiggle.* Then it stops. Then starts again.

Still ten forty-two.

I regard my hands in a detached way and notice they are shaking as if they're resting on the head of a purring cat. A currawong calls nearby: *woo-wit-woooo.* In the distance, the soft, deep hum of traffic.

I turn my head slightly to the left and notice that Matisse's blouse is moving fractionally with each heartbeat. I look down the corridor towards the exit, then back to the clock. Ten forty-four.

It happens before I'm aware she's moved. Stella's got a chair in her hands, hefts it up to chest height, lunges forwards and propels it across the room with a lion-like roar. The plastic crashes against the concrete wall, bounces and hits the floor, clattering away, landing upside down. It doesn't break.

The sound of footsteps comes down the hall, someone running, shoes squeaking on the lino.

Stella leans forwards and grabs the front legs of the chair, lifting it up again then smashing it into the floor. The room echoes with each bang of the plastic against the hard surface. Her face is covered by her hair, which dances, wild and rhythmic, as if she is headbanging in a mosh pit. Guttural, anguished grunts come from deep within her chest.

Warren makes it to her before either Matisse or I can break out of our frozen state of shock. He puts his hands on her shoulders while another officer wrestles the chair from her grip. The third officer stands by, waiting to see what other action is needed. Stella twists around to face Warren, lashing out at him, beating his chest with her fists, screeching. Her face is beetroot purple.

Warren grabs her wrists adeptly, bringing her arms to her sides, disarming her. All the while he is cooing softly, 'It's okay. You're okay. You're okay. Shh. Shhhh.'

Stella quiets quickly and settles her head on his chest, sobbing. He releases her wrists and places a hand in the centre of her back, comforting, protective. Warren was as gentle as a man could be in restraining a woman so ferocious, but I wonder if she'll have bruises later. Yet another reminder of this day, albeit one that will fade.

Still stunned and simultaneously aware that Warren has

the situation in hand, I remain seated. Matisse is staring at Stella, who gulps air and cries into the chest of a man who was a stranger to her an hour ago. Ten fifty-two.

Warren guides Stella back to her chair and she falls into it. He turns to the officers and says, 'Water. Tissues.'

They disappear down the hall. *Squeak, squeak.*

Warren stands back now, observing, analysing, calculating. The radio at his belt crackles and he makes a hand gesture indicating he needs to take the communication. He retreats down the hall, an eye still on Stella.

Stella has her eyes shut tight. Her face is slick with tears and snot. Her chest spasms, each breath a phlegmy rasp. Matisse puts her hand on Stella's shoulder, but her wife shakes it away.

Matisse silently implores me: *What should we do?*

I give a small shake of my head. *I don't know.* Fuck. Fuck.

I check the clock yet again. Ten fifty-six. I glance back down the corridor towards the exit. I silently beg for divine intervention, which is becoming something of a habit of late, even though I'm fairly certain I don't believe in a god. My mind feels like a knotted ball of yarn as I try to make sense of my thoughts. What *do* we do? Surely Stella can't be allowed to go ahead? Can I call Gorski and say that she is not in a frame of mind to proceed? Where's Marvin? Maybe I need to talk to Marvin.

Ten fifty-seven. One of the officers puts water and tissues on the table, all the while observing Stella as though assessing an unpredictable beast. He silently withdraws and leans against a wall a few metres away from us. Warren hasn't returned.

Stella is regaining some sort of composure now. She has wiped her face on her blouse, so the front of it is damp and smeared. She is looking at the door to McDermott's cell. Her face is a mixture of terror and determination. Suddenly I know – know with certainty – that she will not survive this. Call it intuition, gut instinct. She will walk out of the prison alive, of course, but she will not survive whatever it is that she does in that room. My mind's eye shows me flashes of consequences I wish never to see come to fruition. Losses this family cannot bear.

Stella raises herself out of her chair, but both Matisse and I stand faster this time, each putting a hand on her shoulder.

Probably having heard the scuff of chairs, Warren and the officers reappear.

Stella stands to her full height and turns to face Warren.

'It's almost time,' she says in a normal voice, as though her meltdown never happened.

Warren nods, looks at the clock. Ten fifty-nine and eleven seconds. Surely he won't let her in?

His hand delves into his pocket and retrieves a key.

He looks over his shoulder at the two other officers, whose bodies are alert, ready to react at a split-second's notice. He nods at them. I wonder what the nod means.

'Ready?' he asks Stella, and she makes a small squeak, presumably in the affirmative, while staring at the door.

Warren takes a couple of steps towards the door, but they are slow steps, as though he is waiting for the last possible second. Stella follows. Ten fifty-nine and fifty-one seconds.

Do I jump in now? Say something? I feel frozen to the spot. I need time to decide what to do, but I don't have any. Will I regret it more if I do something, or do nothing? I look to Matisse in case she has the answer, but she is staring at Stella.

Warren slides the key into the barrel of the lock and glances again at the time, now referring to a serious-looking watch on his wrist. Does it match the clock on the wall? Perhaps it's slower. Maybe there's more time than we thought.

Suddenly, all three officers turn their heads in the direction of the corridor that leads to the main entrance. They look like a bunch of Great Danes who have heard their owner's car rounding a corner a block from home. I can't hear anything, but Matisse, Stella and I follow their gaze.

Warren withdraws the key from the lock slowly, as though trying not to startle a deer. He slips it back into his uniform pants. Stella opens her mouth, about to say something – object, perhaps, to the removal of the key.

Then I hear it clearly: the door to the building opening. Low voices. Murmuring. I can make out Marvin's voice and another more feminine one. Then, shoes on the floor, one set squeaking, the other clomping, as though a set of heavy boots.

Two figures come into view in the corridor. Marvin, yes, but in front of Marvin, striding ahead, is a woman. A tall young woman taking determined steps. Strong, athletic, self-assured. Hair tied atop her head, straight, glossy, swishing like a horse's tail with every step. Black combat boots. Cargo pants. And a fitted white top with text reading *Justice for Lucy* above a photo of a young girl whose eyes meet mine, innocent and sparkling.

My breath leaves my belly slowly and with relief, as though creating a warm, comfortable space inside me where I can now curl up.

I take a step forwards. Hannah reaches out her arms to embrace me. We hold each other for a second. My muscles relax against hers, which are taut, I know, not just with physical strength but with steely resolve.

Hannah and I turn to face the mothers, whose faces register shock and confusion as they stare at her. Hannah looks to me. Stella and Matisse wear expressions that are fearful and inquiring.

I take a tentative breath, then tell them the words we have rehearsed, which I was never sure I would get to say.

'Stella, Matisse. As you know, Judge Gorski ruled that only family members over the age of eighteen can execute the sentence. This was interpreted as meaning those who were eighteen years of age when the crime was committed. As Hannah was a juvenile at that time, all parties assumed she was ineligible to participate.'

I watch the women as they stare at me. I'm not sure if they're taking this in, but I continue.

'Hannah petitioned the judge, sought clarification of his intention in making this order. She argued that to exclude family members who have come of age in the time between the crime and the execution deprives them of their full rights as an adult, one who has experienced the same loss as the rest of the family.

'There has been some legal wrangling these past few months. Hannah did not want you to be aware of it, because she did not want you to worry. She's been waiting to hear whether she would be allowed to participate today.'

I take a deep breath and look at Hannah. She nods.

'She's here now because Gorski clarified his instruction. He has advised that family members must be over eighteen at the execution date, not at the date the crime was committed, meaning Hannah is eligible to participate in today's execution.'

Stella knits her brows, disbelieving. Matisse's hand covers her mouth.

'Mum,' Hannah says then, looking at Stella and reaching out her two pale hands in offering. Stella takes them in her weather-worn ones.

'I am here to do this for Lucy. I am here to do this for all of us.'

Matisse intervenes, shaking her head. 'Hannah. No. No, you cannot. You are a young woman with your whole life ahead of you. This will traumatise you. It will, won't it, Octavia?' She looks to me, as does Stella.

'In all honesty, I can't predict how this will affect Hannah,' I say. 'But what I do know is that she's been doing everything she could think of to prepare for this. Training for months, both physically and mentally. She has done things she never thought she could: going days without food, sometimes without water even, running in the heat for hours at a time, sleeping in the bush, learning how to use weapons, how to slaughter and butcher animals. She's done these things entirely under her own steam, while largely continuing to function in her daily life. She challenged herself to prove she could keep going when things hurt, be effective under pressure, act in the face of fear, bounce back and do it all over again. And she's discovered she can.'

Stella and Matisse study Hannah as though something is dawning on them. The puzzle pieces of the past months are clicking together in their minds. They are seeing their daughter in a new light. They're seeing her the way I've always seen her.

Stella lets go of Hannah's hands and instead throws her arms around her neck, embracing her daughter. Relief is written across Stella's face. And belief. Belief in her daughter's strength.

'You're sure?' she whispers.

'Never been surer of anything,' Hannah replies, her voice strong and composed. 'And I'm ready. Right now.'

I look to Warren, who is nodding, seemingly satisfied with this turn of events. I don't need to look at the clock. It's time.

34

HANNAH

I SIT ON TOP OF HIM, STRADDLING HIS PELVIS. MY HAIR HAS BECOME untethered; it's wet and tickles my arms. A thousand mosquitos buzz in my ears, and my nostrils are full of copper. His body is slick, naked.

My inner thighs expand in time with his abdominal muscles as he takes slow, laboured breaths. His hair is wet, too. Dark. Viscous. Parts of him are not how they should be but as I want them to be. This is it. We are here.

His eyes meet mine. Then he looks down to my chest, my shirt, and his eyes meet Lucy's. He tries to turn his head and remembers he cannot.

35

OCTAVIA

IT'S THIRTY-SEVEN MINUTES AND NINE SECONDS PAST SEVEN AM when the door cracks open. I am the only one who is awake. Stella and Matisse retired to the cots when the first rays of daylight peeked through the high windows. Warren sent the other officers off to take a break half an hour ago, cautioning them to keep their radios handy. He fell into a gentle slumber in a chair by the cell door not long after, snoring softly. He does not rouse at the sound of its handle turning now.

Hannah steps out and quietly closes the door behind her. She leans back against it. Her white T-shirt is coloured in places now – tie-dyed in watery pink, scarlet and deep magenta. Lucy's eyes gaze out, eternally carefree. The skin of Hannah's face is youthful, delicate and pale beneath her smudges of war paint. Her red hair is loose around her shoulders and has started to curl from getting wet. The curls are crusted, stuck together in places. It doesn't stop them from glowing like a halo in the shaft of sunlight that shines on her from the window above. Her eyes – one blue, one green – are bright. They find mine. A smile plays on her lips.

AUTHOR'S NOTE

When I wrote *What I Would Do to You*, I barely entertained the prospect that it would become something others would read. I submitted it to literary agency Curtis Brown Australia with no other living soul knowing what it was about or having read a single page. The delight of operating that way was that I could live completely in my imagination, drawing simply on my own questions, thoughts, dreams and experiences. This is one of the greatest joys of fiction for me: it is a place to explore things that may never happen, and sometimes should never happen.

It was an interesting thought exercise to create the fictional characters of Octavia and Henry, and to wonder how they might behave in such an unreal scenario. My intention was to capture them as authentic, flawed and vulnerable human beings facing dystopian circumstances – not as some imagined prototype of the perfect future mental health professional.

Although my personal position has always been against any form of violence, when I started writing *What I Would*

Do to You, it was with a question to myself: What would I do, facing the legally sanctioned choice, if somebody harmed my loved one in the way that Lucy was harmed?

Throughout the writing of this book, my thoughts were with the real-world victims and victim-survivors of violent crimes, and I note that their individual opinions on justice and punishment are likely to be as diverse and complex – and sometimes internally conflicted – as they are important for our justice system to hear.

ACKNOWLEDGEMENTS

These might not be typical author's acknowledgements, by virtue of me having largely written *What I Would Do to You* in a bubble. While the support of most of the people below – and that of many wonderful others – was perhaps not of the writing kind, all combined it played a critical role in seeing this book published. My heartfelt gratitude and thanks go to:

Diane, my mother, who instilled in me a love of people's stories and of the land, and George, my father, whose brilliant mind taught me that no idea is too wild to consider. Together they provided me with so many rich experiences from which I now draw, and allowed me to believe I'm capable of big things. I love them so much.

Suzanne, my sister, who is younger than me but whose wisdom and steadiness temper me, and whose love has got me through the darkest days. She's also the original microwaver of the Little Lamb cake. It was terrible.

My brother, Peter, a man of few words who gave me some

good ones in a roadside conversation that helped spark the idea for Stella's farm.

Anna H., a true survivor who is far more incredible than she knows, and who is family always.

Benjamin Paz (aka Stevenson): how lucky I was to have him be the first human to read my manuscript, and to then represent me as my literary agent at Curtis Brown Australia right up until pre-release. His belief in this book made everything possible. But, when you discover your agent's own novel is being turned into a HBO series, you count your numbered days with gratitude and brace yourself for the inevitable break-up call. (Of a list of possible reasons, Benjamin, it was a decent one.) I cannot wait to see what his future holds.

Tara Wynne, literary agent, Curtis Brown Australia: I was thrilled to learn that someone of her calibre wanted to take the reins from Benjamin and help guide this book into existence. I am so excited to be working with her.

Meredith Curnow, publisher, Penguin Random House Australia, who, along with Benjamin, helped make my dream come true. She believed in this book from the outset, and from the moment I met her I had everything crossed in the hope I would work with her. I am so incredibly grateful to be guided by someone of such vision, knowledge and poise.

Kathryn Knight, senior editor, Penguin Random House Australia, whose dedication saw her casting her eagle eye over my manuscript in locations from the Japanese Alps to the cat cafes of Tokyo. I've learnt so much from her and, as I'm editing my second book, I find my fingers pausing over the keyboard to consider what she might say.

Also, to the amazing team at Penguin Random House Australia, including Hannah Ludbrook, senior publicist – who shares a few too many similarities with the fictional Hannah, although none of the scary ones, she assures me – Veronica Eze, lead audio producer, Rebekah Chereshsky, marketing manager, and everyone else who's helped bring this book to life.

Michael C., clinical psychologist, for his valued opinion on the manuscript, and for the things he's done to earn my trust; to small-town boys who grow into good men.

Dr Andrea K., my best friend: the beautiful, dark creature who lights up my brain. Andy, you heal me by meeting me in the places nobody else can, no map needed. Hannah's last chapter is for you. Let's stay, and keep finding the beams of sunlight and basking in them like children.

Claire M., who walked with me down long prison corridors. She has turned up for me over and over again, and I will never forget it. Also, to her and everyone else who plays a role in wildlife rescue and rehabilitation. They are fighting a ceaseless battle to save the ones they can, and would love more help.

Dr Katharine H., whose compassion, collaboration and expertise make my life possible. You are an absolute unicorn, and I hope you know how much what you do means to me.

Carmel, my aunty, who inspires me with her sharp mind and sense of social justice.

Henrietta P., I so miss that blonde mane swishing to Mr Mistoffelees in your London flat.

The Darling Downs Crew – I never intended to stay, but a superb group of colleagues and friends keeps bringing me back:

The beautiful team I work with, for their encouragement during the publishing journey, including Aidan M., Ingrid H., Payal D., Stephen G. and especially Angela O., who has made so much possible for me; Ged D., for his compassion, and

Marcella C. and Rachel M., warrior women who have held space for me without judgement. Also, Danielle S., for always being excited for me.

Nikki Mottram, fellow Darling Downs writer represented by Curtis Brown Australia, for generously sharing her experiences of becoming a published author.

The Shut Up and Write group, where the shutting-up was sometimes scarce but where the company was good, and where I pushed through some final edits.

Louise W., the very first person to make me welcome.

Melanie L., for her friendship, loyalty and incredible brain, and for welcoming me into her circle.

Joanne T., for a new perspective.

Emma H. – finally reunited! – who's been working to save my mortal soul since our teens; it's beyond redemption, Em, but I so appreciate your persistence.

And especially Bridget G., who's embraced me with unconditional love when I've needed it most, and whose family has provided sanctuary despite my presence perhaps occasionally being a reminder of losses they bear with such ferocious grace.

Finally, to those who have had a loved one stolen from them through violent crime, and to every victim-survivor, I honour the journey you travel on the path you did not choose, and the choice you make to take one more step even when you're walking in total darkness. I've seen people whose pain seemed too excruciating to survive take those difficult steps until, one day, they rounded yet another bleak corner to find the breadcrumbs of peace and joy and love they thought they'd lost forever; and, as they follow that trail, life becomes worth living again. Those people aren't braver, stronger or more special than you. Those people are you.

Remember you are not alone. If you need help, please reach out to the many people and services who can walk the journey with you until dark becomes light.

Powered by
Penguin

Looking for more great reads, exclusive content and book giveaways?

Subscribe to our weekly newsletter.

Scan the QR code or visit penguin.com.au/signup